THE

MEMORY

AGENT

ALSO BY MATTHEW B.J. DELANEY

Black Rain

Jinn

THE

MEMORY

AGENT

MATTHEW B.J. DELANEY

47NORTH

Text copyright © 2017 by Matthew B.J. Delaney
All rights reserved.

Published by 47North, Seattle

www.apub.com

Amazon, the Amazon logo, and 47North are trademarks of Amazon.com, Inc., or its affiliates.

ISBN-13: 9781503942691
ISBN-10: 1503942694

Cover design by Damonza

Printed in the United States of America

THE
MEMORY
AGENT

1

September 1933

In the instant before memory starts, I could have been anyone. All worlds were possible. But then like a rusted machine slowly coming, beginning to turn, the gears of memory rotated into place.

I awoke in a bed, my face glazed with sweat, my mouth dry and awful. I was in an ordinary hotel room. A ceiling fan spun lazily, circulating warm air and disturbing the pages of the Pearl S. Buck novel on the small writing desk. A suitcase lay open on the floor, a few stacks of neatly folded clothes visible inside. On the bedside table, an Imperial Airways ticket from London to Cairo.

My room was on the third floor of the Luxor Hotel and looked out across the crowded Jewish quarter of Cairo. Outside, the street bustled. Cairo was a city of the salesman. Vendor stalls were packed tightly together, hawking everything from fruits to rugs to falcons. Anything could be had in the streets. The entire classical world had ended up in Cairo, a counterfeit collection that could rival the world's best museums. Several archeological expeditions that ended in an empty looted tomb could be artificially augmented with a few select purchases from a vendor's cart.

A journal was open on the table. Inside, a list of names.

1. Samuel Clayton
2. Charlotte Gonzales
3. Edward Selberg
4. Nasir Hajjar
5. Elizabeth Blake
6. Bobby Chan

Below the names, a year.

Already the afternoon heat was beginning to fade as the sun set behind the minarets of the old city. Long shadows stretched across dusty streets. I checked my watch. The rest of my team would already be assembling downstairs. I splashed water on my face from a basin, then left my room.

The year was 1933.

The Luxor was one of those large postcolonial affairs, a relic from the old British Empire which was quickly fading from the reaches of the globe. The lobby was large and open-aired. Porters stood at attention in jackets and white gloves, visibly sweating in the heat. In the dining room, brilliantly white-clothed tables were scattered like marbles across the hardwood floor. Charlotte Gonzales stood alone at the bar drinking tea from a clear glass.

Charlotte's skin was luminously pale, her wavy hair a shade more colorless than blonde. The only feature that sparkled with color were her eyes. They were a deep shade of green, big and round as an infant's, but filled with more cunning than naiveté. They were the eyes of someone who had experienced the world, and so far, had not liked what she had seen.

She was the team's linguist and translator.

"Rest of the team is still waking up," Charlotte said.

"You know what this is about?"

"They must have found something in the desert."

Next to arrive was Edward Selberg. He staggered through the main doors of the dining room, holding his head with one hand, a grimace on his face. He had a thin, sharp countenance and narrow eyes, like some minor villain in a Charles Dickens novel. He shuffled forward as if drunk, leaned heavily against the bar, and nodded to Charlotte and me. "Anyone have any aspirin? My head is killing me."

"Lay off the vodka," Charlotte said.

Selberg shook his head. "I don't think I had anything to drink last night. I don't remember a thing."

"Which probably means you had too much to drink."

He continued to rub his forehead with one hand, while with the other he revolved a pair of dice over and over in his palm. He slapped the dice down onto the bar counter, then poured a cup of tea from the silver pot.

The doors swung open again as Samuel Clayton entered. A black man with the misshapen nose and swollen eyes of a former boxer, he wore long boots, khaki pants, and a white shirt held up by a leather bandolier which also carried the weight of a Colt revolver. A brown American-style cowboy hat was pulled low over his brow. He nodded to us, then sat by himself at one of the tables. I brought him a cup of tea and set it down on the table. Clayton and I went back years.

"Selberg's got a headache," I said.

"I've got an everything ache. Head, body. Feel like I just stepped out of the ring. And look at this." Clayton held up his hand. His fingers trembled. "I don't know what's going on with me."

Before I could reply, two more men entered. One was Nasir Hajjar, a tall Egyptian, with a black beard and large, round stomach. He wore khaki pants and a filthy button-down shirt. He was the local guide and he carried with him two painter's easels that he set up in the front of the room. The easels were both covered with canvas. With him was a white man in a tan derby hat with a thick mustache that shone with wax like a new bowling ball. He wore an old-fashioned, tan, sack suit with a red bow tie, and in one hand he held a long, black walking cane. The stranger looked like an illustration from a Victorian novel.

The man with the mustache placed a leather satchel on the table, looked at each of us, leaned against his cane and began to speak. "A month ago, a man stumbled out of the desert into the city of Luxor dying of thirst and claiming to have found a lost city beneath the Earth. He said this city was in the Valley of the Kings and—"

"I'm sorry," Charlotte interrupted. "Who are you?"

"My name is Dunbar. I was sent here as the representative of a group of investors who are funding this project."

"Fine. That's what you do, but who are you?"

"I just told you, I'm here representing the people paying your salaries. As far as I'm concerned, you are aware of everything relevant that you need to know about me. May I continue?"

Charlotte nodded, leaning back against the bar.

"Thank you." Dunbar gave a long thoughtful pull on his mustache. "Not long after being found, this man died, but not before he had drawn this."

Dunbar pulled away the covering from one of the easels to reveal a stencil drawing of what appeared to be a modern city skyline. I could see what appeared to be several tall skyscrapers, architecture that did not exist in Cairo. "This is what the man claims to have found beneath the sand."

"Sounds like a mental patient to me," Selberg said.

"Maybe. But sometimes it's simply easier to dismiss someone as mentally ill than it is to open one's mind to the possibility of the truth," Dunbar said. "But this man was a Bedouin. He had spent his entire life in the desert. He had never visited a western city before, so where could he have seen the model for what he drew?"

"He must have seen a photograph. The Valley of Kings is filled with westerners," Selberg said.

"Possible. But in the man's possessions, we found two other items." From his pocket, Dunbar revealed a small book. The pages were yellowed with age, the cover a dark leather. "The Bedouin cannot read English, but he said he found this book on the remains of a dead man dressed in a red and blue uniform who carried a rifle. Our experts believe this to be the 130-year-old journal of a French soldier named Bouchard who served under the command of Napoleon Bonaparte during his expedition into Egypt."

"But Napoleon's army never made it as far south as the Valley of the Kings," Charlotte said. "His last major engagement was near Cairo, hundreds of miles to the north."

"That is true," Dunbar said. "But while his army never made it that far south, he did send emissaries for scientific exploration throughout the region. It's possible one of these men made it to the Valley of the Kings. Which would explain how the Bedouin also found this."

Dunbar opened his hand like a magician to reveal a single gold coin. On the front of the coin was the familiar profile of a man, the words *Bonaparte Premier Consul* inscribed around the edge. On the back of the coin, *20 FRANCS*. Dunbar flipped the coin end over end along the top of his fingers.

"So you found a coin?" Clayton said. "How impressed should we be by that?"

"As this is a Napoleonic-era coin minted the same year as his expedition to Egypt," Dunbar winked, and twisted one end of his mustache, "I would say you should be very impressed. Wouldn't you?"

Charlotte nodded in agreement. "Have you translated the journal?"

The coin vanished back into Dunbar's pocket. "We have. Bouchard writes about traveling for months along the banks of the Nile, which is consistent with a trip south from Cairo. He arrives in an area described as two valleys in the Theban Hills on the West Bank of the Nile near Luxor. Here he claims to have found an opening that led down to a great city beneath the Earth. A city of buildings higher than anything he had ever seen. A city made of metal and glass."

"There have always been legends of mythical lost cities," Charlotte said. "El Dorado. Atlantis. Perhaps every culture on Earth has tales on the subject. Doesn't mean the stories are real."

Dunbar tapped the journal thoughtfully. "That is very true. Perhaps Bouchard was suffering from delirium. He had been through a war, then traveling through the desert for months, maybe he gets a little frazzled. Or maybe he doesn't."

"You said the Bedouin had two items in his possession," I said. "What else did he have besides the journal?"

"No matter what explanation we might come up with for the journal," Dunbar said, "there is nothing I think to explain the second item."

From his satchel, Dunbar pulled a folded newspaper. The paper was yellowed to parchment, and Dunbar carefully smoothed it out across the table. We gathered around. Across the front was the familiar masthead of *The New York Times* with its Old English font. The rest of the paper was spaced with articles. Some local politician had been accused of corruption. There had been a fire in Manhattan. The stories weren't familiar, but the images were vibrant with color.

"What am I looking at?"

Dunbar tapped just below the masthead to a date.

November 3, 2017.

The silence in the room stretched out for almost a minute. Sounds filtered in through the silence. In the hotel kitchen a dish was dropped, followed by a round of cursing. Two men spoke in the hall outside. In the distance, the call to prayer sounded. Finally, in the dining room, someone coughed.

"That's almost ninety years from now," I said. "I don't understand."

Dunbar shook his head. "We didn't understand either. We checked the entire newspaper. The people, the events. None of them exist in our time."

"I don't know . . . " Charlotte said. "Sounds . . ."

"Too much to believe? That's what we thought too," Dunbar said. "Until we found the tunnel."

◆ ◆ ◆

The Valley of Kings was almost a full day's travel south of Cairo. Nasir had gone ahead and met the rest of the team at base camp. The excavation site stretched a hundred yards along the valley. Khaki-colored tents billowed in a desert breeze, while near the tomb fifty diggers worked with the constant ring of metal against stone. I shielded my eyes against the sun and studied the excavated opening cut into the side of the valley.

"Parker, I am so glad you arrived," Nasir said to me. "We have made great progress on the seal."

"You found a seal?" I asked as we walked toward the tunnel opening.

The seal was a wall of terra-cotta, which traditionally separated the tunnels from the burial chamber. The same type of seal had blocked off the tomb of the pharaoh, Tutankhamen.

"We have found more than the seal," Nasir said.

Beyond the opening, a stone stairway led down into the Earth. The air began to cool significantly as we descended. Electric torches filled the small space with white light and guided us down until we reached a flat area about twenty feet wide. The underground chamber ended with two stone doors, connected by a rod of wood wrapped with rope and sealed with clay.

On the clay was stamped the royal seal of ancient Egypt, an egret backed by an image of the sun.

"The clay is unbroken," Selberg whispered.

"Good sign," I replied. I had seen many tombs before this where the clay seal had been broken hundreds of years before by grave robbers. Sometimes only months after the burial, thieves would find the tomb, break open the door, and take whatever they could. Over the years, the ceiling appeared to have partially collapsed. A heavy mound of rubble blocked the base of the door. It would have to be cleared before we could move forward.

I bent forward and inspected the seal. "And you say it was completely intact when you found it?"

"As if nothing had disturbed it for thousands of years," Nasir said. "And we also found him."

Nasir pointed to the far corner of the room.

In the flickering light of the torch, I saw the remains of a man laid out on the stone. The skin on his face was shrunken and dried, his cheeks and jaw sharp edges beneath parchment. His lips had retracted to reveal uneven teeth set in gums long turned to bone. He wore a military uniform: white pants and a dark blue jacket, both faded and dust covered, but exactly as the Bedouin had described.

Two white leather belts crossed the dead soldier's chest; one supported a cartridge box, the other held a short saber. Near the body lay a long firearm, broken and rusted over by the passage of time.

Selberg bent down enthusiastically. "He appears to be a French soldier of the Napoleonic wars. The uniform is quite distinct. Look, here, on the button, an eagle with outstretched wings. This is the mark of Napoleon himself."

"And the firearm?" I said.

"Definitely French make. It's a Charleville musket, named after the armory in Charleville, France."

"What do you think he was doing in the Valley?" I said.

Selberg tapped his lower lip with a dusty finger. "Napoleon landed with thirteen ships near Alexandria in 1798 and marched inward toward Cairo to cut off the British food supply by capturing the fertile areas around the Nile. It's possible a small band of his troops made it down this far."

"To do what?" I said.

"I have no idea. The Valley of the Kings would have been unknown to the French in 1798. I can think of no compelling reason for him to travel the hundreds of miles from Cairo to Luxor and into the Valley. And at that time, this would have been a brutal trip. Most would die trying."

"Must have been something important. Whatever the reason," I said. I bent down and gently inspected the dead soldier's pockets. This close, the skeleton was frightening. The skin was yellowed and dried, but still intact, as were the man's hair and teeth. The dry climate and the darkness of the tomb had preserved the man's uniform. The blue jacket still felt soft to the touch and the pants retained their original crease. The man's boots, though covered in dust, looked like they would polish up nicely with the right care.

I felt paper inside his vest. "There's something here."

Slowly I retrieved two small items. The first was a strange, small card, like paper, except shiny in the light, and it seemed to be constructed of a durable material the likes of which I'd never touched. Along the top portion, in rich blue lettering was the word *MetroCard*.

"What's a MetroCard?" Charlotte said.

"No idea," I replied. The second item was a square of parchment, which I unfolded on the dead man's chest, being careful so that the creases did not tear in my fingers. The parchment appeared to be a charcoal rubbing off a stone or some other hard, smooth surface. The sheet was the size of a dinner menu and was covered in written characters.

The characters were grouped into three sections. I was no linguistics expert, but the top section of the parchment was obviously Egyptian hieroglyphs. The middle and bottom portions were unknown to me. Charlotte bent down and held the electric torch over the paper.

"My God," she said. "This looks like a portion of the Rosetta Stone."

Anyone familiar with the classical world knew of the Rosetta Stone, the discovery of which allowed researchers to decipher Egyptian hieroglyphics, but I couldn't remember all the details of the story.

"Tell me again about the Stone?" I asked.

Charlotte studied the parchment. "During the two years Napoleon and his men were in Egypt, his soldiers found a stone marked by three distinct bands of inscription. Two of the inscriptions were written in an unknown language. The third was in Greek. And each inscription bore the same message."

Selberg cut her off. "Thereby allowing researchers to use the known language of Greek to decipher the other two."

"What were the languages?" I asked.

"You can see them here," she said. She indicated the parchment rubbing and I could see the three distinct bands of writing on the stone.

"The top portion is hieroglyphics. Demotic script in the middle and Greek on the bottom," Charlotte explained.

"What's Demotic?"

"It's sort of a shorthand version of hieroglyphics."

"So this is a copy of the Rosetta Stone?"

"No way," Selberg replied. "This is most definitely not just a copy of the original Rosetta Stone."

"He's right," Charlotte said. "The Rosetta Stone was much larger. This appears to have been taken from a tablet. The original Rosetta Stone was simply a tax decree written in the languages used in Egypt at the time. Historians always believed that there must be other stones. None were ever found."

"Can you read what this says?" I asked.

She looked down at the parchment. "I can figure it out, but it will take time. I'll work on it tonight."

Carefully, she folded the parchment back together.

The stone wall above the soldier was layered with a coating of dust, but beneath the coating I could see black markings. Slowly, I swiped my hand across the wall. Hundreds, maybe thousands of years of sediment cascaded to the floor. Concealed beneath the layers, more writing. I continued to work until I had cleared a small section.

I expected to see the hieroglyphs common to ancient Egypt, but instead three words appeared written in black paint.

Three English words.

Clayton let out a low whistle. "My God."

I felt my skin grow cold.

On the wall, in a chamber sealed since the time of Napoleon, were English words.

SUBWAY JUST AHEAD

◆ ◆ ◆

Nothing was worse in the academic community than the embarrassment of being taken in by a hoax. It cast such a long shadow on one's career that one could sometimes never find the sun again.

But despite this, part of me wanted desperately to believe that what we had seen in the tomb was real. The world had become too solid. Too rational. Science had removed the mystery behind life and left a population deadened to the possibility of something greater. Something that existed beyond the dominion of the rational.

Darkness began to descend as we returned to the tents. The pharaohs of ancient Egypt constructed their tombs on the West Bank of the Nile. Here they faced the entrance to the east, toward the rising sun, a symbol of their rebirth in the afterlife.

The belief in an afterlife shaped everything they did.

Almost like me now.

My wife was dead.

I watched as they put her body into a box and put the box into the ground. Sometimes the most enduring memories are the ones we wish we could most forget. In the days after her funeral, I would find parts of her life scattered everywhere about our apartment. A closet full of her clothes. Shelves filled with books she had read. In the bathroom, a brush with strands of her hair. All these little pieces had the feel of her, and they all worked together to bring back a full memory of her in life. Her smell. The curl of her hair. The things in life I had never appreciated, but now were all I had left.

She had worked in the history department at Columbia University. The day she died, she had left for work early. I had still been sleeping and her last words to me barely cut through my dreams. There was a whiff of her perfume, the tickle of her hair against my cheek, and the feel of her lips on my forehead as she kissed me goodbye.

"Have a good day."

That was it. That was the last thing she ever said to me.

That was the last memory I had of my wife alive. Me, half asleep, and her voice in the darkness of the bedroom telling me to have a good day. Five hours later she was dead. And I would have given anything to have that moment back again.

So now I needed to believe she was someplace else. Someplace wonderful and eternal. Not just in a box beneath ten feet of earth slowly melting away to nothingness.

Perhaps this tomb was just a hoax. And perhaps there was no mystery left on Earth. That the world we lived in was solid through and through. And there was nothing beyond. But if it wasn't a hoax, if what we had found was real, then maybe the world could be bent, like light through a prism and transformed into an unimaginable brilliance.

And maybe my wife was somewhere out there, waiting for me to join her.

◆ ◆ ◆

We decided to spend the night in the tents. The city of Luxor was only a few miles away, but the hotel was on the eastern side of the Nile.

The ferry discontinued service at night, and since the valley was on the western side, we were left somewhat stranded.

Across the valley I could see the campfires of the dig workers. They had their own smaller tents, donated by the university, which they lived in during the dig. I watched as the men turned something on a spit over the fire, the occasional shower of sparks rising into the air.

"Beautiful night," Charlotte said behind me. She joined me at the edge of the tent and looked across the valley.

I nodded in the darkness.

She wore a white dress, and in each hand she had a glass bottle of beer. She held one of them out. "Beer?"

"Yeah. Thanks." I took the beer from her. Her skin was warm, the bottle, ice cold.

"Wasn't sure if you were a drinker," she said.

"You brought two bottles just in case."

She pulled two more bottles from the pocket of her dress and placed them down at her feet. "Actually I brought four."

I laughed and took a long pull from the bottle. Alcohol always seemed to affect me more than it did most people. A smoldering ember was hidden in me, somewhere. Some deep seed of discontent perhaps. I supposed we all have them. Our own hatreds, which we keep locked up. But for me, alcohol was the master key.

Charlotte took a sip. "So, did you actually stay sober for those Prohibition years?"

I smiled. "I had a place."

"I'm impressed. Second door in the alley, knock twice and ask for Jimmy?"

"Something like that. You?"

"I didn't stay sober. Ever feel sad and you're not sure why? Anyway, most nights . . ." She raised her beer and shook it. The amber liquid sloshed in the glass. "Eventually they'll give it a name."

"They have already. Alcoholism."

"Alcoholism?" she said, as she took another deep pull. "I like that."

In the distance I heard the low rumble of a jeep approaching. The sun had dipped below the horizon and already the desert was dark. I scanned the slow rise of the road leading back toward Luxor, but I saw no headlamps approaching. Whoever it was did not wish to be seen.

Automobiles were relatively rare among native Egyptians, so this was most probably a westerner. European. Or American. The noise of the jeep cut off and the valley returned to a silence punctuated by the gentle murmur of conversation from the worker camp.

I turned back toward the tent. Selberg lay on his cot, pillow propped up beneath his head, reading F. Scott Fitzgerald. Clayton and his rifle were both gone.

"What do you know about Clayton?" Charlotte asked.

"I've known him a long time," I said. "Served with him in the war."

Across the valley, the muzzle of a weapon flashed in the darkness. An instant later, the boom of a shotgun. Selberg sat up quickly in his cot, eyes wide. "What the hell was that?"

Footfalls sounded in the darkness ahead of us. Clayton emerged from the night.

"What happened out there?" I asked.

"Nothing I couldn't handle."

I listened for the sound of the jeep starting up, pulling away back into the distance, but I heard nothing.

Eventually I turned down the lamp, lay in my cot, and fell asleep.

◆ ◆ ◆

Morning came quickly. The sun rose with an urgency in the desert and the cool night air faded into memory. Nasir slept with his eyes open, a strange habit of his. And sometimes he would not awake, even to my heaviest touch. This morning I found him, eyes open, glazed, his face looking out across the valley. I left him to his sleep.

The entrance to the tomb was exactly as we'd left it the previous day. Nasir had posted two guards, lanky men in red caps with antiquated rifles who gazed at me with open smiles as we walked by.

By contrast, the workers were a sullen lot. They stared at me emotionlessly as I passed, bare feet buried deep in sand, backs sweating from laboring with shovels for hours in the sun.

Clayton approached me quietly. "We should keep the soldiers outside."

I followed his line of sight out across the valley. Heat rose in waves from the ridge. "Why?"

"Last night we had visitors. They knew how to find the camp. Information is getting out somehow. This area is crawling with the Brotherhood of Anubis."

"Sounds menacing. Who are they?"

"A bunch of zealots dedicated to keeping ancient Egyptian tombs a secret," Clayton said. "They've been operating in the valley for years."

"Do we need to worry?"

"Don't know yet. Just be aware they're out there and watching us. I think—"

Clayton's words were interrupted by a shout from below. Selberg appeared at the chamber opening, breathless and covered in dust.

"What is it?" I asked.

"We've cleared away the rubble. We're ready to open the seal."

In the chamber below, I inspected what the workers had uncovered.

The door itself was stamped with a series of hieroglyphs that ran in two lines just above the seal. Charlotte approached the markings and began to translate them. "Whoever walks through these doors, I will twist their neck like a bird."

"And that's how legends of curses start," Selberg said.

I took a small rock hammer from my belt and knocked on the seal twice. The clay cracked and fell apart to the ground. Beneath, a length of rope, still surprisingly intact, wrapped around the handles of the door. This I slowly unwound, then pulled on the handles.

The door remained firmly closed. I pulled harder, and from somewhere beyond the doors, sounded the clunk of a heavy weight striking the ground. The door began to slowly open, the stone grating loudly on the floor.

Warm, foul air burst forth. A rush of wind filled the small room and the candles Nasir had placed along the wall all flickered and faded, threatened with extinguishment.

"Is that as ominous as it looks?" Charlotte narrowed her eyes as she watched the candles. The small flames still fought for life.

"Bad air," Selberg said. "The candles are an old miner's trick. You have to remember what these tombs were used for. Burial chambers. They were filled with dead bodies. Clothing. Wood. And over time all this organic matter decomposed, making the air quite toxic to breathe." Selberg rubbed his hand across his chin and I noticed he had a thin layer of stubble. This struck me as odd. He was such a neat and precise man. "And never shave."

"Of course." I ran my hand over my own smooth skin, annoyed at my own stupidity.

"Never shave?" Charlotte asked.

"Shaving opens the skin, allows germs inside," I said.

"Interesting idea," Charlotte replied. "Go back?"

I turned to look back up the stairs toward the small rectangle of light above us.

"Just give it a minute," Selberg said firmly. "As long as the candles don't go out, we're okay."

"You're not the one who shaved this morning," I said.

"Ah, men and their problems," Charlotte said, smiling. "As someone who also didn't shave my face today, I would still like to wait."

We waited in the antechamber. After a few minutes, the old air filtered out and the candle flames burned again with regularity. I approached the open doorway. The blackness yielded to my electric torch, and through the doorway I saw a second stone corridor, which led farther downward into the layers of limestone. The sides of the corridor were smooth, covered in gypsum plaster with reliefs depicting typical scenes from daily Egyptian life. Men fished with spears, standing precariously on the edge of long boats. In other scenes, figures harvested fruits or grains and carried them in wide baskets.

The scene on the opposite wall was much more violent.

"A battle between the Nubians and the Egyptians." I indicated the wall with my electric torch. "Wars between the two had broken out during many of the Egyptian dynasties."

"Who won?" Charlotte asked.

"Can't you tell?" I nodded toward the wall. The Nubians were being slaughtered, their soldiers lying decapitated and bloody while Egyptian chariots rolled over their bodies. The Egyptian soldiers seemed oddly expressionless, only the smallest hint of a smile on their faces. The faces of the Nubians depicted pain. Tongues of the dead hung out, eyes cringed shut. I realized I was staring at the complete annihilation of a people by a more technologically advanced enemy.

"Brutal," Charlotte murmured.

"It was brutal," I said. "The Egyptians had the most superior military of the time. Chariots. Archers. Foot soldiers."

Selberg had continued down into the corridor. He was oddly quiet, and I turned to see him intently studying a portion of the decorations.

"Find something?" I called out to him.

He turned toward me, his face pale, his hand shaking. Charlotte and I walked down the stone corridor toward him.

"God, man," I said. "You look as if you've seen a ghost."

He shook his head, a muffled click arose from his throat, and then he turned his torch toward the wall and illuminated the relief decorations.

We stood at the far end of the corridor, the final last few feet before the tomb abruptly turned ninety degrees to the right, the typical "bent axis" design of the early tombs. The decorations continued the length of the corridor, and in this final portion, the battle appeared to have ended.

"Looks like the Egyptians carried the day." Charlotte flashed her light across the decorations, revealing two Egyptian chariots. The chariots were again both driven by expressionless warriors. And behind the chariots, the men dragged something, a large net filled with the heads of Nubians.

The heads were realistically drawn. The art had a degree of specificity that I had never seen before in Egyptian art. And I could see that not all the heads were men. Some were women. Others were small children, as if an entire village had been massacred.

Charlotte covered her mouth.

It was a ghastly scene. Another of history's genocides. But this one long forgotten, the only evidence of its existence buried in the darkness of this tomb for thousands of years.

I glanced at Selberg, expecting the scientist to be looking at the scene of bloodshed. He was still pale, but his interest was focused at the final portion of the wall.

"What is it?"

"Here, look at this." Selberg jabbed a single finger out. "The soldiers in that battle. They were making an offering. Bringing the heads of their enemy as a gift."

"A gift to whom?" I asked.

Selberg pointed to the painted relief. The last scene. One of the chariot drivers bowed before a single figure. A man with pale skin who wore tan pants and a western shirt. A white man.

A man that looked like me.

Rapid footfalls echoed down the corridor toward us. In the distance sounded a deep boom, followed by the rattle of machine-gun fire. Nasir emerged from the darkness, his face a sheen of sweat.

"Sir, I beg you," Nasir said. "Stay in the tomb! We are under attack!"

Nasir turned and ran back toward the entrance. I followed closely behind him, moved up the stairs, and burst out into the open air. The light was blinding. I shut my eyes, as my brain registered the shock of the sun.

To the east sounded another boom, followed by two unmistakable loud cracks.

Gunfire.

Cautiously, I opened my eyes.

"Sir, get down please," Nasir said. He squatted behind the low rock wall, which led to the entrance of the tomb. He waved at me with his hands to take cover. Without thinking, I ran to him and threw myself against the wall.

"What the hell happened?" I asked.

"The Brotherhood of Anubis has attacked," he said. He nodded his head out across the wall. I looked up. In the distance I saw the peak of al-Qurn, silhouetted tan against the vibrant blue sky. In the foreground were men on horseback. Dozens of them. They wore black robes with white cloth that covered their faces.

The men rode directly toward our dig site, and as they rode, they fired shots at us from expertly wielded rifles. To the east, about forty yards away, a couple of our Egyptian guards hunkered down behind one of the trucks. Occasionally they rose and fired at the horsemen before they ducked down again to reload.

Someone called my name. Selberg, his eyes wide, stared at me from inside the doorway of the tomb. "What's happening?" He ducked as a bullet chipped a portion of sandstone from the side of the tomb. "Somebody is shooting."

"I'm aware of that," I said.

"At us!"

"Just stay in the tomb. We'll handle this," I said. "Has anyone seen Clayton?"

The campsite was a hundred yards away at least, farther down the length of the valley. I tried to think about what firearms we had secured with us. I remembered a long oil-metal box. A few World War I bolt-action rifles. Maybe a pistol or two. Certainly nothing that could repel a force the size of the Brotherhood.

From the direction of the tombs came the crunch of boot on sand. Clayton sprinted across the sand, a wicker basket in hand, and hurled himself against the rock wall next to me. He winked. "Just like old times in the war, right?"

"Yeah, but I'm happy to reminisce in other ways."

"Keep your head down," he said. "I'll straighten this out."

Clayton wiped sweat from his brow, then retrieved a Thompson submachine gun from the basket. He locked an ammunition magazine into the lower portion of the weapon and turned toward the approaching gunmen. I heard a metallic click as he chambered a round.

And then he pulled the trigger.

I had seen the effect machine-gun fire had on men and horses before. A truly awful sight. Never had I seen so many living creatures have their lives taken so quickly and in such a cruel and painful fashion.

And this outcome was just as bloody as I remembered. Where just moments before, a half-dozen men on horseback had quickly approached, now nothing moved, the air silent except for the shrieks of dying horses and cries of wounded riders. And even though they had come to kill me, and would have gladly done so, I could not help but feel sorry at the manner of their demise.

Clayton dropped the machine gun and advanced forward. He pulled a Colt pistol from his shoulder holster and calmly walked among the wounded men and horses, executing each with a single bullet to the head.

I turned away from the horrid sight. Instead I looked down across the length of the valley, toward the east where in the distance I knew the Nile lay, and thought of the images in the tomb. The annihilation of the Nubians by the Egyptians.

With one machine gun, Clayton had done by himself, in a few seconds, a level of devastation the Egyptians could not possibly have dreamed of. I was fearful of what the future held. Of what new weapons we would devise.

"There'll be more coming." Clayton stood over me. He surveyed the upper edges of the valley. "We can't leave now."

"Why not?" I asked.

"We're in a valley. They have the high ground. We won't make it out alive." Clayton checked his watch. "British policy in Luxor is to check on the well-being of all westerners working in the valley."

I was surprised and pleased to hear this. "How often do they check?"

"Every two days."

"So we wait for them?"

"We can't . . ." Clayton looked at me. I saw myself reflected in his sunglasses. Slowly he reached into his pocket and pulled out a cigarette. "We won't make it two days in the open. Not without water. Not without shelter. They'll attack again tonight. Murder us in our sleep."

"So what do we do?"

Clayton put the cigarette in his mouth, lit the end, and took a long pull. Smoke curled around his green eyes. He nodded toward the tomb.

"We go underground," he said. "It's our only chance."

◆ ◆ ◆

"I don't like it." Charlotte stood at the edge of the tomb and shielded her eyes against the sun. "We have trucks. I think we could make it. Drive fast out of the valley and don't stop until we hit Luxor."

"We hit the river first," I reminded her. "If the ferry isn't there, we'd be trapped."

"As if we won't be trapped inside the tomb." Charlotte looked a bit panicked at the prospect of spending the next two days underground. She bit her lower lip. "I just don't know if Clayton should be the one making these decisions. You're the head of the dig. What do you think?"

I shrugged, feeling awkward to be put on the spot. "Selberg doesn't seem to mind." I nodded toward the senior scientist, who was happily unloading a wooden crate from the rear of the truck.

"Of course he doesn't mind. He wants recognition. He's convinced himself this site is real. Not the absurd waste of time we know it is."

"Now hold on, we don't know that," I said. This was my expedition. And while the facts did point to the possibility of our discovery being a hoax, I still didn't like it being brought to my attention.

"No, you hold on. I didn't come out here to die," Charlotte said, her voice growing in fury.

Someone approached behind us and I turned to face Clayton. He held out a rifle to each of us. "You might want to take these."

I took the weapon from him and held it in my palm. I had not held a rifle since the war, and the weight of it now, the absolute certainty of metal in my hand, felt good.

"I'm not taking that thing. Are you crazy?" Charlotte's eyes flared. "We can leave now. Get in the trucks and drive out of here."

"Is that what you think?" Clayton asked.

"That's what I know. They're on horseback for God's sake. We have entered the modern age. We have automobiles. At least we can have some of the workers drive back to Luxor."

"I will not give that order," he said.

"Why not?"

"Because any worker that gets in a truck will be seen as an enemy of the Brotherhood. They will be massacred."

"That's what you believe. I believe they will make it through." She stared at Clayton for a long moment, then turned and began to speak rapidly in Arabic to several of the workmen. She indicated the truck, obviously telling the workers to drive to Luxor. One of the men shook his head and backed away. Most of these men had only seen a handful of automobiles in their lives. They would not know how to drive.

Charlotte became even more frustrated. She threw up her hands and said in English, "Someone drive the damn truck!"

Clayton pushed past her, picked up a heavy brick and a rope from the dig and headed for the truck. He opened the door and began to lash the steering wheel to the inside frame.

"What do you think you're doing?" Charlotte walked quickly toward him. Clayton ignored her and started the engine. "I asked you a question." Charlotte was angry, emotional, her face flushed.

Clayton pushed her back from the truck, then placed the heavy brick on the vehicle's gas pedal. The truck lurched forward on the road, headed, driverless, for the edge of the valley. We all watched the vehicle speed away, a giant dust cloud billowing behind it.

"Oh, that's just great." Charlotte threw her hands up again.

The truck continued straight, gathering speed. As it reached the narrow strip of the valley, an explosion ripped across the desert. The truck flipped forward, launched impossibly high into the air like a toy, before it landed on the front cab and rocked forward onto its roof. A burst of wind struck me an instant later, followed by a low resonant boom.

From either side of a rocky outcropping, a half-dozen men approached the vehicle, firing into the cab with rifles as they moved forward.

Charlotte watched, her eyes wide, then slowly her lower lip began to quiver. I too felt my heart beat faster. I had also considered making our getaway in the trucks. Clayton's face was expressionless. Then he shook his head.

"Shame we had to waste a truck," he said. "We might have need of it later."

Charlotte turned toward him, said nothing, then walked toward the tomb entrance.

We were trapped.

◆　◆　◆

In Roman times, many of the discovered ancient tombs of Egypt had served several other purposes. Some were used as stables, or for storage, and some even became temporary homes. Sitting inside the first chamber, circled around the small electric torch, I could not imagine a more depressing abode.

The gloom of the chamber was oppressive, and I made my way back up the stone corridor to the tomb opening. Clayton guarded the entrance, a submachine gun in each hand. Around the site, the workers had thrown down their tools and were advancing slowly into the desert with their arms raised.

I watched them walk toward the moonlit horizon. "What's happening?"

"They're leaving us." Clayton spit tobacco juice onto the ground. "They're not taking chances."

"Will they be harmed?"

"Probably not. Brotherhood will let them pass through just fine. Hell, some of the workers are Brotherhood members. Wouldn't surprise me to find out we had a few spies in our midst."

"So what happens now?"

"See those ridges up there?" Clayton pointed to an area about two hundred yards distant, where the valley walls sloped sharply upward, forming a long ridge that stretched toward the mountain al-Qurn. "There's a full view of the valley up there. That's where they'll be now."

"Doing what?"

"Waiting for darkness. The tommy gun surprised them. But now they'll be more careful. There won't be any more frontal assaults. The next time, we won't see them coming until they're on top of us."

◆　◆　◆

Night fell quickly in the desert. I stayed at the tomb entrance with Clayton. Charlotte joined us, her arms wrapped in a light blanket she had found in one of the trucks.

We watched the sun slowly lower toward the valley walls. And then, abruptly, it was gone. Night had begun. On the ridge above us, I saw the reddish glow of a campfire. Occasional sparks rose into the darkness, fluttered for a moment, and extinguished into nothing. I detected the faint smell of cooking meat. Instantly I was ravenous. I had not eaten all day, and now that the action had slowed, the feeling was powerful.

"The fires are a good sign," Clayton said. "As long as they've got fires going, we know they're eating. They won't come."

"And when the fires go out?" Nasir said.

"That's when we worry."

I looked back across the valley and saw the flames. Already the night had grown chilly. Back in New York, Susan and I might be getting ready to see a show on Broadway. Or a new motion picture.

I felt a momentary wave of homesickness. I had been away for eight months, two weeks, and four days. That was certainly long enough for any family man. And I missed my wife. Only this time she was not at home waiting for me. The thought of this weighed heavily. I still hadn't accepted her death. Like friends who came back from the war missing arms or legs. Some mornings your eyes open, and for a beautiful fleeting moment, you forget what you have lost. Everything seems right in the world. Then you look down, and see what has been taken and you remember what can never be returned. And the sadness rolls over like a fog.

A chill crept over me, and I crossed my arms to conserve warmth. I looked up to the ridge over the valley. I watched the fires burn. Then slowly, I saw each of them go out, one by one.

They were coming.

◆ ◆ ◆

We waited in darkness. The moon was a half sliver of light. The valley walls held the moonlight and emitted a pale luminescence. The scene looked very much like the surface of some distant and inhospitable planet. I had been in this country for eight months, but the valley tonight seemed as strange to me as if this were my first night. Below, in the tomb, Charlotte, Nasir, and Selberg talked about the rise of the Nationalist Socialist Party in Germany. Next to me, Clayton shifted his weight and slowly raised machine guns to his shoulders.

"Do you see something?" I whispered.

He nodded toward the first ridgeline, where the limestone walls sloped sharply down to the valley floor. He looked uncertain. "Out there, shadows maybe."

"Hit the lights?" I asked.

Clayton shook his head no, and we waited. Above us, the moon slipped behind clouds and the light was extinguished. The moonscape before us turned dark, a complete blackness devoid of any of the ambient light produced by distant cities. Here in the desert, nothing.

From the first ridge to our current location was a wide, flat space fifty yards in length. The area offered little cover, and a direct frontal assault would be cut down by Clayton and his machine guns.

Our weakness came from behind.

The tomb was cut into the valley walls, and the entrance rose about ten feet over our head. Behind the entrance was the gentle slope of the valley, a point from which men could easily climb down and ambush us.

Clayton lightly touched my shoulder, then touched his own ear. I strained my eyes into the blackness ahead of us but could only make out the faint jagged outline of the ridge against the sky.

Someone whispered in the darkness. The voice came from out on the flat plain, maybe twenty yards away. Another voice whispered back, and then someone whistled. I heard the crunch of feet on sand.

"Light it up," Clayton said.

I raised the flare gun over my head and pulled the trigger. A brilliant red meteor erupted from the gun with a *whoosh* and arced upward into the night sky. The entire plain was illuminated in a flickering glare of red light, like a match being struck in the darkness.

At least two dozen armed men in black robes stretched along the road.

Clayton opened up with the machine gun and I banged away with my rifle.

The men dove for cover. Some of them fired back. Bullets impacted around us and a chip of rock flew from somewhere and struck me just below the right eye. My rifle clicked empty and I held my free hand to my eye. My fingers came away bloody.

Voices called out to each other in Arabic, followed by more gunfire, this time much closer. Our position was being overrun.

Clayton emptied another of the machine guns. "We have to fall back into the tomb."

We moved quickly down the stone stairs and into the first chamber. Below, Charlotte, Nasir, and Selberg waited for us.

"What's happening?" Selberg asked. "Good God, man, your eye."

I wondered vaguely what my eye must look like. "Get everything together," I said as I scooped up canteens of water in my arms.

"Where are we going?" Charlotte asked.

"Into the tomb."

Selberg smiled at this, Charlotte frowned, and Nasir sputtered. "But the air, sir, it's still bad?"

"We'll have to chance it," I said, canteens wrapped around my arm. "The air up here has become just as bad. Filled with lead, which is significantly worse for one's health I should think."

From above, machine-gun fire still sounded. The next few moments showed what was most important to each member of the party. Charlotte worked quickly, gathering together her artist's papers and pencils, which she had been using to sketch out the various glyphs and decorations we had come across. Nasir grabbed a few of the wicker baskets containing food. Selberg, his scientific instruments.

From the tunnel entrance came running feet. Clayton half-slipped, half-fell down the stairs.

"Dynamite." Clayton grabbed me and Charlotte both and pushed us roughly toward the back of the chamber. "Everybody down."

A moment of scrambling ensued. Nasir tripped and fell face forward, sprawled out on the rock. Selberg stood uncomprehending in the center of the chamber. I grabbed him and forced him down.

The explosion ripped through the air. I was buffeted back, thrown against the wall as dust and rock debris billowed down from the corridor. My eardrums rippled and almost felt like they would burst as the entire chamber turned upside down. I hit the ground hard. Pain flared through my shoulder and radiated up my neck. I had a last glimpse of something giant and black looming over me. I stared up, my mind trying to piece together the words.

SUBWAY JUST AHEAD

◆ ◆ ◆

I woke in darkness. My mouth was unusually wet and tasted of iron. I knew that I was bleeding heavily somewhere. I sat up and my brain reacted, rolling heavily against the inside of my skull, throwing my entire body into a spinning blur of motion like a drunk in the midst of a world-record binge.

I leaned against the wall behind me and waited for the spins to pass. Eventually they did, and I began to concentrate on my surroundings. The chamber was in complete darkness. At first I feared I was the only one left alive, but then someone coughed to my right.

"Hello?" I asked the darkness.

To my left, someone else coughed, then spit. I reached along the ground and felt for the electric torch I had been carrying before the explosion. My fingers touched the hard base, then I found the switch and turned the bulb on. Brilliant white light illuminated the chamber and the bedraggled crew inside.

At least everyone had survived the blast. Charlotte stood in the corner brushing dust from her shoulders, while Selberg and Nasir shook their heads, a fine layer of sandstone cascading from their hair.

Clayton extended his hand down to me. I took it, and he pulled me upright.

"Thanks," I said as I gained my balance. I surveyed the room and saw what had been the stairway was now completely blocked with crushed stone. "We appear to be trapped."

Apparently the prospect of an immediate death at the hands of the Brotherhood of Anubis had been replaced by the prospect of a much more drawn out death from starvation or thirst deep below ground. I was not sure which would be more painful.

"We're not trapped," Selberg said.

"What do you mean?" Charlotte asked.

"We can still go farther into the tomb." Selberg indicated the second doorway. "There may be another stairwell leading out."

"Or there may just be more chambers," Charlotte said. "More dead ends. I say we stay here."

"What does that gain us?"

"When the rescue party comes for us, we'll be here."

"I don't know, Charlotte," I said. "That's a lot of stone."

She shook her head firmly. "They will come for us. And we should be here when they do."

I saw Nasir frown slightly and I turned toward him. "Nasir, what do you think? How long to dig us out?"

"Oh, I don't know, sir."

"Nasir, this is important. Do not hold your tongue. Speak frankly with us. You are the dig foreman. Your knowledge is invaluable."

Nasir reached up and touched the layer of rock that now blocked the tomb entrance. He rapped it thoughtfully with his knuckle, then shook his head. "Six days sir. And that with a crew of twenty men digging and breaking stone constantly."

Charlotte's face fell. "Six days? But that's almost a week."

"It is, ma'am."

"That is totally unacceptable. I can't be down here for a week."

"I'm sorry, ma'am. But that's my estimate."

"Well you're wrong."

"Nasir's word is worth more than water here," I said. "I would trust my life with what he says."

"So it's settled. Six days we have at least down here." Selberg began to load his scientific equipment into a leather satchel. "Plenty of time to explore the new chamber."

The electric torches would not last for that long. And I was not excited at the prospect of spending the last few days in total darkness.

"Before we go farther," I said, "we should take an inventory of our supplies. We need to know how long we can last down here."

We spent the next few minutes gathering everything together. All told, we had five canteens, tents and bedding, kerosene, plenty of biscuits, four electric torches, several gas railroad lanterns, a host of scientific equipment, and Charlotte's sketching supplies. For armaments, we had two Thompson submachine guns. Two bolt-action rifles. Three pistols of varying manufacture. And several boxes of assorted rounds of ammunition.

"I say we leave the weaponry here," Charlotte said.

"Weaponry comes with us," Clayton replied. He did not even look at her.

"But there is nothing down here that could possibly hurt us. We have no need to carry such heavy items."

"Weaponry stays," Clayton repeated. This time he looked up and fixed her with hard eyes.

Above us, the stone ceiling groaned loudly. Several small fractures were visible in the limestone. Whatever reluctance we might have had to explore farther in the tunnel was quickly eradicated by a long rumble from above, the sound of stone shifting against stone.

Selberg hoisted his satchel over his shoulder, then started toward the second doorway and the unexplored stairwell. He turned back toward us. "Coming?"

Quickly we gathered what we were to carry and followed after him, descending farther into the unknown.

Since I held the only illuminated torch, I took position at the head of the line. We passed by the battle of the Nubians, then reached a second stone corridor decorated with typical Egyptian imagery. I had always found these images to be particularly disturbing. The Egyptian gods were frightening, like characters pulled from a nightmare. Men with the heads of hawks. Giant baboons holding spears. Horrible chimeras of human and beast. The mind projects fears from the world around us. What kind of world had the ancient Egyptians lived in to promote the imaginings of such frightful creatures?

The corridor opened into an area much larger than the previous rooms. I held the electric torch aloft and illuminated the space. My nerves pulsed with anxious energy. I stared at something impossible.

This was not a just a burial chamber . . . this was like nothing I had ever seen.

"My God," Selberg said, his eyes wide. "What is this place?"

Slowly we absorbed the giant open space. Near us, the walls were flat plaster over stone, but soon the plaster gave way to rectangular blocks. Glazed concrete blocks that shone in the light. Support columns ran the length of the room and far beyond an arched opening, which led back into darkness. Black metal bars lined with turnstiles separated us from the darkness.

We stood at the edge of some kind of train station.

The walls were papered with advertisements. Nearby, a large color poster sealed behind glass; a single palm tree on a tiny strip of an island of brilliantly white sand surrounded by blue water. A travel advertisement. Once there had been words on the poster, but over time most had rubbed off. Now, only a single word remained, inscribed in large black letters just over the palm tree, the coloring ominously dark across the blue sky.

Escape.

◆　◆　◆

"What is happening?" Charlotte said.

We sat on benches that lined the wall, our gear spread on the floor below us. Clayton stood by the opening to the corridor.

Buried beneath the sand was some kind of underground transit station.

"I don't know," I said. "But I'm beginning to believe what the Bedouin saw."

"We are obviously looking at the work of a modern civilization with technology far in advance of ancient Egypt. More advanced even than our own," Selberg said. "And not just any technology. Technology specific to a date sometime in the future."

"What if this is like Urashima Taro?" Charlotte reached for her pack, took out a small English textbook and began thumbing through it.

"Excuse me?" I said.

"Urashima Taro was a Japanese tale about a fisherman who visits an undersea palace. He spends only three days there. But when he returns to his village, three hundred years have passed."

"So?" Selberg frowned.

"So what if we're all collectively having a Urashima Taro experience? We've somehow all been sent three hundred years into the future."

"I don't know." Selberg looked thoughtful, then said, "Civilizations are always rising and falling. Mankind makes advances, then loses ground. Look at the Dark Ages. Or Egypt itself. The advances made under the pharaohs were not duplicated again for thousands of years. So perhaps there was an earlier civilization, which has since been forgotten."

I shook my head. "That's impossible. We have archeological records that predate the Egyptians. There is nothing in those records to indicate the presence of such modern technologies."

Selberg's eyes narrowed reluctantly. "You're right." He drummed his fingers against the bench. "But it is here. And there must be a reason for that."

"Urashima Taro," Charlotte repeated.

Clayton pointed toward the end of the chamber. "What do you think that means?"

Set into the wall was a revolving door made of iron bars. I approached the door and pushed against the bars. They were locked in place. Over the door, inscribed in stone, was the word *Panopticon*.

"Panopticon?" Selberg asked.

I shook my head. I had no idea. To the right of the door was a metal box that rose up from the ground about waist high. On the top of the box were two slits, with an arrow that read "Slide Card Here."

From my pocket I retrieved the yellow card we had found on the soldier.

"Wait a minute . . ." Charlotte advanced toward me. "These are not things that man should be tampering with. We don't know what's beyond that door."

"But don't you understand?" Selberg looked at each of us. "That's what's so amazing. We have no idea about any of this. I think we have a scientific duty to move forward. And if none of you will, I'll go first. Alone if I have to."

Nobody moved.

"For Christ's sake . . ." Clayton approached and held out his hand. "Give me the card."

I handed Clayton the yellow card and stepped back. Card in hand, he moved toward the revolving door. He pushed once against the door to confirm it was locked into place. Then he slid the card through the narrow slot in the box near the door.

There was an audible beep.

Clayton pressed against the bars of the revolving portal, and slowly with a shriek of rusted metal, the door began to move. Clayton turned, took a last look back at us, then passed through the door.

"What is it?" Charlotte called through the bars.

Clayton stood on the opposite side of the revolving door. He stared at something beyond our line of vision, completely indifferent to our presence. He was a man transfixed.

"Clayton," I called out. "The card."

Distracted, Clayton nodded and passed the card back through the bars. I swiped once and pushed through the revolving door. Once through I passed the card back through the bars, then took a moment to gather myself. Clayton and I stood on the edge of a concrete platform, which had been painted with a long strip of yellow. The platform extended into darkness.

I held my electric torch up. Something in the darkness reflected the light back. Something made of metal and glass. Behind me, the revolving door spun again and Nasir joined us. He looked out across the platform.

"Praise be to Allah," he whispered, and held his hands up, palms forward.

Parked along the edge of the platform was a subway train.

◆ ◆ ◆

"It appears to be a New York City subway train." Selberg walked along the edge of the train, running his hand across the metal. "Amazing. This is like nothing I've ever seen. What we have back home are drab olive-colored boxes. Red vinyl benches. Riveted steel. This car is some type of composite material. And so sleek. No rivet marks anywhere. We don't have the ability to produce anything like this."

"Not now, we don't," I said.

The train was silver in color, with long glass windows covered in a thin layer of dust. Sets of double doors were closed shut. I wiped at the glass with my finger and held the torch up to the smear. Through the glass I could see rows of empty seats.

"Still think this is a hoax?" I turned toward Selberg.

"No." Selberg smiled like a kid. "No way. Amazing. This has been down here for God knows how long."

"There's a tunnel up ahead." Nasir nodded toward a large arch at the far end of the platform. The subway tracks stretched through the opening and vanished into the darkness. "Maybe we could walk down, see where it goes?"

"Maybe . . ." I approached the tunnel entrance. Already my electric torch was beginning to die. The small bulb flickered desperately in my hand. I was nervous about walking farther into the tunnel with our few remaining torches. "We don't know where this leads. I'd hate to get lost down here."

The light to the electric torch continued to sputter.

"We should light another torch," Charlotte said, "before it goes completely dark."

Her voice came from only a few yards away from me, but already I could barely see her. The darkness encroached quickly beneath the Earth.

Near the entrance to the tunnel, a large switch was fixed on the wall. The switch was the length of my forearm, and beneath it was a sign labeled MAIN SUPPLY POWER. The device was old-fashioned in appearance, large and clumsy, a prop from Dr. Frankenstein's laboratory. I wrapped my hand around it, and as my torch flickered and died, I impulsively pushed upward.

There was a moment of resistance, then the switch gave way and with a loud clunk, moved into the up position. From somewhere behind the wall came a deep resonant hum. An electric hum.

"What's happening?" Charlotte moved toward me. "What did you touch?"

The humming rose in intensity. I heard a pop, then a flare of light appeared from sets of bulbs along the wall of the platform. Collectively we blinked in the light. The train came alive. The headlamps flared with glowing intensity and, with a hiss of hydraulics, each of the double doors slid open.

"Extraordinary," Selberg said. We all stood in silence on the platform. The doors to the subway car remained open, waiting for us to enter.

I could now see the platform was about fifty yards in length, with block columns spaced at regular intervals. The only remaining evidence of the tomb was behind us. We had entered an entirely new world.

The front of the subway car had a glass windshield, which covered the empty motorman's area. There was a crack down the center, as if something heavy had struck the glass. Ahead, the tunnel stretched out into darkness. I looked at the expectant faces of my team. We had come this far. Why the hell not?

"Let's get on."

◆ ◆ ◆

The inside of the subway car was free of debris and the air smelled surprisingly clean. However long the car had been down here, the doors must have remained sealed, keeping out external contaminants.

Windows flanked rows of seats. Each seat was made of a similar material to the yellow card, except much harder and molded into curved shapes. These were pristine, completely clear of dust.

Shining metal poles had been placed at intervals, and the walls featured more commercial advertisements for various products. This was more than any of us could fathom. Selberg ran his hand along the length of glass, stunned by the size of the windows in the car, the futuristic feel of everything around us. Clayton surveyed our surroundings with a guarded quiet, his rifle pressed against his shoulder. Nasir and Charlotte both studied the lengths of advertisements along the wall with open amazement.

I made my way to the front.

At the end of the car was a door that slid back. I opened this, and beyond was a control panel much like the inside of an automobile. I scanned over various lights and buttons, then pressed one labeled Automatic.

Immediately, the doors closed with a snapping finality.

The subway car lurched forward. I was caught off balance, my body swung forward, and I grabbed onto a metal pole that extended from the ceiling to the floor.

"Maybe you should stop touching stuff until we all know what it does," Charlotte said, her hand gripping the pole tightly. The train began to pick up speed, and I wondered if she was right.

"This appears to be a means of local transportation, powered by electricity." Selberg held onto one of the support bars as well. We gained speed at an alarming rate. The train rocked back and forth on thousand-year-old tracks. Through the dusty glass was blackness, punctuated every so often by an electric blue flare of light from below the train.

"Does anyone know how to stop it?" Nasir asked.

"It's probably automated," Selberg said. "Look at the number of seats. It must have been used by hundreds of people. So much larger than what we have now."

"That's not what's most interesting," Charlotte said. "Look at the advertisements. You can tell what a culture values by their advertisements."

I followed her glance and saw posters for Broadway shows and alcoholic beverages and denim pants. All the people were quite good looking. Perfect teeth and flawless skin. They seemed to live a life of ease and convenience. Some of the women wore much less clothing, and I found myself caught between staring and trying to avert my eyes.

There was a beautiful blurred photograph of a Caribbean island. A travel advertisement. The words *Escape Your Dreams* written below. I had seen this before, on the platform.

I could see what Charlotte was getting at.

"They're humans," I said. "From sometime in the future maybe, but they're still us."

"Exactly. They have the same wants, same desires."

"The fact is," Selberg said, "we don't know what's out there. We don't know if it's human. Or not. And if not, we have to consider that it might be hostile."

"That's a very male perspective. That everything might be hostile," Charlotte said.

"Hostile?" Clayton spoke up for the first time since we boarded the train.

Charlotte shook her head. "If there is something down here, it is not hostile. The kind of technology necessary to construct the things we've seen hardly registers as a hostile act."

"So you view all this as an invitation to enter?" Selberg asked.

"Well, it's certainly not a deterrent. Lights that still turn on. A train that still moves. Posters. Advertisements. None of this in any way suggests violence or aggression."

Clayton addressed Selberg. "Why do you think hostility is possible?"

"I don't necessarily," Selberg replied. "But many creatures in nature deliberately entice their prey with attractive colors or scents, only to be hostile in the end. The Venus flytrap, for example."

"So you think this whole thing might be an elaborate Venus flytrap?" Charlotte asked. "And what, we end up being eaten by whatever is down here?"

Selberg smiled sheepishly. "Maybe there's nothing down here. This is all just hypothetical. Academic." The train began to slow. "I mean, it's been a few thousand years. What could possibly have survived?"

With a slight screech of metal, the train came to a full stop. The doors opened and I exited cautiously. I was afraid and excited. Surrounded by the metal and glass of the subway car, I had felt a relative safety. But my heart beat faster as I entered the outside world. Anything seemed possible in this place. I stood on the edge of a second platform similar to the one we had used to board. This one was also well lit, with more advertisements papered on the walls. Nearby, a black arrow indicated a metal-over-concrete staircase that led upward.

"There's something here," I called back to the subway car. "Looks like stairs."

"Stairs?" Selberg joined me on the platform. "Just stairs?" He was sweating and wiped his hairline with the back of his hand. "I was expecting some sort of mechanical transport device." The platform was hot, but from somewhere I felt a slight gust of cooler air. Fan mechanism maybe. "Where's it go?"

I glanced upward, feeling uncertainty rise in my throat. "I'm going to check. You stay down here with the equipment. Clayton, want to join?"

The stairs were typical concrete construction lined with metal on the edges, as if the builders expected heavy foot traffic to wear down the concrete over time. Now, the area was vacant, lifeless. Nothing moved. Not an insect. Not even a scrap of paper. Still, I felt a faint cool breeze. The stairs curved upward, and ahead I could see a square of bluish light. We walked past a token booth, deserted, but ready for use, stacks of change through the glass, a calendar pinned to the wall opened to the month of June, no year listed. Again, I was amazed by the relative smoothness of the construction. In my New York, riveted steel dominated the subway system, everything drab green and blocky in feel. The curves of the booths and the subway here had an elegance that surprised me.

"Strange, right?" I turned toward Clayton. Clayton nodded. "Where is everyone?"

"Don't know." Clayton's eyes scanned the stairwell, weapon at the ready. "Stairs are ending. Look alive."

"You have a pistol for me?"

Clayton glanced at me without surprise. He pulled a Colt revolver from his waistband and handed it to me. Slowly we made our way to the top of the stairs.

The stairs flattened out to a sidewalk, and I recognized our location immediately. We stood at the edge of a large circle of pavement around which stretched tall buildings of glass, metal, and stone. To the west, I saw a multileveled shopping center of glass and white granite. Mannequins layered with clothes stood along the edge of shop windows while at the entrance, a massive marble-lined lobby. To the east, the base of a large park. Not any park. *The* park. The most familiar park in the world. A massive emerald bracketed by concrete and steel. Empty footpaths cut through the earthy green, vanishing around corners into the dusk. A stone wall stretched along the avenue, overhung by crooked branches.

Behind us, at the subway entrance, a sign read Columbus Circle. New York City. Manhattan. I was born no more than twenty blocks from here. And here I was, back again, somehow deep beneath the Earth, buried at the twisted end of a tomb in the Valley of the Kings. This was perhaps the most unique find in the history of humanity, and I was living it for myself. I hovered in a space between dreams and reality, trapped in an experience so fantastical it almost couldn't be believed.

There were no signs of people. It was an eerie feeling. To stand in the center of the busiest city on Earth and see no one. Whoever had built this place had captured every detail of the great metropolis. But without the people, the place felt sterile, like some giant architectural model.

Or, I had the bizarre thought, perhaps the city was a normal model and we were the ones strangely sized, shrunk somehow and dropped into the new vast world. Clayton joined me on the sidewalk. He took in the sight without comment, then said, "What do you want to do?"

"Get the others."

Selberg was animated. Charlotte was quiet. Nasir, who had never been to a western city before, had never seen a building higher than the pyramids, became overwhelmed and fell to his knees in prayer.

"Why, this is wonderful," Selberg said.

Clayton checked his watch. "Clocks are wrong though."

I followed his gaze to a large clock fixed to the side of the shopping mall. The hands on the face were stopped at exactly quarter past nine. Another clock fixed in the center of the circle also read the same. Whether this was a.m. or p.m., I didn't know.

"The clocks are wrong? The clocks are wrong?" Selberg repeated in disbelief. "Who cares if the clocks are wrong!"

Quarter past nine. 9:15. I turned the numbers over in my mind. "It is an interesting point," I said finally. "I mean, why quarter past nine?"

"What?" Selberg turned toward me. "It's insignificant."

"Is it though? I mean, everything in this city is so orchestrated. So well planned. Every detail arranged. So what happened at quarter past nine?" Something bothered me about that time. Some deep memory I couldn't quite grasp. I checked my watch. Outside, in the real world, it was seven p.m., and we had been in the tunnels for hours. Somehow, I had not noticed.

"So what are we waiting for?" Selberg said. "We should push on, explore."

I considered that. Above us, the air was infused with a vague light, like the glow through thick clouds on an overcast day. The glow must be the result of some sort of internal light source, I deduced, as we were too deep beneath the Earth for the sun to reach us. Yet, the surrounding buildings stretched up to incredible heights, not limited by ceilings or barriers. The size of the chamber we found ourselves in was impossible to comprehend. Hundreds of stories in height, at least. If there was a light source somewhere above, it was massive. And I couldn't be certain, but it felt like the light was failing. The air seemed to be slowly growing darker. Perhaps the chamber kept a day and night schedule. This faded grayish light during daylight hours, then darkness at night.

"I don't know if that's a good idea." I hesitated. I didn't want to be caught too far away from the subway entrance if it got dark. Considering this was an artificially constructed world, night inside the chamber might be infinitely darker than in the natural world of stars and moonlight. Here, the darkness could be absolute and impenetrable. And there was no way to know how long it might last.

"Scared of the dark?" Selberg asked.

"Sure, I'm nervous. We don't know anything about this place. We don't know what happens at night." I nodded at our pile of gear. "My vote? We stay here, pitch the tents, and see how the night goes."

"I still think we could explore farther. At least one more street," Selberg said.

I ignored his statement, and Nasir and I went to work setting up the tents. We picked a spot just off the subway entrance, on the hard, paved sidewalk near the circle. While camping inside one of the buildings might be more comfortable, I wanted to stay close to the station in case we needed to make a fast exit.

Selberg pouted for a few minutes, then he and Charlotte moved toward the edge of the park to gather wood for a fire.

"Stay close," I said to their backs.

I had been right, as the light soon began to fade quickly. Nasir and I had a difficult time with the tents. We were unable to bury the tent stakes into the concrete, so we had to settle with tying off the support ropes to the edge of the subway station railing on one side and a fire hydrant on the other. We placed all three tents together in a circular pattern. Each of the doors faced outward.

Selberg and Charlotte returned with armfuls of firewood they had gathered from the park. I inspected the branches, expecting some kind of synthetic materials. Cardboard limbs and rubber leaves, like a set design prop for a theater production. But instead, each branch had fully articulated green leaves and stems of springy, healthy wood. These were real, living branches.

"I wondered about that," Charlotte said. "No sunlight down here. No rain. Where do the trees come from?"

"Don't know."

"Because there looks to be a park filled with them."

"Let's just see if they burn," Selberg said. "It's getting chilly."

I realized he was right. As the light faded, the temperature began to drop quickly. And as dark shadows moved across abandoned streets and the faces of vacant buildings, the city began to feel more and more gloomy. A frightening lost world beneath the Earth. I could tell the others felt the oppression too. Casual glances over the shoulder. A lingering near the edges of the tent. A fire might cheer us up.

"I don't know . . . maybe we should study them," Charlotte said. "We don't know what happens when they burn. They might release toxic gas. They appear to be trees, but are they? For all we know, these trees might be the entities that built this place."

"I'm cold. One way to find out," Selberg said. He dragged over a large empty metal trash can to the edge of the tents, then dropped his branches inside. He doused the branches with a stream of kerosene we had brought with us, then dropped a lit match on top of them.

Flames burst forth, which settled into a slow fire as the branches were gradually consumed.

"Looks normal," Selberg said. "Smells normal."

The fire seemed to burn like a fire should and emitted a welcome heat, which soon had us all gathered around. I used a camp mirror to inspect my face. I had a small gash below my eye from the tunnel explosion. Blood clung to the side of my face in dried rivulets, but the wound had closed and there seemed little danger of infection.

"Wonder if any of these stores have food," Clayton said.

"If they did," I said, "I guess it'd be a few thousand years old."

"Or water. I mean, looks like this place was built for people. So they must have eaten something, right?"

"He raises a good point," Selberg said. "If this place was built for people, then there would need to be supplies of food. Water. Where would this come from? Grown down here? Brought in?"

"Maybe the Egyptians brought it in?" Charlotte asked.

"You think one culture knew about the other? The Egyptians on top and whoever these people are below?"

"Worked in *The Time Machine*. The Eloi and the . . ." My voice trailed off. *The Time Machine* had been one of my favorite books as a child, but now I couldn't remember the name of the monsters. The ones who lived below the Earth. The ones who fed on the Eloi.

"Morlocks," Charlotte said.

"You think the people down here were the Morlocks?" I asked.

"If there was a relationship between the two peoples," Selberg said, "I would suggest it would be one of symbiosis. Mutually beneficial to both. For example, perhaps the city people gave Egyptians access to their technologies."

"And what would the Egyptians give to the city people?" I asked.

Selberg's eyebrows scrunched together. "I'm not sure . . ."

"What did the above ground people give the Morlocks?" Clayton asked.

"The above ground people were food," Selberg said.

"What?"

"The Morlocks ate them."

I hunched my shoulders against the chill and surveyed the circle. Around us was quite dark now, the silhouette of the buildings a faint line against the blue-black sky above. In the darkness near where the park would be, a match head flared and Clayton's face glowed red in the night as he lit up a smoke.

"We should get some sleep," I said. "Not much we can do with the lights out."

"I wonder how long the night lasts here," Charlotte asked.

I pulled back the flap of my tent. Inside was a sleeping bag and a small, gas, railroad lantern. I felt immediate exhaustion and collapsed onto the sleeping bag, the hard concrete of West Fifty-Ninth Street beneath me. The tent undulated slightly, played upon by a slight disturbance in the air. The walls were thin fabric. Nothing could be kept out that might want to get in. And as I drifted off to sleep, I wondered if this might be a problem.

◆ ◆ ◆

I awoke in a sweat, pulled from sleep like one might pull a boot stuck deep in black mud. I wiped my eyes of perspiration, lit a match and tried to read the face of my watch. I was certain it must be well after midnight, but instead I saw it was just past 9:15 p.m. I had been sleeping for only an hour.

The same time as the broken clocks.

I had been having a nightmare. Already the dream was fading from consciousness, and I struggled to remember the details. Somehow it seemed important. There had been a long hallway. Bloody handprints marked the wall. Broken glass on the floor. A bathroom, black and white checkered floor, a shower curtain pulled shut, concealing something beyond.

And then I awoke.

In the blackness of the tent, I breathed deeply. I could feel rivulets of sweat trickle down the length of my back. Outside, footsteps approached the tent's entrance. I pushed myself up onto an elbow and reached for the revolver I had tucked beneath my pillow. It seemed that in Egypt I was not able to get a single night's sleep without having need of the Colt.

The footsteps stopped directly in front of the tent flap.

Clayton's voice came as a whisper. "Are you awake in there?"

"Yes. What is it?"

"There's something out here you should see."

I dressed, then tucked the Colt into my waistband. Fully clothed, I crawled from my tent. Clayton was outlined in darkness.

"Out there." Clayton pointed south, away from the edge of the park. In the distance I could see the jagged silhouettes of buildings along the edge of the circle.

"Third building in from the circle," Clayton said. "Three quarters up."

As my eyes adjusted to the darkness, I saw an apartment building, with tiers of balconies.

A light from a single apartment burned in the darkness.

"There's more," Clayton said. He pressed binoculars into my hands. "Look."

I scanned the dark edge of the building, then oriented myself on the illuminated window. I adjusted the binoculars until the window came into sharp focus.

A single shade was pulled partway down across the glass of the illuminated window. The shade was cream white in color, with a few dark blurred lines creating a mesh of shadows across the surface. I reasoned the shadows must be objects in the apartment, furniture in the real world, but here, in this place I couldn't be certain.

The shade was open about a foot from the bottom edge of the window, allowing me to see a thin strip of view into the room beyond. The distance and the angle from the street made it difficult to see inside, but I vaguely detected a wooden straight line that could have been the leg of a table. I also sighted a thick grayish blob that might have been the edge of a sofa.

Then, a blur of movement. Something passed by the shade. My grip on the binoculars tightened. My heart thudded deep and resonant in my chest. Silhouetted on the shade was a dark outline, clearly human in form. A single shadowy arm reached out, and in an instant, the light snapped out. I continued to peer through the binoculars, but now saw only darkness. The lit room had returned to the uniform anonymity of the hundred glass windows that lined the building.

◆ ◆ ◆

The rest of the night passed excruciatingly slowly. Second by second. Minute by minute. Between my nightmare and the illuminated apartment window, I found it impossible to sleep again. I lay on my back, pistol in hand, and listened to the sounds of the camp. Someone snored. Fabric rustled. A voice called out in a dream. Eventually I fell to sleep, hearing at the far edge of my consciousness a jabbering sort of bark, like the sound of a hyena. But then sleep took hold, and I plunged deep into a dreamless world.

Morning arrived with the suddenness of a light bulb flaring on. Around me, the makeshift camp returned to life. During the night, the small fire had burned down, and Nasir worked now to restore it. Selberg arched his back and grimaced painfully, while Charlotte walked along the edge of the park and inspected various flowers and trees that overhung the sidewalk.

I told each of them what we had seen during the night, then Clayton and I headed out from camp to investigate. The air was comfortable and the light was perfect. Another clear indication that this space had been designed for human habitation.

Clayton spit an inky smudge of tobacco onto the pavement. His rifle rested in the crook of his arm. His body was relaxed, but his eyes scanned our surroundings with intensity.

We had been careful to ration our provisions, but none of us had apparently felt hunger. The excitement of everything had left me with no appetite. We left camp and headed south across the circle. The street was quiet. The air lay heavy across us, nothing stirring in its dead current. The building itself was glass and steel, new construction materials in my time, but perhaps not in the future. I imagined the dull uniform apartments that must occupy its innards. I looked up again at the apartment window, trying to count the floors.

"Fourteen," Clayton said. "Seven windows in from the eastern edge of the building."

The entrance was guarded by two glass doors. Clayton tugged on one and it opened easily enough. A slight gust of wind, barely perceptible if not for the stillness outside, emanated through the open doorway. I wondered if the interior air was safe, but Clayton, with a final resolute spit of tobacco, stepped through the doorway and into the lobby.

The door shut behind us, the air went quiet, and I had the disturbing impression of stepping into a mausoleum. The lobby was standard layout, front reception desk, with a pair of padded leather chairs and a small glass coffee table. On the reception desk was a coffee mug filled with pencils and a pink pen with a feather plume. The elevator was set back into the side wall, with a second door on the back wall, which I presumed led into the stairwell.

"Fourteen floors . . ." I let the words hang, my legs felt heavy already.

"Safe thing to take the stairs."

"Yeah. No. I'm staired out."

I pushed the call button and we waited.

I thought about that pen in the coffee mug, something so uniquely human. It was an odd embellishment to this world and a level of detail that couldn't be randomly created.

The double elevators doors slid back with surprising immediacy, like the jaws of an animal snapping open. We stepped inside and rode up to the floor.

The hallway was neutral in every aspect. Drab white in color, unmarked doors, dimly lit with only a faint odor of almonds as its only identifiable feature. A typical hallway of which there were probably a million variations all across the city.

A window was positioned at the end of the hall, and through it we could see down to our small grouping of tents, small khaki-colored fabric that broke the uniformity of the cement. Nasir and Charlotte reclined against the side of the subway entrance, small puffs of smoke visible around them as they pulled on cigarettes. Selberg sat near the edge of the tent. He appeared to be reading.

"Can see our camp from a mile away," Clayton said. "Too exposed. If these buildings are safe, we should think about moving inside."

Clayton made sense. From this height, our camp did look pretty damn vulnerable. A few fragile tents in the midst of this vast undiscovered wild. And I didn't have a great feeling about this place.

Clayton counted off the doors from the far edge of the window, then tried the knob. The door was locked.

I listened at the door, then said, "So what's the etiquette exactly when you visit the apartment of a totally unknown civilization of potentially limitless power?"

"Knock, I guess."

"Knocking works."

I rapped sharply on the door. The sound echoed in the quiet confines of the hall. We waited, tensely holding our weapons, listening for the metallic clack of a dead bolt. The turning of the door knob.

But there was nothing.

I exhaled and lowered my rifle. "Maybe it only comes out at night?"

Whatever happened, I knew I couldn't be in the hallway for much longer. The silent anticipation was more than I could stand. My feet began to tremble with the desire to run. To move. To be anywhere but here. We listened a minute more, then hearing nothing, we made our way back down the hall to the elevator. I had to force myself not to run. As we waited for the car to arrive, a thought occurred to me.

"Should we try the roof?"

Clayton passed a hand over his chin stubble and then nodded.

The elevator took us to the roof and the doors opened into the diffused brightness of an artificial sun above us. Around us stretched the city. This was the same metropolis I had known, only bigger and grander, with additions beyond the scope of my comprehension.

"Look, there," Clayton said, as he pointed off toward the west. In the distance, where the open space of the Hudson would have separated Manhattan from New Jersey, was a solid wall of fog. As I watched, the fog parted from some unknown current of air. Through the swirling opening, I could see solid, dark rock.

This wall rose impossibly high, higher than any of the buildings, and I realized we were truly inside the Earth. This entire massive structure of Manhattan had somehow been created underground.

I turned to Clayton. "How is any of this possible?"

"Don't know."

To the north, the grassy, wooded stretch of Central Park, to the south, the spires of Midtown, glass and steel shimmering in the false light. Everything seemed in place . . . the layered cap of the Empire State Building, the illuminated neon glow of Times Square, only tenfold what I was used to. Even the bridges were visible. I could see the unique inverted U-shaped structures of the Williamsburg far to the south.

Everything I recognized seemed properly positioned in its correct location. And yet, something still seemed off. Clayton noticed the thoughtful narrowing of my eyes.

"Too clean," he said.

"Excuse me?"

"If you're wondering what's wrong, what's off . . ." Clayton indicated the skyline. "The buildings are too clean."

I looked again and realized he was correct. Every stone, every pane of glass, every beam of steel was spotless. Each building, from older landmarks, to buildings so new I didn't even recognize them, seemed freshly cast from giant molds. This was where the artifice lay. I realized what I regarded now was not a true city, organically grown over time, but an artificially constructed world. And like all constructed things, it must serve some purpose.

Clayton turned and headed back toward the stairs. "Time to head down."

◆ ◆ ◆

Selberg eagerly awaited our return to camp.

"What did you find?"

"Nothing," I said. "Door was locked."

"The door was locked? Why . . . couldn't . . . why don't we just break it down?"

"What if strangers came to your house?" Clayton unslung his rifle. "And broke your door down? How would you respond?"

"I'd call the police."

"And if you had a gun in the house?"

"I . . ." Selberg began, and then stammered. "I'm not sure."

"We don't have any idea what's behind that door. Whatever built all this," Clayton indicated the city around us, "could defend itself with something much worse than a gun. And knocking down doors isn't a good way to start off relationships. Or am I wrong?"

"No . . ." Selberg said. "But if it invites us in?"

Clayton looked back up toward the building. In daylight, the windows looked vacant, black panes of glass that reflected nothing. Casually Clayton opened a tin of chewing tobacco and placed a large wad inside his cheek.

"If something with the power to do all this invites us in," he said, "we won't have a choice. We go."

As the strange, artificial sunlight grew stronger, the air gradually warmed again.

I found Charlotte beneath the low overhang of a tree in Central Park, seated on a bench, intently studying something in her lap.

As I approached, she looked up and smiled. I pointed up to the roof of the building Clayton and I had explored. "You should see the view."

She laughed. "So there are more than these couple blocks?"

"There's the entire island of Manhattan."

"Well, I guess you've got your big find." Spread across her knee was a piece of parchment paper the height and width of a bed pillow. The paper was a rubbing, a thin film of gray black charcoal etched with white lettering. "The Rosetta Stone rubbing we found with the dead French soldier. I think I figured it out."

I reached down and took the rubbing from her lap. The lettering was as I remembered, lines of Egyptian hieroglyphs, the longer scripted lines of Demotic, then the shorter more familiar Greek letters. The paper itself was a heavy parchment, with a hard, waxen feel.

"My Greek was a little rusty," she admitted, "but I worked through it." At her feet lay a leather-bound sketchbook. She handed the book to me. "This is what I got."

Written across the page were the words *The shadow of memory.*

"What do you think it means?" Charlotte asked.

"Not sure. The Egyptians felt that a part of a person's soul was contained within their shadow. So this reference to shadow might have something to do with the soul, or the memory of the soul."

"On the back of the rubbing, there was a single line written in French."

"Written by who?"

"Probably the soldier himself." Charlotte turned the sketchbook page. "I translated that as well."

Across the page, written in Charlotte's careful script were five words. *The start begins in Colomb.*

I studied the sentence, trying to decipher more meaning. I could think of nothing. Charlotte studied the puzzled look on my face. "I'm not sure what it means either," she said.

"Colomb? Is that a city?"

"I don't know," Charlotte said. "I've never heard of it, but maybe in Napoleon's time."

A French soldier had traveled across Egypt and died just before reaching his destination. His body had lain in a tunnel far below the sands for over a hundred years. Whatever mission he had been on had long since been forgotten. But this mission had been of such importance that a man had risked miles of burning desert and given his life for it.

The start begins in Colomb.

The start of what? Even if we found Colomb, we still wouldn't know what we were looking for. The letters began to blur before my eyes, and I looked up from the notebook in frustration. In the distance, farther down the park, Nasir and Selberg sat against their packs, playing cards. Clayton leaned against the base of the statue in the center of the circle reading. Above him towered the giant figure of—

I slapped my forehead. Of course. I growled in frustration at my own stupidity.

"What is it?" Charlotte asked.

"Colomb. That's the French spelling of Columbus. Colomb isn't a place, it's a person." I pointed west, where the statue of Christopher Columbus rose from the center of the circle named after him. "The start begins here."

Excited, we began walking back toward the rest of our group.

Charlotte followed alongside me. "But why 'in Colomb'?"

"Because I think we're meant to look inside the statue itself."

◆ ◆ ◆

The shrine to Christopher Columbus stood atop a granite column decorated with bronze reliefs of the *Niña,* the *Pinta,* and the *Santa Maria.* The column itself was affixed to a large pedestal, the entire monument rising almost eighty feet above the circle. In my New York, it was one of those landmarks that scores of people passed each day without ever noticing the intricacies of its design.

54

The circle itself was composed of an inner and outer ring, each with plantings and benches and fountains. In this place, the fountain was off. But during a normal day, streams of water would jet into the air, while on the outside, traffic packed the roadway, taxis and cars bumper to bumper, fighting for space as they crawled through Midtown traffic. In the silent, empty street beneath the sand, without the distractions of noise and movement, the monument to the famed explorer had a powerful, quiet solemnity.

The monument's base was composed of a few large steps of granite brick, and a pedestal inscribed with raised reliefs that depicted scenes from the exploration. In one, Columbus appeared to have landed on the New World, his foot touching down on the shore, his face looking out away from the sea. In his hand, he held a small, egg-shaped object. I began a slow inspection of this image, looking for anything that might conceal a hiding point. Just beneath the explorer's foot, I saw a thin fissure in the stone about six inches in width. Putting my fingers against the crack, I pressed, and a small square of stone rotated in the pedestal, revealing a hiding place beneath.

Inside was a single United States quarter.

I reached in and pulled out the coin. The metal was cool to touch. The weight and size was as I remembered. The face was inscribed with the familiar bust of George Washington, and in all respects, the quarter appeared normal, except there was no date, only a space along the bottom edge inscribed with the word *Panopticon*.

◆ ◆ ◆

We all took turns inspecting the quarter, but aside from the lack of a date, we could find nothing unusual about the coin. It had clearly been hidden, but for what purpose?

"Panopticon . . . wasn't that in the subway tunnel below?" Selberg said.

Opticon, I assumed, had something to do with the eyes. Or vision. I was pretty sure there was something with a similar name from Greek mythology, but the exact meaning eluded me.

"It's a type of prison," Clayton said. "The panopticon. It's a prison designed so that every inmate can be watched at the same time."

"How do you know that?" Selberg said, his voice tinged with an unmistakable thread of jealousy.

"I know prisons. This one was unique. It was circular, with the cells on the outer edges, and in the center was an observation tower. The jailer could see any prisoner at any time, but was concealed in the tower, so none of the prisoners would know when they were being observed."

"So someone was watching the prisoners all the time?" Charlotte said.

Clayton shook his head. "Not all the time. But that's the point. It didn't have to be all the time. Because the jailer was concealed from view, prisoners never knew when they were being watched."

We stood in silence. I suddenly felt the vulnerability of our position. Manhattan was a city of windows, hundreds of thousands of them, and behind each window could be something watching. This whole place was a panopticon. We were trapped, prisoners beneath the Earth, surrounded by invisible eyes and countless places to hide and observe.

Eventually the excitement over the new find began to dissipate. I put the quarter into my pocket and the rest of the crew wandered off. Only Selberg remained. He surveyed the circle to make sure the others were out of hearing range, then lowered his voice. "I say we take a look around during the daylight."

"What direction?"

Selberg nodded across the circle toward the opening of Eighth Avenue. "Walk down the avenue a bit. See what we see?"

I noticed Selberg had two packs on his back, one strapped over the other. "For samples," he said as we began to walk. "This is our world. Just distinctly more advanced. The technology down here . . . well, to be blunt," he flashed me an awkward smile, then looked back over his shoulder, "would be worth a fortune."

"Ah . . . what happened to the purity of academic research?"

"I spent thirty years of my life in academia. I've got a tired little apartment filled with a couple tired suits, some tired furniture, and a runner-up letter from the Nobel Prize committee. That's the sum total of the purity of my academic research. That's the first half of my life. For the next half, some money would be nice." Selberg nodded back toward the statue of Columbus. The explorer stood, hand on hip, staring out into the vast reaches of lower Manhattan. "What do you think he was doing in 1492? Pro bono work?"

"No. I guess not."

"First thing Columbus and his investors did when they discovered the New World was try to figure how they could make money. Slavery. Gold. This wasn't exploration to benefit mankind. It was exploration for profit. Columbus was a bad guy. And they give him a national holiday. The ends justify the means."

The streets were eerily quiet. No, I corrected myself, this wasn't just quiet, this was the complete absence of sound. And in that vacuum of noise, the drum of our footsteps, the creak of the leather straps on my back, even the occasional muffled pop of an ankle or a knee joint all seemed amplified, until I was sure that if there was anything out there, it could not fail to hear us approaching, the sound of our movements as ear-shattering as the approach of a freight train over rough track.

But if there was anything out there, there was no indication of movement.

As we walked, I inspected the buildings around us. Everything had a too-large feel. A world built for giants. Corporate headquarters surrounded us, barren spaces, sparse and antiseptic as hospital waiting areas.

The only sense of human habitation came from the few small grocery stores with empty shelves, but even those blurred together with their buffet lunch advertisements and bland signage. *Convenient Foods. Lunch Stop. Grab 'n' Go.* Empty chairs and tables set along the curb waiting for customers. A coffee shop with a green awning and photographs of oversized coffee beans in the window. A dentist's office.

I tried to recall the doorways of the Eighth Avenue of my memory but failed. Since arriving in Egypt, my time in New York City seemed to belong to someone else. Another lifetime so completely separate from my own that I felt as if I was trying to connect with someone else's memories. The details were faded and fuzzy, incomplete radio chatter. Broken bits of information between the static.

Selberg stopped short, his head cocked at an angle.

I stood next to him. My hand moved to my pistol. "What is it?"

"I heard something," Selberg said. "There. Hear it?"

Somewhere in the distance, a telephone rang.

Selberg's eyes were half-closed, a man trying to parse out a single distant sound. Then slowly he nodded and pointed. "Sounds like east."

We moved quickly now, eager to reach the sound before it cut off. This city was so empty that sound carried, and the ringing grew louder as we moved but still seemed elusively in the distance. We passed the FAO Schwarz, its rows of limp stuffed animals and wooden soldiers visible through the window, then the Bergdorf Goodman and a Tiffany & Company, both stores ominously dark and quiet, a fortune in jewelry on display in the window.

The phone was on the corner of Fifty-First and Fifth, the spires of St. Patrick's Cathedral rising up beyond. Higher above that, I could see the fog that shrouded the island. The ringing continued, the hollow sound reverberating off the canyon walls of the empty buildings. I broke into a jog, half-afraid the ringing would end before I reached its source.

For such a devoutly clean environment, the phone was surprisingly battered. It was a boxy, metal pay phone, scratched and battered, hanging on a metal column. A sticker of an Easter egg was placed on the phone's side, with loose wires hanging from the bottom. Instinctively I reached to answer the call, then paused. My hand hovered in midair.

Selberg was excited, his cheeks flushed with exertion, his eyes large. "Well you have to answer. Something is reaching out to us."

"What the hell do I say?"

"Make it something good."

I felt an intense crush of nerves. "Something good?"

"You're speaking for the human race now," Selberg said. "This may be a first in the course of human existence."

"You want to do it?"

Selberg shook his head, backed away. "I'm not good on the phone."

Slowly I lifted the telephone from the cradle, held the receiver to my ear, and said the only thing that came to mind. "Hello?"

◆ ◆ ◆

The line clicked dead. I clicked the metal tab up and down. Nothing. Slowly I hung up the handset and stared. The phone remained silent. The street corner around us remained empty. But something out there had reached out to us. Some force beyond my ability to understand had wanted to speak. And for whatever reason, it had chosen a battered, old pay phone as its way to communicate.

Pay phone.

Slowly, I pushed my hand into my pocket until my fingers touched metal. I pulled the quarter out and studied the face of it. Ran my finger over the word *Panopticon* engraved on the front.

I slid the quarter into the pay slot and heard a solid clunk of metal as it dropped into the machine. Then I lifted the receiver from the cradle and held it to my ear. First, silence, then the electric pulses moved over wires from a distant location and transmitted to my ear as sound.

The phone crackled with static, then I heard the sound of breaking glass. I knew someone was there. I could hear heavy, labored breathing.

The sound of someone or something struggling to live? Faintly, I heard running feet. A door slammed. And the breathing continued.

The hairs on my neck began to rise. Something here was familiar. Something ominous. And even if my brain couldn't register what it was, my body instinctively reacted and I felt afraid.

I gripped the receiver and looked down empty Fifth Avenue. I had the fleeting impression that something moved around a corner a few blocks south. The briefest passage of a shadow beyond the corner of a Chase Bank branch. I focused my attention, but whatever it might have been was gone. The phone crackled more static. "Hello? Anyone there?"

The breathing continued, and I felt certain that whatever was on the other end of the line was distinctly human. Selberg met my eyes and mouthed the words, "What is it?"

I shook my head and turned. I couldn't afford to be distracted now. I had a feeling that whatever was about to happen was of immense importance. The breathing labored for a few moments more. Then the person on the line swallowed. Someone was getting ready to speak. And somehow I knew the words would be English. Something that I could understand.

After a painfully long pause, I heard a feeble whisper. A voice made fragile by pain and so tenuous that I could not tell if it came from a man or a woman.

Two words.

"Help . . . me . . ."

And then the line went dead. I held the receiver in my hand dumbly, then clicked rapidly up and down on the cradle. I listened to a long, electric hiss, and then a steady tone hummed in my ear. Carefully I placed the receiver back in the cradle.

From inside the phone box I heard a mechanical clunk. Then something light and metallic pinged inside the change slot. I pushed on the door with my finger, and inside, tucked into the small reservoir, I felt hard, familiar ridges. I dug into the change channel and pulled out the object.

I turned toward Selberg and opened my hand to show him. Sitting on my palm was a single metal key. I thought of the apartment Clayton and I had found. Locked doors needed keys.

I told Selberg what I had heard on the phone.

"Did you recognize the voice?" Selberg asked.

"No. I don't know. Familiar maybe," I said, but already the familiarity was beginning to fade. As if talking to Selberg had somehow broken the delicate spell of remembering and washed everything from my brain.

I pocketed the key and turned away from the phone.

◆ ◆ ◆

By the time we reached camp, the sky had begun to grow dark once more. Here, the day seemed to be slightly shorter than aboveground. Again, like the first night, the heavens grew dark, not by degrees, but in a single swift motion. Like someone blowing out a candle. I was organizing our meager supply of rations when night came. In my surprise, one of the canteens, now only half-filled with water, slipped from my hand and rattled loudly on the concrete sidewalk.

My eyes began to adjust quickly to the loss of light. The blackness faded to a dim gray in which I could see silhouetted shapes of buildings in the distance. Clayton's voice sounded from behind me. "It's time."

In the distance, set high in the shadowed silhouette of the building, the apartment light sparked on again. Clayton and I cut across Columbus Circle. My eyes had adjusted completely to the darkness and I found I could navigate easily. The remainder of our group stayed behind in camp. Charlotte sketched the skyline in her journal by lantern light, while Nasir and Selberg talked quietly around a small fire built inside a metal mesh trash can.

As we crossed the circle, Clayton looked back at the fire. Embers caught in the updraft of heated air rose in spirals before blinking out.

"That fire is the brightest thing in the city right now," Clayton said. "Doesn't make us hard to find."

We reached the lobby and pushed open the front doors. I carried a lantern, and as we entered the building, I pulled back the tin cover. Wild shadows were thrown across the marble walls. In an old gilt mirror, I saw our reflections, two pale faces lit from beneath by lantern light, our skin pocked with shadows.

The elevator ride was short and the doors opened again onto the familiar hallway. Everything was the same as before, only this time we had a key.

A seam of light was visible beneath the closed apartment door. As we approached, a shadow passed across the seam, as if something moved on the other side. The thought fluttered my stomach, and next to me, Clayton raised his rifle and buttressed it against his shoulder.

I paused and listened. On the other side I heard a faint rustle. Barely audible. The sound of feet on carpet perhaps. Clayton nodded, raised his rifle, and stepped back from the door. Slowly I fitted the key in the lock.

The knob turned easily. I pushed the door open and flooded the hallway with light.

◆ ◆ ◆

My first impression beyond the door was of a large, loft-style apartment. Hardwood parquet floors. Neatly painted white walls. A kitchen off to our right with shining appliances. A rug covered a portion of the floor, stretching back toward a bedroom and a series of windows that looked out across the park. I noticed a stain on the edge of the rug, light pink in color. An innocuous splatter mark that looked to me like blood.

In the bedroom area, the mattress was centered by a dark mahogany frame and topped by a thick, white comforter. The comforter was pulled carelessly away, and the sheets were marked by the shallow indentions of a human body. This was a recently slept-in bed. Slowly, I moved through the room, remembering the shadow that passed along the seam of light beneath the closed door. On either side of the bed were two tables, one with glass jars containing candles and the other with a single photograph inside of a silver frame. Over the bed, a painting. Something vaguely familiar to me. Splatter marks of paint across a white canvas.

My attention turned to the bookshelf. Rows of books neatly lined the shelf. I studied the bindings. All of the titles were in English. Some familiar: *Three Musketeers*, *A Tale of Two Cities*. Others I couldn't place. *Catcher in the Rye*. A weathered copy of something called *The Godfather*.

And then I saw the frame and time seemed to slow.

Inside the frame was a photograph of a couple at the beach. The image was of such vivid color, so real that it felt alive in my hand. I had never seen a color photograph, yet this did not seem strange to me. Like the faint remembering of a dream. The beach had white sand, while an almost translucent ocean shimmered in the background.

The couple sat on wood slat chairs in the sand beneath the shade of a large umbrella. The woman had black hair pulled straight back into a ponytail, dark eyes flecked with green. Her face had the slightly weathered look of time spent outdoors. The beginnings of lines formed around her mouth and at the corners of her eyes.

The man next to her in the photo had dark hair turned messy and wet by the ocean. He had a half-crooked smile that warmed a face shadowed by stubble. Everything about this man was familiar. As it should be.

The man was me.

I returned the photograph to the table. I had no recollection of ever being at this beach, and the woman held no familiarity for me either.

And I would have remembered a woman like that. But there was nothing. Yet the man was clearly me. The image itself was so true to life. So filled with color. Beyond anything I had ever experienced. Again, the idea of time travel occurred to me. Yet this man was not my future son. He was me. Of this I felt sure.

Clayton studied me from across the room. He stood in the kitchen, drawers open behind him. "Everything all right?"

"Yeah. Fine." I put the framed photograph face down on the night table. There was something so oddly personal in that photo, something that connected me to this environment, that it seemed strange . . . almost dangerous . . . to share with someone else just yet.

Clayton held up a stack of mail. "Got a name. Looks like a Roger Parker lived here." He squatted down over the pinkish stains on the carpet. "Bloodstains. Washed out. Something bad happened." There were more stains on the wall. A splatter mark that stained the white paint over the radiator.

I studied the marks. "What do you make of these?"

"I'd say a blood spatter." Clayton stood on the rug, formed his hand into a gun, held it to his temple. Pulled the trigger. "Gun goes off, enters the brain, splatter mark to the wall, body falls here. Someone comes in later, cleans most of it up."

"So we're looking at a murder scene?"

"Maybe."

"Whatever is out there wanted us to see this. Why?"

"You're the academic. You tell me." Clayton had moved toward the window. He nodded toward the outside. "There's another light."

I saw only my own reflection in the glass. *Roger Parker.* I rolled the name around in my brain. Tested it out. Tried to get the feel for it, see if there was any faint memory. And there was something, buried deep. We wear our names like skin. They become such a part of us, almost impossible to truly erase. But if this Roger Parker was me, and I was him, and I was the man in the photograph, and this was my apartment, then what was happening here?

I switched off the bedside lamp, the room went black, and I could see out across the dark city. The outlines of buildings were vague shadows. Along the edge of Columbus Circle, our tents were pitched in a jagged line illuminated by lanterns inside, the fabric glowing a faded yellow. A shadow moved inside, distorted and grotesquely huge by lantern light. I couldn't tell who it was. Farther to the east was the dark expanse of Central Park.

And deep in the middle of the park, a single light cut through the darkness.

A cabin in the woods. And a lantern hung from the front porch.

◆ ◆ ◆

We took the elevator back down.

The building lobby should have been as quiet and dark as when we left. It wasn't. Something was waiting for us. A figure moved across the marbled floor, a shadow silhouetted against the lights of the camp visible through the open window. With one hand, Clayton raised the lantern. With the other, he raised the rifle. The shadow figure paused, turned toward us. Then a familiar voice spoke out.

"Hello?"

Clayton exhaled and lowered the rifle. The figure stepped forward and I saw Nasir's face illuminated in lantern light.

"What are you doing here?" Clayton asked sharply. "I almost shot you."

"I came out to see if I could help." Nasir fidgeted with something in his hand. "I found this on this floor."

He held out a brightly colored glossy paper and I took it from his hand, holding it close to the lantern. It was a travel brochure, a montage of rolling orange groves and beaches, *Escape Your World* written in sunshine-yellow letters across the top.

On the back was the address of a travel agency on Doyers Street.

I remembered the same words from the subway station and the train we had boarded. There was something hazy about the brochure. The writing faded somehow. Like a pen running low on ink. I looked for some clue of understanding. Nothing came. I folded up the brochure and stuffed it into my pocket.

"What'd you find up there?" Nasir asked.

"Nothing," Clayton said. "Empty room."

The camp was quiet when we returned. I walked to the edge of Central Park, held up my lantern like some character from *The Hound of the Baskervilles*, and tried to peer through the dense black of foliage. The trees were too thick, and the light we had seen from above wasn't visible from the ground. The park itself was dark and shadowed, incredibly still, but I knew something was out there.

Clayton joined me. "You want to go out there?"

"Of course," I said. "Don't you?"

Clayton shifted his weight. "Don't know. I'm not here to explore this place. I'm here to protect your team."

"Maybe the best way to protect us is to find a way out. We both know about sixteen tons of rock separate us from the world. And nobody even knows we're in trouble. So unless we find food and water soon . . ."

"All right."

"Why did you tell Nasir that room was empty?"

"We don't need panic and fear right now. Everyone is wired tight enough as it is."

"So you lied to him?"

"Yes," Clayton said. "Still want to go out there with me?"

We all had our own secrets and lies. I knew I should tell Clayton the truth of what I saw in the apartment. If he was going to risk his life with me, or for me, he should know at least what he was getting into. But I wasn't sure what I could tell him. I didn't know where to start and I didn't know what the truth was. For now, we had to press forward. Clayton was right, we didn't need panic and fear.

We headed north along Central Park West. To our left, block after block of darkened buildings, each a perfect replica of the original. I wondered how deep the fabrication went. Were these buildings only facades? Movie sets with empty interiors propped up by wooden scaffolds and plasterboard? Or did the replication run deep, to individual apartments filled with the furniture and belongings of real people? And if that were true, who were these people? How had they created this careful mimic of our world, as if this metropolis were one giant mirror of a real city, and Clayton and I now walked on its glass surface.

The street itself was empty of cars and completely quiet. This was the total silence I had only experienced deep inside the ruins of antiquity. I held my lantern aloft. The small gaslight barely pushed back the darkness. The yellow glow of my face floated in the black window glass of a solid granite building. The image was incredibly eerie. I held the lantern down and looked away.

Clayton walked with alertness, his Winchester repeating rifle carried waist high. His head swiveled, his eyes flicked back and forth from the edge of the park to the line of the buildings. From somewhere across the street came the shrill ring of a telephone. The same style of ring that had beckoned Selberg and me earlier in the day.

We stood near the entrance of the Dakota apartment building. The Dakota was famous even in my time, one of the beautiful structures that had been constructed in the late 1800s when the area was mostly farmland. I was pleasantly surprised to see the familiar building. Like running into an old friend on the street. Slender gables rose into the darkness along with a multitude of dormers and balconies, all of which added interesting layers and dimensions to a terra-cotta face.

The ring was muted slightly, as if it came from inside the building. As Clayton and I stood there trying to figure out what to do, an overhead light in the building lobby flickered to life. The light spilled out through the glass front window and onto the dark street, like an illuminated display case.

We crossed the street and pulled open the building's front door. Inside, the lobby had a black and white checkered floor. Gold ornate scrollwork of angels and cherubs lined the edges of the ceiling. Sitting on the doorman's desk, a hospital blue telephone rang incessantly.

I lifted the one-piece handset from the cradle and held the phone to my ear. I heard the faint buzz of static and then a slight electric hiccup, like a needle falling into the groove of a phonograph. Music began to play. The sound was distant and wavering through the small telephone receiver. Chopin. I was reminded of my wife. She had always loved classical music.

As the song played, I looked around the vacant building lobby.

Through the glass, Central Park lay in shadows.

Static cut through the music, then a voice came on the line, sounding distant and muffled. "So you lied to him?"

It was my own voice. The conversation I had with Clayton played back over the phone. Someone was out there listening to us.

"Yes," Clayton's voice on the phone replied. "Still want to go out there with me?"

The static burst again, painfully loud in my ear. Then the background noise cleared, like clouds parting before the sun, and in that moment of clarity I heard another voice. A conversation happening in another place. Somewhere out beyond the walls of this place.

It was a man's voice, speaking to someone else. "I don't know . . . I'm getting feedback . . ."

My fingers tightened on the phone. "Hello?"

The sound of my voice traveled into nothingness. There was no response.

"... yeah, I tried that. Nothing ... I'll keep trying ..."

Then the phone went dead. When I was sure there was nothing else, I hung up.

"What was it?" Clayton asked.

"Music."

"That's it?"

"No," I said. "There was something else. There was someone there. I don't know what it was."

◆ ◆ ◆

Back on the street, we continued to walk north until we saw a yellow glow through the trees. In a land of universal darkness, the light stood in singular illuminated isolation. A gravel path cut off from the sidewalk and led into the trees. The park was especially dense with foliage here, like a forest from an old Grimm's fairytale, thick with creeping vines and twisted elms.

Cautiously, we moved into the cover of the forest. The trees rose up above us, blocking out the darker silhouettes of buildings. The path was knotted with roots, and I could see with horrid fascination the clear scuff marks in the dirt of layers of footprints. This area appeared to be well traveled. The marks all headed deeper into the park.

Something about being in a forest at night brought on a primal fear. Whoever had left those tracks could be out there somewhere, moving silently from trunk to trunk, watching us from a distance, luring us deeper into the park and the unknown.

Our boots crunched lightly on the gravel beneath us, and somewhere through the trees I heard a woman sobbing, a sound made more from fear than sadness. The desperate tears of someone in mortal dread. My heart quickened. Someone was out here with us. Someone in danger. But with a thin stab of guilt, a great part of me wanted to retreat back to the street. The intensity of what was happening almost overloaded my senses, paralyzing me with terror.

Then came a single, long shriek.

It was a chilling sound. A primal cry of pain. Clayton lowered himself slowly, prepping for his attack. I pulled the Colt from my waistband. My doubts broke, and without thinking I ran along the path into the darkness of the park. Clayton followed me, my lantern casting wild shadows across the branches that crowded in on us. The scream came from the direction of the light in the woods, and we headed fast toward the sound. A branch slapped me across the face, momentarily blinding me.

The woman screamed again.

The path turned north. The slope of a rocky hill blocked the light, and Clayton grabbed my shoulder hard. He held a finger to his lip, then slowly moved forward, rifle raised and pressed to his shoulder. The cry had come from the other side of the hill, and we carefully made our way around the path.

As we rounded the curve, I could see a lantern placed in the window of a two-story gingerbread cottage set deep in the woods. The cottage was sided with Baltic fir so dark, it appeared black in the light, with long gables that hung from the roof. Ornate wooden shutters had fantastic, hand-carved scrollwork and large, rounded windows. It was a beautiful cottage, like an illustration from a children's book, but there was something forbidding in this anachronism. The structure didn't belong here.

And neither did we.

The lantern cast a yellow flickering light that created shadows across the bare branches of the dogwood trees along the front. I could see the front door was ajar.

Clayton and I both paused and waited. We heard nothing. The frantic sobs were gone.

In life, I had been here before.

I remembered coming here as a child for a marionette performance of *Hansel and Gretel*. Even holding my father's hand during a beautiful Saturday afternoon in April, I felt a chill of fear in this place.

The imagination of a child can quickly turn the wooden features of puppets, with their limbs artificially jerking and lurching pulled by the strings of invisible hands, into something terrible. A childhood fear is held the longest and the strongest, and standing now in darkness, again before the gingerbread-style cottage, I felt that same fear return, just as strong. I hesitated, and to my shame, I whispered to Clayton, "Should we get the others?"

Clayton surveyed the woods around us, impenetrably dark. "No time," he replied.

I nodded. Clayton was of course right. The woman had screamed in mortal terror. And now the silence weighed more heavily on me than any scream could have. We were here, now, the only ones able to help. And to delay to go back for the others would have been cowardice.

Lantern in one hand, Colt in the other, I slowly advanced. A dog-wood tree hung heavy with large purple flowers, many of which had fallen along the path. They crushed easily beneath my feet, leaving broken petals everywhere the color of blood spatters.

The murmur of the voice died off as we approached, my footfalls loud on the spread of gravel before the entrance. I reached the doorway and pushed back on the solid oak door with my gun hand, extending the lantern deeper into the dark recess of the entrance. Two heavy iron hinges shrieked in protest as the door swung slowly inward.

My light illuminated a small theater.

Ten rows of chairs were set up before a raised stage. The stage decorations were of a Germanic forest, captured in perfect miniature, with a dollhouse-sized gingerbread cottage. The cottage was a replica of the one we now stood in, and my boyhood trepidation flooded back as I recognized the setting for *Hansel and Gretel*. Except for the rows of wooden chairs and the stage, the rest of the theater was empty.

We approached a closed door to the right of the stage. The knob turned easily in my hand and the door pushed back to reveal a small hidden room. At the far end of the space, a single lantern sat perched in the window, illuminating rows of shelves lined with marionette puppets of various sizes and shapes. The puppets were folded over onto themselves in eerily lifeless positions, their operating strings piled in small messy bundles nearby. I recognized a few wooden puppets from fairytales; the rest were an assortment of boys and girls and woodland creatures with menacing faces.

At the edge of the room, a small stairwell led up to a space above the stage. Clayton and I climbed the stairs, our shoulders turned in the tight space. At the top appeared a small walkway that looked down onto the stage below. Here, hidden by a wooden screen of intricately carved foliage, the puppeteer could work the strings of his marionettes, causing the tiny humanoid forms to dance and move on the stage below.

Glowing in the light from my lantern, something postcard-sized lay in the far corner of the catwalk. An advertisement for a marionette theater performance of *Hansel and Gretel*. Across the face of the card was a stylized, art deco drawing of a boy and girl holding hands, looking together at a small wooden cottage. A single window was illuminated, the shadow of an old crone cast in dark silhouette across the glass.

I slipped the card inside my pocket, then Clayton and I headed back down the stairs. I was sure the cries for help had come from inside the cottage, but whoever she might have been had appeared to have vanished. Or never existed.

When we reached the bottom of the stairs, I noticed one of the marionette puppets lay on the floor beneath the bottom of the stairs. It was a little boy carved entirely from wood and dressed in Bavarian lederhosen, with small white socks pulled up at the knee and a black hat tufted with a single feather.

The German.

The word flooded in on me from somewhere, the moniker of someone I had known. But I couldn't remember where. I picked the doll up, and its legs and arms flopped backward, its glassy eyes glinting in the light. Strings hung loosely down from the puppet's hands and feet and piled on the floor.

"Let me see that," Clayton took the puppet and inspected the little wooden body. "There's something inside the mouth."

He forced down the jaw and from inside pulled out a single brass key.

"It would seem that someone is playing a game with us," Clayton said.

"Who?" I asked, not knowing what else to say.

"I don't know. But this is enough to make a man doubt his sanity."

I took the key from Clayton and slipped it into my pocket. To the south, two deep booms sounded in the distance. Gunfire, coming from our camp.

◆ ◆ ◆

By the time we hit the camp, I was breathing heavily, my legs burning. As we reached the perimeter, Nasir came running to us, rifle in hand, face flushed. "I saw something."

Clayton slowed to a walk and pushed past him toward the center of camp. "Where?"

Nasir pointed across Columbus Circle toward the edge of a coffee shop. The window of the shop had shattered. Jagged fragments of broken glass hung down from the frame.

"Saw what?" I said.

"I don't know, sir," Nasir said. "A shadow of something."

Clayton looked at him sharply. "In the future, you must be sure. You can't shoot at shadows."

The rest of the team gathered around us, looking nervous. The campfire flickered shadows across everyone's face.

And then we all heard the sound. A low jabbering bark, then a long howl. Like a wolf, except the bark was deeper in tone. Everyone in the expedition froze and listened. The bark came from somewhere to the west, past the Jazz at Lincoln Center sign, farther down Sixtieth Street.

There was a pause, and then another answering howl. This one came from the east, somewhere in the darkness of Central Park. The two sounds communicated with one another, a back and forth between the howls. I sensed intelligence in the patterns of their communication. And I sensed something else. That whatever these creatures were, they were communicating about us.

Clayton turned and held his lantern aloft. The light penetrated only a dozen or so feet into the darkness of the park, not nearly enough to see whatever it was making the sounds. After a few minutes, the howling stopped.

"I told you I saw something," Nasir said, almost defiant.

"Yes . . . but what?" I asked.

"I saw . . . that," Nasir said.

He stood still, one hand extended, his finger pointed. I followed the line of his finger and saw that it extended directly at the art pad Charlotte still held. Charlotte straightened up in surprise, righted the art pad, and then turned to show the rest of the expedition.

Sketched across the paper was one of Charlotte's earlier drawings from when we had first entered the tomb. As long as I had known her, Charlotte had always been a talented artist. And the drawing on her pad showed her ability. Sketched across the paper was a perfect likeness of the ancient Egyptian god Anubis. One of the more frightening of the ancient gods, with the muscular body of a man and the fierce snarling head of a jackal.

"That's what I saw," Nasir said again. "It was standing in the shadows. Watching us."

◆ ◆ ◆

The next morning I slipped away from camp without being noticed. Nasir preferred not to stay in the tents. He slept outside, his eyes wide open as usual, his body splayed out like a puppet on the ground. I walked slowly down Broadway, no real destination in mind. The photograph in the apartment still bothered me. I had no memory of anything in the apartment or the photograph. And yet, I couldn't say it was totally unfamiliar. There was something there. Some faint wisp of history I couldn't recollect.

I continued south, down Broadway, turned left onto Fifty-Third Street, intending to circle back in a few blocks. Ahead was an empty café, tables and chairs set up along the sidewalk for the dinner crowds. I could imagine the place filled with people, could hear the clatter of silverware on plates, the rush of conversation. But now, silence filled the streets, the building windows black and vacant.

Near the café, an automobile was parked on the curb, the first one I had seen since arriving down below. It was of a futuristic design, more streamlined than anything I was used to, almost like a small van with a large sliding door on the side.

The vehicle appeared to have been in a terrible accident. Its front end was crumpled inward, the windshield smashed and collapsed into the steering wheel. The car listed badly on a broken axle. Through the cracked driver's side glass, I could see streaks of blood on the seats. The vehicle was empty, but nobody could have survived a crash like this.

I stepped away from the curb, filled suddenly with an intense loneliness. More intense than I'd ever experienced. Like a drug injected into my vein by some invisible hand. I paused on the corner, staring down empty streets, paralyzed and lost by my feelings.

So consumed was I that for a moment I failed to notice the light.

In front of a Sheraton hotel, on the corner of Fifty-Third and Seventh Avenue, a subway entrance was cut into the sidewalk. Between a green-painted rail, concrete stairs led underground. And from somewhere below, a dim light spilled out of the entrance.

The stairs led down to a black and white tiled wall. The source of light came from somewhere out of sight, farther down in the station. The air was still, but an unpleasant smell rose from the stairwell. Like something rotted. I paused, shifted my weight, wanting to walk down toward the light. Without knowing when, I found that I had already taken two steps down. The stench was a bit stronger. In a haze, I took another step. I paused, blinked, shook my head, then turned and walked quickly back up. From below I heard a metal gate creak shut and then another sound. Someone called out.

"Help me."

The voice was thin and frail. A child's voice. Like the voice on the phone. I froze at the top of the stairs, listening. "Help me. Please."

The sound came from below. From somewhere underground, inside the subway station. Slowly I turned and looked back down the stairs. Everything was still the same. Above, the black windows of darkened buildings remained still. I could run back to the circle, get the rest of the team, and be back here in twenty minutes. As soon as my thoughts turned to leaving, the voice sounded again, more urgent this time.

"Someone, please help. Please."

Hairs rose on the back of my neck. My heart pumped electricity through my chest. Something in that voice sounded unnatural. A strange imitation of a child. And yet, how could I explain myself to the group if it was a child? If someone really was in danger, how could I explain running in fear? The idea that we were not alone down here was both terrifying and exciting. I thought back to the cottage in the park. I was becoming convinced that something here was toying with us. Something that watched us, explored our behaviors, researched our patterns. But to actually meet the first resident of this place would be a defining moment in human existence. Some part of me wanted that experience to be all mine.

I removed the pistol from my belt and slowly advanced down the stairs.

The odor grew stronger. I thought of garbage left in the sun for too long. But that couldn't be. Everything here was so perfectly groomed for humans, and I didn't believe that this unappealing detail would be overlooked.

I reached the bottom of the stairs. Ahead was a small hallway and a line of thick metal bars painted green, which separated the hall from the rest of the subway platform. As I approached, I heard a buzz and a metallic click. A door in the bars swung open. Beyond was a long platform with more sets of stairs leading down to deeper subway platforms. Signs overhead directed travelers toward trains headed to the Bronx and lower Manhattan.

On the white concrete walls, poster advertisements offered vacation rentals and automobile wonders made of polished glass and metal.

I stood on the threshold of the gate, pistol in hand, listening to the crackle of the overhead bulbs.

"Help me, please, someone help," the voice called out again. Instinctively I moved forward, and as I did, the gate slammed shut behind me. I turned and pulled, but it was securely locked. I tugged hard, a panic rising in my chest, but the gate refused to move. I was locked underground.

Behind me, stairs led down to the lower platform. I stood at the top and looked down, seeing nothing below but a row of wooden benches and a subway system map encased behind glass.

"Hello?" I called down. "Anyone there?"

No response. I moved carefully down the stairs, pistol at the ready. On the second level, a long empty platform stretched before me. On either side, tracks cut through the Earth, disappearing into tunnels as black as rabbit holes.

The smell of rot was almost overwhelming. A putrid scent that seemed to come from farther down the tracks. I thought of an animal that had maybe been struck by a train and crawled off to die. But there were no trains down here. And we had yet to see anything living.

"Help me please. I'm down here."

The voice called again, somewhere below and off to my right. I walked to the edge of the platform. Underneath, subway tracks lay in a bed of gravel about four feet below the platform. The rest of the platform was empty. And somehow, I knew with a certainty, that the voice had called me from inside the tunnel.

My boots crunched against gravel as I jumped down onto the tracks. The platform was now at eye level. Below the platform was a hollow space in which someone small could crouch and hide away from the tracks. I walked slowly forward, checking if someone had fallen down into the space.

I approached the entrance to the tunnel. Ahead was only blackness. A faint gust of air seeped from the opening carrying the foul smell. I stood on the tracks as my eyes tried to penetrate the darkness. I wished I had brought a lantern with me. I remember Clayton had taken his lantern with him, and he was probably back at camp. If I was able to open the gate, I could get back to camp quickly, get Clayton, and we could be back here with lanterns within half an hour.

Faced with the logic of my thoughts, my previous courage began to fade. Slowly, I backed away from the tunnel entrance. I wished I hadn't come down here alone. I thought back to the locked gate. The long hallways. There must be another—

Somewhere in the blackness of the tunnel came the crunch of gravel. I went completely still. My fingers clenched tight against the butt of the pistol in my hand. I listened.

There came another crunch of gravel. The sound of footsteps on the track.

"Help me."

My finger tightened on the trigger and I almost let off a pistol shot. It was that same high child voice. But I knew that was no child. I knew that whatever was in the darkness only pretended. Whatever it was wanted me down here.

Another crunch of gravel. This time closer. Slowly I began to back away. I reached out with my free hand for the edge of the platform. I could lift myself up and off the track, back onto the platform, and then run toward the stairs. My mind formulated the plan and my body only needed to move.

Overhead, the lights flickered. A single strobe, light to dark, with a crackle of electricity. I knew it could only be a moment, but that moment seemed to stretch out an eternity. I heard the crunch of foot against gravel again, and again, faster, as something ran at me from inside the darkness of the tunnel. Whatever it was would soon reach the light and show itself. And I realized this was what I was most afraid of. I turned to run, but found myself unable to move. The lights flickered again, and from the tunnel I glimpsed something humanoid emerge from the tunnel entrance. Human in appearance, but ash gray in color. I had only a momentary glimpse. An impression that lasted no more than an instant.

And then the lights went out and I was plunged into utter darkness.

I stood on the tracks. My breathing ragged and short.

"Help me!" The voice again called from the darkness. This time very close.

A final crunch of gravel, right in front of me, and something hard and cold gripped my arm. I was pulled to the ground with an incredible force. My arm was twisted painfully behind my back and my face was pushed against the sharp gravel of the track bedding.

A hand pressed the side of my head. My cheek burned with pain as gravel dug into my skin. But it was not a human hand. Whatever it was that held me down was cold and dry. Sharp nails dug into the side of my face. I struggled to move, but the thing's strength was incredible. My feet splayed out against the tracks and I tried to push myself back up, but the pressure only grew more intense. I was completely pinned in the darkness.

"You shouldn't be here," a voice said. I felt hot breath on my face, the scent horrible and nauseating. "You don't belong here."

My arm pressed against the cool metal of the tracks and I realized that I could feel something vibrating. As I struggled, the vibrations grew more intense. The track seemed to have come alive beneath me, and with frightening clarity, I realized what it was.

A pale light began to fill the tunnel, gradually growing with intensity until the entire wall of the track glowed white. Two headlights rounded the curve of the track as a train bore down on me.

An intense wave of panic rose up inside me and I pushed against the ground. The force above me crushed down even harder. I tried to twist my head, turn my eyes to see what was above me, but could only catch a glimpse of a single gray finger that wrapped down across my nose.

The train picked up speed and a horn blared. The weight increased on my back until I could barely breathe. I thought back to the camp. I prayed that someone had come looking for me. But I knew there was no one. Vaguely I wondered if I would ever be found.

The train was eighty yards away and moving fast. I closed my eyes.

And then I remembered the gun in my hand.

My left shoulder was pinned, but I could move my arm at the elbow. I raised my hand up and aimed blindly behind me. I expected the gun to be slapped from my hand by whatever held me down. But . . . nothing. The train was almost on me. I held my breath, turned my head away from the barrel of the pistol as much as I could, and pulled the trigger.

Above me came a shriek. I pulled the trigger again and again. The noise was deafening and the gun bucked wildly in my hand. My eyes burned from the barrel flash and my ears rang so painfully that it took me a moment to realize the pressure on my head was gone.

I rolled off the track into the narrow space between the rail and the platform. With a blast of wind, the train roared past me. Flashing wheels hurtled just feet from my face and I braced myself as hard as I could against the wall, feeling wind pull at my clothes.

And then it ended.

The lights flickered back on. With a hiss of brakes and a sigh of hydraulics, the train came to a stop. I stayed motionless and listened for footsteps on gravel. Hearing nothing, I rolled beneath the train and to the other side of the tracks. I stood, pistol in hand. Now I knew at least one thing. That whatever had pinned me to the ground could feel pain. I glanced back under the train, looked for the body of the creature. Nothing. Not even blood. Just a disturbed sweep of gravel where it had crushed my head into the ground. I crossed between two cars and lifted myself back onto the platform.

The subway seemed empty. I moved quickly down the platform and cracked open my revolver as I walked. Two shots left. Behind me I heard the metallic whir of subway doors. I turned and looked back.

The doors of the last subway car stood open. Cold fear gripped me as I stared at that opening. Something was controlling the train. I could feel an invisible hand at work, something that wished me harm. I turned from the open doorway and moved toward the stairs. Then a terror came over me and I broke into a run. I sprinted up the stairs and onto the main floor of the station. Behind me, lights began to flicker out again. I reached the end of the station and pulled on the metal door that separated me from the outside.

The door was locked.

The station grew darker as bulbs flickered out with a buzzing angry snap of electricity. A slow wave of darkness moved down the platform toward me, as each successive bulb of light flashed out.

"Help me!"

The strange voice called out again. A gust of wind blew up from below and I heard the faint click of nails on metal. The rotted odor had increased until the scent almost overpowered me. The stench of two thousand years. I pressed my back against the security gate of the subway platform and raised the pistol.

The darkness moved forward, blotting out the advertisements on the wall, then the subway direction signs. From behind, something grabbed my shoulder. I pulled away and spun around.

Clayton stood on the other side of the gate. "You okay?"

"My God, man, open the gate," I cried as the bulb above my head began to flicker.

Clayton pushed the handle, and with a creak of metal, the gate swung open. I flung myself through the opening and slammed the gate shut behind me.

"What happened?" Clayton asked as I held onto the metal bars for support, my chest heaving, the pistol still clutched in my hand. Together we both looked across the subway station. The lights flicked back on in a single instant, the familiar concrete pathways and walls visible once more. In the distance below us, I heard the sound of a horn and the rhythmic beating of a train pulling away from the station.

I walked back to the camp with Clayton, still feeling very much in shock over what had happened. Only by luck had I managed to escape.

"I have no doubt in my mind. We are not alone here. And whatever is here with us is not friendly," I told the rest of the team outside the tents near the circle.

"But you never saw what it was?" Selberg asked.

I shook my head. "This thing's strength was incredible. I couldn't move. And the way it lured me down there. Away from the group. That shows cunning. Almost like . . ."

"Like what?"

"Like it was hunting me."

"But why?" Selberg asked. "Whatever created this place is clearly of a superior intelligence. What would it possibly gain from hunting or killing any of us?"

"This thing's been down here for a long time. Thousands of years," Clayton said. "Maybe it's bored. Who knows?"

Nasir stood jerkily, then walked stiffly to the fire and stoked it with a long stick. A whirlwind of embers spiraled into the air. "When I was a younger man, I served with the British in Kenya, near the Tsavo River. We were building a bridge over this river, hundreds of workers over nine months. Weather was hot. Hotter than anything I can remember. Brown water. Hot nights. Dust in everything. Worse than being in the desert.

"First few weeks went by without incident. But then, workers started disappearing. Vanishing. Thought maybe some of them had run off. Make a few weeks' earnings, head out to spend the money. Have a good time somewhere. Only they hadn't vanished. See, a few days later, we started finding the bodies. Or what was left of them. Bones picked clean. Clothes shredded up like some big machinery got at them. Only it wasn't no machine."

"What was it?" Selberg asked.

"It was the lions. Two of them. Big males. Seven foot long. After a while, we found out they weren't eating the men they killed. Did it just for the sport. Maybe like this thing down in the subway. We're just sport to it."

A quiet descended on our group. I watched embers from the fire spiral in the air. Clayton finally broke the silence. "But the important thing is that when you shot at this thing, it felt pain."

I nodded. "It seemed to. It let me go anyway."

The academics on the team stared at me wide-eyed. I could see my story had shaken them up. Selberg looked especially nervous, glancing off a few times toward the dark growth of Central Park.

"Well, whatever it is," I said, "it's most likely still out there."

"So we stay in camp," Selberg said. "Post guards."

"We can't stay in camp," I said. "We need to find a way out. If we just stay here and wait, we won't make it."

"Well, at least I don't think we should go anywhere alone," Selberg said.

The rest of the crew nodded at this. Clayton puffed his cigar, then stood. "We should move camp. This place is too open. If there is something out here, we can't defend ourselves from this location. We need somewhere more secure."

◆ ◆ ◆

We divided into teams. The physically strong and the weak. Clayton with Selberg. I paired with Charlotte. Although I wasn't certain who was strong and who was weak in my pairing. As a group, we had to find food and water and scout a location for a new camp. Charlotte and I headed west. Clayton and Selberg, east. Nasir guarded the camp. He still continued to sleep with his eyes open.

After my experience in the subway, I kept my weapon tucked into the front of my belt.

We walked west down the middle of a Fifty-Eighth Street free of cars and people. After a few blocks, we paused in front of an old diner, out of place on a street crowded with tall buildings. The walls had been painted in an art deco black and white, with large windows lining the front.

On the roof was a large sign that read simply EAT.

"Might have some food in here," Charlotte said.

"Maybe." I surveyed the empty street. I wasn't eager to rush into buildings again without the rest of the expedition knowing where I was. Still, if we were ever going to find food, we had to split up at some point. And Charlotte was tough. I felt like I could count on her.

I withdrew the pistol from my belt. "Do you think it's locked?"

I pushed on the door, and with a slow creak, it opened backward into darkness. Charlotte pulled an electric torch from her pack and handed it to me. I flipped the switch and a thin beam of light sliced across a row of laminate tables. I surveyed the room from the doorway, the beam glinting off polished chrome countertops and the glass of the cash register at the opposite end of the diner.

Charlotte pushed past me into the room.

"Can't stand outside all day," she said. She had another flashlight in her hand and she walked past rows of barstools, flipped up the counter and headed toward the kitchen. "I'll see if there's anything to eat."

She disappeared from view, and I heard her in the back kitchen opening cabinets. I surveyed the restaurant. A calendar had been nailed to the wall over a rotating glass cabinet that should have held desserts. The calendar was open to the month of August and displayed a black and white photograph of some crowded Lower East Side tenement street. I ran my finger across the countertop and my skin came away dust free. Everything here appeared newly minted.

I checked two small bathrooms in the rear; both unremarkable rooms with a single toilet and a black and white checkered floor. A third door at the end of the hall led out to a small alley behind the diner with a battered blue dumpster and a handful of garbage cans.

That's when I saw the woman.

She lay flat on her back next to the dumpster in a small, black cock-tail dress. Her face was caked with blood, her hair dark and matted, but pushed to the side by a large gash stretching from her forehead back, to the top of her head. Her eyes bulged terribly, the whites turned a vivid red. Her shoes, small, black heels, were thrown to the side, her bare feet dirty and cut. I stared at her in shock, unable to look away.

Behind me I heard the bang of metal, Charlotte turning over pots and pans. I turned toward the sound. I wanted to speak, but my tongue was dry and unresponsive. Outside came a flash of electric light, followed by a long low rumble. I could feel the crackle of electricity rising in the air around me.

This is for your own good. You won't feel a thing.

Words came unbidden into my head. Some dark recollection of something. Outside the diner, something rumbled once more. I thought of France in the war. We'd been crouched in our trenches for days, waiting for the inevitable charge. A rainstorm had come in from off the coast. We could see the flash of heat lightning and the low rumble of thunder. The memory hit me with unexpected force. An almost physical sensation pushed me against the door frame.

I turned away from the inside of the diner. I turned to look back into the alley.

The dead woman was gone. The alley was slick black pavement, veined with cracks. The dumpster stood empty, pushed against the corner. On the ground where the woman had been lay a single business card. The card was ivory colored, with art deco gold lettering that read:

Feeling Confused? Troubled? Uncertain?

Dr. Joseph Valenstein, DMD, MMS, has answers.

I turned the card over. On the back was an address for a place called the Munroe Film Center just off Columbus Circle with a small drawing of what appeared to be a red Easter egg. I quickly pocketed the card. I wasn't sure what the letters DMD and MMS stood for, but I seemed to remember it had something to do with dentistry. That made no sense. What would a dentist possibly know about my situation? And why was a dentist even here?

A wave of adrenaline coursed through my body, as real and powerful as a drug. I was shaken by what I had seen. The vision of that girl dug into my brain. Certain areas in this place felt more dangerous than others. Like they carried remnants of something. Some hostile energy that coated the surface. The subway station where I had encountered that creature was definitely dangerous. But there was also the cottage in the woods. And the telephones in the lobby of The Dakota and the front of St. Patrick's Cathedral. Certain streets seemed neutral, just frameworks of this system. But others felt edged with fear.

I rejoined Charlotte inside.

We sat across from each other at one of the tables. I had made the decision not to tell her what I had seen. If I was going to be neutral about all this, I had to admit there was another explanation to what I had seen. That I was going crazy. Or at least having some sort of delusions or hallucinations brought about by . . . what? Stress? But if that was true, I wasn't alone. Others had seen something last night too. And Clayton and I both heard something in the cottage.

But I was the group leader, and if my mental state was slipping, I couldn't let anyone know. Outside, through the window, rain began to fall. Droplets trickled down the glass. How was that possible? We were buried underground in a desert, and yet it was raining. I didn't stop to more deeply question this. Impossible rain seemed the least of my concerns at the present.

I wondered where the rest of the team was.

"Guess we don't have to worry about water," Charlotte said as she looked at the rain.

I kept quiet. The memory of the dead girl was still vivid in my brain.

"You okay?" Charlotte asked.

I nodded. I must have looked sick because Charlotte stared at me with concern. I ran my hand across my forehead and felt thick beads of perspiration. "I'm fine. Really. Tired maybe."

"Tired?" Charlotte said. "I've got the perfect thing for you."

She rummaged in her bag and pulled out a single white pill wrapped in wax paper. She held it out to me.

"What is it?" I asked.

"A pep pill."

I took and held the pill. It was made of a finely granulated powder that rubbed off white in my fingers. "What's in it?"

"Don't worry," she said as she unwrapped a second pill from wax paper. She placed the pill on her tongue, then tilted back a long gulp of water from her canteen. She held the canteen out to me. I knew about pep pills. Forced march pills. They were the same as Shackleton took with him on his expedition across Antarctica. The pills were a mix of kola nut and coca leaf extract. The substance was alleged to work wonders. Make the cowardly man brave, and the weak man strong.

I dropped the pill on my tongue and experienced a bitter, aspirin-like wave of taste. I took a drink of water and the pill was gone. Somewhere above the city rolled another crack of thunder.

"Did you hear that?" I asked. "Where does the rain come from?"

"Not sure. Where does any of this come from?"

The rain abruptly stopped after ten minutes. We continued west into a more industrial section. The air was static, the surfaces slick with wetness. Old brick warehouses rose up on either side of us. We walked beneath the West Side Highway, over thin strips of grass that barely covered a layer of gravel and dirt.

A pleasant wave of energy passed over me, and suddenly, I felt better about things. A mild euphoria seemed to settle on my shoulders, like a beautiful phoenix perched on my skin.

"Feeling better?" Charlotte asked.

"I feel great."

Lightning flashed. Giant shadows from the overpass flickered against the street beneath our feet. A second later, another roll of thunder. The low rumble seemed to come from the north. I wondered how high the ceiling was in this chamber.

We reached the far western edge of Manhattan. From somewhere deep inside the shadows of my mind, a memory rose, vivid and fresh.

I'd been here before, looked out across the Hudson, the river shimmering in afternoon light.

My wife had been with me.

I remembered the press of her hand against mine. We had been laughing about something, some shared joke. Then she turned to me and said, "Cut and remember."

"What?"

"Cut and remember," she said. "I'm building a memory scrapbook. I read an article on it. When something good happens, you say 'cut and remember.'"

"What does that do?"

"It's like a mantra. You repeat the phrase and it helps you remember what just happened. Then you can save all these memories in your head like a scrapbook of the mind."

"That sounds insane."

"No, it totally works," she said and squeezed my hand. "We always mock what we don't understand."

"No. We mock what makes no sense."

"Well, I think it makes perfect sense. And I'm going to remember your skepticism for my scrapbook."

It was a pleasant memory. And then like a movie projector that ends suddenly and leaves flapping film trailing around and around, the memory ended. But for a moment I had been there, with her. The feel of my wife's hand. Her smile. The Hudson River shimmering under the sun of a forgotten summer afternoon long ago.

Now I knew. She had been the woman in the photograph with the other me. The photograph Clayton and I found in the apartment over Columbus Circle. Before, I had no recollection of her. But now I knew she was my wife. I didn't know what connection I had to that place. Or where the bloodstains on the carpets and walls had come from. But I was sure now that I had been in that photograph.

I stood on the western edge of Manhattan Island. Where the Hudson River had once stretched out toward New Jersey was now a rocky wall, which rose high above us. I reached out and touched the sandstone-colored barrier. Solid.

"Looks like we reached the end," Charlotte said.

The wall extended as far north and south as I could see, curving slightly to the contours of the island. The euphoria I felt just minutes ago had faded. The memory of my wife had left me sad and lonely, trapped beneath the Earth.

"Head back?" Charlotte asked.

I cleared my head of everything. Tried to put myself in the present. No matter what happened in the past, we had to find a way out of here or we were dead.

"Yeah," I said. "Let's head back."

◆ ◆ ◆

There had been no more thunder. Electricity still hung in the air, and we seemed to walk through it like one might walk through a light fog, particles clinging to our skin. The rest of the team was back at camp. Selberg sat cross-legged beneath the statue of Columbus scribbling furiously in a notebook while Clayton ran a whetstone across an enormous knife. Charlotte went to work on her translations while Nasir sat apart from everyone and watched the group. I slowly walked off to find the address on Dr. Valenstein's card.

No one noticed me as I wandered up Broadway. After a few blocks I reached the wide pavilion of Lincoln Center lined with large concrete and glass buildings. In the center of the pavilion, water spilled into the air from a fountain. In a city of such stillness, the movement was unusual, jarring. Behind the fountain, a banner hung from one of the buildings advertising a ballet company. I stood near the pavilion and scanned the long glass of the buildings.

I had an awareness of how exposed I was. There was no cover for fifty yards in any direction. On a normal day, this would have been beautiful. I imagined hundreds of people, men in tuxedos, women in dresses, making their way through the glass doors into the elegant lobby of Lincoln Center for a night of ballet. The lights would dim momentarily to signal the beginning of the show. Pleasant conversation would die down as people moved in perfumed unison toward their seats.

And somewhere in my brain, a synapse of memory fired. And I knew I wasn't imagining. I was remembering. I had been here before. I had been in that crowd. The memory only lasted for an instant, like the single flare of a nerve cell, but in that moment, I knew.

And then the moment was gone and I was alone once more.

I crossed the empty pavilion, cut between two of the larger buildings, then headed down a set of stone stairs. Giant red lettering across the face of a glass and metal building just off Sixty-Fifth read The Munroe Film Center.

I entered the theater. Inside was a cinema lobby, concessions to the left and two small ticket windows to the right. Concessions was in a typical glass display case with shelves on the back wall, so much like the back of a bar. The display case should have been empty. But it wasn't.

Lined up along the wall, bottles of booze. They stood there in a perfect row, beautiful glass bottles filled with different shades of liquids. I stared at the bottles, the first drinks I had seen anywhere in this strange city. Bourbon. Whiskey. Vodka. My old friends. I held up my lantern, and the glass twinkled in the light.

Prohibition had dried me out. But now I felt the pull of those bottles again, so strong I could almost feel the burn of straight whiskey right down into my belly. My mouth went dry and my fingers tapped a beat on the glass counter.

Slowly, reluctantly, I turned away.

A wine-colored carpet threaded with vines along the edges spread across the floor. I followed this for a few steps, kept my eyes down, until the pull of those bottles made me turn. I swung my eyes back with expectant greed. My tongue worked itself over dry lips soon to be wetted.

The shelves were empty now.

I blinked to clear my eyes, my disappointment almost rising to the point of rage. Of course the shelves were empty. I was in a movie theater. What movie theater stocked booze? But still, I saw what I saw. The bottles had been there. And somehow I was sure that if I had reached for them, they would have all been full, the liquid inside sloshing against the glass.

I turned away from the shelves, then back again. Hoping some trick in the light or movement would bring back my bottles. Nothing. I stood by the counter and listened. No sound. Slowly, I dragged myself away from the counter and through the darkened lobby. A second glass door past the ticket counter swung shut behind me with a frightening finality. My lantern held ahead of me, I moved down a long hall that ended with a gray steel door stenciled Employees Only, leaving the empty shelves behind me.

Through the door I walked up a set of stairs and found myself inside a small projection room. Movie posters for films I'd never heard of were tacked to the wall or lay curled on the floor. *Casablanca. Raging Bull. Out of Africa.* A projection machine pointed out across a vacant theater. In the distance I could see the faint white glow of the screen. On a wooden table, a metal film canister with a handwritten note posted to the top. *Play Me.*

I turned my lantern toward the wall and found a light switch. The overhead bulb flickered to life and I began to inspect the projector. The machine seemed in good order, clean of dust and well oiled. With a clatter of metal, I flipped open the film canister. A reel looped with a short amount of 35 mm film was inside.

I made an educated guess on how to mount the reel. I fed the loose end of film through the projector, depressed a lever, and locked the film into place, then flipped a metal switch at the base of the machine. The machine whirred to life with a burst of light. The two projection wheels began to turn, feeding the film through the lens.

Through the projection window, across the empty rows of seats, I watched the screen light up. I saw a blur of color and an unrecognizable flash of motion. Then the image focused. Onscreen, a man in his late 50s with salt-and-pepper hair, blue eyes, and a deeply lined face sat in a white lab coat, his hands folded on a large wooden desk. He smiled pleasantly, blinked, and tilted his head slightly.

Beside me the projector continued to whir. The man onscreen said nothing, still staring forward. Only I had the uneasy feeling he wasn't simply staring blankly. His eyes seemed focused with purpose. He unfolded his hands in a way that was distinctly impatient. And then he spoke.

"I only have until the film runs out," he said. "So I don't know how much time we have to waste here."

I continued to watch, waiting for him to say more.

"I'm talking to you, you know," the man said. "You up there in the projection booth." The man gave an exasperated sigh. "Well, we won't get very far if we just stare at each other all day."

Next to me the roll began to whine. The film had almost reached its end, the black 8 mm strip running quickly through the machine at a blurring speed.

"Bye now," the man said. The projection roll whirred to empty. The projector shut off and the theater descended back to darkness. Strange. I rethreaded the film and turned the projector back on. There was the same flash of unfocused light on the big screen, and then the man in the white lab coat appeared once more.

"Why, hello again," the man said.

This wasn't what I had seen before. Somehow the film was different.

"It's all right to talk to me. You're in an empty theater. Nobody will think you're crazy." The man onscreen looked directly at me. I was sure of it. I could feel his eyes focus on mine.

"Are you talking to me?" I asked.

"Ah, finally you understand," the man said. "Yes, I am talking to you."

"How is that possible?"

"How is any of this possible? How is it possible that you've found an entire model of New York City buried beneath the Earth? Is that any more or less possible than you talking to a movie screen?"

"Who are you?"

"That's why we should talk," he said. "There's a door just below the screen. See it?" I looked down into the darkened theater and saw a single door with an illuminated red lettered EXIT sign hung over the top. "Go through that door."

"What's there?" I asked, but a moment later the film reel ended. The projector clicked off with a final snap of electricity and once again, the theater descended into darkness.

◆ ◆ ◆

I made my way by lantern light back down the stairs from the projection room and into the theater, passing rows upon rows of empty seats. I approached the single metal door below the giant screen. I hesitated, thinking of my experience in the subway station. If there was something in this abandoned theater that wanted to harm me, it certainly could have done so already. I was far from the rest of my crew and completely alone. I didn't need to walk through doors for something to track me down.

I made my decision and turned the knob. The door was locked. I tried again, harder this time, but the door refused to budge. And then I remembered the key Clayton and I had found in the marionette theater. I still had that key in my pocket. I fitted the key into the lock and turned. The door swung open easily and I stepped forward.

A bright white light seemed to surround me. The light grew in intensity until the theater was blocked out. I shut my eyes against the brilliance, but I could feel it filling my brain. And then it was dark again.

Slowly I opened my eyes.

I stood inside a small, somewhat cluttered office. A frayed sofa flanked one wall. The other wall was covered with a large bookshelf, the bindings of books stacked floor to ceiling. To my right, a set of windows looked out across Manhattan. We appeared to be somewhere in Midtown. Sunlight, real sunlight, illuminated buildings and streets.

The man from the film sat in a chair in the center of the room, legs crossed, in his white lab coat. He smiled at me and indicated the sofa. I sat.

"Welcome," the man said. "You finally made it."

"Made it where?"

"To the deepest recess of your own mind."

"I don't understand."

The man smiled, stood up, walked, and opened one of the windows. Immediately a cool breeze filled the office. Outside I could hear the sound of New York, the familiar mix of horns and rush of tires with the deeper rumble of a subway car passing somewhere beneath us. This felt like a real city. Not the vacant shell we had discovered beneath the sand.

"Feels pretty real," the man said. "Doesn't it? But this world is real only to you. As real as a dream is to any man or woman."

"This is a dream?"

"Not exactly," the man said as he returned to his seat. "It's more complicated than that. But let me introduce myself first. My name is Doctor Joseph Valenstein."

"You're a doctor?"

"I'm your sixth grade orthodontist." The man reached into the front pocket of his white lab coat and pulled out a bright blue plastic box.

Inside the box was a plaster cast of a set of teeth. "Remember this? Probably not. But this is you right after you got your braces off. We saw quite a bit of each other."

I had no memory of what this man said. I ran my tongue across my teeth, feeling their uniform straightness.

"Why are you here?" I asked.

"Only you know the answer to that. You're the one who brought me here. And I don't actually exist. I died years ago. Car crash I think. I don't, or should I say, you don't remember exactly."

"So you're a ghost?"

The man smiled. "No. I'm a projection. A projection that you are creating from your own memory. I don't know why you chose Dr. Valenstein. He was always one of your favorite doctors maybe. I don't know. I could just have easily been this." The person in front of me changed from a man in a white lab coat to an attractive brunette in a low-cut sweater and jeans. "Recognize me? Mrs. Truvani, your next-door neighbor through high school?"

I shook my head. I didn't remember her. Somehow, in this place, I accepted what I was seeing. These faces that morphed and shifted.

"No? You had such fantasies about me back then. Or here's one." The woman changed to become a beefy-looking man with a flattened nose and thick, bushy eyebrows. The man wore athletic shorts and had a whistle around his neck. "Mike Ruben? High school football coach? Anything?"

I didn't know any of these people. The man in the white lab coat appeared before me again. Dr. Valenstein.

"I'll just stay with your original choice," he said. "Some of our strongest memories are created in childhood. Maybe that's why you chose Dr. Valenstein. A trusted parent figure. An intelligent caregiver. Or maybe he's just the first person that popped into that brain of yours. Who knows why our subconscious does anything? But for whatever reason you chose him."

My brain whirled as I tried to catch up. "I don't understand."

"I don't want to break the bad news to you, kid, but this is what prison looks like," Dr. Valenstein said. "Somewhere in your lifetime, the crime rate begins to rise. The cost of prisons rises with it, and people find that freed inmates get out and commit more crimes. That is until Panopticon came along."

I remembered what Clayton had said about that word. "What is Panopticon?"

"I'll show you." Dr. Valenstein stood and walked to the only door in the room. "Right through here."

"But the theater is out there."

"Not anymore."

Dr. Valenstein opened the door to reveal a long, white, tiled hallway. Dr. Valenstein held the door open and indicated the hall with a sweep of his hand. "After you. I promise there are no monsters here."

I walked past him and through the doorway. The hallway led to a large chamber. On either side of me, round windows looked out across water. The floor was dark, polished hardwood, the space the size of a warehouse with the Statue of Liberty visible in the far distance. Artwork ornamented brick walls. A Van Gogh print hung near some sort of classical marble Greek statue. Colorful plastic molded chairs clustered almost randomly around the space.

"Where are we?" I asked.

"This is the inner workings of your brain," Dr. Valenstein said. "This is where you keep your most important memories. You hide them here so the machine can't find and strip them away. I am also a memory planted here. To serve as a guide to explain what's happening. Up until recently, you believed you were some sort of gentleman adventurer. An explorer of ancient Egyptian antiquity. This is not the case."

"What am I?"

"Your name is Parker. On the outside, you're a professional prison breaker for a unique type of prison. And I'm here to remind you of your mission."

We reached the end of the chamber. A set of clouded glass doors remained closed.

"What type of prison?"

"A prison of the mind," Valenstein said.

The door panes suddenly cleared, and I could see into the space beyond, a hospital room with a twin-sized, silvery metallic bed. A man dressed in loose-fitting, pale blue pajamas lay flat on the platform, a metal halo just over his head. A silver cord stretched from the man's arm down to the floor and connected with what appeared to be a heart monitor.

"We are now experiencing your first memory of the Panopticon machine. This was ten years ago."

From an opposite door, a man in a white lab coat entered the room and stood by the bed. He turned to address an unseen audience. His lips moved, but his voice was muted. Dr. Valenstein spoke instead. "At the time, you were an officer in the New York City Police Department. You were given a tour of the machine that was going to revolutionize the prison system.

"The Panopticon was designed as a means to control and reform prisoners. Rather than being held in a large cell, subject to the violence of others, and requiring the cost of guards and various monitoring devices, prisoners could be each assigned a machine and placed into this dream state.

"Prisoners would serve their sentences in virtual worlds of the machine's creation, interacting with other inmates."

I tried to accept what I was being told. To consider it at least. To let it into my mind and play with it, like a new toy. This information. It was no more or less believable than anything I had experienced the last few days. "And the prisoners don't know?"

Valenstein shook his head. "Before entry, the prisoner's mind is erased. New memories are introduced of a new life, scripted by the machine."

I looked again and saw that the unconscious man had a full beard, his hair long and shaggy. As I watched, technicians in white lab coats crowded around the bed. They slid the metal halo off the machine, and slowly the bearded man awoke. He reached out for one of the technicians, then twisted his body and collapsed to the ground.

His entire body shook, and I saw he was sobbing.

"What's wrong with him?" I said. But Dr. Valenstein had already moved away from me. I tried to open the glass doors that would lead out onto the main floor. They were locked shut.

"The doors are locked. They will always be locked," Dr. Valenstein said. "None of what you are experiencing now is real. It is all a memory. Carefully stored and saved by you. But memory is not perfect. There will always be gaps. Holes. Imperfections. That's why the door will stay locked. Your memory of this place isn't strong enough. You can't recall all the details."

I looked out across the room again and noticed that vagueness of the place. The effect was strange. My eyes couldn't focus on portions of the scene. A frame hung on the wall near the window, the canvas a blurry mess of color. A man in slacks and a sweatshirt reclined at his desk rolling a rubber ball between his hands, his face indistinct.

But other details were perfect. The machine was especially distinct, every line of metal, each strand of wire, looked perfectly in place. And the man in the machine, I could see his face clearly.

"Is he a convict?" I asked.

"No, he's a scientist. A volunteer to test the machine. This was before it all started. Come this way."

We continued down the long hall, then through a set of doors that opened into an old-time saloon. A heavy, oak bar backed by a soot-stained mirror with bottles of hard alcohol shone under the flickering light from gas lanterns. The floor was knotted pine, covered by a thin layer of sawdust. More gas lanterns were mounted on the wall, with a piano in the far corner of the room. Chairs and tables were scattered across the floor like jacks thrown from a child's hand. Dr. Valenstein indicated the room. "This was a test model of the first system."

"What do you mean?"

"The Panopticon designers built an entire virtual world to serve as the prison. Each world was populated with prisoners, guards, and artificially intelligent beings who looked and acted human but in fact, served as observers and recorders.

"The first system was a world set in the 1880s. Later systems were set in different time periods. 1953. 1972. 1986. But what every Panopticon system had in common was that they all used the framework of Manhattan Island. So the first system was Manhattan Island of 1890. Filled with the buildings and fashion and technology of the time."

"What was the point of all this?"

"The prison system was overcrowded and expensive. The average cost of housing a prisoner kept rising. The Sleep machine could do the same thing more cheaply. Needed fewer guards, less space. No medical costs. No administration costs. A traditional prison system costs a state billions.

"And brick and mortar prisons weren't even working. These prisoners being released were more violent than when they went in. They served their time sitting in overstuffed cells, surviving cruelty from other inmates and guards, only learning how to be better criminals. The justice system was thus creating new super villains, individuals who were learning no life skills, nothing that would allow them to be reintroduced into society. After a series of prison rebellions in which hundreds were killed, society knew they had to find another solution. And so the Panopticon was devised."

I rapped my knuckles on the bar. "So they built some fake old-timey world and had prisoners live in it?"

"Not exactly. This was a virtual world. A world that existed only in the shared consciousness of the prisoners. As real to them as our world, but still, very much happening only in their mind. And in this place, prisoners would live. They would have jobs. They would interact with each other in normative ways. Their personal histories would be erased, placed in a memory storage facility and returned later as a download. Traumas that perhaps led individuals down the path of criminality would not be remembered. Instead, they could start anew. Not tied to a violent past. The idea being that in this way, they would have a better chance of being reformed. This experience, living in this world, would change them fundamentally as a person, and when they were released, they could be reintroduced to real society."

"But why set these virtual worlds in the past? Why not just have them in present day?" I looked around at the saloon with its gas lamps.

"Because the designers were afraid of confusing the subjects. Of making it impossible for the subjects to distinguish reality from fiction upon their release. Memory is malleable. Memory can be distorted. Changed. Blended together. They wanted prisoners to retain the skills they learned in the system, but still be able to distinguish the real from the created. Setting their lives in different time periods allowed for such potential."

"Does it work?"

"From what you've seen," Valenstein said, "the world in the Panopticon can be as violent and hopeless as the world outside. Even in that virtual world, the rich still have everything, while the poor struggle just to get by. Does it work? I don't know how to answer that. Inside, you're still in a cage, same as in prison, it's just a much bigger one."

"So why didn't they just build a paradise? If the whole point of this is to rehabilitate?"

"They tried that at first," Valenstein said, "and they found the human brain couldn't accept it. We're not made for everyone to be equal. Our happiness is all relative. We look at our neighbors and want more than what they have. The mind rejected the paradise where everyone had every desire fulfilled. The prisoners always sought conflict.

"And politically, society wants prisoners rehabilitated, but victims' families want them punished. Try being a politician and telling a husband that the guy who raped and murdered his wife is doing time in a paradise and see if he votes for you in the next election."

"So why are you showing me all this? What does this have to do with me?"

"Because you worked very closely with this system. You understand the system perhaps better than anyone."

"What do you mean?"

"You lead a very specific type of crew that specialized in prison breaks of the mind. You see, no matter how much this virtual world looks like the real thing, it is still a prison. And prisoners serve years in here. And each prisoner has a family on the outside who misses them. Who wants them back. When that happens, people hire you. You enter the system. Find the prisoner. Break them out."

"How?"

Valenstein nodded toward the dusty glass of the saloon. "Look out there. Tell me what you see."

Through the window, I could see across a rutted cobblestone street leading to a row of tenements, directly across. The buildings were crowded together in a long strip, which extended along the entire block. Gas lanterns stood in the street with hitching posts on the corners. A wooden slat sidewalk traversed the front of the buildings. The scene looked like a film set.

"I can tell you about how the prison breaks work, but there is a memory here, saved for you, that you can experience. You can feel how the breaks work," Valenstein said. "If you want to experience one, go through the door."

Next to the window was a batwing style saloon door, which opened out to the street.

"What happens when I go out there?"

"You will enter a memory of the past. You will experience the memory again as you experienced it the first time. This is necessary for you to know what happens next."

The world had tilted on its axis, and everything I had accepted as truth, I could see now was only variations of the real. A hundred different impressions of reality and of memory were each as open to interpretation as an ink blot. Perhaps there were answers out there that would make sense. I just needed to take the first step.

"Just go through that door?"

Valenstein nodded. "That is the door of memory. And through it you can again experience your past."

I had a moment of doubt. The flame of my commitment flickered for an instant. But then it burned bright again.

I went to the front of the saloon, pushed open the doors, and stepped through.

2

Roger Parker entered with the barest flicker of air. He blinked once in his new body, stretched and flexed muscles as he gathered his bearings. He was seated in a small living room, crowded with people. A half-dozen chairs formed a semicircle around a dead infant in a crib. The chairs were occupied by a rough group that looked on the downswing in life. Cracked plaster was marked by soot from two kerosene lanterns that hung from the wall, along with a map of Manhattan and a black and white photograph of a couple from the old country. Candles, half-melted, were lined around the crib. Street noise filtered in through the open window; the clatter of horse hooves on cobblestone, screams of children, the bark of a salesman, the faraway clack of an elevated train.

A closed wooden door was opposite the window. That was where Parker needed to be. Through that door and out to the street below. He didn't belong here, and they would know it. Parker studied the door a moment too long. He felt the press of a hand against his arm. He turned to look into the faded eyes of an elderly woman seated next to him.

Her hand circled Parker's wrist, her bony fingers surprisingly strong, like the claw of an old crow. Her eyes were narrow, suspicious. "Can you tell me the time?"

Parker paused, considered the question. He looked around the room. *Tried to place the when.* The grip on his wrist tightened and he felt the gnaw of panic in his gut. More faces turned toward him. Each of the half-dozen chairs was occupied by a person in an antique outfit. Only the clothes weren't antique. They were all new. Bought recently, from real stores, stores that hadn't existed in a hundred years. There were men in bowler hats. Women in shawls. A young girl with a bow in her hair and patent leather shoes. The fashion looked late 1800s, but he couldn't be sure of the exact year.

What if he had overshot?

"The time?" Parker repeated the question. "You want to know the time?"

The old crone nodded. One of the men stood, took off his bowler hat, and cracked his knuckles. He had a thick handlebar mustache and eyes swollen half-shut with scar tissue, someone's idea of a saloon bare-knuckle boxer brought to life.

A sound buzzed in Parker's ear. A faint electric whir, then a voice whispered, "Navigator Operator Charlotte coming online now."

The grip on Parker's wrist had the strength of a vise, almost unbearable in its ferocity.

"The time?" Parker repeated. He had to get an answer or this would be a short trip to the past that would end painfully.

"Give me one second," Charlotte's voice sounded in his ear. Fingers tapped quickly on a distant keyboard. He heard a slight beep from the synchrony. "The time. The time. I've got you located. You're at 89 Orchard Street, New York City. It is currently 0830 hours, September 12, 1880."

The man with the bowler hat fitted a pair of brass knuckles over his massive fist. The little girl in the patent leather shoes had moved toward the doorway. She turned the door's bolt, locking Parker inside, and turned to stare at him with the disturbed smile of the criminally insane.

"It's eight thirty, September 12, 1880," Parker repeated aloud. The man with the brass knuckles relaxed, the tendons on his wrist smoothed away. Parker tried to smile, then noticed the grip on his wrist hadn't released.

"Why are we here?" the old woman asked.

Another voice in Parker's ear as the researcher came online. "Archive Operator Selberg online. What'd I miss?"

"Why are we here?" Parker repeated.

"Why are we here, why are we here," Selberg said. "An existential question. Let me see, running 89 Orchard through the historical record. Major events. September 10, 1880, *New York Times* shows a kitchen fire on the first floor. September 9, 1880, census reports show an infant death from influenza. September 7, a garment workers' strike."

"A baby died," Parker said to the woman.

"Dead baby, dead baby," Selberg murmured in Parker's ear. Fingers clicked keys. "Connor Gavin, died, age seven months."

"Little baby Connor," Parker said aloud. "Only seven months. Terrible."

The woman's grip relaxed on his wrist and she turned to stare blankly at the crib. The girl in the patent shoes and the bow in her hair unlocked the door, then returned to her seat.

She looked at Parker. Then with the stillness of a corpse, she said, "We would have killed you."

◆　◆　◆

The crowd sat for ten more minutes, then slowly the mourners broke apart from the cradle and the dead infant. Everyone rose and mumbled thank-yous and apologies to one another. The mother, a thin wisp of a woman in a black dress, sat crying in the corner. Her husband stared stoically out the window.

Parker stood and left quietly. The door led out into the dark hallway of a tenement building. Rough wooden stairs rose unsteadily to the floor above, the walls blackened by years of soot. Behind closed doors he heard the symphony of tenement living: arguing voices, a baby crying, the clatter of pots.

The little girl followed behind as he made his way down the hall.

"I've got a follower," Parker whispered. "I need to change."

"Guard or drone?" Charlotte asked.

He remembered the strange giggle, the unhinged smile of the little girl. "Prisoner I think. Psych services maybe."

"Does she suspect?"

"I don't know."

Parker headed down the rickety stairs, moving to the right to make way for an enormous woman in a soiled dress carrying a dead goose across her shoulder. He reached the bottom floor, then out the back door into a small, stone courtyard area. Limp laundry was strung overhead, dripping brackish water. Several women took turns at a cast iron pump, filling tubs with water and vigorously scrubbing clothes. A row of outhouses lined the back wall. One of the outhouse doors flung open and a rake-thin man stepped out, still pulling up his pants. A few of the women laughed and exchanged dirty jokes.

One of the women stared at Parker as he passed. She was doughy faced with skin pitted from a childhood ailment. Her hair was greasy, her fingernails dark and cracked. At a sign from the little girl, the washerwoman dropped her laundry into the barrel of soapy water and joined the girl to follow him.

Parker ducked beneath the laundry, opened a door at the far side of the courtyard, and entered the adjoining building. "Do we have any drops nearby? I might need a weapon."

"You have a charging drone, third floor of your current location," Charlotte said.

Parker took the stairs two at a time, up past garbage-strewn hallways barely lit with flickering gas lamps. He was still acclimating to his new body. The stairs left him winded. If a fight came, he wasn't sure how the ride would be. He paused on the third floor.

"I'm here, third floor," Parker said.

"Door at the end of the hall," Charlotte said.

One floor below, Parker heard the footsteps of the girl and the washerwoman. They suspected him. He wouldn't have much time before half the guards in the neighborhood were after him.

Parker pushed open the door at the end of the hall and entered a cramped apartment beyond. A large cast iron stove took up most of the kitchen. Dried herbs hung from the ceiling, with a flat iron set to warm near the stove. The floor was uneven hardwood. Through an open doorway, Parker saw a rope bed with a lumpy mattress, chests and battered suitcases stacked almost to the ceiling.

In the living room, a frayed carpet covered the floor. In the far corner was a man. He sat completely still in a wooden chair, and in the faded dusky light from the window, Parker could see he wore faded overalls and the leather boots of a worker. His face was flat and wide, pockmarked, with a thick mustache and black hair.

His eyes were open and glazed over, no life inside the body.

"Got him," Parker said.

"Subject's name is Robert Brown, laborer," Selberg said. "He's a level three drone."

"Can we use him?"

"Of course. I'm accessing him now."

Robert Brown's eyes flickered rapidly. Footsteps sounded in the hall outside the apartment. The woman and the girl had reached his floor. Fear gripped Parker and he scanned the room for anything he could use as a weapon. All he had was his fists—and he clenched them tight. It wasn't pretty smashing a little girl in the face. That's probably why they always chose them. That moment of hesitation could make the difference in an escape.

"Transitioning," Selberg said. Parker gritted his teeth as his stomach plummeted and his brain went light. His vision went black. In the darkness, he heard a rattle of metal as someone tried the locked door. His senses returned.

He was alone in the same room, seated in the wooden chair. He rose and looked into the warped mirror that hung from the wall near the window. The flat, rugged face looked back at him. He was inside Robert Brown.

"We're good," Parker said. He moved quickly around the room, testing his new reflexes and balance. Something in his brain wavered and dizziness swamped his body. He held onto the chair for balance. "Whoa . . . feeling a bit wobbly here."

"I can see that. We're only at 80 percent."

Parker took a cautious step forward. The room seemed to spin around him. "Can you tighten it up?"

"I'm trying. Perfect synchronization is tricky. Should have gotten a synchronizer for this job," Selberg snapped.

"Ouch," Charlotte voiced.

"I'm not paid enough to archive and synchronize," Selberg said.

Parker's grip tightened against the chair as his brain continued to swirl. "I've got guards at the door. Just fix it."

"Trying to. Hang on."

The dizziness increased and a wave of nausea overcame Parker. And then he was locked in. His stomach still felt queasy, but the world stopped turning. He opened his eyes.

"Good," he said.

"Told you. Just be patient."

Parker's previous body lay in a pile on the ground. Seeing him now from the outside, the man had been weak, sickly looking. Maybe one of the garment workers along Orchard. Parker had to hide the body.

There was a sharp knock on the door to the apartment, then a metal click as someone tried the knob again. Parker's heart flared with adrenaline. "They're at the door."

"That's the only way out," Charlotte said. "Better get moving, cowboy."

Parker hoisted the body over his shoulder. The man was heavy and limp, but Parker's new vehicle was strong and able to handle the weight. Parker kicked open the lid to a wooden chest in the corner and dropped the body inside. He folded the legs up, trying not to think of this thing as human. It wasn't. Not really anyway.

The rough banging on the door sounded again, then the lock broke up with a crash. Parker dropped the lid on the chest and stood. The child and the washerwoman stormed into the room. The little girl held a pistol.

"Where is he?" the girl asked.

"Who?" Parker replied. He felt a wave of relief as his voice worked normally. He hadn't remembered to test out his new vocal cords.

"We had an intruder," the girl said, her voice young, but her bearing completely adult. Parker had no doubt she would shoot him if given cause. The washerwoman vanished into the back bedroom. She overturned the mattress to the ground. "You didn't see nobody?"

Parker shook his head.

"What's your name?" the girl demanded.

"Robert Brown," Parker said.

"Prisoner?"

"AI. Drone."

The washerwoman returned to the room and shook her head.

The girl glanced around the room, still not satisfied. "This is your recharging quarters?"

Parker nodded. The girl moved forward, her eyes flickering to the windows. Parker tensed the muscles of his arms, ready to spring forward if the girl moved toward the chest.

"Remember, Parker," Selberg's voice sounded in his ear. "She isn't an eight-year-old girl. She's a violent adult prisoner and would shoot you down in a moment if she had to. So whatever happens, don't hesitate."

Parker said nothing. The girl passed by Parker and began to walk slowly toward the chest. The washerwoman stood near the exit, blocking the open door, her beefy arms folded across her chest. Parker sighed. He hadn't wanted this to happen. It was supposed to be an easy job. But Charlotte had dropped him into the middle of a funeral. He was bound to be noticed.

The girl flipped open the heavy lid of the chest. She had a moment to glimpse the crumpled body inside before she swung back toward Parker. Parker's fist impacted her face and knocked her off her feet. The gun clattered to the floor. Parker picked it up and turned as the washerwoman charged at him, a metal pipe in her hand. Parker shot the woman once, the pistol incredibly loud in the small space. The woman twisted and collapsed.

A sharp pain and intense pressure electrified Parker's shoulder. The little girl hung on his back, her teeth buried into the meat of his upper arm. Parker screamed and spun, trying to flip her off him. Sharp fingernails dug into his cheek and he felt blood on his face. She bit down into the side of his neck like a crazed vampire. Parker slammed his body against the back wall. There was the hard jolt of impact and the girl's grip loosened enough for Parker to reach up, grab hold of her hair, and fling her forward to the floor. She hit the ground hard, scrambled to her feet, and charged at him again with a shriek.

Parker unloaded the pistol into her body. She fell back to the floor, twitched for an instant and then lay still. His surge of adrenaline passed. Parker bent over and vomited in the corner of the room.

"Rowdy stuff. You all right there?" Selberg asked.

"Go easy on him, Selberg," Charlotte's voice cut in. "He just shot an eight-year-old kid."

Selberg scoffed. "More like a forty-year-old rapist."

"Well, I guess we'll never know."

Parker wiped the sides of his mouth, then stood. "I'm fine. Just get me where I need to go. Those kills are going to set off alarms."

"I see someone doesn't want to be cheered up," Selberg said. "Fine."

"I'm here," Charlotte said. "You need to get to 176 Stanton Street. Go out the door before you have company."

Parker straightened himself, pocketed the revolver, then walked into the hall. The firearm hung heavily in his pants and he pressed his hand against the weapon to keep it from swinging. Several apartment doors were open, light spilling out into the dark hallway, curious tenants staring at him, drawn out by the gunshots. Parker kept walking, hoping none of the onlookers were guards.

Nobody stopped him, and he stepped out the front door and breathed thick air. Orchard Street was jammed with street vendors, horse drawn carts, and people. The air was heavy with the smell of manure and baking bread. Wooden and brick tenement buildings crowded around him, blocking out the light.

"Head north. Stanton Street is one block away," Charlotte said.

Parker moved up the block, trying to blend in with the tradesman who hawked their wares and filled the crowded sidewalk. The men around him all sported mustaches and hats, most wearing filthy aprons and cracked boots. Small businesses were crowded between and inside the tenements. Hat makers, cobblers, shirt makers . . . everything was bustling and alive. The depth of detail was incredible—the place felt real.

The noise was deafening. Men shouted and cursed, iron wheels clattered on stone, horses whinnied, leather harnesses creaked, and in the distance he heard the jarring rattle of an elevated train. Added to the din was the general scuffle of feet as an incomprehensible number of people bumped and jostled each other along the sidewalk.

A sickly looking mule pulled a vegetable cart slowly down the street. A woman in a filthy ankle-length dress swatted the mule half-heartedly with a long thin stick. The mule kept pulling, bells around his harness jingling morosely. In its day, this was the most crowded section of Manhattan, filled beyond capacity with the newly arrived poor setting foot in the New World to chase their dreams through the mud and violence of America. Even in this version of history, the same idea held. The prisoners without connections lived down here, in the bowels of Manhattan. Unable to buy their way up the food chain, they toiled in the same backbreaking labors as their ancestors had a hundred and fifty years earlier.

The system was built to rehab the convicted. But like any system, there were flaws. This one took on a life of its own, and some prisoners continued to experience the harshest of circumstances.

Parker crossed the street behind the cart and paused on the corner beneath a leaning gas lamp.

"You're on Stanton now," Charlotte said. "Look for the brick tenement with the red door, about fifty feet to the east."

Parker spotted the building next to a white clapboard house that leaned dangerously to the side. An alley of rutted cobblestones could be seen between the two buildings. Laundry hung limply over the alley, wooden barrels stacked up against the wall in a pool of stagnant filthy water. As Parker approached, two toughs stepped out wearing high-crowned derbies and carrying wooden clubs.

Charlotte's voice sounded in his ear. "I'm showing the building has security."

"Yeah. I'm looking at them now. Times two."

The toughs were heavily muscled for the time, both in dirty long coats with checkered vests. They had the casual amble of men used to getting their way and stepped onto the street to block Parker's path.

One of the men pointed the club at Parker. "What are you doing here, boy?"

Parker stopped short, put up his hands. "Just minding my business."

"Why don't you mind your business the other way," the man said. "Street's closed."

The man jabbed Parker painfully in the ribs with his club. Parker took a step back. His fists clenched, and he took a breath against the pain. The body he was in was stronger than most. The pistol still weighed heavily in his pocket, but he wanted to keep it quiet.

"What am I looking at?" Parker spoke aloud for Selberg's benefit. The Archive Operator had the ability to scan prison records, and for listed prisoners, he could match up the faces of their new bodies with their records. The point of this whole system was rehabilitation, but some convicts were too far gone. They would never leave this place.

"Both prisoners," Selberg replied. "Lifers for homicide."

"Am I authorized?"

"You have a green light."

The two toughs glanced at each other as Parker seemed to speak to himself. They took another step toward him. One of the men had a thin face, a twisted lip marked by an old scar. The street that teemed with 1880s tenement life suddenly went quiet. From his periphery, he sensed the crowd stepping back onto the sidewalk. A prostitute in a wine-red velvet dress draped in folds walked by and quietly whispered at Parker, "Don't want to mess with those two."

Parker smiled and nodded at her, then turned back toward the men. He spread his feet out into a boxer's stance and dug his back foot into the dirt of the street.

"But I like this street," Parker said to the men.

"That's your mistake, then."

The blow of the club was easy to predict. The first man pulled his arm back, then swung the club in a wide looping motion at Parker's head. Parker ducked the move easily, the club whistling over his head, then delivered a kick to the gut of the tough. The man doubled over, and Parker caught him across the temple with a right hook.

The second man took a tentative step back as he watched his companion fall unconscious into the dirt. Parker picked up the fallen man's club from the ground and hefted it expertly in his hand. It was solid oak, with a leather handle.

"You shouldn't pick fights with strangers," Parker said, then buried the point of the club deep into the man's belly. The man crumpled to his knees, and Parker smashed the man's face with the point of his elbow. The tough shrieked in pain as his nose broke and blood gushed over his mouth.

"Time is ticking," Charlotte said.

"I know, I know," Parker replied as he advanced across the rutted street. The front door of the tenement burst open with a single kick. He stepped into a narrow dark hallway littered with broken glass. The roof was layered in dented tin. Peeling, rose-colored wallpaper layered black with soot spread raggedly along the wall. A kerosene ceiling lamp flicked a feeble, blue flame behind its glass enclosure.

"Second floor," Charlotte said. "Wooden door number three."

Parker pulled the pistol from his pocket as he took the stairs two at a time. The upstairs hallway was empty. The door to the shared hallway bathroom was left open, a toilet on a wooden platform visible inside. Somewhere a baby cried. Parker pressed his ear to the third door and heard nothing.

"Door three?"

"That is affirmative," Charlotte replied.

Gripping the pistol in one hand, Parker kicked the door hard, and with a snap of wood, the rickety lock snapped open. Parker advanced quickly into the two-room apartment beyond. The kitchen was empty. A wood fire boiled a kettle of water on a large cast iron stove. The air was stiflingly hot.

The target was in the back bedroom. He jumped up from the bed as Parker moved into the space. He was in his early 30s, with a cunning and unlikable face. He was shirtless with dirty slacks and suspenders that hung around his waist. His eyes went wide and he raised his hands. He stepped back and almost tripped on an oak chest on the floor. A woman sat on the edge of the bed, a baby cradled in her arms. She screamed and moved toward the wall.

From below, a police whistle sounded and Parker heard booted feet on the street below.

"What's your name?" Parker asked, the pistol leveled at the man's head.

"What do you want?" The man's hands began to shake.

"Your name."

"Edward Rafferty."

Charlotte's voice sounded in Parker's ear. "That's our guy. Prison snitch. LifeSleep for bank robbery."

Parker pressed a finger to his lips, then the pistol to Rafferty's forehead. Outside, the footsteps of the coppers moved by. When the hall was quiet, Parker turned back to Rafferty. "You know why I'm here?"

"No, sir." He kept his hands in the air. "I work in a tinner's shop on Essex."

"Bullshit. You got a twenty-year sleep sentence for a dozen armed bank robberies."

Rafferty's eyes flicked slightly to his woman. "I never robbed no banks. Honest. Just work with tin."

Parker looked around the small, squalid apartment. The place stunk of cabbage and old grease. An ash barrel stood in the corner, overflowing with garbage. The view from the window was blocked by the fire escape. Rafferty's wife cradled the baby against her chest. She wore a dress the color of dirty snow that hung limply on her pale frame. The baby shrieked, its little face blistering red.

"My wife. Doesn't know," Rafferty whispered. "Thinks she was born and raised in here. Perfect synchronization, total memory wipe."

Parker nodded to the woman. "Take a walk. You see any coppers, you keep your mouth shut. Got it?"

The woman crept silently out like a ghost, the shriek of the baby getting farther and farther away as she descended the stairs.

"Why do you live in this shit hole?" Parker waved the pistol around the room.

"Flats are expensive. Do I look like a Fifth Avenue man? Elevators and steam heat?"

Parker raised an eyebrow and frowned, kicked the edge of the bed with a foot, then lifted up the mattress. Hidden underneath were two *Hustler* magazines, naked girls rubbing each other on the cover. Typical contraband. For a price, hackers on the outside could insert modern-day items into the system. Every once and a while they would show up. Same thing had been going on for years in the real world. Used to be drugs or cigarettes smuggled in. Now it was all virtual. The idea of something.

Parker held up the magazine. "Get this in your tin shop?"

Rafferty shrugged. "Never seen that before in my life."

Parker rolled up the magazine into a tight club then struck Rafferty across the head with it. "I'm going to toss every inch of this place. Every anachronism contraband I find, I'm taking it all."

"No, no, wait a minute, wait a minute. We can talk about this, friend. You know how hard it is to get that contraband in here. The drops are harder and harder to find."

"So talk."

"Don't make me a rat."

Parker struck Rafferty again across the face with the magazine. "Hey, Tinman, I don't care about your misplaced prison code of ethics."

Rafferty ducked his head like a cowered dog. "All right, Jesus, what do you want to know?"

"I'm looking for someone."

"Prisoner or guard?"

"Prisoner. Name on the outside was Donald Lancaster. Investment banker, doing ten years for fraud."

Rafferty rubbed his chin thoughtfully. Then, like a mask pulling away from his face, he smiled and his eyes grew sharp. He touched the cut beneath his eye, then licked the blood from his fingertip. "Yeah, sure, I think I know him."

"And?"

"And that's it? I just tell you? I got twenty years in here, you think I'm going do that time reading Charles Dickens and going to the burlesque? I'll lose my mind."

"At least you're walking around—plenty of guys in solitary."

Rafferty held up his hands. "Hey, listen, I'm not complaining. But why the 1880s? Put me down in the 1990s at least. Whores, drugs. Television. God, what I wouldn't give just to turn on a television. Here I work in a fucking tin shop and step in horse shit every time I walk out the front door of my hovel."

"What do you want?"

"Money. Mobility. I can do 1880 on Park Avenue, but not in these tenements. Put me in someone else, not some off-the-boat mick laborer with a second grade education and no prospects. Give me someone uptown. Not a Jew though, I want to be able to eat pork."

Parker shook his head. "I can't transfer you. And I can't get anything out-of-period. Nothing after 1880. Nothing anomalous. Prison security would detect it."

Rafferty exhaled, then mumbled. "So what can you do for me?"

There was a buzz in Parker's ear, then Charlotte's voice sounded. "On the outside, Rafferty had a thousand-dollar-a-day cocaine habit. We could try that."

"Try it."

"I'm sending something now," Selberg said. "Try the dresser in the bedroom."

Parker turned and saw a cheap oak dresser in the corner. He opened the top drawer to find colorful paper boxes decorated with images of a little boy and girl playing in the street. Across the top of each box in Victorian script was written Hadley's Cocaine Toothache Drops. Parker showed them to Rafferty.

Rafferty raised an eyebrow. "How much is in there?"

"Even for a party boy like you, it's enough of a bump."

"This is real?"

"Available in any drugstore of the period. Nobody will pick up on it."

Rafferty looked at the box thoughtfully, then smiled. "Who are you looking for again?"

"Lancaster, Donald."

"Yeah, yeah, I know him. He's connected in here. Paid his way up the ladder."

Parker flipped one of the boxes to the snitch. Rafferty ripped open the box of cocaine toothache drops. Inside was a small glass bottle filled with clear liquid.

"Where can I find him?"

Rafferty took a sip of the liquid and swished it around his mouth. His eyes widened as the coke reached his gums. "Oh wow. You weren't kidding. There is a fucking bump in here."

Parker snapped his fingers. "Stay focused."

"Yeah. Yeah. Sure. Let's see. Lancaster, banking guy right? He's a Fifth Avenue man. Heard it's a beautiful flat. Elevators. Servants and carriages. Real plumbing, don't have to shit in a hole in the ground."

"Where on Fifth?

"Nice place. Funny name." Rafferty tapped his forehead, trying to remember. "The Hyacinth. It's Fifth Avenue and Sixty-Fifth Street. Fucking prison. Got me down here in the slums, he's up there eating caviar and getting rubdowns by showgirls."

"Does he know?"

Rafferty looked up. "Does he know he's really in prison and all this is just a product of a Sleep machine? I don't think so. Not many people do."

"So how do you know?"

"They never got full synchrony when they put me in the machine. They're supposed to put you through the memory wringer first, remove all your memories, put them in storage. Then when you get out, they give them back to you. But it didn't work for me."

"How do you mean?"

"Don't know. I still have all my memories of before. Of my regular life before this. That's how I know this world is just an illusion. That I'm really in a Sleep machine. They say these places are supposed to be for rehabilitation, but this is no paradise down here. How can you rehabilitate yourself when you're worried about just putting food on the table all the time? There's a few of us pretending to be regular citizens. Then of course you have the guards. And you have some of the prison snitches. Get certain benefits to keep an eye on the rest of us. They know the deal, but stay away from them, they're all certified psychos."

Parker thought of the little girl and the laundry woman. "Yeah. I met some of them already. Got attacked by a few of them the instant I touched down in this world."

"Yeah, the machine don't work on the real crazies sometimes. They're always on the lookout for intruders. Those are the real bad ones. They know the truth, and they love it down here. They can be as violent as they want.

"Most of us, like me, don't cause problems. Just serve out our sentences. Better than being on the outside. At least in here we get some kind of life. How is it on the outside?"

"Bad. Whole world is falling apart."

"Like I said, sometimes it's better to be in here."

Parker took a last look around the cramped tenement. Then he turned to leave. He reached the door when Rafferty called out to him. "This guy you're looking for, Lancaster. You're trying to break him out?"

"Family has money. They want him in the real world, not lying in a coma in a machine somewhere."

"Well, be careful," Rafferty said. "The guys that don't know the deal, that don't know this whole world is an illusion, they don't want you to break them out. No matter how much you explain it, they just think you're crazy. Wealthy guy like Lancaster is going to have security down here. Just watch yourself."

"Appreciate your concern."

"Self-concern. When you do get caught, do me a favor: forget my name. Living in the slums is still better than in a cell somewhere."

Parker nodded. "Thanks for the tip."

◆ ◆ ◆

An omnibus, pulled by a team of horses and brightly hung with advertisements for hair cream, clattered over the rough cobblestones on its route up First Avenue. Nearby, a boot maker's window was lit by electricity, casting a bright, cheerful square of light onto the sidewalk. The boot maker himself was visible inside, bent over strips of leather, holding a half-dozen nails between his lips as he worked his craft.

Parker paused beneath a streetlamp to watch the man work. He wondered who he was. A prisoner. A guard. A drone. There, sitting in his shop, hard at work under the electric light, he looked so real, so animated, though he was just a skin inhabited by the consciousness of a criminal.

The omnibus came to a stop and Parker boarded, dropping a nickel into a tin box and climbing into the back. Inside, two benches ran the length of the bus beneath the windows. The benches were already crowded, and he found a seat between two well-dressed men in hats. As he squeezed down, Parker felt the hard metal of a pistol strapped to one man's hip, hidden beneath his suit jacket. A misty rain, thin and cold, blew in from the street as the horses strained forward in their harness, and the omnibus jerked north.

"They found the bodies of those two toughs you took out," Charlotte said. "They're sending in more guards to the island now."

"What's their appearance?"

"Coppers."

They turned west, then north. The Third Avenue elevated train roared by in the distance with a belch of smoke and the loud clank of metal. The omnibus crossed Fourteenth Street, passing by Brentano's bookstore and the wide muddy field of Union Square.

"They're sending out your description now," Charlotte said.

On the sidewalk, a newsboy ran from a dark alley, a stack of papers in hand. He stopped at a light post and tacked one of the papers to the pole before scampering off up the street. As the omnibus pulled closer, Parker saw an uncannily accurate stencil drawing of his current appearance, the word WANTED in bold gothic print written below. More newsboys appeared on the corners, holding out the wanted flyers and handing them off to the crowds.

The security system moved quickly without breaking the rules of the time and set into motion an entire population designed to hunt Parker down.

Parker's seatmate turned with curiosity to look at the commotion on the sidewalk outside the omnibus. Parker looked to the ground, rubbed his eyes with the palm of his hand, feigning a headache, while doing his best to hide his face. At the next stop, Parker stood and jumped off the back of the omnibus. He searched his pockets, found a few coins, and stepped inside a hat store just off Broadway. He left minutes later, wearing a new Bollman bowler pulled low down over his eyes.

Keeping his head down, he passed through the crowds along Fourteenth Street. His wanted poster was circulating quickly. Inside this world, the coppers and street thugs were the system security, while the newsboys were like a virus. Alarms were generated by some internal server and pushed out all over the city. They were totally artificial, incapable of speech other than to spread their preprogrammed message in the dialect of the time.

Another newsboy appeared suddenly on the corner, looking almost identical to the others on the previous block. He swung his hand in wild circles. "Coppers hunting their man! A fiend if there ever was one!"

"I need a new look," Parker spoke to his handlers.

"Yes, I would say you do," Charlotte replied. "Security is already shutting me out. I'm not going to be able to transition you into an AI from here."

"What about an internal link?"

"We've got an old one. Never used him before. But he should be able to connect you with a new body. Head to Fourteenth and Avenue A. Find the German."

Parker moved as quickly as possible without drawing attention. A copper ambled slowly along the opposite side of Fourteenth, twirling a wooden club on a leather handle. He was a big man, his knee-length blue police coat with gold buttons tight against his broad shoulders. On his head, the British-style custodian helmet added another few inches to his height, making him seem even more imposing.

The misting rain continued, slicking the streets and adding a shine to the buildings. Parker entered the East Village neighborhood of Little Germany, filled with oyster saloons and beer halls. This section of the city was cleaner than the other immigrant areas, but the people on the streets still carried the hard-edged look of suspicion. A group of workers in long, dusty coats and stovepipe hats with impossibly thick mustaches and weather-beaten faces huddled beneath the ragged, blue awning of a dilapidated hostelry, muttering among themselves in German. They looked up, flinty-eyed, at Parker as he passed by, one of them reaching to the saddle roll of a horse hitched to a post. Parker assumed that man concealed some sort of weapon.

"Look for a place called Zum Schneider," Charlotte said. "It's a beer hall."

Parker kept his eyes on the cobbles of Fourteenth Street, filled with pastry-sized piles of horse dung, and passed by the workers without incident.

Zum Schneider took up the entire ground floor of one of the larger tenement buildings. A wooden sign hung from an iron bar over the two saloon-style swinging doors that guarded the entrance. Girded by the clinking of heavy glasses, a cacophony of voices and accordion music blared incredibly loudly through the open doorway. The place sounded packed, and as Parker pushed through the doors, he saw the large hall stretch out before him, crowded to capacity, the sheer volume of noise and movement almost overwhelming him.

Hundreds of men, mostly working class in appearance from their worn clothes and leathered hands, stood together shoulder to shoulder, ten deep around a solid, hand-cut oak bar. Tables, also made of thick oak, were packed tightly with chairs, on which more men sat holding massive glass or pewter-capped steins filled with frothy beer. The floor was covered with knotted pine and sagged beneath the feet, while above, kerosene lamps hung from smoke-blackened beams.

Fairly pretty girls wearing traditional flower-patterned Tyrolean blouses and green and black dirndls moved nimbly through the crowd, ferrying trays of beer steins back and forth to the bar. There, the bar-keep, a squat man in a black and red jacket with a green cap, worked to refill glasses from a bronze spigot inserted into a large wooden barrel. Barely visible through the crowd, a band in lederhosen played their hearts out, the music adding to the clamor.

"The man you're looking for is Hans Moeller," Selberg said. "Census records show him on the second floor."

"Across the room should be a door. Through the door, up the stairs, first door on your right," Charlotte said.

Near the end of the bar, Parker saw an oak door. He pushed his way through the crowd, then opened the door and continued up a set of steps. The stairs were rickety. Gas lamps burned in flickering shadows on the walls. At the top, a dimly lit hallway seemed to lean to one side. The noise of the band sounded dully from below. Parker knocked once on the first door. A girl of about six sat in the corner of the hall, almost obscured in darkness, bouncing a dirty porcelain doll in her lap. She eyed Parker with suspicion as her little fingers tightened around the doll's neck. Parker's arms fell to his side, his hand resting on the butt of his revolver. He really hoped he didn't have to kill another kid.

From inside the flat, a voice barked, "Komm!"

Parker pushed open the door and found himself in the kitchen of a cramped filthy apartment. On a table, a candle sputtered weakly next to a tin plate of moldy cheese and a bottle of soured milk. An old man sat at the table, bent over the cheese, picking away the mold with dirty fingernails. He turned as Parker entered.

The man mumbled something in German, then he took a long sip of beer from a dusty stein. The sound of a fight broke out somewhere below. Chairs overturned. A glass broke.

Parker kept his hand on his revolver. "Are you Hans Moeller?"

The man nodded slightly.

"English?" Parker asked.

"Ja. Of course." The man's voice was heavily accented.

"I've heard you can help me."

The man put down the beer stein and wiped his upper lip with the back of his sleeve. He held the candle aloft and peered through the darkness at Parker's face. Dark bags of loose skin hung beneath the man's watery eyes. His teeth were mostly missing, and the ones that remained were badly discolored. His clothes, dirty and ragged.

"I don't know you," the man said.

"I'm from the outside."

The man's lower lip trembled slightly, then he closed his mouth. "Have you come to kill me?"

"No, old man, I've come for help. I need a change of outfits."

Moeller nodded. He pushed himself up from the table, then shuffled down the dark hall toward a back room. "I haven't had many visitors lately. I thought the outside was quiet."

"The outside is the same as it's been for years," Parker said. "Just been harder to get anyone inside."

"When the system was new, whole world was more free. Guards weren't as hard. We'd have breaks every month. I'd see someone like you all the time."

"System is better now. More secure. How long have you been in here?"

"Oh, many years."

"What did you do?"

"I had a puppet show. Many years ago. In Central Park. I had the cottage to myself. They found a woman murdered. They said it was me." The old man paused in front of a locked wooden door. "Raped and murdered. Terrible what we do to one another."

He unlocked the door with a key on a leather strap that hung around his neck, then fiddled with a mounted gas lamp. There was a hiss, then a flame appeared inside the glass ball. In the yellow light, the room was dingy and windowless. A table was bolted to the floor in the center of the room. Slumped over against the wall were the bodies of three men and a woman. The men were varying ages. The woman looked to be in her late twenties.

The forms were lifeless, arms and legs spread at odd angles like forgotten dolls. Their eyes were closed, but their mouths hung open, swollen tongues protruding from teeth. A layer of dust covered some of them.

"Little dirty," Parker said.

"They'll get it done." The old man used his boot to nudge the leg of one of the men. "The connections good. Balance and coordination both good."

Parker raised an eyebrow. "When was the last time they were operational?"

"Six months."

"I don't know," Parker said doubtfully.

"They're good models." The old man pointed at a thick-necked man. "He's a good strong one. Good in a fight. Can be a laborer. Get you most places in the bad areas."

"Any trouble before?"

The old man sighed. "Last time he got taken out, he knifed a man on the Bowery. Coppers might be looking for him still."

"Can't use him. How about her?"

"She's reliable. She'll get anywhere you want. Go up to Park Avenue, the good houses take her on as a scullery. Wander the Bowery as a whore or a washerwoman. Lot of options with her."

"How's her health?"

"She's fit. Everything works. Don't sell no lemons here."

Parker thought for a moment about being a woman. The process was disorienting enough without switching genders. Each move to a new body, Parker had to get used to differences in height and strength, like learning to drive a new car every time, never sure where all the levers and pedals were.

But as a woman he might have better access to where he needed to go.

"All right, sold," Parker said. "Make a good connection."

"Do you have gold?"

Parker took a step back. "Selberg, can we pay the man?"

"I'm on it," Selberg said. "I've got a connection. Tell him to check the cabinet in the kitchen."

Parker turned to the old man and told him to look in the cabinet. Hans left the room, then reappeared a few moments later holding a canvas bag. He opened the bag and held it before the feeble light of the lantern. Inside, a mound of gold coins. He nodded and placed the bag in his pocket.

"Good choice, the woman." The old man's smile showed his row of bad teeth. He swiped his hand across the top of the table. A cloud of dust swirled up into the air. He bent down and took hold of the woman's legs. "Help me with this."

Parker held the woman's arms, and together the two men lifted the lifeless form onto the top of the table. From inside a metal case, the old man removed a rusted metal helmet with long wires attached to a suitcase-sized wooden box on the floor. Connected to the box was a metal crank.

"You are having problems connecting from the outside," Moeller said.

"Security shut it down."

"I see. They will do that." Moeller placed the helmet on Parker's head. The metal was sharp and heavy and dug into Parker's scalp. "Have you ever done an internal transition before?"

Parker shook his head. Moeller went to the hand crank and began to turn it. The crank revolved with a shriek of metal. Moeller laughed, showing his rotted teeth. "It can be a bit painful."

Moeller turned the crank faster. Small blue electric flickers flashed within the box. The hair on Parker's head began to rise.

"How painful?"

"Worse than anything you could imagine."

Moeller pushed down on a large black switch on the side of the box. There was an electric pop and a flash of light. A surge of pain crashed like a wave onto Parker's brain. He gritted his teeth and shut his eyes as every nerve in his body seemed to fire with razor sharpness. His spine snapped into a lock position and he felt himself falling.

The world went black.

◆ ◆ ◆

Parker's consciousness roared up in the darkness. He slammed into his new body with an unexpected shock. Something felt wrong. He felt somehow heavy. The presence of his new being was around him, but he could see only darkness. Parker tried moving his legs, but he felt a great weight on them, seeming to pin him to the table.

"—you hear me? Parker? Can you hear me?"

Charlotte's voice sounded far away and Parker struggled to remain conscious.

"You're in trouble Parker, wake up!" Charlotte's Navigator voice cut through the fog and powered Parker to alertness. His eyes opened. Parker lay on the table inside the same cramped room. He struggled to sit up, but something pushed him down. His legs were forced painfully open and heavy weight gripped the top of his knee. Parker looked down, momentarily disoriented by his own female body. Then the confusion changed to fear and disgust. Moeller was on top of Parker, his pants down to his knees, as he tried to force Parker's legs open.

"Wake up!" the Navigator screamed in his ear.

Suddenly fully conscious, Parker bolted upright. The German slipped sideways, his breath hot in Parker's face, stinking of old meat. Moeller pulled back and punched Parker hard in the eye. The blow caught Parker by surprise and his head rocked. A sickening flare of pain erupted through his brain and Parker feared for a moment he might lose consciousness again.

Moeller moved sideways, crablike, snatched a length of rope from the table, and tried to tie Parker's ankle down. Parker brought his knee up hard. The German grunted in pain and rolled off the edge of the table. Parker swung down and kicked again at the old man who lay curled on the floor.

"Please, just one time . . ." Moeller cried out. "It's been so long."

"What the hell is going on?" Parker said. "What happened?"

"The minute you made the transition," the Navigator said, "the old man climbed on top of you, hard as a rock."

Parker looked down at the sickly old man and felt a surge of revulsion. Links of rope were stretched out on the table. A few more minutes, and the old man could have tied Parker down. No escape. Parker barely suppressed the anger. He clenched his fist and advanced forward. The old man cowered on the floor.

"We're on a clock," Charlotte said. "Parker, just get out of there. Forget it."

Parker took a last look at Moeller, sniveling on all fours. Disgusted, he turned and walked out.

In the kitchen, Parker took a moment to inspect his new appearance in a mirror. He was a pretty woman in her late 20s, with dark brown hair and hazel eyes. His nose and mouth were small, age lines already formed around the corner of his mouth. He looked the part of a girl of the streets, grown up in hard poverty. A bruising could be seen over his left eye where Moeller had hit him.

That would make it harder to get into the Park Avenue mansions.

"There should be a trunk in the bedroom," Selberg said. "I hacked a pistol and silvers in there."

Parker moved quickly around the room, tearing open drawers and overturning the mattress. He found an old captain's trunk. Inside was a pistol, some loose rounds of ammunition, and two silver bullets. Silvers were the only thing that would wake people up in the system. He loaded the pistol with both, then found a bit of twine and tied the pistol inside his dress against his thigh. He thought for a moment of going back and putting a bullet in Moeller's brain, but better to leave him alive. Security would pick up another prisoner death.

Parker pushed open the apartment door and stepped back into the dingy hall.

"Where to now?"

"Make your way uptown," the Navigator said. "Find the target."

Below him, a door to another apartment opened suddenly. Parker stepped back into the shadows as a woman bearing a basket of laundry appeared in the hall. She barely looked in Parker's direction as she moved quickly down the stairs and out onto the street. Parker waited, then followed her. The stairs were quiet except for the muffled music from the beer hall. Parker had almost reached the ground floor when a door banged open behind him.

"Parker, watch out!" the Navigator voiced in his ear. Footsteps thudded down the stairs toward him. Parker turned and saw one of the male units from the German's apartment bearing down on him fast, his face twisted with rage.

The man held a wicked looking knife, and he slashed at Parker from above. Parker sidestepped and knocked the big man off balance.

The knife clattered down the stairs. The man grabbed Parker by the throat, and with incredible strength, hurled him against the wall. Parker's head struck the solid wood, and white light flashed in his brain. The pressure on Parker's throat was crushing; within moments, he felt himself losing consciousness. Pushing through the fog, Parker reached down beneath his dress. He felt the hard metal of the pistol and tore away the twine holding the weapon to his thigh. He pressed the barrel of the pistol against the man's stomach and pulled the trigger.

The noise of the gunshot ripped through small space. The big man fell back with a grunt. The pressure released on Parker's throat and wonderful oxygen rushed into his lungs. Parker bent over, gasping, his head still swimming. On the floor, the big man rolled onto his side, his hands pressed against his stomach, a flower of red spreading around his fingers.

Parker stood, raised the pistol, and pressed it to the man's head.

"Parker, no! Let him live!" the Navigator said. "The guards will register a retirement."

Moeller began to crawl back up the stairs toward his apartment. If he could transfer to a new body, he would live. Parker hesitated for a moment, then tucked the pistol back beneath his dress, turned, and walked out the door.

◆ ◆ ◆

The street was crowded with late afternoon shoppers. Parker pushed his way through the dense population, hailed a passing omnibus and found a seat on the packed bench.

"The target should be sitting down to dinner soon," the Archivist said.

"How many people in the house?"

"Between the servants and family, at least eight."

Eight was a big number. Lot of witnesses. And one of the eight could be a guard. Parker didn't want to have to shoot his way out.

"How's Moeller?" Parker asked.

"Alive," the Navigator said.

All along First Avenue, the newsies were still handing out wanted posters for Parker's old body. The elevated train rattled by overhead, the noise deafening, before it veered off at Twenty-Third Street toward Second Avenue. Shopkeepers and laborers began to filter off the omnibus as they continued north, until only the domestics were left on board. At the cusp of the modern age, the roads were a strange mix of transports. Small, two-seater surreys and carriages clattered by carrying the Park Avenue crowd while an electric car sped by with a gong.

Parker paid his fare and jumped from the omnibus at Sixty-Fifth Street. He walked quickly west toward Fifth Avenue until he found himself at Central Park standing in front of The Hyacinth, an elaborate sandstone apartment house that stretched almost the entire block.

A doorman, hands folded behind his back, stared out across the park. His eyes narrowed as Parker approached. He had a muscular build, his neck bulging over his collar, the faint mark of a tattoo visible below his ear.

"Can I help you?"

"Here about a placement," Parker said, his voice completely feminine.

"What placement?"

"Lady's maid."

The doorman stepped back, looked Parker up and down, then jerked his head toward the lobby. "Take the back elevator."

"Thank you, sir." Parker nodded, then entered the public foyer. The doorman followed close behind and together they boarded the small service elevator.

The top floor of The Hyacinth was a sprawling, richly furnished apartment house. Parker was led through a well-decorated sitting room and into the kitchen.

"I'm looking at the building plans for your location now," Charlotte said. "Ten rooms. Two elevators. Takes up the entire floor. From the kitchen, there's a staircase leading up to the roof."

The kitchen was large and devoid of people. A large, wooden table took up the middle of the room, with a zinc-lined sink and a hooded range. The black handles of knives protruded from a wooden block.

"You have papers?" the doorman asked.

Everyone in the system had papers. In his new body, Parker had nothing. He made a show of patting down the front of his dress.

"You're going to have to kill him," the Archivist said.

Parker ignored the comment.

"Do it now before he puts out an alarm," the Navigator said.

"I'm not sure if I have my papers," Parker said to the doorman. "I might have dropped them in the omnibus."

The doorman took a step forward. His hand reached beneath his jacket and rested on something hidden there.

"Do it now, Parker! Take him out!"

Parker thought of his hidden pistol. He would never have time to get to it. He cursed himself for forgetting to get identification for the body from Moeller. Nobody moved inside the system without papers. The doorman took a step closer to Parker. Parker's hand flashed out and his fingers wrapped around the handle of one of the butcher knives. The doorman stepped back. A pistol appeared from beneath his jacket. Parker stabbed the man in the chest. The knife slid between the door-man's ribs while Parker gripped the pistol with his free hand.

The man's weight sagged against the handle of the knife. Parker lowered him to the floor.

"That's a kill," the Navigator said. "Alarm is going out. Get moving."

Leaving the dead man on the floor, Parker unstrapped the pistol from his own leg and moved quickly out of the kitchen. He passed down a long hallway, opened a set of double doors, and walked into the music room. A maid knelt before a large, marble fireplace emptying ashes into a metal bucket. She looked up as the door opened, and Parker shot her once. She fell back. The metal bucket overturned and spilled ash onto the floor.

Everyone who saw him now had to die. Any of them could be guards. Parker couldn't take that chance. And it didn't matter. The alarm had already gone out.

Parker entered the library at the same time as one of the valets, a young man with dark curly hair and bright green eyes. He stopped short at the sight of Parker.

"Ma'am, is everything—?" the valet began. Parker shot him twice and walked into the dining room.

"Multiple alarms going out now," the Navigator said.

"Got it."

Parker found the target in the master bedroom. He was a small man, narrow shoulders, a thin, fragile face. He had a slightly twisted upper lip, the deformity of a cleft palate. His hair was neatly groomed and parted on the side, shining with oil. He stood, arms raised, half-dressed, his dinner clothes laid out on the bed. Through the window beyond, an electric airship powered over Central Park, filled with guards coming for the intruder.

Parker checked his pistol. The last two rounds were silvers. One for the target and one for his own exit.

"What do you want?" The target's eyes were wide. His mouth hung open. Parker could tell he had no idea of the truth.

"Is your name Donald Lancaster?"

"Yes. Do I know you?"

Parker ignored the question. "You're the investment banker?"

"I'm a banker, yes."

"What year is it?"

"It's 1880," Lancaster said, his mouth parted slightly. He licked his lips and blinked nervously. "I have jewelry and money in the cabinet here. Take what you want."

"I'm not here to rob you," Parker said. "I'm here to set you free."

"Free?"

The Navigator shouted in his ear, "Just do it Parker. He's never going to understand. He has no idea what you're talking about."

"You're in a prison right now. A prison of the mind."

Lancaster shook his head. Parker studied the room. The clothes laid out on the bed were expensively tailored. The room itself, beautifully furnished. Even on the inside, Lancaster lived richly. If he didn't know he was a prisoner, he would never want to leave.

"Please," Lancaster said, "just put the gun down."

"Just kill him and move on," the Navigator said. "You're wasting time."

"I can talk to him," Parker responded, his voice sharp.

Lancaster frowned. "Who are you talking to?"

Parker shook his head. "I'm trying to explain things to you. The truth of things. So you know. So you're not shocked. If you don't understand what's happening before it happens, it can be too much to handle."

"I don't know what you're talking about."

"You were convicted of crimes. You were sentenced to prison. Your family wants you out. That's why I'm here."

"Who are you?"

"I help people like you escape back to real life. I find them, and bring them out. The world you think you're living in, you're not. The year you think it is, it isn't."

"I can assure you, ma'am. I am in no need of help."

From behind, angry voices, the clatter of boots, the splinter of an axe into wood.

"They're at the door," the Navigator said.

Parker sighed and cocked his pistol. "Don't say I didn't warn you."

Lancaster screamed once, then Parker shot him. Outside, the door broke open and feet ran down the hall. Half a dozen guards burst into the bedroom dressed as nineteenth century brawlers. They fanned out.

One of them held out a hand. "Easy now, ma'am. Put down the pistol."

A thin curl of smoke still wreathed from the barrel as Parker held the pistol against his temple and pulled the trigger.

3

I stumbled back through the saloon doors like a drunk, my mind reeling. My foot caught on something, and I fell forward. I crashed hard to the floor, where I rolled over on my back and covered my eyes, a wave of nausea rising up from my stomach and threatening to spill out.

"Pretty wild ride," a voice said. I turned over on my side and opened my eyes a crack. Dr. Valenstein sat on one of the barstools looking at me.

"Oh my God," I said. "What was that?"

"That was your most recent prison break. This is what you and your team do. You enter the Panopticon. Find your target. And break them out."

I crawled along the floor and propped myself up on the bar. The spinning in my head began to slow. That world had felt so real. So full of life and detail. I could still feel the pain of it. The fear. Smell the layers of filth and horse shit and food. It had become a part of my memory now. I understood why the Panopticon had to use different time periods. The only way I knew what I had experienced wasn't real was because of the era. A marker for reality.

The nausea slowly passed. I rested my head on the bar.

"So now you know how it works," Dr. Valenstein said. "You understand the principles of the Panopticon machine."

With my eyes still closed, I nodded. "It's like the world's most expensive hangover." Dr. Valenstein chuckled. Or maybe my own sub-conscious chuckled. Or a lost memory. I had begun to lose track of what was happening. "So what am I supposed to do now?"

"Can you walk?" Dr. Valenstein said.

I nodded. My eyes opened and slowly, I stood up. The spinning in my brain had slowed to a gentle rocking. I found that I could walk, my arms outstretched for balance, and with each step my coordination improved.

"I want to show you something else," Dr. Valenstein said. "Follow me."

I walked behind him as we passed through the first doorway of the saloon and back into the long corridor. Valenstein counted off doors, then stopped before one with a large letter *C* stenciled on the front.

"The brain's filing system is amazing," Valenstein said. "Now, these memories are laid near each other in this small space, because they needed to be hidden."

"Hidden from who?"

"From the Panopticon program security." Valenstein pushed open the door. We entered a dimly lit warehouse space the size of an air-plane hangar filled with what looked like giant museum display cases. Thousands of them. Rows upon rows, stacked on top of each other. Inside each case was a human. The humans were vacuum sealed inside clear plastic bags with air masks over their faces. The cases rose toward the ceiling, some ten stories above us.

"This is a memory taken from your tour of the Panopticon storage facility," Valenstein said.

"My God," I said. "These people are all prisoners?"

"Every one of them," Valenstein said. "This is where they actually store the physical living bodies."

"How many people are in here?"

"In this particular storage unit, about eighty thousand. Each prisoner in a deep state of suspended animation, all connected to each other, all sharing the same virtual reality. In your memory, when you assassinated the client in the system, you woke up his physical body in one of these storage facilities."

"Then what happened?"

"He had people here waiting to remove him," Valenstein said. "You never took part in that aspect of the missions. You only hacked into the system and did the executions."

Valenstein walked back through the door, the heavy metal slamming behind us, and once again we were in the corridor. We walked to a final door, which opened automatically for us as we approached. This time he led me into a beautiful Japanese garden. A cherry tree in full bloom overhung a small pool while stone benches lined a path of crushed, white stone. Fish swam fat and lazy in a koi pool. We sat together in the shade as distant cicadas hummed.

"I was sent here to explain to you what's happened," Dr. Valenstein began. "Sent here by you, as an insurance policy. To make sure you remembered. To make sure you are aware that you are now inside the Panopticon."

"My team that's here with me. Do they know the truth?"

Valenstein shook his head. "You are the only one who knows. And right now, you're in the middle of a mission. A very dangerous mission into the new supermax prison system to break someone out.

"This new prison has security that you've never encountered. To get in, you can have no memory of who you are. The security system scans your mind, searches memories. If people are aware they are going into a prison, they never fully accept their new lives within that system. You can't pretend to be something you're not, forever. You can't live this new life in this system, be fully immersed in it, if you remember that it's a lie. So to eliminate cognitive dissonance, the impossibility of holding two contradictory beliefs—I am in a prison, and I am free living my life in 1880s New York City—all memories of each person's past must be eliminated completely.

"If you know the truth, it will reject you. You won't be able to hack in. So you had to enter the system in a way you believed. As an archaeologist in ancient Egypt making an amazing discovery."

"So I'm in a prison now?"

Valenstein shook his head. "Not yet. Now you are in the memory storage facility of the Panopticon. When prisoners are brought into the system, their memories are downloaded and stored. That's where you are now. This entire city serves as a storage area for those memories."

From somewhere above us sounded a deep rumbling. The sound of dynamite against rock. The Brotherhood of Anubis was out there somewhere. Trying to get in. Or if they weren't, if they didn't exist, then what was happening? A cherry blossom petal shook loose from the tree and twirled slowly down the length of my arm. I caught the petal and rubbed it between my fingers. It felt real.

I looked at Dr. Valenstein. "What is happening out there?"

"The Brotherhood of Anubis is attacking."

"But I thought you said none of this was real."

Dr. Valenstein smiled. "Your perception of being an Egyptologist isn't real. But the machine itself is very real. It's a very complicated computer system. And like any good system, it has its own security features. You are under attack. The security system is becoming aware of your presence here. Is looking for you. How you perceive that attack is in your mind. You've created the Brotherhood of Anubis because it fits with your belief that you are in Egypt of the 1930s."

"So can the system hurt me?"

"Of course. You are an invading computer virus. And the Panopticon security system is designed to find you and destroy you. If you are killed in here, the mission will fail." Another deep boom sounded from somewhere above them. The trees shook petals to the ground. Something splashed inside the koi pool. "This is only the beginning of your mission. There is a backdoor here, a way for you to get into the real prison system."

"Where?"

"I don't know. I haven't been given that information."

"But you're my memory," I said. "Wouldn't I have made a point to remember something like that?"

"I'm only the memory you have left. The Panopticon works against me all the time. Perhaps at one point I could have helped you more. But now those memories may have been blocked.

"Memory is almost a living organism. Capable of change. Capable of adapting. The machine does its best to block memories of the past, but the mind adapts, tries to preserve what's important."

I thought back to the wrecked apartment I had explored with Clayton. The photograph of myself I had found inside that apartment. The scene made sense now, if that was some vestige of my past that I was still able to cling to. Something buried deep, which even if I couldn't consciously recall, still existed somewhere.

And there was my wife. For an instant when I was with her, at the edge of this world, I had remembered my wife. I remembered the feel of her hand in mine, the view across the Hudson. That had been real. I had seen the small scar below her eye, and I knew that was from when she had fallen against the corner of a table as a child. On her finger, the engagement ring I had saved to buy, around her wrist, the bracelet we had found on our first trip to Paris. These were things from real life beyond this world.

"So why can't I remember more?" I asked.

"The memories have been hidden in this world. Hidden from the Panopticon. Look out across the city, all these buildings, all these rooms and apartments and doors. And behind these doors lie the memories you need. The memories of your life. Of how you got here and where you need to go."

I thought of the vastness of the entire island of Manhattan. How many apartments there must be. How many doors. How many places to hide something. "How do I ever find anything?"

"It will all be catalogued somewhere. Your brain is a complicated filing system. Storing away millions of bits of data, simply waiting to be recalled. You must find the key to the filing system. But do not trust anyone."

"What do you mean?"

"Your crew down here now, do not tell anyone we spoke, what you are looking for, or that you know any portion of the truth. The Panopticon system creates artificial intelligences that can mimic human behavior. The system may have sent one of your crew here to monitor you. I have no way of knowing."

A cherry blossom drifted down and landed quietly at our feet. Dr. Valenstein bent down, lifting the blossom up to inspect it. "Very beautiful. All the details perfect. Each petal perfectly in place. This must have been very important to you somehow," he said. "To remember something so small in such great detail. I wish I could tell you why."

"Me too." I looked out across the garden and watched as more petals drifted into the pond. The structure of my reality had been pulled apart, and I was left with something so unrecognizable that I doubted my own sanity.

And yet, this expedition had filled me with doubt. Something had always nagged at me, that this world was out of tune. That it was more a product of fantasy than anything that could have been created in reality. In some sense, the truth was reassuring. Or at least what my mind was telling me was the truth in this current moment. I felt slightly saner, even if what I had just learned was totally and completely crazy.

"Unfortunately our time here is up," Dr. Valenstein said. "You can never stay too long in one memory."

"Why?"

"The system will know something's wrong. It will seek you out. There are dangers here you can't possibly imagine."

I already knew of some of these dangers. The woman who screamed in Central Park. That creature that Nasir had shot at. And even worse, what had happened in the subway tunnel. "I was attacked by something," I said. "I don't know what it was. But it spoke to me. It said I shouldn't be here."

Valenstein looked thoughtful. "That was Panopticon security most likely."

"It was a monster. Some kind of creature." I thought of the weight pushing my cheek into the ground, the horrible twisted fingers.

"It will be probing the city now, searching for you. And when it does, it will send something terrible after you. There will be more monsters."

"But I felt pain. If this is only in my head, how could it hurt?"

"Pain is electrical impulses. The firing of nerves to alert the brain to danger. The brain makes what happens down here real. The pain you feel is real," Valenstein said. "And there's also leakage."

"Leakage?"

"You are inside a system designed to contain the consciousness of criminals. Every once in a while, one of these memories breaks free. Gets lost in the system. You may find certain places in this city are, for lack of a better word, haunted. Some of the prisoners have done terrible things. Not all monsters live in fiction."

The scream we heard in Central Park had been like the reliving of a memory. But the pain in that woman's voice was real, maybe one of these broken memories. The remembrance of some terrible crime that had happened and now lived in the mind of a prisoner.

Valenstein checked his watch, then stood and extended his hand. "I'm afraid we're out of time."

"So that's it for now?" I asked.

"That's it for now."

I stood and shook his hand. I had no idea what I was shaking. Some vestige of an old memory I had dragged up? Or some fantasy I had concocted while sleeping? But the hand I shook felt real enough.

"I cannot leave this room with you," Dr. Valenstein said. "So here is where we say goodbye. But I'm here to help you."

"How do I find you again?"

"Think of me like a concierge. Just ring and I'll be there," Dr. Valenstein said. "And when you leave, don't forget to exit through the gift shop."

I walked down the path toward the metal door imbedded into the side of a grassy hill. I turned and looked back. Dr. Valenstein still stood at the edge of the pond. He raised his hand to wave. I waved back, then opened the door and stepped through.

I found myself back in the dark theater. Behind me, the door was locked shut. I made my way up the empty aisle into the lobby. To the right of the concession stand was a small gift shop. Thinking of Dr. Valenstein's parting words, I entered the shop and found an assortment of movie-related knickknacks. Sweatshirts and keychains. Near the register, a glass display case filled with snow globes. Inside each round ball of glass, miniature buildings, the base of the glass covered with white flakes. Something caught my eye.

A purple Easter egg hand drawn on the base of one of the globes. I picked up the toy and the motion swirled the white flakes up from the bottom, filling the water with a miniature snowfall.

Inside the glass was a building sculpted in ceramic miniature, roughly twenty floors in height with a colonnaded entrance. Each floor had rows of tiny windows made from little flecks of gray paint. The base of the snow globe was inscribed with hand-painted lettering: Historic Hotel Pennsylvania. I turned the globe over. On the bottom was a small music box crank handle and the words *Room 1612*.

I wound the crank handle and tinny music began playing. Some kind of waltz. Inside the globe, the snow swirled in eddies around the building faster and faster until the building was completely obscured by a blizzard. The movement began to make me feel nauseated. My stomach turned and for a scattered moment, I had a vision of a long hotel hallway. Bloody handprints on the wall. A door slammed shut in my face. Someone cried out for help.

I shut my eyes and the vision faded away.

◆　◆　◆

"We need a vantage point," Clayton said. "Somewhere to look out over the entire city."

After the theater, I had returned to camp without incident. No one questioned my absence, and I mentioned nothing about what I had found.

Charlotte had the rubbing spread out on her lap, studying it. She glanced up. "Where do you propose we go?"

Clayton pointed to the south. Rising above the skyline was the iconic multi-tiered cap of the Empire State Building. "We should go there. It's the middle of the island. We'd have a clear view of our entire surroundings."

We packed up our camp in twenty minutes and began heading south along the avenue. As we walked from the confines of the circle, I took a last look back. Already the light was fading, deep pockets of darkness spreading through the forest of Central Park. If there was something living in there, the darkness would conceal it perfectly. I had little doubt that it would have no trouble finding us, wherever we might make camp.

Our small group formed a straggling line as we progressed down the middle of an abandoned Eighth Avenue. Clayton at the lead, I brought up the rear. Selberg was ahead of me, struggling under the weight of his pack.

We walked along Thirty-Fourth Street until we found ourselves at the base of the Empire State Building. Each of the thousands of windows was dark, the glass exterior cloaked in shadow. I craned my neck back to take in the full scale of the building, but it was too large to comprehend from a single point on the sidewalk below.

We pushed our way through the revolving doors of the front entrance. The main lobby was tiled in gold and sand and glimmered beautifully in the lantern light, like stepping inside a Faberge egg. At the end of the long hall was an aluminum relief of the building itself. Long rays of light were cast down from a halo over the central spire of the building. Just below the relief of the building, a fixed clock, hands paused at quarter past nine.

We rode to the top in silence. Clayton had his rifle ready as the elevator doors opened, but we stepped out onto an empty observation deck. The view stretched out the length of Manhattan. The stillness was almost unbearable. There was no wind. No sound of sirens and traffic filtering up from below. No blanket of lights spreading out before us. Only darkness and silence and the black silhouettes of turned off buildings.

"So empty," Charlotte said.

"No . . ." Clayton said, his eyes fixed forward. "There's something out there."

I wandered to the southern edge of the deck and had a clear view all the way to Wall Street. Something flickered in the darkness.

As I watched, a single window of light suddenly illuminated in a distant building overlooking the park. One apartment in the vast city and its light burned bright as a star in the darkness. Another light flashed on somewhere to the east. Then streetlamp turned on. Slowly a multitude of lights began to appear across the reaches of the city. Everywhere I looked, there they were. These were my memories. Places

I had visited. People I had known. Each bit of light like slivers of quartz trapped inside granite, throwing out reflections of my mind.

I still felt undone by everything I had seen. But the human brain was a marvelous device capable of great adaptability. Already, I was beginning to accept my changed circumstance. Manhattan was my palace of memory.

"My God, get over here and look at this!" Charlotte's voice sounded scared. I moved quickly to the north of the observation deck. She stood against the railing, her hands gripping the support, staring out toward the park.

I joined her at the railing.

"What is it?" I said.

"Look." She pointed north. In the distance I could see the thick foliage of Central Park. Something was moving through the trees, something massive. Even from thirty blocks away, I could hear the crack of timbers breaking. Fifty-foot-tall trees, bent forward like saplings in a storm. Whatever was out there was enormous, still concealed by the thick growth of leaves, but headed this way. I could see the giant rippling of water that swept across Central Park Lake, five-foot-high waves that crashed against the boathouse, almost as if this entity had risen up from the lake's depths.

"My God," Selberg said. "It's huge. That must be twenty stories tall."

"We've got to move," Clayton said. "Now."

From deep in the park, we heard a tremendous bellow, a deep booming sound that echoed like lightning down the avenues. A primordial, otherworldly scream. I froze and stared, my body going numb. Blocks away, the one-hundred-year-old trees parted, crushed to the side like blades of grass. Clayton pulled my arm and we all ran to the elevator.

We piled inside the car and I jabbed my finger at the ground floor button. Quietly the machine began its descent down. Selberg was pressed against the wall, one hand on his chest. His cheeks puffed in and out. "What was that thing?"

"I have no idea," Clayton said. "But this city is a maze. We just need a place to hide."

Charlotte turned toward me. She snapped her finger. "Maze. Maze. What's the Greek word for maze?"

I looked at her, startled. "How would I know?"

Excited, she dropped her backpack to the floor of the car and started rummaging through it. She pulled out her notebook and ran her finger down the lines of script. Outside, I heard another bellow. The deep bass carried through the building.

"I know what's out there," Charlotte said. "The translation from the stone. I know what it means." She pointed at a word in her notebook. "I didn't know what this word was. But now it makes sense. Now I know."

She smoothed out the notes with her free hand. I could see scratched handwriting in several languages across the pages. She read the translation out loud. "Deep in the maze of horrors lies a perilous beast. It protects the secrets and slays any who find their way into his presence. It is the keeper of the maze, a creature half-man and half-bull."

Selberg shook his head. "What does that mean?"

She looked up at us. "I think it's a Minotaur out there. From Greek mythology. This giant creature with the head of a bull and the body of a man. It guarded the Cretan labyrinth."

"That doesn't sound good," Selberg said. "That actually sounds terrible."

And then I knew. The Minotaur was the security system for the Panopticon. The machine knew we were here.

The elevator opened onto the lobby and we piled out.

"The security doors!" Clayton pointed at two large metal doors that were open flat against the building. The doors were each two inches thick. "Close them both."

Together, Clayton and I put our weight against the heavy metal. The thick hinges shrieked in protest, but slowly the doors rotated closed. Nasir came running to help, and the three of us slammed shut the first door. The second door was even harder to close, and it took all of our strength to get it rotating on the two massive hinges.

"Let's go boys . . . push," Clayton gasped.

From outside we heard another tremendous roar. Whatever was out there was moving fast and getting close. I pushed with everything I had, my back and legs straining against the door. Slowly, it swung shut. The security door had large bolt locks, which we drew across. The metal locked into place with a satisfying clunk.

Everyone except for Nasir turned off their lanterns and waited in silence. I could hear the thing coming from blocks away. Its stride was massive, each step a thunderous crack against the street. It roared again as it came, and I could hear the chuff of its breath, like a bull before the charge. The footsteps grew louder and louder. Above us, the chandelier shook, the hundreds of little crystals tinkling together. We backed slowly away from the door.

The thing was right outside. I could smell it through the door. The thick odor of horseflesh and a slight rotten scent. Through a small crack in the door, I glimpsed a massive human-shaped foot covered in thick, black hair.

Something snorted, then pushed tentatively against the door. There was a slight creak of metal. Then nothing.

Nasir's lantern began to flicker, then the bulb died. Even though it must have been tremendously hot, Nasir reached inside and pressed his fingers against the glass, trying to get the light to return. The room became incrementally darker. Eventually all our lamps would go out, the more nights we spent here. And then we would be trapped down in the blackness.

The sudden impact on the doors was tremendous, like a bulldozer driving full speed. Charlotte screamed and the entire frame bent backward with a shriek of metal.

Again, something slammed against the door. The security bolts twisted, but the metal continued to hold. We all waited, frozen, and again came another impact. The doors, several inches thick, were beginning to break.

"Those doors can't hold," Selberg said. "We should move now."

"Move where?" Clayton asked.

"Anywhere but here," Selberg replied. "We've got to hide."

The doors groaned loudly as another impact fell against them.

We scrambled to gather our stuff and ran down the hallway toward an exit sign near the elevator. I pushed through the door, and we passed through more hallways and down a flight of stairs. In the distance, muted by the building around us, came a terrific roar of frustration.

We ran through underground corridors and an employee locker room before I pushed open a black metal door. We collapsed onto Thirty-Third Street, one block south of the main entrance.

In the dark, I listened for the sound of feet, for the bellow of whatever great beast was after us. I heard nothing.

"We should put distance between us and this building," I whispered.

"I agree with that," Selberg said. "Let's get the hell away from here."

I turned my lamp on to get our bearings. My first thought was the Hotel Pennsylvania. Room 1612. I knew the hotel was only a few blocks from here, due west. I started walking quickly in that direction. The rest of the group followed.

"Where are we going?" Charlotte said.

"West."

"What's west?"

"A hotel," I said. "Someplace that might be safe for the night."

She met my eyes. "No place is safe."

◆ ◆ ◆

We moved quickly. Every few minutes I flashed on my lantern to reorient myself. In those moments of light, I saw empty streets and vacant buildings. The Minotaur was out there somewhere. I could hear the deep boom of its footfalls sounding toward the park.

We reached Seventh Avenue without incident and headed south. I turned my lantern on quickly and flashed it around the intersection. My single searchlight beam cut through the darkness. To our right, a book store and the entrance to Penn Station and Madison Square Garden. On our left, the marquee for the Hotel Pennsylvania.

"Where to now?" Selberg asked.

I nodded toward the hotel. "I vote we go in there. Plenty of rooms. We can hide out, find a room, maybe try to get some sleep."

"And what about this thing, this creature out there?"

"Seventeen hundred rooms in this hotel," I said. "Pretty good place to hide."

Selberg turned toward Clayton. "You're the security guy, what do you think?"

"I think standing out here on the street isn't doing us any good. We should get inside, wait until daylight. Then we'll have a better chance to figure things out."

Selberg tapped his fingers thoughtfully against the side of his hip. "Fine. Let's go."

Together we crossed the street and entered the front door of the Hotel Pennsylvania. Inside, more darkness. My lantern illuminated a shining marble floor patterned with squares and circles. Pink granite columns were spaced evenly around the room near small groupings of overstuffed green chairs. The lobby doors were glass, but thick velvet curtains hung to the side.

"Let's close those curtains," I said.

Nasir and Selberg drew the curtains together and the rest of the team turned on their lanterns. Nasir stumbled forward, like a drunken man, and Selberg had to catch him by the arm and hold him in place. His face looked waxen. His eyes rolled without focus.

"You all right?" I asked.

Nasir nodded. "Yes, sir. Just lost my balance."

He straightened himself and wiped a hand across his forehead.

"Looks like we have the place to ourselves," Selberg said.

In truth, the place made me uncomfortable. This was one of the oldest hotels in Manhattan. So many thousands of people had passed through these doors that I couldn't believe that only my memories were associated with this place. Every grand hotel had its share of scandals. Of murders and suicides. Of sleepless nights spent on lumpy hotel beds plotting evil. There must be others in this hotel with us. So many people had passed through the doors of this venue, there could be dark memories lurking down every hallway.

And I wasn't eager to run into a memory in one of these dark empty halls.

I walked behind the great stone slab of a reception desk. Behind the desk was a long metal locker, which I easily opened. Inside were rows of keys, each carefully labeled by room.

I pocketed the keys for rooms 1612 and 1712. I addressed my team. "We can each have our own room, all be on the same floor? I've got 1712."

"We should share rooms," Selberg said.

Charlotte joined me behind the counter. She surveyed the keys and took one for room 1714. She jingled the key between her fingers. "I, for one, am tired of group living. I'll take my own room."

"I really don't think that's safe," Selberg said. "We should stay together."

"You're welcome to bunk up with whoever you want. I need some space."

Selberg had a slight look of panic on his face. "Clayton?"

Clayton had closed the main lobby doors. "As long as we're on the same floor."

I needed to be alone for my plan. "I agree," I said. "Same floor."

Outnumbered, Selberg nodded in agreement. We filtered behind the desk, each member taking a key from the same floor, then we took the elevator up to the seventeenth. Clayton checked his watch. "We'll meet in the hotel lobby at six a.m."

"Fine with me," I said.

"Get an early start on the day."

"Early start for what?" Selberg asked. "We have no idea what we're doing here."

"We're remaining calm," Clayton replied. "We're not going into a panic. And we are finding a way out of here."

"What if something happens during the night?" Nasir asked.

"We wait in our rooms," Clayton said. "That way we all know where everyone else is. Nobody goes running around the hotel getting lost."

Selberg tapped his key nervously on the counter. "Wait in our rooms and then what?"

"I'll come find you," Clayton said.

The elevator doors opened onto the dark hallway of the seventeenth floor. Each of us went to our own room, key in hand, then one by one we disappeared behind the doors.

My room was small and generic. King-sized bed. Television on a cheap wooden bureau. Bathroom in the corner. The sort of depressing place people ended up in the downspin of life. I drew the curtains and looked down onto Madison Square Garden below.

Empty streets.

I laid my pack on the bed, then went into the bathroom. The faucets turned in my hands, but no water came out. I looked at myself in the mirror. By lantern light, I looked ghoulish. My skin was pale. Dark circles hung beneath my eyes. I wondered if this was still my face. How long had I been in the machine? What if I got out and found myself an old man? All youth gone, my body broken down and feeble.

These were not constructive thoughts.

I left the bathroom and listened at the door. The hallway was quiet. As much as I didn't want to creep around the dark hotel in the middle of the night by myself, I had to get to room 1612.

Slowly, I opened the door.

The hall was silent. From behind one of the closed doors, some-one was talking. A male voice, unrecognizable, but it sounded deep in argument. I crept to the stairwell and made my way down one floor below. The sixteenth floor was exactly the same as the seventeenth. The carpet was threadbare from years of use, but at one point had been a deep burgundy. The wallpaper was faded, peeling. I turned the key in the lock for 1612, heard a click, and quickly entered.

The room was identical to upstairs. I set my lantern on top of the television and surveyed my surroundings. A card was on the bed. I picked it up. On the front, elaborate script read:

You are cordially invited to the hotel bar.

◆　◆　◆

I returned to the lobby.

I heard music from behind the closed doors of the hotel bar. Cautiously, lantern in hand, I pushed open the doors and stood on the threshold. Sets of tables and chairs each hosted a flickering candle inside a glass globe, their wood polished and shining, ready for guests. Two large ferns in clay pots stood by windows. Along the back wall, a full bar. Bottles lined glass shelves fronted by a mahogany wood bar and red upholstered stools. Standing behind the bar was Nasir. He wore a white tuxedo and was carefully polishing a glass with a white bar towel. He placed the glass on the bar and nodded at me.

"I've saved a place for you," Nasir said.

Carefully, I approached. The rest of the room was empty. I took a seat on the barstool, catching a glimpse of my reflection in the glass behind the bar. I looked afraid.

I studied the man before me. "What's going on, Nasir?"

"Ah, first, would you like a drink, sir?" Nasir turned to the shelves behind me. He ran his hand over the bottles, then selected one and turned back toward me. "I imagine you must have many questions right now."

"I don't understand what's happening here," I said. "I received this invitation in my room," I lied.

"Yes," Nasir bowed. "I wanted to be able to speak to you alone."

Nasir spoke in perfect English. The slight trace of an accent he used to carry was gone. Even the tone of his voice was different. Slightly deeper, softer somehow. But his movement seemed strangely jerky.

"Speak about what?"

Nasir blinked. His mind seemed to reset. "Would you like a drink, sir?"

"Nasir, you asked me that already."

Nasir nodded, spun back to the left and walked to the end of the bar. He stood for a moment, stared vacantly across the room, blinked again, spun to the right and strode back before me.

"Are you feeling okay?" I asked.

"Very fine, sir," Nasir said. "Why do you ask?"

"You're acting very strangely."

"Ah, yes, well, I am afraid I do not have much time left with you," Nasir said. His mouth moved as he spoke, but somewhere the voice no longer seemed to line up with the movement of his lips.

"What do you mean?"

Nasir's head cocked down like a piston, then came back up. "I am finding the connection very difficult down here. The further we go. I find it hard to control my behavior."

"What are . . ." I began to speak, but then in a flash it came to me. Nasir, sleeping with his eyes open. Nasir, always ready to help. "My God. You're not real. You're not human. You're a drone."

I thought of the AI drones I had met in my past memory in 1880s New York. They had been so lifelike initially, until something broke down inside of them.

Nasir nodded, his face trembling spasmodically. "You are correct, sir."

"Sent by who?"

Nasir opened the bottle of whiskey and attempted to pour it into the glass in front of me. His arm jerked and twitched, most of the liquid spilling out across the bar. "I am terribly sorry, sir. I seem to be rapidly losing control."

"Can I do anything for you?"

"Oh no, sir. I feel no pain," Nasir said. "You should drink your drink, sir."

I stared at the glass, half-filled.

"What happens when I do?"

"You will learn new things," Nasir said. He swiveled away from me, looked out through the window. "I wonder what happens when I go away. Where . . ."

Nasir's voice trickled down, like a radio running out of battery power. His head swiveled away from the window and slowly sagged down toward his chest. He was gone. I picked up the glass from the bar, held it up to Nasir's expended body, and drank it all.

4

Parker awoke in his own bed. His heart pounded, his hands ice cold. The sound of gunshots still rang in his ear, his nose still tingled with the sweet burn of gunpowder. He breathed deeply, tried to slow the painful contraction in his chest. He pulled himself up and glanced around the room. Photographs hung on the wall, him and Clayton in police uniform standing before an unmarked police sedan. A bonsai plant, as brown and brittle as a Christmas tree in April, sat on a wooden writing desk with one cracked leg boosted up by a dozen *National Geographic* magazines. He stood, stretched. A headache lingered just above his eyes.

Lately he'd begun to suspect the world around him was not real. Or perhaps he wasn't real. Although he felt solid enough. He rapped his knuckle against the wood of the table. Solid. He looked around his kitchen, opened the refrigerator, smelled the sour, expired milk, tasted the kung pao shrimp from Panda House. Those things felt believable. But for the past few days, he couldn't shake the nagging doubts.

He placed his gun on the kitchen table and looked out the window at the Malone kids playing stickball in the street near the furniture factory. In the distance, across the river, rose the spires of Manhattan. A brown sedan slowly circled the block on a squeaky suspension. The Malone kids, all four of them, stopped their game long enough to watch the car slide by and disappear around the corner of the factory.

Everything in Parker's neighborhood was a factory. Cabinet factory. Glass factory. Jacket factory. The air always smelled deliciously sweet from the bread factory across the street. Even his apartment was located in a factory. An old ceramics place, the large column of a kiln still visible in the rear yard, various rusted pieces of machinery bolted to the floors near the perennially broken service elevator.

Everything seemed so normal, but the mistakes were always in the details. He looked down at the white Chinese takeout carton in his hand. Why was he always eating this crap?

A menu was stapled to the side. Panda House. 13-20 Queens Boulevard. All his food seemed to come from there. Funny. He had never been.

The menu was crowded with those generic photos of Chinese food dishes. Everything labeled and priced. Nothing out of the ordinary. A rotary phone hung on the wall over the refrigerator. He picked up the handset and dialed the Panda House number. The line was busy. He dialed a random series of numbers. Another busy tone. Always busy. He hung up the phone. Looked like he wouldn't be ordering Chinese.

In the distance to the north, the Fifty-Ninth Street Bridge stretched out across Roosevelt Island to Queens. The bridge carried no traffic. A blinking LED sign flashed BRIDGE CLOSED DUE TO CONSTRUCTION. Beneath Parker, one of the Malone kids hit a solid shot with his broomstick bat. The rubber ball bounced off the metal-gated window of the cabinet place and ricocheted down the street. The brown sedan circled the block once more.

Parker glanced around his apartment as if for the first time. A secondhand-looking flower patterned sofa sat opposite a Zenith black and white television. A few Hummel figurines lined the window sill. The carpet was a deep burgundy color and from the wall hung a Norman Rockwell knockoff of some American village. This crap couldn't be his stuff. Knickknacks and country kitsch. Parker never felt like this could be his life.

A shoebox sat on the kitchen table. On a whim, he opened the lid. Inside, stacks of hundred dollar bills. He pulled out the bundles, flipped through them, and tossed them back in the box. A sticky note was glued to one of the bills.

"Welcome back."

His wife had left Parker sixteen months ago. His wife, snatched from his arms by a judge and jury and sent away. He still remembered that moment. The bang of the gavel. The handing out of prison time. Ten years inside. Work was the only thing that made him forget. He'd turned into one of those guys who had always depressed him. Working nonstop so they didn't have to sit at home alone, staring at the walls. Those were the sad sacks you'd see hanging around the precinct all the time. Sleeping in the lounge. Showering in the locker room. Picking up as many overtime tours as they could.

Parker sighed, holstered his Smith & Wesson, and left for work.

The man had been dead for a week. A crackhead found him in the basement of an abandoned building on Avenue D. He was tucked in the far corner behind a rusted boiler, curled into a fetal position, a dark stain of dried blood on the concrete floor beneath his head, his only recognizable feature, the twisted upper lip of a cleft palate. Dirty heroin syringes littered the floor like pine needles. Parker drank more coffee and tried to think of something else.

Clayton rubbed vanilla lotion on his hands, then palmed his nose. The dead body smell was clichéd for a reason. Clayton looked like he'd been dredged up from a swamp as a solid block of granite and chiseled into the shape of a man. Everything was squared off angles and solid mass, except for his nose, which hung at a crooked angle between the promontories of his cheek bones. His eyes were set back beneath the overhang of thin, almost hairless eyebrows. His ears looked like coiled roots clinging to the side of a cliff.

"Overdose?" Clayton asked.

Parker frowned. "Pretty big pool of blood for a simple OD."

"Maybe he OD'd, fell over, hit his head?"

"Possible."

Footsteps and the squelch of radios sounded from upstairs. The uniform sector who found the body waited around on the first floor to be relieved. Down below was just Clayton and Parker. And the dead guy. Bodies were always turning up in these kind of shooting galleries. Junkies filtered in and out of abandoned buildings all over the Lower East Side, getting high, passing out. Sometimes they got too high and that was that.

Clayton bent over the body of the dead man. He frowned, looked closer. The man wore a filthy T-shirt and jeans. Parker knew that face from somewhere. He reached back into memory, trying to place the man, but came back with nothing.

The rest of the basement was empty. Graffiti-covered filthy walls. Urban detritus lay scattered across the floor, parchment-colored fast food wrappers, rusty spoons, puddles of urine, and shitty wads of toilet paper. A single bowl was half-buried upside down in the dirt.

Clayton moved slowly around the room, bent over at the waist, inspecting the edges of the floor. Swirl marks could be seen in the dust, and small spatters of blood trickled toward the stairs. As a crime scene, the room was a disaster. A hundred people had probably come and gone in this basement in the last week, probably many of them with yardstick-long priors. Whatever prints the officers got could match up with half the prior population of Rikers.

The part of Parker that wanted to feel sad about the death of another human being had been spirited away years ago in the war. He had seen what one man could do to another. Take a boy and send him off to war, and whatever man he might have become simply vanishes.

Instead, you're left with anger and hatred wrapped in skin. If we each had a conscience, Parker's had long since burned away.

◆　◆　◆

Parker and Clayton circled the neighborhood for the next hour, drinking coffee and looking out the window of the unmarked sedan as the crumbling East Village slid by. Block after block of abandoned buildings, shadowy figures moving in and out through broken doorways. The radio crackled with 911 jobs. A marked patrol car flew by, lights flashing blue and red across the dying trees of Thompkins Square Park.

Clayton chewed the nub of a cigar and tapped his fingers against the steering wheel. Finally, he turned toward Parker. "The next time you go out, I want in."

Parker shook his head. "I can't do that."

"Why?"

"You know why. It's illegal. They find out, you go to jail," Parker said. "Me. I got a reason. The risk is worth the reward. My wife is out there somewhere, rotting in a prison. But for you, you've got a family . . ."

"I got a daughter who hasn't spoken to me in four years. I got an ex-wife who I give half my paycheck to every month so she can buy her boyfriend a new motorcycle. I can't sleep, I have these dreams. My head's all fucked up. So, what do I got that's so great here?"

"But at least you're here. You're living. You cross that line, you might not come back," Parker said. "You know what these jobs do to you. Last three days of my life. Gone. I can't remember a damn thing. Wake up this morning in my own bed. Box of money on the table. No idea where I've been or what I've done. That shakes your reality."

"What's it like?"

Parker thought of the sound of gunfire. The smell of burnt metal in the air. Someone screaming just on the horizon between wake and sleep.

"It's like coming out of a bad dream. You can feel it in your body. Your heart is racing. Your adrenaline is pumping. And you can almost . . . almost remember why. And then it all just kind of fades. And you're in a room. And you don't know how you got there. And there's this, like, terrible moment where everything is gone. All your memory. And you can't even remember who you are."

"Why do they do that?"

"Part of the job. Erase all your memory of what you've done. Of who you escaped with."

Clayton pushed his cigar to the corner of his mouth, his fingers clenched on the wheel as we drove down Avenue D. Someone had painted an enormous Minotaur on the side of an abandoned building. The Minotaur stretched out his giant bull's head, sharp horns rising up from its skull, plumes of smoke billowing from flared nostrils.

Parker checked his watch. They would be expecting his call. They pulled over near a dented pay phone. Outside the car, Parker retrieved a business card from his wallet. It was a plain, bone colored card, no images, with Muninn, Inc. printed on the front, a phone number on the back.

Parker deposited a quarter into the pay phone and dialed the number.

"Muninn Incorporated," a woman answered after the second ring, her voice cheerful, her accent neutral.

"Just checking on job openings," Parker said.

Parker heard her fingers clatter on a keyboard, then she said, "We do have an opening."

"Tell me about it."

"This requires a personal meeting. Twenty minutes. Avenue D and Tenth Street."

Parker hung up the phone and went back to the car. Clayton's face was still caught in a frown. He turned away from Parker and stared glumly out the window.

"What are you, mad?" Parker asked as he started the engine.

"I need this, brother. I need the money. I don't sleep. I got to get out of here. Get away from all this."

Parker pulled away from the curb and headed north. "I've got a meeting with these people now. You want to sit in and decide, be my guest. Just don't pout about it like a six-year-old."

Clayton turned back toward Parker and slapped him hard on the shoulder. "My man."

"Don't say I didn't warn you."

◆ ◆ ◆

The meeting took place inside an abandoned biscuit factory, a grand old structure from the glory days of the neighborhood. The building was a half-block in length, with ornate wheat sheaves carved into the side. Most of the windows were now broken, the elaborate cornices over the loading doors covered in graffiti, the stonework crumbling into ruin. The officers parked and entered through a creaking metal door inside the loading dock. Beyond the door was an industrial elevator that carried them to the factory floor.

"Who are we meeting?" Clayton looked nervous. He straightened his suit jacket, smoothed down his hair, prepared himself like a man before a job interview.

"Don't know. Never met with them in person before. Always farmed out jobs over the phone."

The elevator ground to a halt and the duo stepped out onto an expansive, empty floor. Light filtered in through the dirty glass. Silt and broken needles littered the ground. Industrial machines rusted in the far corners of the floor, dust-covered and long forgotten. A man leaned against a thick support column, waiting. He wore an elegant suit with a vaguely vintage feel. His face was partially obscured by scraggly muttonchops that advanced down each of his cheeks, framing a thick nose and mustache. On his head, a large black stovepipe hat. He was a complete anachronism, like someone who just stepped out of a black and white Victorian-era photograph.

As Parker and Clayton crossed the floor, the man smiled. It was a beautiful smile, the kind of smile actors dreamed of having. But there was nothing welcoming about his expression, and Parker grew wary.

"You brought a friend," the man said. He spoke with a vague accent. The words had a nasal tone, the sound of some lost East Coast American dialect long ago smoothed out.

"My partner," Parker said.

"The partner of the legendary Parker is always welcome here." The man indicated the decrepit warehouse.

"You know me?" Parker asked.

"You need no introduction," the man said. "I, however, do. My name is Dunbar. I am the representative of the organization that has employed you for various projects. And we have marveled at your success."

"I've been lucky."

"Luck has nothing to do with our success in life. Our destiny is in our own hands. Believe anything but that and you'll become a prisoner yourself."

"What did you want to see me about?"

Dunbar smiled his actor's smile again. "Your last job, how did you feel?"

"Like a blank space."

"We have a contract for you."

"What's the job?"

"What the job has always been."

"Escape."

"Bingo," Dunbar said, the term sounding strange as it sprung from his Victorian era mouth. Dunbar indicated a map stretched out on a work table near one of the industrial machines. The paper was faded to a burned yellow. It was a map of New York City. "I think you know this place."

Parker studied the map. Manhattan and Brooklyn were meshes of streets and parks and subway lines. Queens was still filled with the open farmland. Parker had become something of an expert in maps. The physical lines and spaces helped ground him in reality, which was good, because losing grip on reality was always a danger in his profession.

"What is it, early 1950s?"

"1953," Dunbar said. "This is the mindprint for a New York State max secure mind penitentiary."

"How secure?"

"Very," said Dunbar. "Lots of guards. Lots of drones."

Parker studied the map. The 1950s were a dangerous time. Lots of weaponry had made it back from the war. Lots of guns. Lots of anger. People were quick to fight, even the ones who weren't guards or drones. He preferred an earlier time, when settling things with a fist rather than a loaded gun was a more likely option.

Parker looked up. "Who's the mark?"

"The only son of New York State Senator Ted Scott."

"What'd he do?" Parker asked, still studying the map.

"Does it matter?"

Parker studied Dunbar. "Of course it matters."

"Ah, yes, I've heard of your moral reservations. Well, this one's different. You're being paid for it not to matter."

Parker shook his head, then wiped his hands together. He suddenly felt very dirty. This had always been a dirty game, but there were rules. Bankers. Fraudsters. Tax evaders. Money launderers. These were guys he could bust out. They weren't clean exactly, but they weren't violent. He didn't have to worry that six weeks later he'd read about some ten-year-old they found dead in a ditch somewhere with a Parker escapee's fingerprints all over the bloody knife that cut the kid's throat. No thank you. This life was bad enough without serving time in hell in the next one.

"Can't do it," Parker said. "But thank you for your time."

Parker turned to leave. Clayton took the hint and followed him. They had almost made the elevator when Dunbar called out, "The mark is in the same system as your wife."

Parker froze, felt the world around him begin to close in. His wife. His wife who he hadn't seen in sixteen months. His wife who'd had too much to drink one night, drove off, and crushed a kid with her Volvo. His wife, now doing ten years in the system.

All Parker's fault.

He turned slowly around. "How do you know?"

"We know," Dunbar said. "We don't know her virtual identity, but we know she's there. And we know the senator's son will have that information."

"How?"

"He has money. Money buys information. He has a guard who has been helping him."

Even if Parker found her, she wouldn't know him. She wouldn't remember him. She would be so wrapped up in her world, there would be no convincing her of the truth, of their love. But he knew he had to find her. And somehow, a deeper part of him, the part of him that wasn't rational, that didn't listen to just reason, felt that when he found her, she would know him. And maybe he could bring her back.

"I'll go," Parker said. "I'll get your man. I'll break him out. And then you leave me in there until I get done what I need to. Deal?"

"What you do on your own time is no concern of mine," Dunbar said. "But this is time sensitive."

"What do you mean?"

"Our man has to get broken out in the next forty-eight hours."

Parker's stomach contracted in a laugh, but the sound died before it ever reached his lips. Dunbar's face was expressionless. No hint of a smile. The man was serious. Clayton kept quiet. He had no idea what went into a mission, but Parker did.

"That's impossible," Parker said. "We need weeks to plan. I need to know my Navigator, my Archivist."

"Pick your team. There's money in this operation. Anyone you want to work with."

"The history of the era. I need to study. I don't know the weapons, the lingo . . . I'll get made in the first five minutes."

"Forty-eight hours from now, the Panopticon owners shut the system down for good. Nobody in or out. You want to wait, you lose your wife. It's a reach, sure. But sometimes the reach is worth the reward. Or did I overestimate your feelings?"

"What about guards?"

Parker thought of his wife. The last time he saw her. She had smiled. Her eyes filled with tears. Then she hung up the intercom phone and pressed her hand against the Plexiglas window. Right before a guard came and led her away. And he never saw her again. But she was out there somewhere. Living a new life in the system.

Dunbar extended his hand. Cold to the touch. Parker gripped it tight.

"We have a deal," Parker said. "Tell me when we go."

◆ ◆ ◆

The precinct locker room looked like a German bunker at the end of the war. Low ceilings, flickering lights, cracked concrete walls. The showers crawled with roaches flitting in and out between loose tiles. Lockers were rusted out boxes, stacked like old refrigerators along the walls. The fronts were covered with the requisite "Police, Don't Move" stickers, reminding cops what to say in gun encounters. The only sacred space was occupied by a pair of posters, one of Don Mattingly, the other, Cindy Crawford. Everything else, pure government shit.

Parker changed quickly. Jeans, sweatshirt. He tucked his gun into an ankle holster. His shield he slid into his wallet.

"So what happens now?" Clayton said.

"Now we go get the team," Parker said. He slammed shut his locker.

They took Clayton's car, a maroon sedan the size of an ocean liner. The Navigator lived in uptown, and they headed north on the FDR, the East River flashing by. Traffic was light. Clayton drove with the windows down. The air smelled of cigarettes and wet concrete.

"You've never been inside before?" Parker asked.

"No, buddy. I just lock them up. I don't really know what happens after. How many times you been in?"

"I'm not really sure."

He could always remember little bits of things. Immense skyscrapers that stretched so high, you could barely see the top. Streets crowded with people and cars, everyone jostling each other, moving about their lives with purpose. He thought of the German. And the bodies he'd been inside, used up like candle wicks. "It's unbelievable. Unless you knew it wasn't real. You feel hunger. Fear. Pain."

"Pain? What happens if you die inside?"

Parker had died plenty of times. Most he hadn't even seen coming. Kick down a door, a man inside with a revolver. You're gone in a flash of smoke. Eyes suddenly open in another place. Another time. Those were the disorienting cases. But dying wasn't the problem. Dying was how you came back.

"You die, you wake up," Parker said. "Living is the problem."

"What do you mean?"

"You get captured, you don't wake up. Ever," Parker said. "They'll throw you in prison and keep you there in the system. That's the danger. The only way to leave the system is to die. That's how we break out the prisoners."

"Dying doesn't hurt?"

Dying was the worst pain Parker had ever experienced. Excruciating. Like his mind was being ripped from his skull through his ears and nose. "Just try to get it over with. Die fast."

The Navigator lived in one of those beautiful doorman buildings on the east side of Central Park. A marked police car was parked with its lights on, rotating strobes of blue and red flashing across the stone face of the building. Seated inside, two uniforms made entries in their memo books. The driver looked up, startled, when Parker tapped the window with his shield.

"Everything all right?" Parker asked.

The uniform shrugged. The smell of hamburger wafted up from inside the car. Two patrol guys about to park somewhere and eat when they got called out on a job. The aggravation wafting from the police car was almost palpable.

"Emotionally disturbed person job," the uniform said. "Some lady took a shitload of pills, changed her mind, called 911."

"Get her name?"

"Yeah," the uniform checked the Aided hospital card. "Charlotte Gonzales. Female, white, 35 years old."

Charlotte Gonzales. Even before he heard the name, Parker knew it would have been Charlotte. She was a ship lost in the night, far from land, surrounded by fog and taking in water.

"Where'd they take her?" Parker asked.

"Bellevue," the cop replied.

A minute later, Parker collapsed back into Clayton's car.

"Problem?" Clayton asked as the big engine rumbled to life.

"Slight," Parker said. "There's something I didn't tell you about our Navigator."

"What's that?"

"A few years back, her son drowned in some kind of boating accident. After that, she sort of lost it. Now she's mentally unstable."

"Aren't we all a little mentally unstable?" Clayton pulled off from the curb. "But she's good at what she does?"

"She's the best Navigator I've ever worked with."

"Let's take a ride to the psych hospital."

171

Bellevue clung like a barnacle to the edge of the highway, overlooking the East River. Streetlights flashed by overhead in a blur. Across the water, Roosevelt Island stretched out, the ruin of an old mental hospital barely visible through the trees.

"What is a Navigator anyway?" Clayton asked.

"A Navigator is like a guide. She accesses historical archives. Maps of the city through different time periods. She gives you routes, street names, building numbers. After Charlotte's son drowned, her whole life fell apart. Since then, she's been in and out of psych hospitals."

"Can't you get someone else?"

"I could always get someone else. But there's nobody I trust. She's the best. And the work steadies her," Parker said. "You're my partner out here. She's my partner in there."

"So what do we do to get her out? She's in psych. We can't get near her if she's been committed."

"I know the doctor at Bellevue. He released her to me before," Parker said. "Hopefully he will again."

They pulled into the ER lot outside the hospital. Bellevue was the collection center for most of the psych cases in the city and for the entire population of male psych prisoners. The ward itself was part Rikers, part *One Flew Over the Cuckoo's Nest.*

The waiting room was filled with men handcuffed to hard metal chairs. It was feeding time. Some of the prisoners were drinking orange juice from plastic cups or eating peanut butter and jelly sandwiches. Their uniformed escorts looked bored or tired. Prisoners and patients shuffled about together, most of them in pale blue hospital gowns. A television bolted to the ceiling played *Murder, She Wrote.*

Doctor Chandler was in his late 50s, salt-and-pepper hair and a car dealer's smile. He wore a white coat, his nametag fixed to the pocket. His office was physician bland, diplomas on the wall, a framed photograph of two kids in braces, a shelf of medical reference guides.

Chandler leaned back in his chair and laced his fingers together. Nothing but all the time in the world.

"Sure, Charlotte Gonzales," the doctor replied after Parker explained the reason for their visit. "I can't discuss the details of her case with you. But I'll tell you what you already know. Just brought her in an hour ago. Acute stress disorder. Depression. Suicidal thoughts and actions."

"She lost a child," Parker said.

"I know. Terrible. Depression is the inability to imagine a future. And since one never truly gets over the loss of a child, one is always fighting depression, fighting to imagine a future, if you will."

"I need you to release her to my care," Parker said.

"And why is that?"

Because she's my Navigator. I need her to enter another world and break someone out of prison.

Parker tried to keep his face neutral. "She's a friend."

Chandler sighed, rocked back in his chair. "I don't know if that's going to be possible. She made a legitimate suicidal attempt."

"I know she did. But I can help her. Better than being in this place. Zombies walking into walls. *Murder, She Wrote* on loop. Any sense of normalcy she might have had before will just evaporate in this shithole."

Chandler considered this. "I might be inclined to be insulted. But the care and safety of a patient is more important to me than my ego. And I admit you may have a point. With her consent, I will interview her with you in the room. And then make a decision. Agreed?"

Parker hoped Charlotte was lucid enough to hold a conversation. If she wasn't, it would be a very short interview. But no matter what happened, Parker was not leaving this place without her.

"Agreed."

Charlotte looked terrible. Her hair hung in greasy vines from her head. Dark circles floated under her eyes like pools of dirty water. She stared sullenly at the ground. Her lower jaw hung open slightly, a pearl of saliva caught on the corner of her mouth.

Even through the mask of sadness, Parker could see she had been a formidable woman once. But more than just her child had been lost in that water. Her future, her reason for being, her soul had also slipped beneath the surface on that day.

That was her in the real world.

As a Navigator, she was the best Parker had ever seen. Her damaged mind accepted and understood the world of the system and she could move through its imagined intricacies without the blocks of a strictly rational brain.

Chandler, Parker, and Charlotte sat in the doctor's office. Clayton paced the intake waiting room outside.

The doctor leaned forward, a yellow writing pad balanced on his knee. "Charlotte, can you hear me?"

Charlotte nodded slowly, not taking her eyes from the floor. She's almost gone, Parker thought. There's nothing here but the shell of a human. The skin. The hair. The clothes. But whatever existed once inside was lost.

The doctor indicated Parker. "Do you know who this man is?"

Charlotte glanced up momentarily and Parker had the frightening feeling that she looked right through him. Not recognizing who he was. But then she nodded, almost imperceptibly, before she dropped her eyes back to the ground.

"Who is he, Charlotte?"

"Parker. He's my friend. I look out for him."

"You look out for him? What do you mean?"

"I protect him. I help him find his way home," Charlotte said. "Can I have some water?"

"In a minute. But first, tell me, how are you feeling?"

"Sad. I feel sad. And lonely."

"Why do you feel sad and lonely?"

Charlotte sighed, some of the life coming back into her. She twisted her fingers together. "You know why."

"Do you want to tell me?"

"Because I lost my son."

"What happened to him?"

Charlotte looked past the doctor toward some invisible point on the wall. "I was on vacation, at the beach with my son. He swam out too far, away from me, and this riptide . . . just carried him out."

Parker had heard this story before. Each time it was recited with the same rote consistency of an actor reading lines, as if she had no emotions left to give.

"And does this make you want to hurt yourself?"

"I did," Charlotte said. She looked up finally and met the doctor's eye. "I didn't want to live anymore."

"Do you still feel that way?"

Charlotte glanced at Parker. "Why are you here?"

Parker said nothing. He only nodded slightly.

Charlotte pushed matted hair from her face. "A job?"

The doctor waved his hand and turned toward Parker. "It's easier if I conduct the interview."

Charlotte looked at the doctor, a spark of life in her eye. She frowned, then sat up straight in her chair. "I did want to hurt myself. But now I don't."

"What do you mean?"

"I feel much better now," Charlotte straightened her clothes. "Now I have a reason to live again."

◆ ◆ ◆

They had released her after Charlotte made a bunch of promises about long-term therapy. She and Parker had both signed various forms. Some other doctors had come in to look things over. But in the end, she was like a fish no one wanted, thrown back into the water.

Clayton drove, Parker in the passenger seat, Charlotte in the back. She still wore her bathrobe and stared out the window, tracing the patterns of light on the glass with her fingers. Clayton glanced over at Parker. "You sure about this buddy?"

"I can hear you back here," Charlotte said. "I'm crazy. Not deaf. And you two clowns just made yourself responsible for a depressive suicidal wreck. You should be careful of your tone."

"She'll be fine," Parker said. "Right?"

"Yeah. Yeah. I'll be fine as long as there's work. Probably blow my brains out when the job is over. But for now, I'm great." Clayton drove past the Kip's Bay movie theater. Crowds of people filled the brightly lit lobby. "There is a job, right?"

"There's a job," Parker said. "Escape. Five person team."

"What era?"

"1953."

"What'd the guy do?"

"Don't know that."

"You don't know? I thought that was like the Parker Golden Rule. Never bust out anyone if you don't know what they did. This guy could be like a serial killer of nuns for all you know."

"I'm willing to take that risk."

"Why?"

"Because my wife is in with him."

Charlotte shut her mouth. "Fair enough."

Clayton headed back toward the Upper East Side. Charlotte smoothed down her hair, tried to straighten her clothes. She sighed. "I'm a fucking mess."

"You really try to kill yourself?" Clayton asked.

"That's what my stomach pump results tell me."

"You kill someone at the brain stem. Bullet. Knife. Any kind of sharp object really," Clayton said.

"Okay crazy, next time I'll try stabbing myself in the back of the neck. Thanks for the pep talk," Charlotte said, then turned to Parker. "Who is this guy?"

"Don't mind him, he just . . . some lasting trauma," Parker said. "From the war. Antisocial."

"Cave man is going in with you?" Charlotte said.

"I object to that term," Clayton said. "Despite my aggression and violent tendencies, I am a product of my environment, not heredity. I like things. Culture. Film. Art."

"Have you ever been into the system before?" Charlotte asked.

Clayton shook his head. "Never."

"It's a real mind fuck," she said. "You need someone stable in there or you can get a brain break."

"What's a brain break?" Clayton asked.

"Inside the system, you inhabit the world created by the machine, or in essence the world created by the machine's programmers. This is a fully articulate world composed of other prisoners and guards, all interacting in a completely realized environment," she said.

"When we enter the system," Parker said, "we essentially hack into the machine, inserting my consciousness into a drone in the world of the prison. To increase the population of the system and make it harder to tell the difference between prisoners and guards, the system fills each world with drones, preprogrammed humanoids who act in a predictably unpredictable way. Like humans. But there's no human consciousness backing them. They're just empty shells. This is how we enter and stay in the prison world."

"But you need a stable psyche," Charlotte said. "Someone not prone to mood swings."

"Why? What happens?" Clayton asked.

"You can't bond with the drone. The system detects the instability and sends every guard after you," she said. "Stable mind. Stable drone."

They reached Charlotte's building. The marked patrol car had vanished. A lone doorman stood in front, smoking a cigarette and staring off down the street toward the diesel belch of a garbage truck.

"Do you have an Archivist yet?" Charlotte asked.

"Working on it," Parker said.

"Going with Selberg?"

"Rather not. But probably."

"The guy is a degenerate gambler."

"Good eye for details."

"He's also a self-centered ass. Who knows what secret delusions he's harboring. At least I'm open about my depression. That guy is wound tight. He'll break if you put him under pressure."

"That's why he's not going in with us," Parker said.

"When are we going?"

"Tomorrow sometime. I'll let you know."

Charlotte blew the two men a kiss, then hopped out of the car. She was no longer the sullen shell that had shuffled out of the psych ward at Bell. She had something to do now. A job.

"She calls *me* unstable," Clayton said as they both watched her skip into the lobby of her building. "That one is bat shit crazy."

"She's not crazy. Just lost and sad. We just gave her something to hope for."

Clayton pulled away from the curb. It was just after eight. Carriage horses made their way slowly around Central Park. A light fog rolled in from the west, giving halos to the streetlights and shrouding the clattering beat of hoof against pavement.

Parker thought back to a few of the late century breaks he'd pulled. The horse and carriage jobs, he called them. Those were tricky. People were tougher back then. They led more physical lives. They were more desperate. And desperation brought violence. Men seemed quick to throw a punch, and weapons were everywhere. Brass knuckles. Lead saps. Billy clubs. And if the body of a stranger turned up dead in a barrel, it barely made the papers. So many people floated in and out of the city, carried in on the winds of immigration, that one or two going wouldn't raise an eyebrow.

Only the guards would notice.

"Where to?"

"Brighton Beach," Parker said. "Russians have a social club down there. All night poker. That's where we'll find our guy."

"Far trip. We need this guy?"

"We need an Archivist."

Clayton gave him a blank stare. Parker sighed. The man wasn't ready to go into the system. The first time was hard enough, even with training, and Clayton barely understood the basic concepts.

"Archivists run historical research," Parker said. "The system is designed off historical databases. So each system is populated with historically accurate figures pulled from census records. They all interact with each other in real buildings and locations. Sort of a collective consciousness. The Archivist runs the history of the buildings and the people. He determines the time periods and helps prevent you from saying something stupid and getting the guards on you."

"Your guy is good?"

"He gets it done. He has a master's degree in history from Yale. But he's also got a gambling problem. Business like ours, sometimes you have to take what you can get. He knows the system. Needs the money."

"You trust him?"

"Can't trust anyone. You know that."

"I'm trustworthy."

"You, my friend, are an American classic."

They took the BQE along the outer edge of Brooklyn, the Verrazano Bridge shimmering in the darkness over the water. The Volga was a little Russian restaurant on the boardwalk in the midst of drab, yellow brick apartment buildings. A couple of heavy hitters in suits stood out front, smoking cigarettes and giving the eye to a girl walking her dog. Clayton parked on the corner.

"Is this a heavy job?" Clayton asked.

Parker looked at the two Russians. These games were invite only, and they weren't the sort of players to welcome anyone in off the street. Especially two cops. The building itself was small. The front door was probably the only way out.

"Maybe."

"Ten-four."

"If things go bad in there, might be tough getting out."

"That's what you brought me for," Clayton said. He popped open the glove compartment, rooted around beneath a pile of gum wrappers and retrieved a pair of brass knuckles. He slipped the knucks into his pocket. "Ready?"

"Let's go."

◆ ◆ ◆

The two Russians straightened up as Clayton and Parker approached. One of them flipped away the cigarette he'd been holding and slipped a hand inside his jacket. Parker could feel the energy shift in the air. Clayton had both hands in his pockets. Parker held his hands up and out to the side.

"Help you?" one of the men said as Clayton and Parker approached.

"Yeah, know any good borscht places around here?" Clayton asked.

"Oh, you a funny guy?"

"Listen, fellas," Parker said. "We're just looking for a friend of ours. Think he's inside. We really don't want trouble."

"Joke like that," the Russian nodded at Clayton, "and you'll get trouble."

"I get it," Parker said. "We just want to find our friend."

"Who's your friend?"

"Selberg. Little guy. Ferret looking."

"Don't know him." The eyes were the best lie detector ever invented, and the man's flickered like a dying light bulb. Behind his shoulder, lights were on inside the restaurant. Parker heard the dull bass of Russian pop music playing.

"He's not really worth knowing," Parker said. "But maybe we could check out the restaurant. Might run into him."

The Russian shook his head. "Private party."

Parker sighed. This was going to be trouble. He could feel Clayton slowly coiling up, tightening like a spring.

"We're not asking permission," Clayton said.

"Oh no?" The second Russian laughed. Then he took a step forward. He moved with the easy confidence of a big man used to getting his way. The Russian put up his hands to push Clayton away. He palms were outstretched, lazily moving forward, when Clayton's right hand flashed out from his jacket pocket. He bent down, then the spring uncoiled ferociously, as he swung for the stars. The brass knuckles around Clayton's fist crunched against the Russian's jaw, and everyone heard the snap of breaking bone.

The Russian went down hard.

The second man backed away, hands up in the universal gesture of "please don't hurt me." Parker and Clayton walked by him and pushed open the Volga restaurant door. They didn't have long before the guys out front got a group of their friends together and half of Little Odessa showed up with baseball bats.

Inside, the restaurant was dark, but Parker had the impression he was surrounded by lots of gold-plated furnishings, polished wood floors, and mirrors. Pop music blared loudly. A handful of down-on-their-luck women flitted around a large, round table like fish circling a fat piece of bread floating in the water. At the table sat a half-dozen men holding cards. Cigarette smoke clouded the air like diesel exhaust.

The men turned toward the door and stared.

"We're looking for Selberg," Parker announced to the room.

Dead eyes stared back at the officers through the smoke. Then one of the men stood from the table. He was in his late forties, with loose sagging skin and a nose that looked like it had been drawn by a drunken child with a crayon.

"Selberg is a friend of yours?"

"Well . . ." Parker said slowly, reluctant to admit Selberg was a friend. "We're looking for him."

"I'm Boris." The man approached them. He laid his hand over Parker's shoulder. "Come, I'll help you find your friend."

Boris led them through the restaurant. They passed a buffet table piled with lots of meats in fried pockets and soups. Bottles of vodka glinted in the dim light. Clayton had his hands back in his pocket and followed a few steps behind. From the shadows behind the bar, another man stepped forth. This one walked on the other side of Parker.

"How you doing?" Parker addressed the second man. "What's your name?"

"Boris," the man said.

"Ah. I see. Popular name here."

Boris Number One guided Parker to the back of the large space, through a set of maroon curtains and into a private room of glass-topped tables and crystal chandeliers. Parker felt the slow burn of fear crawl across his heart. He had to remind himself that this was real life. This wasn't the system. Whatever happened now would really actually happen. If these men chose to shoot him, he would actually die. Not just wake up.

He suddenly wished they'd just tried to get a new Archivist. Selberg was good, but he certainly wasn't worth a bullet in the brain. Parker didn't even like the guy.

They passed through a set of swinging double doors and into an industrial kitchen. Stainless steel countertops gleamed in fluorescent light. Knives and cleavers clung to a magnetic strip on the wall. The burner of a stove built to cook for an army flowered with blue petals of a gas flame.

Selberg was in the center of the room.

He was stripped to his boxers and tied spread-eagle to a wooden table. His face was a mask of blood. Two of the fingers on his right hand were bent so severely they looked almost torn from his hand.

"This is your friend, yes?" Boris Number One said. "Maybe since he's your friend, you pay the big fucking debt he owes us."

Selberg turned toward the sound of the voice. His eyes went wide when he saw Parker, two white circles in a slick coating of red.

"Oh, Jesus, Parker, help me," Selberg said.

Parker turned toward Boris. "I need this man alive."

Boris shrugged slowly. "We all need something. I need the seventeen thousand dollars he owes me."

Parker shook his head. Stupid Selberg. Just pulled a job and gambles everything away and goes in even deeper to some crazed Russian gangsters. This would be the last time Parker worked with the man. And if this job wasn't so important, Parker would have walked out of that kitchen, gotten back in the car, and driven away, never giving a second thought to how many cigarettes they put out on Selberg's balls.

Parker rubbed his chin thoughtfully. "I need this man for a job."

"What kind of job?"

"Personal. But after the job, he'll have your money," Parker said.

Still strapped to the table, Selberg nodded vigorously. "Yes. Yes. That's exactly what I said."

A man stepped out from the shadows and punched Selberg once in the stomach, producing a wet slapping sound. Selberg grunted in pain. He turned his head slightly, then white vomit bubbled out of his mouth.

Boris patted the top of Selberg's head. He looked thoughtful and dangerous. "Must be a pretty big job, one man in the crew can come up with seventeen thousand in a day."

"Big enough."

"I'd like to get in on that," Boris said, a sly look in his eyes. "I can help with certain things."

Parker shook his head. "We're all full on this one. But give me Selberg and you'll get your money."

Boris grabbed a thatch of Selberg's hair and shook. The sound of hair being ripped from scalp echoed in the kitchen. "How do I know I'll get my money?"

"You'll get it. And think about it this way. You kill Selberg now, you'll get nothing."

From behind the group came the sound of running feet. Clayton sidestepped quickly away from the door. His hand went to the revolver that Parker knew was tucked in his partner's waist. The swinging double doors flung open, and three men burst into the kitchen. Parker recognized one of the men from outside the restaurant.

The three newcomers paused when they saw Boris. One of them held a length of pipe, which he slowly lowered. A quick exchange occurred in Russian between the men. Quietly, Parker unsnapped the holster inside his jacket, the revolver sliding free into his hand.

Boris waved the men back toward the interior of the restaurant.

One of them made hard eye contact with Clayton. "I see you soon."

"You see me right now," Clayton responded. "Why wait?"

The three men retreated back into the restaurant. Boris turned to Parker. "I will give you Selberg. When you are done with this job, you pay me my money. Or something very bad will happen."

The two officers wrapped the blood-soaked Selberg in trash bags so he wouldn't ruin Clayton's car, then laid him out on the backseat. He groaned and curled his knees upward, his eyes fixed on the floor. Clayton pulled away from the curb, the crowd of Russians standing outside the restaurant watching him. He lit up a cigar and gazed through the smoke as the Volga grew smaller in the rear view.

"Selberg, you dumb asshole!" Parker said. "You can't make it one day without doing something stupid."

"I'm sorry, Parker," Selberg said. His voice was raspy, like his mouth was filled with crushed ice. "I'm still good. You can count on me. God is my witness."

"You're lucky this job is last-minute, because there is nothing I would not do right now to get you off this team. With everything going on, we need this Russian mafia heat?"

"I'm sorry. It was stupid of me."

"Get some scratch tickets like a normal degenerate gambler. That way, if you lose, you don't have your knee caps blown off."

"Fucking Russians," Clayton said.

Parker studied Selberg. "You look like shit. You need a hospital?"

"I'm good. Might throw up again. But I'm good."

Clayton looked concerned. "Not in the car."

"Just get me home."

Selberg lived in a single resident occupancy in Hell's Kitchen. He had a room with a single window view of an air shaft and a bathroom down the hall that he shared with a mob of mentally unstable homeless people. Once a month someone would end up getting slashed in the hall.

Before it all went wrong, Selberg had been a history professor at NYU. Then the gambling bug bit hard and the descent soon followed. He would hop the bus to Foxwoods Casino in nearby Connecticut and disappear for days. He started missing classes. Becoming more erratic. NYU denied his tenure and warned him about his behavior. Selberg couldn't quit. Eventually the school tossed him from the faculty, and without a steady paycheck, the money went fast.

Parker never understood what addicted Selberg to the dice. Perhaps some men just liked the edge. Beneath the academic's professorial demeanor, there seemed to be an always shifting wildness.

They stopped in front of a dilapidated building in Hell's Kitchen. A few neighborhood characters sat on the stoop out front, smoking cigarettes and drinking from brown paper bags. Bachata music blared from a parked car. Someone argued behind closed doors.

Selberg sat up. "Home sweet shithole."

Parker turned to look at him. "So you'll be ready?"

Selberg fished in his pocket for a loose cigarette. "How much is the payoff?"

"Enough."

Selberg gripped the cigarette with swollen lips. "I'm in or I'm dead. You know that. Not much of a choice. I'll have about five hundred bucks left after I square with the Russians."

"Big gambler like you, double that in no time."

Selberg lit the cigarette and laughed as smoke swirled around his face. "I'm a real monument to success." He sighed then pulled himself painfully from the car. He leaned in on Parker's window. Parker could smell cigarettes and cheap booze on the man's breath. "What's the era?"

"1953."

"I know I'm a fuckup. But despite the booze and the gambling, I'm still the best Archivist out there."

"There are others."

"That's bullshit and you know it." Selberg pushed himself off the car and began to slowly stagger toward the front stairs of his building. "You'd be lost in a storm without me, looking for any safe shore."

"Sober up. Stay inside," Parker called out. "I'll call you."

Selberg waved a dismissive hand, stumbled up toward the door, and disappeared inside.

◆ ◆ ◆

The team met in the abandoned biscuit factory. Dunbar greeted them at the elevator. He wore another old-timey looking suit, like something a carnival barker might wear. The space in the center of the floor had been cleared and a large table set up. Spread across the table was a gargantuan map of mid-twentieth century New York City.

"Ladies and gentlemen, thank you for coming," Dunbar said as the team stepped off the elevator. "Excuse the conditions of this space. It has certainly seen better days."

Parker looked at the crew. Clayton looked healthy and rested, but the others looked like old sneakers. Selberg's eye was almost swollen shut, his lips puffy and split open. Charlotte shuffled in behind Selberg, her hair still matted and greasy, her skin pale, dark circles ringing her eyes.

Dunbar seemed to sense the desperate, nervous energy in the group. He frowned as he watched them filter in. They crowded around the table and looked down at the map.

"Anyone have some water, juice, anything?" Charlotte held a hand to her forehead, her right eye wincing in pain. "My head is killing me."

Parker realized they were all totally unprepared for this. And entering the system did not work out well for anyone who went unprepared. Parker normally would have backed out of this job. But if what Dunbar said was true, and Parker's wife was in the same system as their target, the job might be Parker's only chance to see her.

Parker ignored Charlotte's question and smoothed over the map with his hand. "This is the period?"

"Yes sir. New York City, 1953," said Dunbar.

"This is a new time period," Selberg said. "I've never known them to do a 1953 before."

"New time period. New system," Dunbar said.

"Oh wait . . ." Selberg took a step back and shook his head. "This isn't . . ."

Dunbar nodded. "I'm afraid so."

"Oh man . . ." Selberg ran fingers through his hair. "Fuck, man. This is not good at all. I heard about this. I didn't think it was operational."

"It is."

Parker had no idea what they were talking about. "Can someone fill me in, please?"

"It's the new supermax Panopticon," Selberg said. "Totally different security. You can't just enter the system anymore."

"Why not?"

"Because the system is self-enclosed now," said Dunbar. "It's built to detect intrusions from the outside."

"But we just went into the system," Parker said. "Our last breakout."

"That was the old system. This is the new one, supposedly unbreakable. You can't just hack into a drone. The system monitors all consciousness and checks for any breaks. The instant you land in a new drone, guards will be all over you. The drone itself will shut down. You'll be trapped in this lifeless, immobile body."

Trapped. Parker's worst fear. To be trapped inside the system meant capture. And capture was worse than death.

"But you can get in, right?" Parker asked.

Selberg smiled. "We'll figure out a way. Just more complicated."

"Complicated how?"

"They have a new program security. Called the Minotaur. It constantly monitors consciousness to detect intrusions. Supposed to be pretty kick ass. And also, as I said, it's a closed system. People on the outside can't communicate with people on the inside. So the Navigator and the Archivist will have to be inside the system with you."

Charlotte frowned. "No. No. No. I didn't sign up for that. I'm a technician. I'm not running around killing people in 1950s New York City."

"You wouldn't have to actually interact with anyone," Selberg said. "You could go into the system and find a comfortable hotel room to work out of. Or a car. Or wherever. But the only way you'll be able to communicate with Parker is by being inside with him."

"Everyone would have to be inside? Even you?" Parker asked.

"Even me." Dunbar coughed politely, then stroked his mustache. "Is that a problem for you?"

Parker shook his head and cast a warning glance at Selberg. "No. There's no problem."

Selberg sighed, sat back in his chair, and raised his hands. "Let's talk about money."

"Fair enough," Dunbar said. He wrote something on a legal pad, then tore off the page and slid it across the table toward Selberg. The Archivist smirked, then turned over the paper, and stared at the number. His eyes opened wide.

"This is for real?" Selberg said.

Dunbar nodded. "I hope you will find our compensation package is adequate."

"Shit yeah." Selberg turned toward Parker. "Looks like I'll be going in with you."

This is really all happening, Parker thought. "So what's the next step?"

Dunbar handed out a packet of information to each member of the team. Parker flipped through the stapled stack of papers and saw poorly photographed maps of New York City and statistical charts.

"This is what we know about the prison," Dunbar said. "New York City in the early-to-mid-1950s. Population of about one million prisoners. Five thousand guards. And a few hundred thousand drones."

"My God, that's huge," Clayton said. "One million prisoners?"

"The supermax facility is the largest in the world to date," Dunbar replied. "Every prisoner from the entire Eastern Seaboard has been consolidated into one facility. They've memory erased all of them and put them in the new system."

"And the reality translation was perfect?" Charlotte studied one of charts. "None of the prisoners know what they are?"

"Nobody knows," Selberg said. "I only know because I'm tapped into the systems all the time. I hear things. But nobody else knows this place exists. It was all programmed and built with private money. Kept totally hushed."

Dunbar looked thoughtful. "I'm sure there are a few imperfections. Every system has a handful of prisoners who know the deal. Who know the world isn't real. But we don't know who they are. Or what they're doing with that information."

"And our guy could be anywhere?" Parker asked. "That's like finding a pebble on a beach."

"Not anywhere," Dunbar said. "Your target's name is Andrew Scott."

"Senator Scott's son?" Selberg said.

"That's correct."

"What did he do to get locked up?"

"That doesn't concern you," Dunbar said. "I'm only giving you this information as it might assist in your finding your target. Andrew Scott is 22 years old. Wealthy and connected. We believe he knows he is in prison."

"Why do you think that?"

"We have a guard," Dunbar said. "We haven't communicated with this guard since lockdown, but he was given instruction to seek out Andrew Scott, protect him, and give him the truth of his identity."

Parker asked, "When was the last time you had any positive contact?"

"About a year," Dunbar said.

"A year is a long time," Selberg said. "Your boy could be anywhere in this population by now."

"Perhaps," Dunbar said. "Scott was a big boxing fan on the outside. Liked nice things. Women, cars. He's going to be living a high profile life on the inside. His isn't a personality that understands keeping quiet. So you can start with that."

"I don't know. This whole thing is a stretch," Parker said.

"I was under the impression we were paying the best. If that's not the case, we'll find someone else. I'm sure your wife will be very disappointed."

Parker stared at Dunbar for a long moment. In that instant he hated the man. But he was ready to go inside.

Dunbar walked toward the exit. When he reached the door, he turned back and faced Parker. "Oh, one last thing. Once you get inside, if you have any second thoughts about the mission . . . I don't know, like maybe looking for your wife and forgetting about the job you're being paid to do . . ."

"Yeah?"

"Scott is the only one who knows where your wife is."

"How would Scott know that?"

"We've been planning this for a while now. Your name always comes up as being the best," Dunbar said. "But sometimes the best needs motivation. Find Scott, you find your wife."

5

The memory ended, and I was back in the hotel bar. I made my way back to my room. Now I knew why I was here. To find the senator's son and bring him out. But I needed to find more memories. I needed to know what had happened. There were supposed to be a million prisoners in that system. How did I end up on an empty island?

But most important, I knew more about my wife. She was out in the system somewhere, in this prison. That's the real reason why I was on the mission. She wasn't dead. Now I had hope.

I walked in a slow circle around the room, trying to clear my head. Before I went into the system, my memory had been erased. I had used the existing blueprint of Manhattan as a cognitive palace to store and hide my most important memories, thus preventing the system from finding them. It seemed some of the areas were formed strictly from my own memory, like those places I had visited with Valenstein.

But many places were new to me. Someone else's memory had brought them into the machine. I looked around the room more closely, curious now, trying to remember if I had been here before, and I began to notice something odd.

This was the same room that I had been in upstairs.

Not in the way that generic furniture and drab bedding made all hotel rooms appear the same. But the two rooms were actually identical.

The same nicks were visible on the bureau. The same peeled section of wallpaper. The same dark stain on the carpet.

I felt the presence before I saw anything.

Something cold wrapped itself around the base of my spine, then crawled its way up to cling to the back of my brain. I froze. Faint rock and roll music played somewhere. I shut off my lamp and followed the sound out into the hallway. Without my lantern, the blackness was so complete, it felt as if no light had ever penetrated these halls before. A complete and total void.

But in the void, I felt a small breeze and had the distinct impression that something walked past me in the hall. There was nothing definite, just the small movement of air and a vague unease that spread through me. Down the hall, a door slammed. It was an unusual sound. Heavy and metallic. Not a room door but something else. Without thought, I flicked on my lantern and ran toward the noise. At the end of the hall was a stairwell door. I pushed it open and found nothing. Only blank, metal-lined concrete stairs. I heard another door open and close farther down the stairwell. I moved quickly down the stairs after the sound and pushed open a second metal door, which led out of the stairwell.

The light was almost blinding.

I stood on the edge of a huge party. Banquet tables were lined with shrimp and steak and bowls of freshly cut fruit. Champagne was everywhere. And on a parquet wood floor, a well-dressed crowd danced awkwardly to a cover band. I looked around, tried to piece together when this was. The styles were distinctly 1970s. Women in fringed miniskirts, men in flared jeans and trousers. Then the world went fuzzy. Like a wax-covered screen had been placed in front of my eyes, and the details faded away. I turned my head from the dance floor and the scene sharpened.

This wasn't my memory. This belonged to someone else. And parts of this world were better stored than others. I walked slowly through the crowd, following the path of sharpness. When details faded, I moved away until things became . . . *better recollected.* The phrase felt right, the only way I could understand what I was experiencing.

The crowd of thirty blurry people continued to dance on the parquet floor. I followed the line of clarity, past the food tables and the cover band, until I found myself standing before a red painted door to the men's bathroom.

Inside, the bathroom had orange painted walls with a black and white tiled floor. A row of shiny porcelain urinals lined the wall. Orange walled stalls were in the back of the bathroom, and from one of them I heard someone humming. A man pushed open the stall, his head down as he worked his thumb over something on the front of his shirt. He wore a camel-colored leisure suit with a striped butterfly collared shirt. He stopped in front of the mirror, took off his suit jacket, and turned on the faucet.

His undershirt was stained with a wide spray of blood. The man sighed, then went to work on the spots with a wet paper towel. He hummed to himself, and as he dabbed, the blood turned pinkish under the water. I moved toward him. Like a vampire, I had no reflection in the mirror. The man continued to work on the stain, dabbing with the paper towels. The facial hair and sunglasses had confused me. He sported a scruffy beard and wore light-tinted aviators. His hair was longer too, falling down around his ears and neck. But beneath all that, I was looking at someone very familiar.

Edward Selberg.

The door opened and a man and woman barged into the bathroom. They were falling over one another in drunken laughter. Selberg saw them and straightened up, stopped rubbing at the bloodstains. The couple froze with embarrassment. The man nodded an apology and they slowly backed out of the bathroom. "We'll find somewhere else."

Selberg shook his head good naturedly, worked the stain a few swipes more, then tossed the paper towel in the garbage and put his suit jacket back on. He did a line of cocaine off the sink, splashed water on his face, straightened his jacket, and stared into the mirror. He pointed at himself. "You. You. You."

He turned and walked from the bathroom. I followed ten feet behind. We passed back through the crowded party, the music deafening. Selberg headed for the elevator, and I joined him in the car before we traveled upward. Alone with him, I studied his face. The same Selberg I had on my expedition. Only his eyes were different. Something harder behind this one's eyes. Like he wore a Selberg mask over a monster's face.

We exited and walked down an empty hall. Then this Selberg fitted a key into a door lock and we entered an anonymous room. Inside was the familiar queen-sized bed with nondescript carpeting, this room the same as the others except for the outdated black and white television on the laminate bureau and the bloody man handcuffed to the radiator.

Selberg took off his suit jacket again and sat on the edge of the bed. Next to him, already laid out on the bed, was a metal crowbar, a handgun, and a knife. The man handcuffed to the radiator cringed in fear. He was stripped to the waist, a gag shoved in his mouth, one eye swollen shut.

"You know, you ruined my shirt," Selberg said. "Blood doesn't come out as easy as the commercials make you think."

"Please . . ."

Selberg held up a hand. "Let me speak. Now you're going to tell me what I want to know. Or I swear I'm going to pull you apart bit by bit like Legos and stack you up on the floor right here. Do you understand?"

"Oh Jesus, yes, please, whatever you want to know."

I stood in the far corner of the room feeling more powerless than I ever had in my life. There was nothing I could do to change the past, and there was a very real possibility this man was going to be killed in front of me. I wanted to leave the hotel room. To forget what I had seen here. But this memory was important. This was a memory of someone I was trapped inside the machine with. And I had to know why he looked like Selberg. Or why my Selberg looked like this bearded psycho.

"Where's the money?" Selberg asked.

"I don't have it."

Selberg hung his head and reached for the crowbar.

"No, no, no, wait," the man said. "I really, I don't have it, but I can give you something better."

"What?"

"My car, my car, I'll fucking sign it over to you right now."

"What kind of car is it?"

"It's a Chevelle. Orange and black. Beautiful car."

"Interior?"

"Beautiful interior," the man said. He could see salvation, and his enthusiasm showed through. "Leather. Got everything. More leg room. More power."

Selberg paused, his hand still clenched around the crowbar, his eyes distant and thoughtful. Finally he bit. "Keys?"

"My pocket." The man nodded toward a bloody bundle of clothes piled on the far side of the room. "In my right pocket."

Selberg reached into the bundle and pulled out a set of keys jangling on a ring.

"That car is worth three times what I owe you. Just fucking take it."

Selberg slipped the keys into his pocket. "I will take it."

The man exhaled in relief. "Thank you, God."

"But that still don't change the fact you owed me money," Selberg said. He swung the crowbar hard and fast. The man let out a squeak, then his skull was crushed by the hard iron. Selberg continued to swing the crowbar again and again, red, wet sap spraying everything.

When he was done, Selberg dropped the crowbar to the ground.

I tumbled backward. The stench of blood was foul and thick in the room. I fell out through the door and into the dark hallway beyond. The memory was over, and I was left in the blackness.

◆ ◆ ◆

I returned to my room, turned the dead bolt, and pressed my forehead against the thick wood. I breathed deeply. The thwack of the crowbar against bone was still in my head. Selberg had been some kind of enforcer. I must have been inside his memory because Selberg was here in the machine with me. What did that mean?

I had no idea. I needed to find another memory. I needed to move forward. I needed to know more. There were so many gaps in the story . . . I needed help.

There was a knock on the door.

My heart jumped. We never should have come to this hotel. There were too many rooms. Too many memories. Outside, I heard a shuffle of feet on carpet. Just beyond the wood of the door. Something was out there waiting for me. I thought back to the subway tunnel. To that creature that lurked beneath the earth. What if it had returned?

The knock came again.

Slowly I crept across the room, my feet silent on the carpet floor. I put my eye to the peephole and looked. Outside was black, too dark to see what stood before my door.

"Who's there?" I yelled.

Suddenly the hallway lights flickered to life.

And I could see Charlotte.

Somehow, she had changed her clothes and now wore a light blue dress that reached almost to her ankles. Her hair was different too, longer. And there was a strangeness to her. Her face had a vacant expression, her eyes blank and staring, her mouth almost slack-jawed, like she was high on something.

And then I noticed the smell.

A rotting scent of death. I knew something was wrong. I opened the door a crack, the chain still on, my pistol in hand hidden behind my back.

"Charlotte? You okay?"

Nothing moved on her face. Like her skin was made of wax. She didn't even seem to know I was there. Then, slowly, she turned away from the door and began to walk down the hall. I followed. Stepping into a hallway that I immediately knew was from a different time. This was not real. This was memory. Charlotte's memory. And like what had happened with Selberg, somehow I was trapped inside.

I walked twenty feet behind her. The scent of rot was strong now. It was more than just a smell, it was a feeling. A memory of something terrible that had happened. Of something so thick with disgust and despair that it reeked of death. As I followed Charlotte, I began to feel terrified of our destination, of what we were going to see.

She entered the stairwell and I followed, gliding as quietly as a ghost. Or a memory. Below me, the stairs revolved downward like the whorls of a shell. My lantern in hand, I followed Charlotte to the floor below. Faintly, from somewhere inside a room, I heard a baby begin to cry, a long, drawn-out wail of loneliness and fear.

Rows of doors stretched down the length of the hotel. Behind each room was a hidden story, a thousand moments lost in time, but now captured in this machine, destined to be repeated over and over again. Saved on some of kind of memory hard drive that could never be erased, only hidden from view. And maybe some things were better hidden from view.

I could never forget what I had seen Selberg do.

And now, if I followed, I felt certain I was going to see something else I could never forget. There was no reset on this moment. No delete.

Charlotte had a set of keys in her hand and entered one of the rooms. I followed, drawn forward, my feet seeming to move on their own. The door to the room had been left ajar and I was able to slide through the opening.

The room was the same as all the others, only this one was filled with someone else's stuff. A suitcase half-open on the bed, clothes spilled out onto the floor. A ceramic ashtray on a cheap dresser, stubbed-out cigarette butts forming a shotgun blast pattern on the base. The room was shadowy save for the flashing glow of a television set. The sound was muted. A cartoon cat chased a cartoon mouse in an endless loop around a living room, casting flickering shadows across the wall.

The bathroom door was open slightly, yellow light spilling onto the carpet.

I knew it was there. Whatever I was meant to see was beyond that door. Somewhere in that room. I stood fixed by the doorway. From the bathroom, I heard running water. A woman began to sing a lullaby, her voice no louder than a whisper. There was a slight splash of water. The baby no longer cried. The water turned off, but the woman continued to sing.

The door to the bathroom opened and Charlotte came out. Her arms glistened with water, her dress wet and clinging to her body. She walked past me and went to the open suitcase. She removed a baby blue blanket and laid it carefully down on the bed, folding it over into a neat square. She hummed to herself.

I walked forward, moved through the opening of the door, and looked in.

The bathroom was small and perfectly square. Black and white tiles lined the floor. A large, white vanity was littered with toothbrushes and a hair dryer and bunched up towels. A mirror reflected the room, but I was invisible.

Opposite the mirror was a bathtub. From the faucet, a single droplet, fat and round, hung suspended for an instant before it kerplunked into the bath water.

Inside the tub, something soft and pale lay beneath the water.

It was a child of about five. A boy, in trousers and a sweatshirt with small cartoon dinosaurs on it. His eyes were open. His hair floated around his head in the bathwater like seaweed. Drowned. I fell back against the wall. My hand covered my mouth.

Charlotte returned to the bathroom. She lifted the boy from the tub, water cascading off his little body, and carried him into the bedroom. She laid him down on the blue blanket, carefully wrapping the edges around his body.

Anger and disgust rose up inside me at the futility of all of this. Of seeing these things and not being able to make a difference. On the bed stand was a letter, half-finished.

I picked it up and read the scripted handwriting.

> *My Dearest John,*
>
> *By the time you read this, it will be done. I once told you that with family, one could never be lonely, for with children you would always be surrounded by friends. Where I go, I cannot bear to be alone. Either of us. I know what I have done is terrible, but please find it in your heart to understand.*
>
> *I hope you are happy now in the new life you have chosen. I cannot fault you. I know how hard these things have been. You are a good man, and I know our death will pain you greatly. I live, but do not live. One must make a choice. And so I do. And begin a new chapter with my only friend. Forgive me.*

"Oh no," I whispered. "No, no, no . . ."

I fell on my knees in front of Charlotte. I begged her, tried to shake her, slap her. But there was nothing. I was in another world in another time. My body was immaterial, as if I didn't exist. Charlotte slowly turned her head, reached into a bag at her feet, and pulled out a revolver.

No . . .

She held the revolver first to the side of her head. Then changing her mind, she opened her mouth and placed the barrel between her teeth.

All I could do was close my eyes.

In the blackness I heard the gunshot.

I stood, eyes closed, in the darkness, my entire body trembling. I knew these things had been real. As surely as I knew my own memory. This had happened to Charlotte. She had done this. Her child hadn't drowned in an accident. She had drowned him in a bathtub in a hotel room, and then she had put a bullet in her head.

Someone banged on the door. My eyes flicked open. Expecting to see the dead little boy, Charlotte on the ground, her head blown off, a pool of blood soaked into the carpet. But I was alone in the room. The television was turned off, the bed carefully made, the closets empty. In the bathroom, the tub was dry.

Someone banged on the door again.

I went to the door and opened it.

Charlotte stood outside.

I pulled back in shock. Her face was as I remembered, healthy, alive, not a blank shell. She no longer wore the blue dress but instead wore denim pants and a button-down shirt. A rifle was slung across her shoulder. She looked at me with concern.

"Where've you been?" Charlotte said. She pushed past me into the room and slammed shut the door behind her.

My tongue was sluggish, my brain barely responding. "What?"

"I was looking for you. Are you okay?"

I felt such an enormous relief to see her that without thinking I reached out and hugged her. I felt her startled body push back against mine, then slowly yield. "What's wrong?"

I couldn't even begin to explain what I knew. How I knew it. Or what she was capable of. This was a Charlotte freed of these memories, memories that had been erased from her mind and stored here in this hotel.

I wiped my eyes with the palm of my hand.

"Nothing. Nothing. I'm fine."

"You sure?"

"Yeah. I'm sure."

She nodded uncertainly, then for the first time glanced around the room. She froze, her eyes suddenly wary. Her jaw tightened, her head cocked thoughtfully. She walked toward the bed, then stepped into the bathroom. "It's the strangest thing," she said. "I feel like I've been here before."

You have.

You drowned your son and blew the back of your head off right there on that bed.

But that couldn't have been right. Charlotte must have lived. She must be in the machine with me. That's where the memory came from. She had pulled the trigger, but somehow she hadn't died. She had lived and been arrested for the murder of her own child.

"All these rooms look the same," I mumbled.

"I guess so," she replied doubtfully. "But still. I wonder." After a long moment, she snapped her attention back to me. "I don't think we should stay here. I don't have a good feeling about this room. Something feels . . . off."

The ring of a telephone cut through my thoughts.

On the bedside table was the source, a single hotel phone. The phone rang again, piercing the room's silence. Charlotte looked at me and nodded her head. I answered the phone.

There was a long crackle of static. Then the line went dead.

Next to the phone, the radio alarm clock turned on. Some kind of 1950s doo-wop song filled the room. I jumped back. This wasn't a memory. This was happening live. Some invisible force was in here with us.

I turned to scan the room and stopped to gaze at the nearby window. I hadn't noticed before, but the view through the glass was strangely flat. Outside, I could see the silhouettes of buildings in the darkness, but they had no dimensionality, almost as if they were hand drawn. I reached out to touch the window, but instead of the smooth, coolness of glass, I felt a papery, coarse surface.

The window wasn't real.

I wasn't looking at a city through glass, I was looking at a painting set inside a window frame. I tightened my fingers and slowly pushed forward against the paper. There was a tearing sound, and the paper gave way, ripping open with a gust of warm air and exposing a long corridor beyond.

The corridor was shiny and metallic, like a ventilation duct, and stretched out of sight, beyond the reach of the light from my lantern. A breeze came from the duct, the air warm and odorless. Whatever lay beyond here, whatever memory or experience, wasn't terrible. It had no scent. Wasn't saturated with the odor of rot like the others.

Charlotte watched me from the doorway.

I wasn't sure if I could bring her with me, but I didn't want to bear this burden of knowledge alone anymore. I reached out my hand to her. Tentatively she approached. "What is that?"

"It think it's a backdoor to somewhere else," I said.

"Where?"

"I'm not sure."

I climbed up through the window and into the duct. If I stayed bent over slightly, I could stand inside. I took my first step forward. The floor was solid. I held my lantern aloft. The duct continued forward, the walls clean and smooth.

"If we get separated," I said, "I will meet you back here."

Charlotte nodded. "This is crazy."

"You have no idea."

I moved slowly forward. Deeper into the duct. Behind me the hotel receded, falling farther and farther away, ultimately vanishing in a single pinpoint of light.

6

Roosevelt Island was a thin strip of land that lay in the East River between Manhattan and Queens. For years it had been known as Blackwell's Island and operated as a home for New York City's various unwanted. Over the years, the locale had hosted a prison, an almshouse, and a typhoid hospital. The island was perhaps most famous for its treatment of the insane, and several large facilities had been constructed over the years to facilitate the care and treatment of mentally disturbed patients. Unfortunately, since this had been during the late 1800s, the care and treatment had been barbaric, so much so that an exposé was written in the early 1890s by an author who had secretly posed as a patient. The book detailed the brutal treatment of the persons in the care of Blackwell's Island Lunatic Asylum and led to a period of reform.

Eventually the asylum was abandoned, though it still stood near the East River. Like most New Yorkers, Parker had forgotten the place even existed; one of the many buildings left over from a bygone era, all but lost to the passage of time. Which is why he found it strange that Selberg had wanted to meet here.

The building was a ghost.

Parker pulled in along the dirt road that circled the front of the old asylum. It was after ten p.m., a cloudy night. High above, the moon slipped in and out of cover. Parker's headlights illuminated the over-grown vegetation that curled up over the road. A stand of oaks covered in vines crowded in over the road, their greenery so dense that the ground would be shadowed even on sunny days. Scattered among the thick trunks were the castoff refuse of a city: plastic bags, a rusted shopping cart half buried in mud, a truck tire. The sweep of Parker's headlights flashed over everything before they settled on the main building.

In its day, the structure must have been glorious, but now what was left of the old asylum was a frightening wreck out of someone's nightmare. The main building was octagonal, made of solid granite blocks covered with graffiti and the ever-present choke of vines. Most of the windows were broken, jagged shards of glass jutting out like teeth from rotted wooden frames. A cupola topped the rising building, the night sky visible through a roof that looked torn apart by a giant hand. The long hospital wing was crumbling, most of the vacant windows boarded up by listing pieces of plywood. It was a sad, lonely place, a feeling made stronger by the waters of the East River glittering in the moonlight, and past that, the spread of the Manhattan skyline.

A few cars parked out front indicated the rest of the team had arrived. Parker pulled in next to Clayton's sedan and cut off the engine. Insects buzzed in the night. Clayton stepped out from the open doorway. The lantern in his hand cast his shadow, stretched and distorted, across the entire face of the old asylum.

"Cozy place to meet," Parker said.

"Lots of charm." Clayton turned and walked back through the open doorway. Parker followed. Inside, Charlotte and Selberg stood huddled near each other. A handful of lanterns were spaced along the floor, illuminating the interior lobby of the asylum. A circular staircase rose up through the central octagon, rotting bannisters slowly receding into blackness as they stretched away from the lanterns.

Parker turned toward Selberg. "Why are we meeting here?"

Selberg looked exhausted and worn, dark bruises from the beating still patterned on his face, while his lips were a chapped mess. "There's something I have to show you here. But first, the job. I can't get it done.

The problem is with the new system," Selberg said. "I can't guarantee I'll be able to get us in."

"What's the problem?"

Selberg began pacing back and forth in the abandoned lobby, the lanterns casting weird shadows of his movement across the peeling paint of the walls. "As part of prisoner processing, right before they put you into the mind machines, they wipe your memory clean of your past life. If you remember who you were before, then you know you're not really a carriage driver in 1880 New York City. There's too much cognitive dissonance. You never accept your new environment."

Parker nodded. That was how the whole system worked. But sometimes people slipped through the cracks.

"They take all your memories and download them out of your brain, put them in a storage facility. You go into the system with no memories of your past. Then when your sentence is done, they give you back your memory and you can reenter the world. But this wasn't a hundred percent foolproof," Selberg said.

"You're talking about a glitch," Charlotte said.

Selberg snapped his finger. "Exactly."

Clayton looked at each of them. He scratched the back of his head, then sighed. "I'm sorry. I'm a little new at this. What's a glitch?"

"Every once in a while, a prisoner is introduced to the system who hasn't had a full memory erase," Parker said. "So he knows he's a prisoner. He remembers. Sometimes he'll have a freakout and the guards will catch him, kill him, wipe his memory clean, and reintroduce him. Or sometimes he'll pretend. He'll live his life in the system, pretending he has no memory of his past, but knowing full well he's a prisoner."

"And you guys use this glitch to get in?" Clayton asked.

"Sort of," Parker said. "The only way we can do what we do is because we know the real world from the system and the system allows us entry without a full memory wipe. So we can enter the prison world knowing we're not really in New York City of 1880. That's what differentiates us from the prisoners."

"What about guards?"

"Guards are different," Selberg said. "They know the truth."

Clayton frowned. "So why don't you just find a guard, pay him off, and have him break out the mark? Seems a lot easier than going in ourselves."

"Because of the silver bullet," Selberg said. Clayton stared blankly at Selberg, then Selberg turned toward Parker. "Jesus Christ, didn't you tell him anything?"

"We didn't get to that yet," Parker said.

"You've got a guy going in with you and he doesn't even know what the silver bullet is?"

"Yeah, I get it," Clayton said, indicating himself with both thumbs. "This guy doesn't know anything. But can we just skip the part where you make fun of what an idiot I am and actually get to something constructive?"

"I just figured he would have told you," Selberg said. "Since it's kind of like one of the most important things that we do. But, yeah sure, I'll tell you. You know how you kill a werewolf, right?"

"Shoot it with a silver bullet," Clayton replied.

"Exactly. You can only kill a werewolf with a silver bullet. Same as in the system. You can only break someone out of the system with a silver. Well, not really a silver bullet actually, but it's a uniquely designed bullet that separates the consciousness of the target from the Sleep machine. It's the only thing that allows them to wake up."

"But wait," Clayton said. "I'm confused. I thought if you got killed in the system, you automatically woke up."

"No. That would be a terrible prison," Selberg replied. "Would never work. This is a real-life world we're talking about. A world populated by thousands and thousands of people, all living their lives. Even on a good day, someone is going to kill someone else. Murder is a fact of life. So every time there's a murder, you can't have prisoners waking up into the real world. That's not secure."

"So what happens?"

"Someone gets killed in the system by anything other than a silver, they just get recycled. Their memory gets wiped and they get put back into the system as someone else. Meaning, you're a boot maker one day, you get shot, stabbed, whatever . . . the next day you wake up and you're a bricklayer. Still in the same system. Your consciousness never separates itself from the machine. You never really wake up," Selberg said. "In order to truly awaken, you have to be killed with a specially coded bullet, what we call a silver."

"I don't understand," Clayton said.

"Everything in there is a computer system. It's not real. It's all coded by someone. Billions and billions of lines of code. When you die, the program tells the system to retain your consciousness and just regenerate it into someone else. The silver bullets are actually little computer viruses. They break up the coding. So in the system, when you shoot someone with a silver bullet, you're actually introducing a computer virus into their system. This virus disrupts the attachment of consciousness with the machine. Forcing someone to wake up in the real world. That's what makes prison breaks possible."

Selberg was right, Parker thought, the silvers were what made the breaks possible. If you got killed any other way, the guards were alerted, and your target just regenerated somewhere back in the system.

Selberg continued pacing back and forth. Just outside, the horn of a passing tugboat bellowed deeply in the night. "Now that we've got remedial prison break out of the way, let's move on. The problem with the new system is the memory erase."

"What do you mean?" Parker asked.

"The old systems, we could insert you inside with your memory. The new system, we can't do that."

"Meaning what?"

"Meaning if you remember who you are, if you know that you're actually going into a prison, the system will be alerted and won't grant you access."

"So how do we get in?" Charlotte asked.

"That's the thing. The only way in is if you don't know you're going into a prison. If you think what you're experiencing is actually real."

Parker rubbed his chin. This was what he had always been afraid of. What every person in his position feared the most. Of losing track of what was real. In his world, memory was never taken for granted. Memory was as malleable as clay. Always changing. Never constant. Part of Parker's job was letting his memory be erased. And like an old VHS tape recorded over and over again on the same ribbon, he sometimes felt his memory getting weaker. But to not know what was real. That would make him no different from a prisoner.

"So what are you saying we should do?" Parker asked.

Selberg shook his head. "From what I've heard of this system, it's good, man, like real good. I'm probably one of the best hackers in the world, but this is too much for me. We need someone else."

"Who?" Parker asked.

Selberg went silent, kicking at the dust-covered floor with the toe of his shoe. Charlotte looked at him sharply. "Nooo . . . you don't mean—"

"He's the only one good enough."

"Is he even still alive?"

"Yes. He's alive."

Parker waved his hand to get their attention. "What are we talking about?"

Charlotte turned toward Parker. "He's talking about Bobby Chan."

Parker drew a blank. The world of prison hackers was a small one, populated by anxious conspiracy theorists like Selberg. Parker had always been on the operational side, reliant on the hackers to get him into the system, but never knowing much about their world. But he knew enough to know that the good ones were like celebrities in their own little spheres of influence. "Who is Bobby Chan?"

Selberg clapped his hands. He had everyone's attention. "Bobby Black Hat Chan. The best prison hacker I've ever seen. He cut through any system like a knife through butter. He's the only guy that stands a chance to get in."

"But what's the point? Nobody has heard from him in years," Charlotte said.

Selberg held up a finger. "Ah. Exactly. And do you know why nobody has heard from him? Because three years ago he went to prison. Where he continues to be."

"What prison system?" Parker asked.

"System 1972."

Parker shook his head. "That's impossible. They shut that system down. Moved all the prisoners out."

"Yes and no," Selberg said. "The system was shut down for instability issues. But not all the prisoners were moved out. A core group of prisoners was left behind in 1972. The real troublemakers. They just locked the doors on the system and walked away. But Chan is still inside. No guards. Should be easy to get him out."

Parker had never heard of a system being abandoned with prisoners still inside. The guards preserved a sense of law and order. Without that, he wasn't sure what such a world would look like. But he could very easily imagine the chaos of a system filled with only the worst prisoners and no rules.

"Whoa, wait," Parker said. "You're telling me this guy has been in an unstable system for three years?"

"Exactly."

"Even if we find him and break him out," Parker said, "we don't know where his physical body is. We have no idea where he would wake up."

Selberg smiled, bent down, and picked up one of the lanterns. "Yes, we do. Why do you think we're meeting here?"

◆ ◆ ◆

Selberg led the way through a set of rusted double doors and down a dark corridor lined with open doorways. Parker spotted old examination rooms and laboratories, many littered with leaves and animal droppings.

"After this place was abandoned, they used it as a holding center for the bulk of the prisoners," Selberg said. "And when they shut the system down, they just left the prisoners here."

"How do you know this?" Charlotte asked.

"I tapped into the old prisoner records," Selberg said. "Found out where they were keeping him."

The hallway opened into a large open space. In another time, this had been the facility dining hall. Through an open serving window, the shadowy bulk of industrial-sized kitchen equipment was visible. A yellowed menu of items was posted on the wall behind glass. The rest of the room was open space, the floor lined with what looked like hundreds of coffin-sized boxes. A series of lights from a generator blinked red and green in the far corner of the room.

"My God, man," Clayton said, approaching one of the human-sized boxes. "What is this place?"

Parker knew exactly what this place was. Although he had never been to one before. His job had always been to go into the system. To find the subjects, and wake them into the real world. He never knew what happened to them afterward. "These are Sleep cells."

Each cell was made up of a black matte metal, like giant display cases, with a viewing pane on the top portion. Through the glass of the viewing pane, Parker could see a male face. The man's eyes were closed, the rest of his face covered by a ventilation mask. He was vacuum sealed inside a clear plastic bag, reminding Parker of freeze-dried meat.

"Who is this guy?" Clayton asked.

Selberg joined them. He inspected the face of the Sleep cell. "Don't know. These Sleep cells always have identifiers on them so you know the prisoner name and number. Someone removed these though."

"So this guy is a prisoner?" Clayton said.

Selberg nodded, waved his arm to indicate the entire floor filled with thousands of Sleep cells. "Yup. All these people. Everyone in this room. They're all prisoners. Tried and convicted of crimes and then sentenced. And now they exist together in the same system."

"But what are they doing here?" Clayton said. "I mean, this place is abandoned. No security. Anyone can just come by and open up these coffins and wake them up."

"You can't," Charlotte said. "Nobody can just wake them up like that. The cells monitor brain wave patterns, remaining locked until subjects wake up. The mind is immersed in the reality of the Sleep system so deeply that you can only wake them up from being on the inside. And as long as the person sleeps, their cells can't be opened. An ingenious security system."

Parker surveyed the rows and rows of Sleep cells. "Which one is our guy? Which one is Chan?"

"Not sure," Selberg replied. "And since they removed the identifications, we'll never know. But he's definitely here. He's one of the forgotten ones."

"These are human beings," Charlotte said. "How can they just leave them here?"

"Transfers are expensive," Selberg said. "It's not like they have visiting hours. Who's going to know the difference? Family can't complain. Most of these guys are hardcore felons. Long sentences. By the time they're due for release, most of their family will be dead or have forgotten about them. The prisoners will continue to age and eventually die in their sleep."

"So what do we do now?" Parker said.

"If you want to move forward with the job, we need Chan. He's the only hacker good enough to get into the new system. To get to Chan, we need to break him out."

"When?"

"I was thinking right now," Selberg said.

Parker laughed. Even for the easiest jobs, he generally took months to plan. Parker had to study the history of the time period, the people, the fashion, the technology, or he couldn't function. The success of any breakout was based upon being invisible. You had to be able to move seamlessly through the world. The guards were everywhere, and the more waves you created, the more mistakes you made, the easier it was for them to spot you.

Selberg read the look on Parker's face. "It's not as crazy as it sounds," Selberg said. "Think about it. The time period of the system is the early 1970s, not that far off from today. And there are no guards. Nobody is going to notice if you come crashing into the system like a meteor. You can use any techs you want and it doesn't matter. Nobody is looking to keep you out."

Parker bit his lip thoughtfully. He hadn't thought of that. No guards. He had never been in a system like that. That would make his job easier. And they really didn't have much of a choice. Selberg was conniving and untrustworthy, the proverbial snake in the grass. But he was good at what he did. And Parker could think of no reason for Selberg to lie. If they cut Chan into the deal, Selberg's share of the profits went down. So if Selberg said they needed Chan, Parker had to trust the advice.

"How would we get in?" Parker looked around the filthy room. This wasn't exactly the laboratory environment he would have preferred to work in.

"The servers for the system are right here," Selberg said. "The security is totally antiquated. I can easily hack in. Drop your consciousness right into the system. You find Chan. Bring him out. Easy."

"Why do I think that is a gross oversimplification of what's about to happen?" Parker said.

"I want to go in with you," Clayton said. "Practice run."

Parker turned to Selberg. "Is that a problem?"

Selberg shook his head. "Not really. I can get you both in."

Charlotte coughed slightly. The sort of attention-getting cough that indicated there was an issue. She had her arms folded thoughtfully, her eyes squinted with concern. "I think I should warn you. I don't know how positive it is there are no guards. I mean, for all intents and purposes, this has been a world abandoned for years now. With no law. We don't know what we're going to find. But I think there's going to be chaos and violence like we can't even imagine. Imagine *Lord of the Flies*, but on steroids."

Selberg nodded. "That is possible."

"More than possible, I think it's fairly likely," Charlotte said. "I'm not saying don't go in. But I am saying, be prepared for the absolute worst."

"Which would be?"

"Open tribal warfare. I think various groups will have aligned with each other and we'll be in a constant state of violence with each other. Rape. Murder. Torture."

"I thought you couldn't be murdered in the system?" Clayton said.

"Oh no," Charlotte replied. "You can be murdered. You just end up right back in the system. Imagine how horrific that would be. Like living a nightmare you could never escape. The constant reliving of violence over and over again would destroy most people. I think you're going to a system filled with violent psychopaths with no sense of humanity left."

"Or on a more optimistic note, you could find a peaceful commune that values art and literature," Selberg said. "There's really no way of knowing."

There was no way of knowing until Parker went in. But he tended to believe Charlotte's point of view. You take a few hundred violent recidivist felons and throw them together on an island with no rules or law long enough . . . eventually things would go bad.

"Just remember the Boy Scout motto," Charlotte said. "That's all I'm warning."

◆ ◆ ◆

Parker crashed into the system. His entire brain shook on the way in. Pain surged through him, deep into his bones as the world spun like a centrifuge. The vibration poured through his body, every cell seeming to resonate with the hum of a tuning fork until his entire being felt on the verge of breaking apart into a billion separate atoms. He screamed in brute pain, but no sound was heard in the darkness that surrounded him. And just before he blacked out and yielded to the nothingness, the pain ended.

He had arrived.

He lay flat on his back, his eyes still closed, a rumbling somewhere beneath him. Slowly, carefully, he opened his eyelids, his fists clenched, ready to fight. He appeared to be alone. He was in some kind of small transport vehicle. Above him, a metal roof, windows on all sides. The floor was rubber, with support poles that ran to the ceiling. Parker rolled over on his side and vomited.

A voice sounded in his ear. "Navigator Operator Charlotte online."

"Hi, Charlotte," Parker barely managed, his stomach slowly finding itself.

"Archive Operator Selberg online," another voice sounded. "How you doing, buddy?"

"I feel like a bag of golf balls in a blender."

"Sorry about that. The entry system was a little out of date. Bit rougher than I thought."

"Where am I?" Parker said. His strength was slowly returning, but he needed another few moments of lying down. The floor beneath him was definitely moving. And that made him worry.

"I was trying to get you onto one of the buildings on the east side. But looks like I'm showing you . . ." Selberg's voice trickled off.

"Showing me where?"

"He's on the tram," Charlotte spoke to Selberg. "That's why he's moving. Parker, you ended up on the aerial tramway that connects Roosevelt Island with Fifty-Ninth Street in Manhattan."

Parker rolled over onto his stomach, then slowly pushed himself up. Using the pole for support, he pulled himself to a standing position. The inside of the tram car was about twenty feet wide, windows on all sides. He stumbled toward the glass and looked out. He was two hundred feet above Manhattan and moving fast. On one side, the skeletal beams of the Queensborough Bridge. Empty of traffic. The pillars rusted. A half-dozen metal cages hung from the bottom of the bridge, suspended out over the water far below. Inside the cages, Parker could see men. Living men. Some lay huddled, knees pulled up to their chins. Others stood, looking out through the bars, watching as the tram passed by.

Two hundred feet below, the waters of the East River ran in swirls of current, the waves incredibly dark. Then Parker passed from water to land, the lanes of the FDR visible below him. Wrecks of cars were piled up along the median. The vehicles were empty, stripped to almost nothing. Then the view was gone as the tram swept into a valley of residential apartment towers. Even twenty stories up, a massive tower of glass and steel rose above him, reaching out of his line of vision. The tram passed within two dozen yards of the building, level with the twentieth story, allowing Parker to look in through the windows. He could see the line of apartments, all empty. A fire burned in one unit, flames engulfing the side of the building, sending plumes of smoke into the air. From a smashed window hung a giant banner made from bed sheets.

In red paint someone had written PLEASE HELP US!

Around him, farther away, other residential buildings were burned-out shells. Glass broken. Smoke blackened. Like old photographs of Berlin after World War II. It was night, and the city lay dark. Only a few pockets of light were visible across the vast Manhattan skyline. The effect was surreal.

"Looks like the city is running on generators," Charlotte said. "Power and lights for only a few."

Below him, First Avenue was empty. He gazed north. For fifty blocks, not a single car. Machine-gun fire sounded somewhere to the west. The reddish hue of a large fire painted the horizon in the vicinity of Central Park.

It was the apocalypse, and Parker was about to touch down in the middle of it.

"I need a weapon," Parker said. "Fast."

The car began its descent. Through the front glass, Parker could see the tramway station quickly approaching. The station appeared empty, two large concrete slabs with a giant conveyor wheel that wound the metal guide wire of the tram. The tram was the only thing moving, bound to attract someone's notice. And whoever it was, Parker was pretty sure it would be worse than guards.

"I'm getting you a weapon," Selberg said. "There's a furniture store on the corner of Fifty-Ninth and First Avenue. There's an office in the back of the store. I'm sending you a weapon there now."

"Got it," Parker said. In the distance, he heard the rumble of a truck engine. Two blocks north, a pickup turned the wrong way down First Avenue, tires squealing on the pavement and the engine roaring as the truck accelerated toward the tram station. Three men sat in the rear gripping onto the sides of the pickup, machine guns slung over their shoulders. "Just hope I can make it there in one piece. Got some company. Where is Clayton?"

"I'm looking for him now," Selberg said. "He hasn't made contact."

"Is he in the system?"

"Should be. But it was a rough landing for both of you," Selberg said. "I tried to synchronize your arrival together, but I don't know, I lost him somewhere."

The tram slowed as it reached the station. The pickup was only a block away and moving fast. Parker wasn't going to get out of the car in time.

"Can you open the doors of the car?" Parker said.

"One sec," Selberg replied. A moment later, the double doors slid open with a hydraulic hiss. Outside air flooded in. The ground was twenty feet below. Parker steadied himself for an instant, then pushed off hard from the opposite wall of the tram. He ran the length of the car, then launched himself into space, the movement of the car propelling him forward. The concrete platform rushed up to meet him and he slammed down hard. He rolled forward to keep his momentum and save his joints from absorbing the bone-shattering impact. He skidded to a painful stop.

Parker stood and moved quickly down a stairwell that led from the platform to the sidewalk below. He was at the edge of a small park lined with benches and burned out streetlamps. Behind, a row of storefronts stretched the block of First Avenue. Most of them were small spaces, no room to hide, nothing more than dead ends. Around the corner, he saw the familiar marquee of a movie theater, the black lettering advertising for some forgotten movie dangling from the signage at odd angles.

The weapon Selberg had sent Parker was on the opposite side of the street, toward the pickup truck. Parker would never make it. Instead, he turned and sprinted toward the theater, the only place large enough for him to hide inside. He pushed open a shattered glass door, passed by the empty ticket seller's window and entered the front lobby. The area was littered with dried leaves and trash, which had blown in over the years from the open doorway. A few yellowing movie posters lay behind dusty wall compartments. The concession glass was broken into sharp fragments, the racks beneath empty except for a handful of dead roaches.

Behind him, the pickup drove onto the curb and screeched to a halt, the men in back piling out. He could see them closely now. Their faces were covered with white and red war paint, vertical strips just beneath their eyes and down the length of their cheeks. Each carried a machine gun, belts of ammunition over their shoulders, and wore military-style camo pants and black boots laced up past the ankle. One of the men, his hair chopped into a shaggy Mohawk, wore a torn white T-shirt clearly stained with blood.

Parker had no idea who these guys were, but he had no intention of any further introductions to the tenants of this system. Charlotte had been right.

"I need a weapon, fast," Parker said as he moved away from the door. "I'm in some kind of movie theater, just off First Avenue."

"The Apple Cineplex," Charlotte said. "Do we have any drops there?"

"Checking now," Selberg said. "Hang on."

Several long hallways branched off from the main atrium toward each of the individual screens. Parker chose one at random, running down the length of the hall and through a door into the blackness of a theater. He found utter darkness. The air was hot and stank of mildew. He could sense the rows of chairs sitting vacant around him, waiting for patrons who would never come.

Parker heard the distinct shuffle of feet against carpet. The sound was somewhere ahead of him. Something moving in the theater. Something in here with him. He lowered himself to the ground, his fists clenching together. Outside, somewhere in the hallway, he heard the low murmur of voices of the men.

In the blackness, a sudden light flared up, bursting with such intensity it temporarily blinded Parker. There was a rush of movement. Something brushed past him and headed for the door. Parker knuckled his eyes, trying to rub out the flares of white light that still floated in his retinas. He heard the theater door slam open, then running feet.

A moment later, a woman screamed.

Blinking away the last of the floating light from his eyes, Parker moved quickly and quietly to the doorway of the theater. Cautiously, he peered out into the hall. About thirty yards away, the men from the truck had cornered a woman. She must have been hiding in the theater and Parker had scared her outside, right into that group of psychos. She was wearing filthy, oversized chinos and a gray T-shirt a size too small. The men each held lanterns and had spread out forming a line, like the open mouth of a net moving toward a cornered fish.

"You been hiding in here this whole time?" the Mohawk asked. "Pretty thing like you?"

The woman backed slowly away from him. "Please, don't."

"We been looking for a little fuck toy like you," Mohawk said. "Gets real lonely out there. Getting tired of those lady boys we got chained up under the bridge. Could use some real, genuine pussy."

The woman moved to run back toward Parker and the theater. She made a half-step before one of the men knocked out her leg. She fell face first, her nose shattering on the ground, blood pouring onto the carpet. She grunted in pain, her hand going to her face. She rolled over on her side and curled into a ball. Mohawk put the lantern and his machine gun on the ground and advanced, his hand unbuckling his belt.

The woman saw him coming and whimpered, sliding away on the floor, her hand going up protectively.

"How are we coming with that weapon?" Parker whispered. "Got a situation here."

"Got a gun for you," Selberg said. "Revolver, hidden inside the cash register at the concession stand."

The cash register was on the other side of the men.

That gun might as well have been in New Jersey, because there was no way Parker would make it past them without getting killed. He might have had a chance against the four in unarmed combat, but they all had machine guns. It would be like jumping into a wood chipper.

Mohawk kicked the woman hard in the stomach. She gasped with the violence of the blow and cried out. He turned back to one of the other men. "Check the theater she came out of. See if she's got any friends who can join the party."

One man nodded, reluctantly turned away from the woman on the ground, and began to walk toward Parker's position. He was a big man, heavy in the chest and arms, with a thick beard and long hair tucked beneath a baseball cap. He held a lantern in his left hand, the machine gun in his right. That gave Parker a slight advantage. In a fight, the man couldn't fire as accurately with just one hand. He would have to pause to drop the lantern. That might give Parker an extra second. With a combination of surprise and luck, he might have a chance.

Parker retreated into the shadows of the theater. He felt along a section of seats, crouched down between the rows, and waited.

The theater door opened and a beam of light scattered away the darkness. The bearded man moved sloppily. His size and his gun made him overconfident, and he walked without fear. He held the lantern over his head and scanned the rows of seats. He walked toward the front of the theater, giving his back to Parker. Parker crept out from behind the seats, moved quickly toward the man, and wrapped a forearm around his neck. Parker pulled tight, instantly cutting off the man's air. With his free hand, Parker gripped the machine gun, holding it in place. The man lurched backward, throwing Parker off-balance. Their two bodies fell to the ground. Parker wrapped his legs around the stranger, keeping him controlled, as he pulled the choke even tighter. The lantern crashed to the floor, the glass breaking.

A human can go without oxygen for a frighteningly short period of time, especially under stress. And quickly, he felt his prey go limp. Parker kept applying pressure until Charlotte said quietly, "He's done."

Parker rolled the dead man off him, then reached for the machine gun on the floor. It was an old style British Sten, short and stubby with a long magazine column stretching horizontally from the side. Most of the weapons in the system were smuggled in from the outside. Parker held the Sten at waist level and slowly moved from the theater. In the hall, a man laughed and cheered.

The woman screamed.

Carefully, Parker peeked around the corner. The woman lay on her back, crab like, her legs and arms in the air, desperately kicking at the three men who circled her like jackals after meat. One of the men feinted, sidestepped a kick, then grabbed the collar of the woman's shirt. He pulled down hard and the shirt ripped. The woman swung her body like a pendulum and swept her leg along the ground. She caught the man in the back of the knee, his leg buckled, and he dropped to the ground. Immediately she pulled herself upright and elbowed the man hard in the face. There was an audible clunk of bone on bone and the man's nose collapsed.

The man cursed and fell backward. In an instant the woman was up on her feet, carefully moving, she surprised Parker as her hands came up in a boxer's stance. The fun was over. The men's smiles were gone, their expressions stone. They weren't playing around anymore. The guys were going to beat her and then rape her.

"No guards to worry about here," Charlotte said. "If you're going to do it, take them all out and be done with it. Don't hesitate."

Parker stepped from around the corner into the hall.

The men had their backs turned to him, but the woman glimpsed the movement. Parker's appearance startled her, and she turned her attention from Mohawk and his friends and stared wide-eyed at Parker. Mohawk saw her reaction and paused, then slowly followed the line of her eyes, turning around and spotting Parker.

"How you doing?" Parker said politely. "Am I interrupting?"

Mohawk recovered his composure. He didn't move or flinch. His hands stayed down, inches from the Sten slung over his shoulder. "How you doing, friend? Passing through?"

"Well, that depends. I'm looking for someone."

"Who's that?"

"Name on the outside is Bobby Chan," Parker said. "Not sure what he goes by here."

Mohawk licked his lips. The fingers of his shooting hand moved slowly, like the tentacles of a sea anemone caught in an ocean current. His friends slowly moved apart from each other. Parker could still catch them all in one sweep of the machine gun, but they were trying to flank him.

"Name is familiar," Mohawk said. "Let me think."

"Don't think too long. My trigger finger has a short timer when it comes to bullshit."

Mohawk actually managed a smile. "You really think you can get all three of us in time? You picked the wrong fight."

"What's it matter to you? I'll kill you first. So I don't expect you'll much care after that."

"You must be new here," Mohawk said. "You think you can kill me?"

Parker was so focused on Mohawk, he barely registered the woman. In a flash, she sprang forward, grabbed the nearest soldier by the neck, buried a knee in his back, and flipped him backward to the ground. She tore the machine gun from his shoulder, buried her foot in his neck, and spun toward Mohawk. She fired once, accurately, putting a single bullet in the man's leg. Mohawk grunted in pain and fell to a knee. Forced into action, Parker turned and opened up with the Sten on the third man. The machine gun bucked wildly in his hands, a spray of bullets tearing the man open.

The woman dug the heel of her boot once more into the neck of the man on the ground, then shot him in the head.

"Jesus," Selberg said. "I like this girl."

Parker turned the Sten toward Mohawk, ready to finish it. Mohawk faced him, eyes narrow, ready to die. Blood seeped through his pant leg, forming a pool on the ground. Parker's finger tightened on the trigger.

"No!" the order came from the woman. "Don't kill him. That's what he wants."

She came up behind Mohawk, yanked the machine gun from his shoulder, then kneed him hard in his bullet wound. Mohawk grunted in pain. She grabbed a handful of his hair, then pulled him backward, almost lifting him off his feet, and dragged him across the hall to a thick metal bannister. He reached up to push her away and she brought the butt end of her rifle down on his face. His cheek split open instantly, blood pouring out. Ignoring the injury, she bent down and expertly tossed him. From the pocket of his cargo pants, she pulled a set of handcuffs.

She held them up. "You going to use these on me?"

"Fuck you."

She struck him another blow with the butt of the Sten, then with the handcuffs, she chained the man's wrist to the bannister. Mohawk had a machete strapped to his back. She pulled the weapon from him, turned toward Mohawk's dead partner, raised the blade up over her head and brought it down on the dead man's neck. She did this again with each of the dead. Mohawk watched her, his face registering no surprise.

"I'm going to go outside, and I'm going to set my friends free from those cages," she said. "And I'm going to tell them you're in here. They're going to set to work on you with metal shears. Cut you up into so many little pieces they'll be able to use you as parade confetti."

"They kill me, I'm going to come back for you," Mohawk said. His voice sounded tough, but Parker could see fear in those eyes.

Parker checked his watch. He was on a tight schedule and wanted to spend as little time as possible in this terrible world. Whatever happened here was none of his business. He turned away and began to walk back down the hall.

"Hey," the woman called out. Parker kept walking. He wasn't here to make friends. Just get in and get out. Focus on the job. "You're from the outside, aren't you?"

Parker kept walking.

"I know where he is," she called out to him.

Parker stopped. He turned back toward the woman.

"The guy you're looking for," she said. "I know him. I can take you to him."

"Where is he?"

The woman laughed and stood. "Nothing is free."

"What do you want?"

"I asked you before, you're from the outside?"

Parker was curious about how much these people know about their reality. Most prisoners in these systems had no idea. But something seemed different here. Something was off. "What do you mean, outside?"

"From somewhere other than here," she said. "This place."

Parker shook his head. "I don't do deals with unknowns."

"You won't last a minute out there without me."

"Last I checked, I saved you."

"But what you don't know is that we have about four minutes before those guys you killed, they come back here looking for us." The woman smiled. "And I think you don't have a clue how this world works or how to deal with that."

"She's probably right," Selberg said. "This is a totally unknown system."

Parker sighed. "So what do you want?"

The woman checked her watch. "We can discuss my terms on the move. But right now, we need to get out of here."

They left Mohawk chained to the pole and headed back onto the street. The pickup was parked up on the curb. It was a battered and rusted-out old truck, with metal grates over the windows and machine-gun ports in the doors. A human skull served as a hood ornament. The woman went to the truck, popped open the door, and looked inside.

"Keys are here," she said. "Let's roll."

"Why would they leave the keys in the ignition?"

"Because everyone knows who owns it."

The woman sat behind the wheel, and the big truck rumbled to life. She revved the engine, which emitted a massive resonant sound. An engine way too big for this to be stock. Someone had built this truck from scratch; a vehicle modified for war.

Parker joined the woman inside.

"My name's Blake," she said.

Parker slammed shut the passenger door without responding.

"Okay, then," Blake said. She gunned the engine and powered off the curb back onto First Avenue. She headed toward the Fifty-Ninth Street Bridge. The two-level, cantilever structure stretched out over the dirty green waters of the river, spanning Roosevelt Island, before vanishing into a wall of fog that seemed to engulf the entire eastern edge of the island.

They smashed through a series of blue NYPD wooden barriers that formed a semicircle around the base of the bridge. The bridge itself rose above them, beginning in a series of stone archways that pushed the roadway higher and higher as it headed out across the river. Fixed into the side of the stone was a winch, a thick cable wire pulled taut, that bore the weight of cages holding people suspended off the side of the bridge a hundred feet above them.

"Who are they?" Parker said as they pulled up along the winch.

"My friends," Blake said. "The people I was with. They have to keep them alive."

"Why?"

Blake got out of the truck and went to the winch. "Because whoever you kill just comes back." She pushed a button on the winch, and with a grinding of gears, the cable wire began to unroll as the cages slowly lowered to the ground. "So your true enemies, you never kill."

"Why don't they kill themselves?"

"With what?" Blake said. "And if one of them does manage to die, his friends will be tortured even more for it."

Parker watched from the truck as the four cages, all of them containing men, reached street level. Blake pulled open each door with a shriek of metal. The men inside look like starved dogs, bones protruding, ribcages standing out like ventilation covers beneath tattered shirts. Their faces were covered in bruises and cuts. One of them stumbled forward and collapsed to the ground. Blake helped the man up, then pointed to the cinema. Parker couldn't hear her words, but he was sure she was telling them about Mohawk still chained up inside. The men's eyes went hard and narrow as railroad spikes. They shuffled off painfully, like zombies, lurching across the avenue toward the desolate movie theater.

Blake got back in the truck, and she and Parker headed north.

"What's going to happen?" he asked.

"Same thing that always happens when the group getting tortured captures their torturer."

They drove up First Avenue, the bridge receding behind them in the side view mirror. The street was empty, but Parker glimpsed occasional movement inside some of the buildings. He had the sense that people were everywhere.

Every building was a wreck. Some had plywood put up over windows with various cryptic messages scrawled graffiti style over the front. *No Food Here.*

Beware the Passage of Days.

Revenants Inside.

The sidewalks were littered with broken glass and trash, surrounded by an unearthly quiet. Beyond the low rumble of their own truck engine, Parker could hear nothing. Manhattan, the loudest, busiest city on Earth, had gone completely quiet. And it wasn't a peaceful quiet. It was the quiet brought about by fire. The quiet of someone hiding beneath the bed from a burglar. Whoever lived here was afraid.

"Why did you cut the heads off those men?" Parker asked.

"To keep them from coming back."

"Coming back?"

"When you kill someone, their . . ." She paused, trying to find the right word. "Spirit. Comes back. In a new body. They are the same person, more or less. But the body they left behind, their dead body, comes back to life too. But there's no consciousness in it. No soul. No thought. It just wanders. We call them revenants."

"Are they dangerous?"

"They're the most dangerous things out here. Violent. Unpredictable. They're all trying to find a consciousness. So any humans they see, they attack."

"And chopping the head off keeps them from coming back?"

"Yup."

"Lovely."

Blake pulled the truck over on the corner of First Avenue and Eighty-Second Street. She dropped the gearshift into Park, then shut off the ignition. The rumble died out. The silence of the street was overpowering. What she said about the revenants made sense. The bodies must be AI, but since nobody was running the system, they operated without guidance.

"We got a read on Clayton." Selberg's voice sparked suddenly in Parker's ear. "He's coming into the system on a Metro-North Railroad train arriving at Grand Central in twenty minutes."

Parker didn't reply. He and Blake sat in front of a grocery store. Through the empty glass panes of the front windows, Parker could see overturned racks. Under one of the racks, a pair of legs. Someone dead beneath, like a dog, crawling beneath a porch to die.

"What are we doing here?" Parker said.

"We?" Blake said. "You're getting out and walking. There is no we."

"Walking where?"

"I don't really care. But I don't have time to spend babysitting you anymore for free. I need a guarantee."

"What guarantee?"

She turned and looked at him for the first time. Her face was hard lines and sharp edges, her nose busted from the earlier fall. She was a woman who had seen bad times and knew they were only getting worse. But her eyes were a soft green. Like a field just after dawn. "That you get me out of here," Blake said.

"How do you even know I can? Or what's even out there?"

She looked away from him, her big, green eyes growing distant as she stared up the length of the avenue. On the horizon, the wrecks of cars had been piled up in front of the lobby of an apartment building. The vehicles formed a makeshift pillbox. On the opposite side, a fixed machine gun was mounted into the ground. A man smoked a cigarette, his hand casually resting on the barrel. Above him, the apartment building rose about twenty stories. Parker could see the first real signs of human habitation. Clothes hung out to dry along the railing of a balcony. Cook smoke wafted from one of the windows. A shirtless man sat on a plastic beach chair on another balcony reading a book, a sniper rifle slung over his shoulder.

"They call these places Peace Colonies," Blake said. "After the guards left and things began to fall apart, the good people barricaded themselves in these towers. They created their own defense systems. Working together, they formed a little ecosystem of protection against the rovers."

"Who are the rovers?"

"The rovers are the gangs that run the streets. Thousands of them out there. Like our friend with the Mohawk back at the theater. They take what they want. Rape. Torture. Doesn't matter to them. They have no law. Only the law of the gun."

"Why did you leave the Peace Colonies?"

"Rovers grabbed some of my friends," Blake said. "I've been searching for them."

Parker reached over and turned the ignition back on. The engine rumbled to life. "Keep driving. Let's talk."

Blake put the vehicle into gear and they continued west down Eighty-Second Street, the small quiet brownstones all gutted and blackened by smoke.

"You remember when the guards left?" Parker said.

Blake nodded, navigating around a torn-up section of the road. "This place wasn't so bad before. There were peacekeepers here."

"When did they leave?"

"About two years ago," Blake said. "It was like, we all woke up one day and ten percent of the people were just . . . gone. Not too long after that, the chaos started. But I remember, every once in a while, someone would show up. From the outside. They would come for one of us. And just vanish."

"What do you think the outside is?"

"Someplace that's not here," Blake said. "I know there's something going on here. Something that doesn't make sense. Like, how can you kill a person, then they keep coming back. How is that possible? And why has nobody ever left Manhattan? I mean, when the peacekeepers were here, we all believed that this island was all there was in the world. But why have bridges? You know, if you walk out on a bridge here, you come to the fog. You've seen it, that fog that surrounds the whole island."

"I've seen it."

"You walk into the fog, you just come right back to the beginning of the bridge again. I mean logically, why have a bridge that doesn't go anywhere?" Blake said. "So there's got to be somewhere else, other than here."

They were quickly approaching Central Park. Blake accelerated, then braked hard, their truck lurching up over the curb at the wall of the park. Only the park wasn't there anymore. Instead, Parker saw a vast open space of dirt that yawned out toward the reservoir. The Metropolitan Museum of Art had been burned to rubble. And along the open space, uneven rows of wooden grave markers stretched forth into the thousands. Central Park had been turned into a cemetery.

"This is what the last two years have been like. One big graveyard. Everyone who has been killed, they keep coming back, but the bodies pile up. Sever their heads and bury them so they don't turn to revenant," Blake said. "I find your man for you, you get me out of here."

Selberg's voice crackled again in Parker's ear. "Got a lot of movement at Grand Central. Clayton is headed for a hornet's nest."

An old man with a salt-and-pepper beard walked along the edge of the cemetery. A massive pit bull on a length of chain wrapped around the man's hand walked with him. The dog must have been a leftover from when the system had been live, like the horses in the 1890 system.

"You do what I say," Parker said to Blake, "I'll get you out."

"How?"

"It doesn't matter. But I will. I promise."

Crossing over from Eighty-Second Street, another man dressed in rags pushed a shopping cart filled with lengths of metal pipe. He walked slowly toward them. One of the wheels of the cart spun mindlessly. Blake looked uncertain. Her fingers drummed against the edge of the steering wheel.

"Blake," Parker said, "we don't have a lot of time here. So you need to make a decision right now, or I need to get out and find another way. I have to get to Grand Central."

"What's your name?"

"My name is Parker."

Blake's hand tightened on the wheel. She put the truck into gear. "Well, Parker, hang on. You see that guy with the pit bull? And the other guy with the shopping cart?"

"Yes."

Keeping one hand on the wheel, Blake slowly raised the Sten. "See how they're coming up on both sides of the truck?"

"Yes."

"That's a sign that it's time for us to go."

Shopping-cart man stopped walking in the middle of the street about thirty yards ahead of them. He moved slowly toward the front of the cart and began rummaging among the pipes. Parker gripped his own machine gun, bringing the barrel up to just below the level of the window. The man with the cart spun around fast. In his hand he held a bolt-action rifle. He fired once from waist level, the bullet shattering the windshield. Parker felt the impact just inches to the left of his head, the frame of the truck vibrating as the bullet tore into the cab.

Blake put the truck into reverse and pumped the pedal to the floor. The truck lurched backward. Along the cemetery, the other man bent down and released a clip on the pit bull's collar and shouted something in the dog's ear. The muscular beast tore away from its owner, streaking across the front of the truck, closing the distance on the vehicle. Blake braked hard and spun the wheel. The truck skidded and swung in a half circle, Central Park sliding wildly past the windshield until they faced south. She put the truck into Drive and slammed down the accelerator again. The vehicle shuddered, then tires caught on concrete with a squeal of rubber and the duo jolted forward. On Parker's side, the pit bull caught up with them, legs pumping, mouth hanging open. The animal launched itself up through Parker's open window, its compact body slamming into his shoulder.

The pit bull was in the small cab with them, eighty pounds of muscle and teeth snapping and twisting. Its jaws snapped shut on Parker's forearm, incredible pressure and pain charging through the length of his arm. The dog's head twisted and snapped back and forth, the teeth digging through leather and flesh. With his free hand, Parker reached for his weapon. An instant later, the cabin exploded with the ear shattering crack of Blake's machine gun. She fired with one hand, the bullets striking the dog's body. There was a yelp of pain and Parker felt the pressure subside, like the easing off of a steam valve.

"Oh man," Blake said. "I hate shooting dogs."

The dog's dead weight was heavy in Parker's lap. The truck was traveling fast down Fifth Avenue. Parker pushed the animal out the window of the truck and it disappeared from view. He tore off his jacket and inspected his arm. The skin was dark red, already bruising from the crushing force of the jaws, but the leather had kept the dog's teeth from tearing skin. Parker felt a wave of nausea rise from his stomach to his mouth.

"You okay?" Blake asked.

"Ask me in five minutes."

"Welcome to my world," she said. "Sucks here."

Parker put his jacket on and rubbed the length of his arm. They sped past St. Patrick's Cathedral. Graffiti scrawled across the front read "There is no God here."

That was the truth.

"What's at Grand Central?" Blake asked.

"My partner is coming in."

"Grand Central is filled with rovers," Blake said. "So I hope your friend is worth it."

Blake turned off the avenue and headed east down Forty-Second Street. Parker had never worked with anyone on the inside before. And definitely not a prisoner. But this place was different. He had never seen a system this violent.

"We're going to have to go in fast," Blake said. "Snatch up your man before the rovers even know we're there. But that's not the worst of it."

"What do you mean?"

"This guy you're looking for," Blake said. "He's holed up in the Waldorf Astoria hotel."

"Sounds classy."

"Not exactly," Blake said. "That place is like ground zero for revenants. The entire building is crawling with them. Your guy is basically trapped there."

"Do you know where?"

"I heard he's got a top floor penthouse. Not sure though. Either way, we're going to have to fight a lot of revenants to get to him. And they don't go down easy. So I hope your friend we're meeting is good in a fight."

"Sam? Oh yeah, he's the best."

Grand Central approached rapidly, the large granite structure blackened by smoke and ominously quiet. They screeched to a stop beneath the Park Avenue viaduct and Blake was out of the truck in an instant, moving rapidly toward the main glass doors. Parker followed and they entered the central walkway, which led toward the main concourse.

Even in this awful place, Grand Central was still the most glorious station Parker had ever seen. It was the one constant in nearly all the systems he had broken into. The timeless anchor in a city of change. Someone must have hooked up the station to generators, because overhead, the chandeliers cast a pinkish hue off the Tennessee marble that layered every surface. Abandoned shops were spaced at intervals along the Vanderbilt Hall before the space expanded into the giant main concourse.

Above them, the domed ceiling soared, covered in the pattern of constellations on aqua-colored plaster. Light streamed in through three arched windows the size of small buildings that lined the far wall, while the iconic four-faced clock stood in watch over the main information booth; each clock frozen at 9:15. The familiarity of the concourse comforted Parker, but its emptiness made him uneasy. There was little cover here, the perfect place to be trapped.

"Track 19," Selberg said. "Coming in now."

Parker turned and scanned the arches for the correct track. Over the ticket windows, the arrival board suddenly came to life, the black and white tiles fluttering like shuffled playing cards.

"This way," Parker called out. "Track 19."

The platform was empty. The rails were already beginning to hum, and in the distance, farther up the line, they saw the slowly increasing brightness of train headlights approaching. Blake took up a position behind a support column, her Sten trained out toward the main concourse.

"Get your friend and let's go," Blake said. "By now the rovers know we're here and they'll be coming for us. And don't let yourself get taken alive."

"What do you mean?"

"Unless you want to spend the next five lifetimes in a cage, if things don't go your way, make sure the last bullet in that machine gun is for you."

"What happens if I get killed?"

"We call it getting recycled. You'll wake up somewhere else in the city. Could be anywhere."

The train chuffed its way along the platform. A silver locomotive, blue stripe along the side, with Metro-North printed in white painted letters. Behind it, eight passenger cars.

The cars rolled to a stop and the doors opened automatically. No sign of Clayton. Parker entered the first train and found rows of empty seats. He moved quickly through a handful of cars before finding his partner. Clayton had kept his original form. Sometimes it was difficult getting into these systems and they had to jump into other bodies. But security here was easier to break so both Parker and Clayton could be hacked in as themselves.

Clayton wore a business suit, seated in the back of an empty car, his head slumped over onto his chest. His eyes were half closed, thin strips of white visible beneath his lashes. His body was limp, the only movement coming from his thumb and forefinger as they tapped a random pattern against each other.

"I'm showing a lot of activity headed your way," Selberg said.

Parker bent down over Clayton, took his shoulders, and shook him hard. He was lifeless. "What's going on with him?"

"I'm working on getting him synced. He's a first-timer. It's taking longer."

Out on the platform, Blake's voice called out. "Hurry up in there. We're about to have company."

Parker checked Clayton's pulse, feeling nothing. He shook him again, then stepped back to the open doorway and looked out along the platform. Blake hid behind the support column, machine gun at her side. Beyond her, a dozen armed men moved quietly along the length of the main concourse. They wore a rough assortment of civilian clothes. Some in jeans, some in cargo pants. Most were in filthy T-shirts. Each carried at least one rifle.

They looked like trained civilian militia, serious and cruel, but they didn't know where Parker and Blake were. They walked in a line across the concourse, headed for the ticket windows. Eventually they would begin to check each platform. And Parker and Blake would be trapped.

Parker shook Clayton again. "Come on, buddy. Wake up."

"Almost got it," Selberg said. "There!"

Clayton's eyes flew open and he gasped for breath. His hands came up to his chest and he looked around wildly. He jumped up from the seat, then fell backward, grabbing the wall with his hand to steady himself.

"Be calm. Be calm, Sam," Parker said.

Clayton rubbed his eyes, blinked, then looked around. He focused on Parker. "Wow, that's intense."

"You okay?"

"Yeah. I think."

"Good, because we have to move out of here. Fast," Parker said. "Can you run?"

Clayton nodded and they moved quickly out of the train and onto the platform. Blake eyed them as they approached. Clayton was unsteady, but he could manage well enough. And the sync would improve over time.

"Sam, this is Blake," Parker said. "Vice versa."

Blake and Clayton nodded at each other, then Blake turned back toward the concourse. "I think we've got about a dozen rovers in there now. All armed. Probably more outside."

"We've got to get to the Waldorf Astoria," Parker said to Charlotte. "Can you find us a route?"

"You could try the Waldorf Astoria line," Charlotte said.

"The what?"

"It's in the other systems. During the 1930s, a secret railway line was built connecting Grand Central Terminal with the Waldorf Astoria. You should be able to use that tunnel to get to the Waldorf."

"Is it in this system?"

"I don't know," Charlotte said. "But probably."

"Probably. Great," Parker said. On the concourse, the rovers moved to the row of ticket windows. They were going to start checking each of the platforms. The secret railway sounded like a long shot, but Parker would have to take the chance. "All right, tell me where."

"Across the concourse, go down the platform for Track 9," Selberg said.

Parker turned to Blake and Clayton. "You ready?"

Clayton nodded. His face still looked pale. He hadn't adjusted yet to being in this world. The trio moved in a crouch-walk along the edge of the platform. When they reached the edge of the concourse, Parker held up a hand, keeping them out of sight. The rovers had moved off onto an adjoining platform, leaving the main floor free. Quickly, Parker and his team sprinted out onto the concourse and headed for Track 9.

As they reached the central information booth, a man shouted behind them. Then, the loud crack of gunfire. The trio took cover behind the booth. The rovers were running toward them from the opposite platform. Parker pulled the trigger on the Sten, the weapon spraying metal across the concourse. Chips of pink marble shattered off the far wall and the rovers scattered for cover.

"Poor old building," Parker said. "I'm sorry, Grand Central."

Parker fired another burst from the Sten, then headed toward the Track 9 platform, Blake following close behind and Clayton in the rear. The platform was the single depressing concrete slab that stretched out like a pier for almost a hundred yards. Railroad tracks ran below ground in long parallel lines that vanished into the tunnel.

"There should be two sets of tracks," Selberg said. "Jump down onto the track bed on your right, follow it for thirty yards, then you should see a door."

Parker took the lead and landed with a thud on the gravel-covered rail bed.

"You sure you know what you're doing?" Blake said. "This looks like a dead end to me."

"We'll find out."

"Your confidence is not inspiring."

Ahead was a metal door set into the concrete wall of the tunnel. It looked little-used, traces of rust visible over the front, with graffiti covering the face. Parker reached the door and pushed hard with his shoulder. It swung open with a shriek of metal and a puff of stagnant air. Inside, concrete stairs led down into blackness.

From her pocket, Blake handed Parker a long-tube, metal flashlight. Parker turned on the light and swung the beam down the stairwell. A strange glimmer flickered back from below. Parker moved down to get a closer look.

"Oh no," Parker said.

Blake and Clayton stood at the top of the stairs. "What is it?"

"Selberg, we've got a problem here," Parker said. "The stairwell is totally flooded out."

Parker passed the light once more across the bottom of the stairs. Below him dark water filled the stairwell, reaching the level of the roof and completely blocking the passageway.

"I heard you," Selberg said. "Stand by one second."

Parker turned toward Blake and Clayton. "How we doing up there?"

Blake shouldered her Sten and fired a burst up the tunnel. "Not good."

Clayton joined Parker on the stairs. "What's the problem, buddy?"

"Whole tunnel is flooded out," Parker said. The water lapped on the stairs just below their feet.

"All right, listen," Selberg said. "That tunnel is about twenty yards long, then there are stairs leading to another track at your elevation. If you can make it twenty yards, the water should clear when you hit the other stairs."

"Should?"

"I don't know," Selberg said.

Parker sighed. Above them he heard the static burst of gunfire. Blake came hurtling down the stairs, chips of concrete flashing off the tunnel wall behind her. "We've got company coming. Fast. Tell me you found something." Blake saw the flooded tunnel and stopped abruptly. "What is that?"

"It's supposed to be clear in twenty yards. Can you swim?"

"I can swim," she said. "But if it's still flooded, we're going to drown down there."

"Nobody is going to drown," Parker said. "We'll make it."

"Not like we have a lot of choice," said Clayton.

Parker studied the surface of the water. If they stayed, they would die. But what did that mean here?

"What if they kill us?" Parker said. "We just get recycled. We'll just end up somewhere else."

"Yeah," Blake said reluctantly. "There's something I didn't tell you about that."

"What?"

"You do get recycled, and you do come back. But there's only a handful of return points in the city. And they always have rovers there waiting. They'll grab you the moment you come back."

"Then what happens?" Clayton asked.

"They'll throw you in a cage and torture you in unimaginable ways."

Clayton nodded and bent down to take off his shoes. "Looks like we're swimming."

"Fuck, man." Blake slid the strap of her weapon off her shoulder. "Why did I even get mixed up in this?"

"All right, everybody, be calm," Parker said. "This is all going to be fine. We'll just swim and I will see you all on the other side."

Parker studied the surface of the water, as black as oil. He took a last look at the light in the tunnel above, pulled in a deep breath and dove into the water.

The cold hit him immediately.

The flashlight in his hand flickered out. And then it was absolutely pitch black. He wanted to move forward as cautiously as possible, one hand in front of his face, like a newly blind man walking through a room. But already he could feel the slow burn in his lungs from the lack of oxygen. He abandoned all restraint and kicked out his legs hard to propel himself forward. Anything could be down here. He thought of the revenant Blake had described. Living but not living. Waiting, reaching out to grab his leg with one of their cold, rotted hands and pulling him down into the darkness.

He swam faster, using both his arms now, trying to pull himself forward. Twenty yards was nothing. He could walk twenty yards in a few seconds. But here, under water, his legs and lungs already burning, that twenty yards felt like eternity. And what if Selberg had been wrong? He was outside the system, hacked in. That was an imperfect science. What he thought might be twenty yards could really be fifty. A hundred yards.

His lungs were burning now. Behind him, he heard three distant cracks. The sound was muted through the water, but he knew they were gunshots. Parker kept moving, yearning to breathe, his eyes squeezed shut. His fingers reached out and he felt the hard corner of a concrete stair.

He pushed up with his legs and his head broke the surface of the water. The air was heavy with the staleness of many years, but he breathed it in deeply, the oxygen filling his lungs and pushing away the pain. He was still in complete darkness but he slowly felt his way forward and pulled himself up the stairs.

An instant later, he heard someone else break the surface of the water.

"Who's there?"

"Blake," she said. "You friend is coming behind me. He was holding off the rovers. That guy can shoot, man."

Parker heard her swim forward and reach the stairs next to him.

"Selberg," Parker said, "can you read me?"

"Who is that you keep talking to?" Blake asked.

"A friend," Parker said, not sure how to explain the system. "It's complicated."

"Okay."

There was a burst of static, then Selberg's voice came online. "You made it. Congratulations."

"It's a little dark here. Any way you could get us some light?"

An instance of silence. Then a flicker of feeble light. A string of bare bulbs hung along the wall above them. Parker watched as the filaments inside slowly began to glow, gaining in brightness and pushing away the dark.

"Found some old construction lighting," Selberg said quickly. "I had to reroute the power to the tunnel. You should be operational for a while."

A stream of bubbles broke up from the water, followed by Clayton's head. He gasped and choked, his hair slick against his forehead. Blood streamed down the side of his neck.

"These guys are coming right behind me," Clayton said as he hauled himself out of the water. "We've got to move."

Together they ran up the stairs and onto the track bed of another railway line. This line had no platform, only a narrow tunnel that stopped abruptly with a brick wall at one end, extending into the dark mouth of the tunnel toward the other. The train, constructed of dark gray metal plates with a series of small windows high on its walls, looked more like an armored troop carrier than a passenger vehicle.

"That was the personal train for FDR," Selberg said. "When he traveled to New York City from Washington, he'd go directly to the Waldorf Astoria. The tracks run right below the hotel. It's about a quarter mile jog."

"What, we can't get the train?" Clayton said.

"Stop being lazy. This system was engineered to age naturally. Nobody expected it to be abandoned for this long. Those train wheels are rusted solid."

Behind them, they heard a splashing. One of the rovers had broken the surface of the water in the tunnel. Together, the trio took off at a quick jog along the railway line, then around the abandoned train. The tracks offered no cover at all, which meant the rovers would have clean shots. Parker and his team had to put some distance between their position and the tunnel entrance.

Parker's feet pounded over the gravel of the bed. Behind him came the sound of voices, then a long, low whistle. He ventured a look back and saw three flashlights bobbing in movement up the track.

"They're coming," Parker said.

Clayton was huffing alongside them. He was a big man and ran with slow steady strides. Blake moved faster. She was long and lean and carried herself almost effortlessly. Ahead of them, Parker saw a fully illuminated train platform. They were making time but still had a hundred yards to go. The rovers were catching up fast. Parker knew his team wasn't going to make it. They had to make a stand now.

He turned quickly, his hand tightening on the Sten. He only hoped the water hadn't damaged the weapon's firepower. His finger tightened on the trigger, then he froze in surprise. The flashlights were moving away from them. The rovers were retreating back down the tunnel.

"They're going away," Parker said. "They had us . . . and they're pulling back. Why would they do that?"

"Because they know about the hotel. Everyone does," Blake said. "It's just one of those places you don't go."

"Why not?" Clayton asked.

"Because of the revenants. This place is infested with them. Imagine a beehive colony. That's what the Waldorf Astoria is like."

They slowed to a walk as they approached the hotel platform, another stretch of concrete with several well-oiled industrial-looking machines with gears and large crank shafts. Several sets of lamps were affixed to the wall, each electrically lit and filling the space with an uneven glow.

"Selberg, you've got the power on here?" Parker said.

"Nope. Not me. For some reason I'm actually having trouble accessing your location. It's blocked for some reason. I'm working to find a way around it."

"Your guy has generators hooked up everywhere," Blake said. "That's how he keeps the place running."

"And he's here by himself?"

"As far as I know," Blake said. "The guy is like this total recluse weirdo."

Parker pulled himself up onto the oil-spotted platform. The trio boarded a cargo elevator large enough to transport a car. Inside were two black buttons, one with an up arrow, the other with a down. Parker pushed the up button and two metal doors slid shut. The elevator groaned and with the heavy crank of gears, they began their ascent.

"How long has he been here?" Parker said.

"Since the system went bye-bye," Blake said. "About two years. The first year was the worst. The rovers were everywhere, raping and murdering everyone. We didn't know about the revenants back then. They came later. In the second year. That was bad too. Now we've got both. Your guy just sort of retreated into the hotel. Nobody has seen him since."

"Wait, nobody has seen him in three years? How do you know he's even alive?"

"No, he's alive. He's got a sniper rifle. Every once in a while he'll come out, take a shot at a rover or a revenant on the street. And we can hear him playing music."

"Music?"

"Yeah, big Michael Jackson guy. But not Jackson 5 Michael, more like an older Michael Jackson, I think, sometime after our time. He figured out a way to access things outside our system. Rovers tried to go in and get him out. But there are too many revenants in the building now. He uses them as sort of a security system."

"Sounds like an interesting guy," Parker said.

The elevator slowed, then came to a stop. The doors slid open with a grind of metal.

The elevator car opened onto a grand ballroom. It was a vast, open space, with cathedral-style windows that looked out across a deserted Park Avenue. Sets of crystal chandeliers hung from the vaulted ceiling, still glimmering brightly beneath a coating of dust. A carpet was rolled up and abandoned in the corner near a half-dozen overturned chairs and a piano obscured by a faded felt covering. Above the piano was a mirror that stretched the entire length of one wall.

Someone stood in the center of the ballroom. He was a man of nothing particularly remarkable, slim in build and of average height. He wore faded blue jeans, work boots, and a flannel shirt. His back was to the elevator, his focus toward the windows. He seemed to sway slightly back and forth, reminding Parker of bits of debris rocking on an ocean current. Everything seemed normal about the figure, and yet Parker felt his skin grow cold. He was witnessing something terrible. Next to him, Clayton's hands were clenched into fists, his eyes wide with fright. Slowly, Blake's hand reached up and gripped Parker's arm. She nodded at the man, then whispered, "Revenant."

She held a single finger to her lips and quietly stepped out of the elevator. The man continued his trancelike rocking, his arms at his sides, his feet planted on the ground. The three of them quietly edged along the wall, making their way toward the set of double doors that led out onto the hotel lobby. As they moved, Parker glanced up toward the mirror on the back wall. The man's face was reflected in the glass, the face of a nightmare. The bottom of his jaw was missing and ragged bits of flesh dangled from below his nose, partially obscuring a few broken teeth. Parker imagined the creature had taken a shotgun blast to the face, the bottom portion blown away. But what was even worse were the man's eyes, covered with a white, gauzy film of death.

Parker found himself staring at those eyes. Being drawn into them, utterly repelled at the same time. And then to his horror, the man's eyes shifted toward the mirror. And even though the eyes were clouded jewels, Parker knew the man was looking at him.

The revenant spun around, its rotting face turned completely toward them. It crouched down and emitted a terrible shriek of surprise before it charged at them, running with abandon across the ballroom floor.

"Watch out!" Blake said.

Shocked by how fast the thing moved, Parker stood frozen, the Sten clutched in his hand. Blake raised her weapon to her shoulder and fired a burst. The bullets struck the creature and spun its body full around, knocking it back to the ground. It was up again in an instant and as it charged once more, its mangled upper lip snarled back. Parker had a faint impression of Blake's hand as it flashed down to the machete clipped to her waist. She brought the sharp weapon up, and as the creature reached them, she stepped to the side and swung the machete like a homerun hitter cutting for the fences. The blade struck the revenant in the neck and cut through already-dead flesh. The body still moved forward, headless for a few crashing steps, before collapsing to the ground in a pile of twitching limbs.

"Fuck! Fuck! What the fuck?" Clayton said as he jumped back from the still-moving pile. "What was that thing?"

"That was a revenant. And now you know why the rovers don't come around here."

"There's a whole building of these things?" Clayton said, his knuckles still clenched, the skin tight across the bone.

"Yeah. That's what I've been saying." Blake shouldered the Sten gun. "Let's get moving. There will be more around here soon. They can smell when one of their own gets killed. They all come running."

The three crossed out of the great ballroom and into the lobby of the hotel. The floor was carpeted in burgundy and peach, stained with streaks of long-dried blood. The front reception desk was vacant and dust-covered. Another glass chandelier hung partially torn from the ceiling, the layers of crystal dangling like broken branches. The front doors were sealed shut from the outside by heavy boards. A grand staircase curved up from the main floor to the terraced second floor. Beneath the stairs, two more revenants stood. They both faced the wall, their chins against their chest as if sleeping while standing. Their clothes were shredded almost completely off their bodies. One of them had dried stab wounds covering his back.

Quietly, Blake led the team up the stairs toward the second floor. She pulled them inside a bathroom and quietly shut the door. "Their sense of sight isn't great," she whispered, "but their sense of movement is excellent. If you see one, stand still. They might not know you're there."

"How do we kill these things?" Clayton said.

"Only way to truly kill them is to cut off the head."

"What did you say earlier, they can smell the dead?" Parker said.

"If one of them dies, they emit this odor. I think. Anyway, other revenants seem to be able to sense it and they come running. So try not to kill one unless you absolutely have to. And if you do, get away as quick as you can."

"How's their hearing?"

"Good. Like ours."

"What were they doing down there? Sleeping?"

"Something like that. They seem to sort of shut down after a while. But if they see a living human like us, they wake up pretty quick. Like, instantly. And you do not want one of these things getting ahold of you."

"So this is pretty much the most awful place I've ever been," Parker said. "And where is Bobby Chan in this whole mess?"

"The guy you want is on the top floor, penthouse. But like I said, nobody has actually seen him in years. I don't know anything more than that."

"Why would he stay here?"

"Doesn't like people, I guess. I mean, the revenants are a good security system. Nobody is going to come bother you."

"Except us."

"Well, nobody smart anyway," Blake said.

They reloaded their weapons, then quietly left the bathroom, returning to the second-floor hallway. The hall was empty. In the reception lobby below, Parker saw that the two revenants beneath the stairs had vanished. He wondered if they had gone into the grand ballroom to look after their fallen.

The hallway was carpeted with intricate designs and the trio's feet moved silently along. Ahead, a fire alarm was fixed to the wall, beneath it a red glass-and-metal case that housed a long axe. Quietly, Parker pulled open the door to the case and eased out the fire axe. He hefted it with one hand. The axe had a heavy, wood handle that ended in a wicked-looking steel blade.

They passed through an open doorway into a smoking room. Shelves of books lined the walls, the jackets molding and yellowed. Big game heads were mounted on the wall, elks with massive antlers, a grizzly bear and a giant moose over a fireplace littered with trash. The skin on the animals was peeling off, revealing taxidermy stuffing beneath. Several leather chairs faced each other. Empty snifter glasses stood at the ready on small glass tables. Tiffany-style floor lamps cast a yellowish glow across the room.

From somewhere in the hotel came a long, inhuman shriek. The same sound that thing had made in the ballroom below. Parker spun around, expecting to see one of the revenants, its face torn apart by bullet wounds, racing toward him down the hallway.

Nothing.

"They do that sometimes," Blake said. "I think it's a way they communicate with one another."

"You think?"

"I don't know. Nobody has fucking spent the time to study these things. Usually you go the other way when they're around."

Parker sighed. "Where do we go now?"

"I don't know, man, I've never been here before," Blake said.

The floor lamps flickered twice, then cut off. Enshrouded by darkness, Parker felt his heart accelerate, threatening to pump its way out of his chest. In the lobby below, he could hear the shuffle of feet. The slow creek of old joints, like bones wearing against each other.

"What the hell is going on?" Clayton's voice whispered.

"The place is powered by generators," Blake said. "I'm sure they cut out sometimes. Just give it a moment."

They stood in the shadows, too afraid to move. After a minute, the lights flickered back to life. Parker swung up the axe, ready to defend himself against an attack, but the room was empty.

"Let's go find an elevator."

Outside the smoking room, the hallway cut back around, the lobby visible one story below. One of the revenants shuffled out of the ballroom, its head cocked to the side. Blake froze immediately, holding her hand up to Clayton and Parker.

"Don't move."

The three went completely still. Below, the single revenant moved aimlessly across the lobby floor, wearing the same cargo pants as the rover militia from Grand Central. It had on no shoes, its feet filthy, the nails black and long. It shuffled beneath them and out of sight, never once looking up.

Without a word, the trio continued forward. Parker thought of his wife, trapped in a place like this. She had been away for years. And Parker had possibly been in a system with her. These were entire worlds populated with hundreds of thousands of souls. He could wander them for decades and never find her. To imagine her in some awful place like this was more than he could take. He had to find her.

Blake reached the elevator and pushed the call button. The elevator door was leafed with gold, an image of a woman in a long, flowing dress molded onto the front. The three waited as the car descended toward them.

"What happens when we find your guy?" Blake asked.

"I'll tell you later," Parker said. "How did you get in here?" he asked, wondering if Blake had recovered any of her real-world memories.

Blake shook her head. "I can't remember. I don't know. I remember before everything fell apart, I worked in a bank. Village Credit Union on the Lower East Side. I was a teller. We all had jobs. And at night we went to classes. I was taking Spanish."

"Where were you living?"

"I had an apartment. A studio on Eleventh Street. I lived there with my boyfriend. Then one day I came home and he was gone."

"Like he broke up with you?" Clayton said.

"No, idiot." Blake rolled her eyes. "Like, he just vanished. A lot of people started vanishing. It was strange. Every day the streets getting more and more quiet. People started putting up flyers for the missing. At first, there were just a handful. Then there were hundreds. Then one day, all the police vanished. That's when it started to get really bad. There were weapons everywhere. Not enough supplies. Fear. People started rioting. Forming up into these militia groups that became the rovers. But you know what's really crazy?"

"What?"

"Everybody was scrambling to stockpile food and water. And we realized, nobody was even hungry anymore. It was like the people that were left stopped needing food. That was when a lot of us started questioning things. Like how come nobody could ever leave the island? And when the killing started, people would just reappear. And so did the revenants. That's when it was all over. Total chaos," Blake said. "But you know what? We had everything we needed. I mean, after the disappearance, we had the city to ourselves. Any apartment you wanted. We didn't even need food. We wanted for nothing. And yet we still destroyed ourselves. Still destroyed this city. It was like it was in our nature. Which makes you wonder who we were before all this."

"You don't remember anything outside of this world?"

Blake shook her head. "No matter how hard I try. This is all I got."

The hallway lights flickered again. Then went out. They stood in the dark hallway, listening to the shuffling of the revenants below them. The elevator continued to move. Parker realized different portions of the building must have separate generators.

The elevator chimed and the doors slid open. The car was completely dark. Parker felt a flicker of unease at that, but he was ready to get off the floor. Completely blind, he reached forward and touched the frame of the elevator, then stepped into the car.

"Should we wait until the lights come on again?" Blake asked.

"I don't think we should wait," Parker said.

He could hear Blake and Clayton join him in the elevator, then the wheeze of the elevator door as it slid shut.

"I can't even see the number panel," Clayton said.

"Hang on, let me get my light," Blake said. Parker could hear the rustle of fabric, then the rattle of metal. A click, and Blake's flashlight came to life, emitting a narrow beam that revealed the button panel on the wall near the door. Blake pushed the top floor button, and the elevator began a creaking ascent.

Then they heard the sound behind them. A low wheezing, like the death rattle of a dying man, the sound of something breathing. Slowly Parker turned. Behind them in the elevator car stood a revenant, facing the corner, swaying back and forth. Slowly, the creature turned toward them, its milky dead eye seeming to see through Parker. Its skin was pale white, the color of bone, and peeled away in places. It opened its mouth and the rank smell of rot filled the air as it shrieked. Its hands came up fast and Parker had a glimpse of nails caked black with dirt before fingers encircled his throat. He felt a crushing pressure on his windpipe, the flow of oxygen gone in an instant.

Clayton charged forward and smashed an elbow across the bridge of the revenant's nose. The grip on Parker's neck barely loosened. He kicked upward, his foot buried into the soft flesh of the thing's stomach, but with no effect. Blake hit the thing with the butt of her machine gun, the beam of her flashlight swinging wildly around the elevator car. Blackness began to encroach from the corners of Parker's vision.

He felt Clayton's hand pull the axe from his grip. Parker could feel himself beginning to pass out. The world swirled in darkness, and in the void, he heard the whistle of the axe and the sickening wet thump of metal hitting flesh over and over again.

The pressure lifted from his neck, and Parker collapsed to the ground, beautiful oxygen rushing into his lungs. The revenant lay on the floor of the car, leaning against the closed doors of the elevator, head disconnected from its body and staring with vacant eyes at the ceiling. Blake moved the flashlight over the scene and said, "You okay?"

Parker nodded and slowly stood while rubbing this throat. His head began to clear. He could still feel that creature's hands around his neck. The thing's strength was amazing. Clayton held the fire axe in his hand. "Close one, buddy."

"Yeah. Thank you," Parker replied. "Let's find our guy and get the fuck out of this place."

The doors opened and the revenant flopped out onto the floor beyond. They stepped over the creature as they exited the elevator onto a carpeted hallway, which led to a closed set of double doors. The doors were constructed of solid oak, with faded brass handles, at least six inches in thickness. Parker pulled hard on one of the handles. The door refused to move.

"What if this guy doesn't want to come with us?" Clayton asked.

"I'm not going to give him a choice," Parker said. "We'll give him the hard sell."

Parker pounded on the closed door with his fist. No response. Above the door was a silver closed circuit camera the size of a shoe box, pointing down. They were being watched.

"You think there's another way into this place?" Clayton asked.

"Doubt it," said Blake. "This guy created a fortress here. There's not going to be another way in."

Parker did a quick inspection of the space. Opposite them, the headless body of the revenant lay on the floor. Farther on were two large, stuffed leather chairs, and behind them, a set of three windows facing a commercial building across the street. The building was occupied by a half-dozen men seated on an overturned filing cabinet playing cards on a desk. Around them, the office was a mess. Papers and old furniture littered the floor. The windows were broken and laundry was hung to dry from the frame.

Something made Parker uneasy about the whole scene. Something nagged his brain, like a piece of grit inside his skull.

"Put me in that building across the way with a sniper rifle and a silver bullet, I'll take out our man," Clayton said.

"I was thinking that," Parker said. "That's about a two hundred yard shot."

"No problem. Just get Selberg to get me the right equipment and it's a wrap."

There was a slight cough behind them. Parker turned and saw Blake standing behind them, her eyes wide. "Uh, guys, I think we have a problem."

"What?"

"We've got a dead revenant up here," Blake said.

"So . . ."

"I told you, the revenants know when one of their own is killed," Blake said. "They're going to come."

With a flash of clarity, Parker realized that's what had been bothering him. The body of the revenant. How could he have been that stupid? Every system had its own rules. And Blake had told him.

"In everything that happened," Blake said, "I totally forgot."

Parker ran to the stairwell, opened the door, and looked down. He could see them below, scores of revenants moving fast up the stairs in their terrible, lurching walk. Dozens of them, with their rotted skin, some of them missing limbs, and their gunshot and stab wounds. Each of them having been through death in some horrible way, but now stuck in the system. Refusing to pass on.

Parker slammed the door shut. "They're coming up. A lot of them."

Clayton grabbed one of the leather chairs, pulled it across the hall, and pushed it up against the door. Parker and Blake grabbed the other. The chairs were heavy but would barely slow the things down. Parker had felt the strength of just one of them—he couldn't imagine a whole legion.

The trio piled the two chairs on top of each other, both braced against the stairwell door. The barrier wasn't going to be enough.

"We get rid of the body," Parker said. "Out the window."

"It's too late," said Blake. "Dead revenants leave a scent behind. The others will still come."

"We'll go to another floor," Parker said.

Something pounded on the door and the metal impacted the chairs with a heavy thud. Parker reached for the call button on the elevator. Blake grabbed his hand and pulled it away. "No. There could be more inside. We left this thing's head in the elevator."

She was right. The car could be filled with revenants. The elevator would carry them right up to their floor. Outside, something pounded again on the door. The chairs pushed back a few inches. The door opened a crack and long fingers reached around the edge of the frame. Clayton braced his back against the door, his feet planted into the carpet. With a frantic intensity, the revenants began beating on the door. Throwing their body weight against the metal, the entire frame vibrated. The chairs slid back another inch.

"I don't know how long I can hold them," Clayton said. Beads of sweat ran down his cheeks, his legs beginning to shake.

Parker looked wildly around the area. The only exit was the locked set of doors. He thought for a moment about smashing the window, trying to lower themselves down to another floor. But they were twenty-eight stories up and he saw nothing they could use to climb down. They were going to have to make a stand here. They were going to have to fight.

Parker turned to Blake. "I'm sorry for getting you into this."

"Don't," Blake said. "Wasn't doing anything today anyway. Not like I haven't died before."

Clayton looked at them. "Alamo time?"

"The last stand."

Clayton moved away from the door and joined them at the far end of the room, and hefted up the axe. Outside, the impacts grew louder. A revenant let out a shriek. They could hear the scuffling feet of hundreds of them, packing the stairwell landing, crawling over each other to get inside, like a pile of maggots on decaying flesh.

"Selberg, you there?" Parker said.

"I'm here."

"I don't think we're going to make this one, buddy. When we get spit out somewhere, try and find us."

"Good luck."

There was a final crack, the two heavy chairs fell backward, and the door swung open. A revenant with only one eye, the other gouged out and missing, stood in the doorway, his teeth chattering and clicking together. Behind him were others, faces pale and ghostly. Parker felt an almost paralyzing fear take hold of him like he had never experienced before. His hands began to shake. He gripped the Sten, ready to fire.

A dozen of the creatures spread across the floor. Slowly they shuffled forward, lurching, the stench of death heavy in the air. They formed a line as they came closer, stepping together. Parker's finger tightened on the trigger of the Sten.

The line of revenants stopped. From two large speakers set on the wall, loud music began to play. An iconic rhythm Parker recognized immediately.

The revenants stared forward, then their heads jerked in one swift motion to the right as their right shoulders shrugged up in time with the bass of the music. In perfect synchrony, the dozen revenants pivoted to the side . . . then shuffled forward . . . then back.

Their feet slid together and they all clapped overhead.

"Uh . . . guys, what is happening?" Blake said.

"My God . . ." Parker said. "I don't believe it. 'Thriller.'"

"What the hell is Thriller?"

Clayton looked at her like she'd lost her mind, then said, "I forgot, you haven't reached the 1980s yet."

"But someone obviously has," Parker whispered.

"Chan found a way to hack out of the system," Selberg said. "I knew he was our man. He went out and grabbed music he liked outside of his world. He probably hacked the revenants too. I told you, this guy is brilliant."

Behind them sounded the creak of a door.

"You guys going to hang around outside all day?" a voice said behind them. "Or did you want to come in?"

Parker whirled around. The thick wooden doors were open, music blaring even more loudly from inside. A short, muscular man stood in the doorway in a gray T-shirt and jeans, his skull shaved bald, his face covered with a full black beard.

"Bobby?" Blake said.

"At your service."

Not hesitating further, Parker, Blake, and Clayton moved quickly through the open doorway. Parker turned for a last glimpse of revenant choreography in the open space of the floor before Chan shut the door.

The man rubbed his hands together, then bowed. "Bobby Chan. Welcome to my humble abode."

Clayton let out a long deep breath, lowered the axe, then bent over at the waist as if he were about to vomit. Parker placed both hands over his face, and held them there for a moment, enjoying the blackness. Enjoying anything that took him momentarily away from this place.

"Jesus," Chan said. "What's with the glum faces? You look like you've never been chased by a pack of crazed revenants that break out into dance."

Parker took his hands from his face and looked around.

He stood at the edge of an incredible suite jammed with expensive pieces of furniture. The room stretched out the full floor of the hotel, filled with marble and paintings and crystal chandeliers. It was like a museum exhibit on the Palace of Versailles, gold and pink and white everywhere, shining in the light that streamed in from the wall of windows.

Chan moved to a blender on the wall. He began cutting up pieces of fruit and putting them into the machine. "So, you seem to know who I am, but I'm at a loss for who you are. But I can guess, first experience with the revenants, so that means you're not from here. Which means you're from out there somewhere. And since the only people who come here are prison breakers, I'm guessing that's what you are."

"You know this is a prison?" Parker said.

Chan laughed. "Oh wow, I'm sorry. Were you hoping to come in here and overwhelm me with your revelation that this whole island isn't real? That I'm actually inside a virtual prison of the mind. Did I totally just steal your thunder on that one?"

"I just didn't know anyone here knew."

"Do you want me to pretend I don't know, so you can do your big reveal, and I can be all surprised?"

Clayton looked angry. "Hey, asshole, we risked our lives coming here to get you."

Chan snapped his finger and pointed first at Parker, then at Clayton. "I get it. Good cop. Bad cop."

Parker rubbed the bridge of his nose. "I'm sorry. I'm just trying to figure this out. How did you know about this?"

Chan finished cutting a banana into the blender, then opened a plastic tray of strawberries. "I'm the best hacker in the world and they imprison me inside a computer system. Did they really think I wasn't going to be able to figure it out?"

"But you couldn't figure a way out."

Chan looked genuinely confused for a moment. "What makes you think I would want to?"

"What do you mean?"

"I'm God in here. Why would I want to leave?"

He finished packing cut strawberries into the blender, then turned on the device. The powerful engine whirred loud enough to drown out the possibility of any conversation. After half a minute, Chan turned off the blender, disconnected the mixing cup, and held it up to Clayton and Parker. "Smoothie?"

"So you're telling me you could leave at any time, but you choose not to."

"Duh. I mean, listen, don't get me wrong. The rovers suck. But I figured out how to control most of the revenants. What'd you think of my dance show? Pretty good, right?"

"How can you do that?"

"The revenants are just bodies without consciousness. I hacked into their core, changed the programming around a little. I don't control all the revenants. But the ones I do, man, can they move."

"But what about the ones that attack us?"

"Yeah, sorry about that. Don't have control of all of them."

Parker heard the unmistakable sound of a woman's high heels. A tall blonde in a shimmering silver cocktail dress walked out from the back bedroom. Chan drank his smoothie from the blender cup and watched their reactions. "Not bad, right? She's an AI drone. Left over from before. I reprogrammed her for all sorts of nasty things."

Parker wasn't sure what was happening. "Selberg, what's going on?"

"Selberg?" Chan interrupted. "Don't tell me you rely on that washed-up, degenerate gambler. He's still in the business? Oh man. What a dinosaur."

"I told you he was an asshole," Selberg's voice said in Parker's ear.

Chan downed the rest of his drink, then wiped his lip with the back of his hand.

"I thought you guys didn't have to eat in here?" Clayton said.

Chan snapped his fingers. "Yes. Yes. That is an excellent point. But do you know why I eat?"

"Why?"

"Because I like it. Because in here, I don't *have* to do anything. I don't have to eat. I don't have to drink. I don't have to fuck. But I do, because it's pretty goddamn fun. Everything I do is for pleasure," Chan said. "Do you know anything about Easter eggs?"

"Probably not as much as you, so let's skip the part where you make me feel dumb and just go ahead and tell me," Parker said.

"Easter eggs are like hidden messages or items left inside computer programs. Like a video game where if you go into a certain room and touch a certain part of the wall, it reveals the name of an uncredited video game designer, or some political message, or whatever. Like this hidden thing that only the video game creator knows about, and everyone has to find on their own. And that's why it's called an Easter egg, because you have to hunt for them."

"So?"

"So this whole place is basically one big, fucking video game," Chan said. "And these Easter eggs are everywhere."

"What do you mean?"

"Well, when I first got here, I had no idea. Like everybody else. I'm just living my life in 1970s New York City, the Big Apple. And it's pretty fucking cool. Disco is in. The place is like dirty and dingy, but at the same time, alive. The cops are here, kicking ass. People doing drugs. I was working at a record store on Avenue A in the Village. And I'm just like this normal dude. Trying to fuck chicks. Going to school at night. Keeping up with my mandatory education like everyone else. And one day, I'm at work and the place is empty and I'm just killing time, so I go to put on a record in the store. I'm flipping through some of the old records in the back, and I find this album called Miles Larson

Overdrive with, like, a photograph of this New York City street scene on the front cover.

"So I figure, something new, I'll try it out. I put the record on to play it, and it's just like this guy speaking. I almost turn it off thinking it's some hippy bullshit about peace and getting out of Vietnam. But then he starts talking about these things called the AI, which he designed, that look just like people, but operate on their own, independent from human control. Then I look at the cover of the record, and I realize it's a photograph of my record store. But from a different time. It's not a record store anymore, it's this place that just sells coffee. And I can tell from the cars on the street and the clothing, that it's, like, way in the future. So, at first, of course, I think it's a hoax, but the more I think on it, I'm not so sure."

"And that was the Easter egg?"

"Yeah man, that record was the Easter egg. This secret that Miles Larson, some low-level designer, left in the game just as a fun thing so he could get a little recognition. Sort of a fuck-you to his bosses. But turns out, these Easter eggs were everywhere. You just had to know where to look."

"Where was that?"

"Well, I scoured my entire record collection at the store. Listened to all of them. And I found three more Easter eggs. Other designers basically just giving their names and crediting themselves for the different parts of the system that they designed. Then one of them mentions a backdoor. A way to move in and out of the system. So by now, I'm starting to really get interested. And I keep doing more research."

Chan moved to the windows and looked out across the city. Parker had heard stories about Easter eggs being left in the system. But he had never found one himself. He knew the system could be manipulated, objects moved in and out, but he was never certain how flexible the world really was. There were rules to every system, and Parker had always been bound by them. But what if he could find a way to bend those rules? That might be the key to finding Susan. If the system could be manipulated so that people could be more easily located, then Parker might be able to find her.

"Tell me about the backdoors," Parker said.

"They're like portals, in and out of the system and into other systems," Chan said. "See, when they designed these worlds, they all share one thing. What is it?"

"They're all set in Manhattan," Parker said.

"Yes!" Chan snapped his fingers. "Exactly. They're all set in Manhattan. They keep reusing the same code over and over again and just changing the population. Come here, follow me, I want to show you something."

The blonde had vanished. Chan walked alone through the penthouse, down a long, opulent hallway lined with paintings, the kind of stuff that even Parker would recognize from museums. He paused for a moment to study the canvas of the *Mona Lisa*. It looked amazingly real. But of course, this was all just illusion.

They reached a large, open room containing Grecian statues of naked men wrestling, a couple of vases on display pedestals, and a beautiful Steinway grand piano flanked by a view out across the city. The room was a strange mix of art and music, like the work of a collector with too much money and not much taste.

The centerpiece of the room was a twenty-foot-long conference table topped by an enormous map of Manhattan. Chan walked to the map, running his finger along the edge of the table.

"The basic grid street structure of Manhattan was designed in 1811. Then they made a few changes, but by 1850 or so, things were pretty much as they are today," Chan said. "So if you can take this grid structure and keep reusing it over and over again . . . different time periods, different people, but it's the same basic framework. It saves the designer time. You follow?"

"I follow."

"So if there was a backdoor in one framework, in the original pro- gramming, you would be able to travel from one system to the next. From one time period to the next," Chan said. "Now, you live outside the system. And you're able to brute-force hack into the system. But once you're inside, you can't jump from system to system. You have to commit. Right?"

Parker nodded. He had never traveled from one system to another. It was only from the real world, then into one specific time period, and back out. Never between systems.

"But this is all just theory?" Parker said.

"It was just theory," Chan said, tapping his fingers on the map. "Until I found my first backdoor."

"Where?"

"Here, in the hotel," Chan said. "There are forty-seven floors here. But we're on the forty-eighth. The entire top floor of the Waldorf Astoria is one big Easter egg. It will never show in any plans or models. It was put here by one of the program designers. And once I found this place, that's where I knew I had to live. Because you don't make this big of an Easter egg as a joke. There had to be a reason. And I totally fucking found it, man. It's awesome."

Chan led them through a sliding glass door that opened onto a large terrace with wooden decking and several beach chairs. An open cooler was filled with ice and bottles of beer next to a sniper rifle set up on a tripod overlooking Park Avenue.

"I come out here sometimes to think," Chan said and nodded at the sniper rifle. "And also try and pick off some of the rovers. Discourages them from hanging around. Getting killed here is always a risk. Never know who might be waiting for you when you come back."

Farther down from the sniper rifle was a set of old-timey, coin- operated observation binoculars. The binoculars were mounted on a metal tower, with a slot to deposit coins and two eye holes. It was the kind of thing seen at tourist vantage points all over the world, but it seemed a little out of place at a hotel.

"So I found this little device up here," Chan said. "These things are everywhere. Pay like fifty cents and get to look through the binoculars for a minute. But why is it here? Little odd, right? I mean, this isn't a tourist destination, this is someone's private terrace. Normally I would think it's no big deal. But now I question everything that doesn't seem right." Chan handed Parker two quarters. "Try it out."

Parker deposited the quarter into the coin slot and pressed his eyes against the lens. At first there was nothing but blackness, then came a mechanical whirring as the lens cap was lifted away and he could see a magnified view across Park Avenue. The binoculars looked down on the destroyed office building Parker had seen before. The men still played cards amid the rubble of furniture. Farther up the avenue, to the south, Parker glimpsed the Empire State Building. A large banner hung from the windows read, Revenants Here, Keep OUT!

Parker pulled his eyes away from the lens. "Same shithole as before, only closer up."

"Yes. Same shithole," Chan said. He fished another quarter from his pocket. "Now try this. But before you do, look at the quarter, see if you notice anything different."

Parker took the currency and inspected it. On the face was the familiar silhouette of George Washington, but along the bottom edge of the coin was something unusual. Instead of a year of mint, the word Panopticon was inscribed.

"I think that coin was left here by some system programmer who wanted the people in the system to know the truth," Chan said. "Try it out."

Parker deposited the coin into the binoculars again, put his eyes against the lens, and waited as the black cap slid upward again with the same mechanical whir. Immediately, the Empire State Building came back into view. Only this time everything was different. The iconic skyscraper looked brand new, every window shining and clean, the top populated with groups of tourists.

Parker swung the lens down along Park Avenue. The first thing he saw were the cars. Their bright colors jumped into focus, like spots of light pressed against the eye. They were all early 1950s models and seemed to sparkle like new toys on Christmas.

Parker saw a bright orange and white hardtop Chevy Deluxe, a light blue Chrysler Saratoga, and a cherry red Crosley Super Roadster convertible. And there were people everywhere. Parker had already grown accustomed to the empty streets of this system. But down below, he saw hundreds of people making their way along crowded sidewalks, cutting across bumper-to-bumper street traffic. Men wore suits and houndstooth patterned shirts, almost all of them in hats, while the women wore print dresses and striped skirts and coat sweaters.

This was a different system. Something set in the early 1950s. Somewhere Parker had never been before. It was amazing, so full of detail, so vibrant with life and movement. Most of the other systems Parker had visited felt real, but there was still something faded about them. Details sort of blurred out on the edges. But this was clear and focused. He studied the hundreds of people below him, trying to tell the guards apart from the prisoners, but he found it impossible.

"Pretty wild, right?" Chan asked. "Now, turn the focus knob there."

Parker turned the knob on the side of the machine, then pressed his eyes back against the lens. It was the same view of Park Avenue, only this time, instead of 1950s cars, there were horse-drawn carriages and a scattering of early model Cadillac V-12s. A policeman in white gloves and a full, button-down, reefer coat stood at the corner of Park and Fiftieth Street directing traffic. At the front of the office building across the street, a large sign advertised Warner Brothers' production of *The Public Enemy* starring James Cagney. Fewer people were on the street.

Parker pulled back from the binoculars. Clayton took his place and looked through the lens.

"Every time you turn the dial, it's like a different view into another time," Chan said. "I've counted eight different periods."

"Can you physically visit them?"

Chan shook his head. "Not that I've found. But there's got to be a way. This is just one backdoor into these different places. The connection is there. If you can view into the world, you can physically walk into it."

"What if I told you a way to do it?" Parker said. "Would you be interested?"

Chan looked away, out across the burned out shell of the city. "Why would I trust you? Here, I've got something. Some control. Some truth."

"You have no idea what the truth is. You live here sheltered up from the outside. Too afraid to even leave your home. Totally alone."

"That's not true," Chan said. The woman they had met earlier stood at the edge of the terrace. She watched them with a blank look on her face.

"Oh right, I forgot about your friend," Parker said. Chan had reprogrammed an AI drone to come alive, but there was no intelligence there. Only following commands. A completely binary program of action. "Have a lot of good conversations with her?"

"You come here to my home to tell me this," Chan said. "I'm on the edge of discovery here. I'm on the edge of finding things out. I know about your world too. I know about Selberg. I know about you. You're what they call mind stalkers. You go into these places and you bring people out."

"Do you even know what these places are? You know all about the programming, but you don't really have any idea about what the point of all this is, do you?" Parker said. Then he turned toward Blake. "Do any of you have a fucking clue?"

Blake shook her head. "I just know I want to get the fuck out of here. Anything is better than this."

Chan looked at her and shook his head. "You don't know that. You don't know what's out there."

"What's out there isn't perfect. But at least you would know the truth."

Chan ran a hand over his bald head. He paced back and forth on the terrace. Then he made a fist and lightly punched the palm of his hand. Clayton pulled away from the binoculars. "Amazing," he said.

"Why did you come here?" Chan said.

Parker thought of a million different lies he could tell Chan. In the waistband of his pants, he felt the pistol with the silver bullets. He could pull it out and end this now. Wake Chan up. But he needed Chan to cooperate, to want to leave the system. To want to help. And if they were to wake him up, the programmer would find out the truth anyway.

"I'm here because I need your help."

"Help with what?"

"Exactly what you've been doing here. Figuring things out. Getting into other systems."

"In all my time here," Chan said, "I still haven't found out what these places are. What they were made for. Who we are. Why we're here."

"I can give you those answers."

Blake stepped forward. "No matter what he says, I can go with you, right?"

Chan went to the railing of the terrace and looked out across the city. A thin trail of smoke rose from one of the buildings in Midtown, giving the sky a greasy film. Gunshots rattled off in the distance. From somewhere in the building below moaned a revenant. This was a dying city. Trapped for eternity inside a never-ending loop of despair and violence. Chan had to see that.

"I'll go," Chan said. "What do I have to do?"

Parker turned to Blake. "You too?"

"Shit, yeah, I'm not hanging around this dump anymore."

Parker nodded, for he had already decided how he was going to do it. The explanation only scared people. Gave them second thoughts.

"Both of you, just look over the edge down to Park Avenue. You should see a bright light."

Curious, Blake joined Chan at the railing of the terrace. They both leaned over, looking forty-something stories to the street below. With their backs turned, Parker pulled the pistol from his waistband, walked up behind Chan, and shot him in the back of the head.

Blake spun around at the noise, her eyes wide.

"Jesus, what hap—" she uttered, before Parker shot her too.

Parker reentered a state of consciousness like a satellite crashing through the Earth's atmosphere. There was utter blackness, then light burned at the edges of his brain. He could feel himself erupting back into wakefulness. And he prepared himself for the memory gap. But there was none. He could remember everything that had happened while inside the system. For this first time, he knew where he had been. What he had done. Because this time, he wasn't working for anyone. There was no memory erase.

Slowly he opened his eyes. The usual slow burn of a headache wasn't present. There was always the mild hangover caused by the memory wash, and Parker lay on his back, enjoying the absence of pain. He turned his head to inspect his surroundings. He lay on a military-style cot in what appeared to be one of the old rooms of the asylum. Through the window, he could see the East River passing slowly by, the skyline of Manhattan glittering in the early morning sunlight.

He swung his feet out over the side and sat up. Near him was Clayton's cot, and Selberg and Charlotte's work station. Both were empty. The room had green tiled floors with whitewashed walls marked by graffiti. Behind him, a door banged open. Blake strode in. The real

Blake. She wore cargo pants two sizes too big and a men's button-down shirt that hung down to her knees. She walked up to Parker and pushed him hard.

"Jesus Christ, you asshole, you couldn't have told me you were going to do that?" Blake said, her mouth twisted with outrage.

"Do what?"

"Shoot me in the fucking head, man! I mean, what the hell was that?"

"Oh . . ." Parker sighed, stood up, and stretched. "The first time it's easier not to know it's coming. The anticipation is the worst part."

"Well next time, let me know first."

"Next time? Whoa, wait, there is no next time," Parker said. "That's it. You helped me, so I got you out. Congratulations. Go live your life."

"No, it's not that simple. I need to know things."

"What things?"

"Like my whole life? Every memory I have is a lie. Some make-believe bullshit that some computer nerd made up for me. I want to know who I am. Jesus Christ, I was in prison. I don't even know what I did."

Parker studied her. He had never actually met anyone in person that he had brought out of the system. All the people he kill-waked came alive in some distant Sleep machine somewhere. But then he realized, maybe he had met someone from the inside before? He wouldn't have remembered. But somehow he felt like this was the first time. And to see her standing before him in this totally new environment was a little surreal. Like dreaming of a person, then waking to find her standing before you.

"I appreciate what happened to you, I really do. But I don't take tourists. I go back for a reason, and there's no room for extras."

"I can help you," she said.

Parker walked past her and into the hallway beyond. In daylight, the hospital wasn't anywhere near as gloomy as it had been the night before. Except for the occasional rusted beer can or smashed bit of glass, the halls were fairly clean.

Blake followed him. "I can fight. I'm tough. I survived years in that hellhole. Every single day there was a battle."

Parker found himself in the old cafeteria, the Sleep machines still spread out across the floor, hundreds of prisoners in their suspended states. Blake stopped and stared.

"This is it?" she said. "This is where I spent the last few years? Strapped into one of these machines?"

"Yup," Parker said. "You and every single person in that system with you. The machine keeps you in a sleep state, and puts your consciousness into the system. You then share that world with everyone else. The machine feeds you, keeps your muscles from atrophying."

"But why?" she said. "Why do they put you into this weird, terrible world? Why not just put everyone to sleep for ten years then wake you up."

"Well, the whole point of it is to rehabilitate people. In most of these systems, there are supposed to be mandatory classes. So you learn a skill. Learn how to get along with people. Manage anger. That sort of thing. Like a cross between getting a prison GED and some serious psychological smoothing over. You learn how to live in the regular."

"So in order to find out how to become human, we need to go into a computer program," she said. "So what was I supposed to be learning in my world? If you kill someone, you better chop their head off or else they'll come back to life as some zombie undead creature?"

"Well . . ."

"Or, no wait, never let anyone take you alive, because they'll throw you in a cage and rape you seventeen times per day and torture you whenever you're bored. What the fuck am I supposed to learn from that? How much the world sucks and how shitty people are to one another when things go bad? Do you have any idea how fucked in the head I am right now from the last couple of years? And you just want me to live my life?"

"Your world was different. A mistake. I've never seen anything like it before. They shut the system down, but they forgot you inside. Or maybe they left you deliberately. I don't know. But it wasn't supposed to be like that."

"Oh, well, that's great. Me and Chan are the lucky ones."

"Speaking of your friend, where is he?"

"He's not my friend."

"You seemed like you two knew each other in there."

"Everybody knows everybody in there. You don't really have time for friends. You have allies and enemies. People who want to kill you and people who don't."

"Which was he?"

"He didn't want to kill me."

"Well, that's a start."

"I guess," Blake said. "He's in the back with the others."

Along the back of the asylum stretched an old wooden porch, half-rotted, but still standing. The view was impressive: out across a short stretch of grass, then toward the water and the city beyond. Parker imagined a time when patients must have been brought out here in wheelchairs or in their beds by nurses in starched white uniforms with high-peaked hats and white shoes. Tortured minds looking out across the water at a normal world off limits to them.

It was a beautiful morning. The air was still cool, a thin layer of dew covered everything, sparkling in the sun like minerals in sand. Several old rocking chairs faced the water, and seated in them, engaged in a heated discussion, were Selberg, Charlotte, and Chan. Unlike Blake, who looked pretty much the same on the outside as she had on the inside, Chan was much skinnier than he had been in the system. His elbows formed sharp points that jutted out from the dirty T-shirt he wore. His fingers were long and bony, his neck so thin it barely seemed able to support his head. And his face wasn't quite as handsome as it had been on the inside either.

He must have found a way to modify his appearance virtually. To actually change the coding for his projection in there to make him look better. Fill him out with muscle. Make him more handsome.

A guy who could do that was exactly the kind of guy Parker needed. Clayton stood on the porch, looking out across the water. He nodded to Parker. "How you doing, buddy?"

"All right. Made it out alive. Congratulations on your first trip. How's it feel?"

"Strange. Like I just woke up from a dream."

"You did."

"But it feels like it actually happened. Feels so real. I can still remember everything."

Parker nodded. "Enjoy that part. Most of what we do, you'll never remember. Never even know about."

Parker joined the small circle of Selberg, Chan, and Charlotte. Chan nodded at him. "I knew it, man. Everything they've been telling me. I knew it. I knew there had to be more out there."

"They told you about the supermax system?"

"Yeah, yeah . . ." Chan leaned back in the rocking chair and interlaced his fingers. "Selberg and Charlotte were just bringing me up to speed. You can't know you're going into a prison. You have to trick the system."

"Is that something you think you can handle?"

"Of course I can handle it. I have to handle it," Chan said. "I have to go back into the system. My memories are out there somewhere."

"Exactly," Blake said.

"What do you mean?" Parker said.

"They took away my memory of who I was before I went to prison. I get it, Selberg's been filling me in. I was some bigtime hacker. Convicted, sent to prison. Whatever. But I can't remember any of that. I can't remember anything before my life in the system. But they don't destroy your memory. I have this theory they just download it from your brain and sort of store it somewhere. Like in a systems version of an off-site server. So my memory is out there somewhere. And I need to find it," Chan said. "So yeah, I'll get you in. Just tell me about this system."

Selberg cleared his throat. "Well, I think it's like this. There's no way we can get into the supermax system from the outside. It's impossible."

"Why?" Parker asked.

"Because the system is completely shut off from the outside. Nobody in or out."

"What about guards?" Clayton asked.

"Sure, plenty of them. But they all signed on for long-term contracts. Those guys are in for years at a time. We can't get to any of them."

"What about new prisoners?"

"None. No new prisoners. And no prisoner is scheduled for release for another ten years. I'm telling you, this place is vacuum sealed."

"So what do you do, like, whatever it is you normally do?" Blake said.

Parker shot her a "why are you talking" look. She stared right back at him. Selberg ignored both of them and rocked back in his chair. "Well, as Chan mentioned, there are plenty of backdoors in the older systems. We've been able to exploit that to circumvent the security. Think of it like a firewall on your computer. So a firewall acts as a barrier between a trusted world and something that may or may not be trusted. So the prison system, the island of Manhattan, is considered trusted. And whatever is coming onto the island is considered a possible threat. Once you get past the firewall, the only security within the system itself were the guards and other prisoners who might decide to turn you in. But once you had boots on the ground inside the prison world, it was just a matter of staying disguised and not bringing attention to yourself."

"So what changed?" Clayton said.

"Well now, security added a new layer. Sort of like a holding stage. Where everything that comes into the prison is memory-monitored to determine reality awareness."

"Meaning what?"

"Meaning, if you're aware of the truth, if you're aware that you're actually entering a prison, the system won't let you in. But the problem is, if you're not aware that you're going into a prison, if you think the world you're entering is real . . ."

"You can get lost in there," Parker said.

"Exactly. Forget the mission. You'll just start living a new life. And the system now has one more prisoner."

"So we need to get someone past security," Chan said. "And once we're inside, we need to somehow have them be able to retrieve their memory?"

"That's exactly right," Selberg said.

"Well, that's exactly what my theory was," Chan said. "They download the memory to a facility and store it. Then when they release you, they give your memory back. So if we can download the memory of the person going in and somehow store it inside the system where he can find it, then we're good."

A sailboat made its way down the East River. Already the sun had risen above the horizon, dull orange giving way to brilliant blue. The day was fast approaching.

"We don't have much time here," Parker said. "These theories. Will they work?"

"I'm really not sure," Selberg admitted.

"Well, what's the worst case scenario?"

"Worst case is we strip your memory completely, we get you inside, into the memory storage facility, then we can never connect you again with your memory. So you go on living as a prisoner forever. We can never get you out."

"That's bad." Parker had spent enough time in these machines. He wasn't going to die in one.

"Yeah. And you haven't even heard what the second-worst scenario is," Chan said. "Because I think it might actually be a little worse than first worst scenario."

"Okay, so what's second-worst?"

"Second-worst is that something goes wrong and somehow the security system catches you and kills you."

"So that's not too bad. I just wake up."

"No, you don't just wake up. The security system is designed to follow your connection out to the real world, track down your Sleep machine, and shut off your breathing apparatus. If security kills you on the inside, your real body will die."

Parker had never heard of that happening. He had no idea there was a security that was able to leave the system and affect outcomes in the real world. Frightening.

"Enough with the negative, man, what's the best-case scenario?" Parker said.

"Well, of course, best-case scenario. We strip your memory, we somehow get you into the system without you having any idea you're really entering a prison. Then we give you a series of clues . . ."

"In the form of Easter eggs," Chan said. "Hidden messages for you."

"A series of clues that somehow lead you to a spot where we've hidden your memory of what's real."

Parked pressed his fingertips together. "Okay, then what?"

"Then, when you have your memories in place, you actually remember what your mission is. You seek out the target and you kill him. Kill yourself. Wake up, and everyone gets paid."

"What's the chance of all that happening?"

Selberg exhaled. "I really can't predict that. And you know I love to lay a bet. But this one, no bookie in the world would touch."

"Worse than fifty-fifty?"

"Probably. I don't know. Depends on how well Chan and I can do our jobs. And how well you can do yours on the inside. Even if we're able to smuggle your memory inside, you still have no idea how to find the mark. And if you stand out in any way, the prison guards are going to be all over you. I mean really, this mission would be like if Fort Knox was put inside the Pentagon, which was then placed on the moon and we were told we had to find a way in."

"So yeah, I guess you'd say that's a long shot," Chan said. "Jesus, thanks for the motivational speech."

"He should know the truth of it."

Parker turned away from them and walked the length of the porch. To the south, the Queensborough Bridge stretched across the river. He stared at the expanse, deep in thought. This mission wasn't about money. Wasn't about getting paid. This one was about finding his wife. He didn't care what happened to their client. Some rich kid who had a daddy trying to get him off the hook. If Parker got him out, fine. If he didn't, fine. What really mattered was finding her.

"So every system shares the island of Manhattan in common," Selberg said. "I think Chan's theory on backdoors is accurate. I think each system has a series of backdoors somewhere inside. So my idea is this: If we can get you into the memory storage facility, then you can use a backdoor to get into the supermax system."

"How do you mean?"

"You've got these prisoners going into the system, but they have to download their memories and store them somewhere. So they made this memory storage facility. They put the memories of the prisoners into the facility before they go into the system. Then, when they get released, the memories are uploaded back to individual prisoners.

"Now, the storage facility and the supermax system are connected. So we need to start by breaking into this memory storage facility. Security monitors for intruders constantly. The base grid is well defended. So you can have no conscious awareness of the reality. In other words, you can't know that you're entering a prison."

"So, what, you just happen to stumble on this huge abandoned island of Manhattan? How is that explainable?" Parker said.

"We would need a cover story. One the mind would accept. Like, I don't know, there's been a nuclear war and all the people have been killed off and you're the lone survivor."

"Maybe," Parker said. "But how do you explain that I can't leave the island? And what would happen to the people? They would be dead, bodies everywhere. They wouldn't have just vanished."

"It would have to be a closed system," Blake said. "Not only is the city abandoned, but you can't leave."

Clayton snapped his fingers. "Seattle. They have this city there, all underground. The first city was destroyed in a fire, so they rebuilt on top of the remains of the old city. What if you had something like that, only with Manhattan."

"Maybe that could work," Selberg said. "I like that idea of an underground city. We could keep it enclosed that way."

Chan spoke up. "Okay, so what if you're an archeologist who finds this city under the ground?"

Parker thought for a moment. He could see how that might work. "You make some grand discovery. Almost like discovering the lost city of Atlantis. There's precedence for that. Petra wasn't discovered by the western world until the 1800s," Parker said.

"Exactly. A lost city, a Manhattan, beneath the Earth. Not logical exactly. But believable enough. Your brain would hold on to that story, rather than knowing the truth that it's really the unpopulated framework for a prison," Chan said.

"So we enter the framework, believing it to be a lost city, then what would happen?" Parker said.

"Well, once you're in the grid," Chan said, "there's nothing preventing you from downloading your memory again. The security system checks for conscious recall at the admission to the grid, but not while you're actually in the system itself. So we would have to store your memories of the mission somewhere in the city."

"So how would I find where we hid the memories?"

"I could leave you Easter eggs," Chan said. "Hack into the memory storage facility and leave you clues to guide you along."

"Of course, the facility is still going to have its own security. The Minotaur system will sweep the grid for intruders. You're going to have to stay out of its way," Selberg said.

"So then what would be the next step?"

"Well, after you've secured your memories, you would need to find a backdoor from the memory storage into the supermax facility of 1953. But you would need to get all your memories."

"Where will the backdoor be?"

"I've been looking at the terrain." Chan spread out a map on the ground. "I think I can get a backdoor from the memory storage facility into the 1953 system here. There's an old travel agency on Doyers Street in Chinatown where I think I can get a connection into 1953."

"How?"

"Doyers Street was the old pathway they used to get prisoners into the 1953 system," Chan said. "They stripped their memories, then transported them into the new system. The old coding is still there. I can get it working again. I can get you in."

"What about me?" Blake asked.

"You stay out here with me," Chan said. "I'll need help on the outside."

"So you and Blake stay here in this system," Parker said. "You guide us from the outside, and make sure we find our way into 1953."

"Once you get to 1953, I should be able to get your memory back," Chan said.

"Should?"

"Should. If I can't, you'll wake up in 1953 and have no memory you're in prison. You'll just be another resident of the Sleep machine world, walking around not knowing the truth."

"And if that happens?" Parker said.

"If that happens, you'll be lost forever."

7

"Parker, wake up!"

My eyes were closed, but in the darkness, I heard someone call my name. The voice was far away and feeble, a sound that traveled over a great distance to reach me. My body rocked gently at first, then harder.

"Wake up!"

The cushion of air I seemed to float on hardened suddenly. My mind snapped to attention, and I opened my eyes. I lay on the floor of a hotel room. Charlotte knelt over me, one hand on each shoulder, shaking me, her face concerned.

I focused on her, then waved my hand. "I'm up."

Beneath me, the entire floor trembled. I heard a tremendous roar of anger that seemed to pulse through the walls of the hotel. Outside in the hall, wood splintered and something crashed against metal, the sound of a door being torn from its hinges. My mind was still reeling from the intensity of the memory I had just experienced. I was trying desperately to right myself again, like a gyroscope gone off kilter.

"Something's outside," Charlotte said. "It's searching the rooms."

Whatever it was that had attacked me in the subway tunnel and that Blake had taken a shot at was here now. I smelled that horrible, rotted odor. My stomach turned.

There was a strange bluish glow in the room with us. I sat up and inspected the area for the source. It came from a small nightlight plugged into the outlet opposite the bed—a small cartoon cow jumping over a moon. It was a child's nightlight. The kind a five-year-old boy would have.

A five-year-old boy like Charlotte's son.

Charlotte sensed the absence of darkness too and she followed my gaze until her eyes fixed on the nightlight. Her expression faltered. Confusion. Uncertainty. She walked toward the nightlight as if in a trance.

"I know that light," she said. Her voice wavered. The sound of someone on the verge of discovering a terrifying truth. "I know it from somewhere." She bent down before the nightlight, ran her fingers over the cartoonish figure. "There was a room. In another time. A child's room."

"Charlotte . . ." I called her name, trying to bring her back to the present. To save her from the horror of a memory she had been stripped of by the Sleep machine. She didn't look at me. She was fixated on the light. The smiling cow jumping over the smiling moon had become the center of her world.

"Something bad happened . . ." She held her hand to her mouth, her eyes slowly widening. She turned and looked toward the bathroom, studied the bathtub. "There was a child."

Heavy footprints stomped down the hall. There was another terrible shriek. I wondered where the rest of the team was, if they were still in the hotel with us or if they had fled somewhere else. The creature was checking each room, tearing open the doors. Its claws ready to tear flesh. Its breath reeking of death. We didn't have much time. I went to Charlotte and crouched next to her. She turned to look at me, wide-eyed, confused. "What's happening?"

I put my arm around her shoulder and held her. She burst into tears and buried her head in my shoulder. "What's happening to me? My brain is splitting. I feel like I'm going crazy."

The thing out there was coming closer. Smashing its way down the hall. There were only a few more doors before it reached our room. I turned Charlotte in my arms and looked into her eyes. I had never noticed her eyes before, an enthralling shade of green.

"I don't know what's happening," I said truthfully. "I've had the same thoughts as you. The same feelings. You're not going crazy. But whatever this is, I promise you we will figure it out together." Outside, another door was ripped from its hinges. "But right now, something is out there coming for us. And we have to be strong."

Charlotte nodded. Her eyes lost their softness and a bit of their old shimmer of life returned.

"Okay?"

"Yes. I'm okay."

She reached out, pulled the nightlight from the outlet, and put it into her pocket. The room returned to total darkness. Outside, the beast was too close. We had no chance of leaving the room now. We were trapped. The duct we had crawled through into the memory of the past had shifted back to a window. Through the glass was a seventeen-story drop to the ground.

"I'm sorry," Charlotte said.

"Don't be sorry." I reached for her in the darkness and she found my arms and hugged me back. For a moment we were two people sharing loss and grief together in this strange city. Then she pulled away and I heard the metal click of her rifle.

"I'll check the window," she said. Her lantern came to life and she moved quickly to the window. The glass slid open slightly before a security bar locked it in place. The only other logical place to hide in the room was under the bed. We had guns and could fight, but caught in this tiny space, we wouldn't be able to get off more than a few shots before that thing was on us.

Another roar from the hall reminded us that time was running out. We slid beneath the bed and lay as flat as we could, our heads brushing the underside of the box spring. We didn't have long to wait.

The door virtually exploded open. Splinters of wood fragmented into the room as the door crashed against the opposite wall. I huddled under the bed, pistol in hand, and waited. From there, I had a narrow range of view across the floor of the room. Two feet entered. They were bare and human in shape, but massive, with streaks of dirt and long nails. A closet door was torn open. The bathroom was next, accompanied by the sound of breaking porcelain. Then the television hit the ground hard and smashed, bits of glass landing near my face. Charlotte's hand closed around my arm. The air was thick with animal stench. The mattress springs shrieked as something hit the bed hard.

And then it was gone. I heard it farther down the hall checking more rooms. Quietly, we slid out from beneath the bed. I took Charlotte's hand and we slipped out into the hall and carefully made our way to the lobby. We could hear these creatures everywhere in the hotel, tearing the place apart, looking for us. The lobby was quiet. The rest of the team was gone, either hiding somewhere or having fled the hotel.

"We need to get to the travel agency on Doyers Street," I said. "From the memory. There's going to be a connection there we can use to get into the system."

◆ ◆ ◆

We left through the front door of the hotel and found ourselves back on Seventh Avenue. To the north was Macy's. A giant hole was ripped in the side of the building, the skeletal interior visible, racks of clothes spilling out onto the street. The Minotaur was still out there somewhere. I wondered if one of the crew had tried to hide in the department store.

The avenue was wide and open, no place to hide. It would be impossible to outrun anything here. If we stayed in the open, the Minotaur would find us. We were blocks north of our destination, and I didn't think we would make it above ground. We needed to travel where the Minotaur couldn't follow.

The subway tunnels.

I thought back to what had been lurking in the tunnels before. But we didn't have a choice.

Across the avenue was the marquee for Penn Station and Madison Square Garden. In all my time living here, I had never been inside, but I knew it was one of the larger transit hubs for the city. From there we could make our way through the tunnels, and the Minotaur wouldn't be able to follow.

"We need to get to Penn Station." I pointed across the avenue. "We can take the tunnels and find our way south. We won't last two minutes above ground."

"Looks like it's about seventy yards away," Charlotte said. "We can run for it."

"Keep moving until we get underground," I said. I surveyed the length of the avenue. The street was empty. The buildings towered above us in shadows. But I knew the Minotaur was still there.

We readied ourselves, then Charlotte nodded, and we sprinted out from beneath the hotel awning across Seventh Avenue and headed toward Penn Station. As soon as we hit the avenue, a tremendous roar sounded off behind us. I turned to look back as I ran and saw a massive creature the size of a building come crashing around the side of the hotel. The beast was enormous, twenty stories high at least, with the head of a bull and the body of a man. Its shoulder crashed into the side of the hotel. Shattered glass and stone broke free and cascaded down to the street below.

Its footsteps were deep and thunderous, leaving spiderweb cracks in the street. I accelerated, keeping pace with Charlotte. We crossed over the centerline of the avenue and kept moving. The Minotaur charged after us. I felt the pavement heave and tremble as it gained ground. We just had to get underground.

We reached the Penn Station entrance and sprinted down the main stairwell. Thirty yards below, the stairs ended and the main floor stretched out of sight. I had almost reached bottom when my foot caught on something. I fell forward, arms pinwheeling in space. The stairs rushed up at me and I closed my eyes before impact.

Nothing.

My eyes still closed, my body curled into itself, I felt nothing. Slowly my lids opened. I stood again at the top of the stairs. I was alone. Disoriented, I looked around the platform and down the stairs again.

At the bottom stood Charlotte. To my right, a door which led to the elevator. I pulled on the handle, but thick chains rattled and kept the door closed. I looked back down the stairs and realized what was wrong.

I had never been inside Penn Station before.

And except for the connections between worlds, I didn't think I couldn't enter anywhere I had no memory. This entire city was based upon memory. There was no new creation. These places existed, and if I had never visited them, I had no way to know what their interior looked like. I could only travel where memories existed.

I turned and saw the Minotaur running with enormous strides across the avenue. It saw me and its snout opened as it roared, exposing lines of sharp teeth stained with blood.

"Go, just run!" I called down to Charlotte.

"What's wrong?"

"I can't come with you. I've never been to Penn Station. It's not in my memory."

"But I have," Charlotte said. "It's in my memory. Join me here."

I moved down the stairs as she ran up to meet me. The world began to blur. The railings became indistinct lines of black. The sharp edges of the stairs turned soft, wavered. I could feel myself slipping away, like being on the edge of wakefulness and sleep. The Minotaur was almost on me. There was a blast of hot stinking air from behind.

Charlotte suddenly stood below me on the stairs and reached up to me through the fog. I took her hand. The world cleared as if a giant lens snapped into place. Charlotte kept her hand in mine and guided me down the stairs. The dizziness lifted from my brain and I could focus again. We reached the bottom, and the lower level of Penn Station stretched out before us.

The large, flat Penn Station marquee shielded the stairwell from above. The Minotaur smashed into it, tearing away metal and glass, roaring and roaring. Charlotte and I sprinted farther into the station, deeper into the safety of the underground.

I had expected an empty, dark station, like the rest of the places we had visited, but the lower level was filled with life and light. Thousands of commuters flooded past us and stopped in shops filled with snacks and books and newspapers beneath bright fluorescent lights. Loudspeakers rattled off announcements of travel delays and I could feel the distant rumblings of subway trains passing by. The effect was so real, so vivid, I had to remind myself that this too was only memory.

We were in Charlotte's memory. And it was so much sharper than mine had ever been.

"I guess my memory is stronger than yours," she said. "I must have come here a lot."

We moved like shadows through the crowd, ran across the populated causeway, and entered a wide rotunda hived with food vendors on all sides. Stairs and escalators led to different floors. We followed signs for the subway. I turned to look down the crowded corridors and saw nothing pursuing us. Only thousands of anonymous strangers who formed the crowd.

A Long Island Rail Road train had pulled into the station.

Hydraulic doors hissed open, and a stream of people flooded the already crowded causeway. Charlotte's hand tightened in mine. I followed her gaze deep into the crowd. And there I saw another Charlotte. The same woman I had seen in the Hotel Pennsylvania. She was wearing the same dress from the hotel room, and as she moved toward us, I saw she held the hand of a little boy.

My Charlotte stopped on the causeway and stared at her own image. The boy practically skipped along with his mother. He was so full of life and energy, it was almost impossible to imagine him floating dead in the bathtub, an inanimate water-logged doll.

The other Charlotte looked happy too. She had a bright smile on her face, and she bent down to say something to the boy. They passed by us, only feet away in the crowd, so close I could hear her say, ". . . meet Daddy for lunch . . ." and then they were past us, carried off again in the crowd.

My Charlotte stretched out her arm toward them. Her hand was visibly trembling. The crowd was thick and moved sluggishly along, but soon the other Charlotte and her child were carried from our view. My Charlotte reached into her pocket and pulled out the nightlight.

"This was my son's. I had a son. I remember now. I remember this day." She turned and looked back toward the LIRR. "We took the train in to meet my husband for lunch. My son, Eric."

She looked at me, and I had never seen a more plaintive expression in anyone's eyes before. Never in my life. So filled with pain and hurt but so desperately wanting to know the truth.

"You know what happens. You saw something in that room. You saw something."

I shook my head, not wanting to lie, but knowing I couldn't tell her the truth. I had worked so hard to find these memories. And now there were things I wish I could forget. I took her hand. "I'm not sure what I saw."

Her entire body trembled. Fearing she might collapse, I took her in my arms. She sobbed into my chest. "I want my son. I want my baby." She grabbed my shirt and looked into my eyes. "What happened to him? Why am I here? Oh God . . . please God, help me . . ."

I held her while around us the indifferent crowd passed us by like time.

I understood now what the machine was. Torture . . . for those trapped inside. It made you lose your mind, each horrific memory forever fresh. How could Charlotte heal? The memories never went away. They would always be there, in this memory city, in a particular hotel room, waiting for her. The pain and anguish as immediate as the moment it happened.

Charlotte had put a gun in her mouth and pulled the trigger. But she hadn't died. She must have lived. She must have survived. And now she was in the machine with me. Sharing time in this space that was neither alive, nor dead. But there was still a chance for Charlotte. She still didn't know about the hotel room. She suspected, but she didn't know.

We had both just seen her exit the train with her son. I was sure it was the same day she was going to drown him. What had happened to her that day that could have caused such pain? That could have forced her to do something so terrible? The woman who I saw exit the train was a good person, a good mother. She was not the same woman who I saw sitting on the edge of the bed in the hotel room.

As I continued to hold Charlotte, I studied the crowd. It was a strange feeling to be so unnoticed, not warranting a moment's attention from the thousands who passed by on the concourse. I was invisible.

And then I wasn't.

At the far end of the station I saw a police officer staring at me. Not staring in my general direction, but staring at me. Meeting my eyes. As I watched, he slowly began moving through the crowd. He raised his radio to his mouth and spoke into it. Down here, the system's security took many forms. This was one of them. And it had found us.

I pulled away from Charlotte. "Someone is coming for us."

I looked quickly around the station. There was another cop in uniform. This one by the bathroom. Like the first, his eyes locked on both of us as he quickly made his way toward our location. Charlotte saw them too. "Who are they?"

"Let's not find out."

Together we took off at a run through the crowd, heading toward the subway entrance. I hopped a turnstile and turned and helped Charlotte over the top. Beyond us, the two cops were running hard, equipment jangling on their belts. We ran down another length of stairs onto the subway platform. A train sat waiting, doors open, the car filled with passengers.

I pulled Charlotte onto the train. The train heaved a sigh of hydraulics and the conductor advised everyone to stay clear of the closing doors. From the stairs above, one of the cops appeared. He bounded down, two stairs at a time. He raised a handgun, and without pause, he fired at us. I ducked beneath the open door. A bullet struck the window above me and the glass shattered. The crowd in the subway remained unaware, quietly reading newspapers or listening to headphones. From a crouch in the doorway, I fired back.

The sound of my pistol was incredibly loud in the small subway car, and I saw the cop go down hard. He rolled down the stairs and came to rest on the platform. We could fight back. We weren't helpless against security. My bullets had worked against the creature in the subway, and they worked again now.

The doors slid closed and the train slowly began to roll out of the station.

I slumped back against the door. Next to me, an old man in a baggy suit turned the page of the *Daily News*.

"Where's this train going?" I asked.

"South," Charlotte said. "I think."

The train rumbled on the tracks. The lights flickered. I checked the map. We were on the 2, headed south. We made stops. Each time more people boarded and exited and we were on our way once more. The lights flickered again.

"How could those cops see us?" Charlotte said. "I thought we were in a memory. My memory."

"It's system security. Like a virus detector. It knows what doesn't belong. We're in the memory storage facility now, and the system is trying to kick us out."

We passed south of Houston Street. The lights flickered again. This time longer. With a shriek of metal, the train lurched on the tracks. I grabbed the rail and held on. The lights went out completely. Through the glass, I could see a whoosh of motion as another train passed us on a nearby track. The train shook violently.

The passengers began to slowly fade out until I saw we were in an empty train.

"What's happening?" The clatter of the train had become so loud I had to yell.

"I just realized something," Charlotte said, her knuckles white around the railing. "I never took a subway south of Canal. I won't have any memory of this. And if there's no memory, there's no train."

Around us the train began to break apart. Seats and fragments of window and advertisements flew away and vanished down the length of the tunnel. Brakes screeched and the car tore away beneath us. The rest of the train gave way and we skidded onto the track bedding.

After we gathered ourselves, we turned our lanterns back on. The beams arced across the curved tunnel wall and exposed a red metal door set into brick.

"Now what?" I asked.

"I guess we can't keep going south on the tracks," Charlotte said. She turned the handle on the door. "Might as well see where this goes. We'll have to go above ground."

"You sure about that?" I asked, feeling cautious about going through unknown doorways.

"Of course I'm not," Charlotte said. "But I remember there was a fire on the tracks years ago, and we evacuated through here."

Charlotte pushed open the door to reveal a narrow chute with a metal rung ladder embedded in the wall. The ladder led up.

I went first, and together we climbed until we reached a metal sewer cover. I pushed, the cover bumped up, and I slid it off. I climbed out of the opening and onto the street. I helped Charlotte out of the hole and we found ourselves standing in the middle of the avenue on a crowded New York City summer day. Traffic blurred by us. A bus passed inches from my face without stopping. We dodged taxis and cars and reached a sidewalk packed with late afternoon shoppers. I saw a smudge of blue in the crowd, and there again, was the other Charlotte. We were in her memory. No matter where we went, she would always be there.

"We're almost there," I said. "Can you make it?"

Charlotte nodded. "Let's go."

We started walking, always in the shadow of the other Charlotte, headed for the travel agency where I hoped we would have a way out. As we walked, Charlotte reached and took my hand. She kept her eyes down on the sidewalk. It was too painful to see her old self and her son. I walked for both of us, guiding us south down the sidewalk. The day was sunny. The sky, brilliant blue above us. I had forgotten how blue the sky could get. How the sun could feel on the skin. I was forgetting what it was like to live.

I wondered why my memories were so desiccated compared to those of Charlotte. I seemed to remember the places, the details and the feel of buildings, but not the surrounding humanity. I could only remember certain specific events, but not the general flood of people and moments that had filled my life.

Wanting to take her mind off the events around us, I said, "Your memories are amazing."

"I've always had a good memory," Charlotte said. "I have all this information, I don't know, hermetically sealed in my brain. Still crisp and new."

I looked around the world that she remembered. So filled with detail. So filled with life. I could even smell the world around me. The acrid tang of car exhaust. The metallic odor that drifted up from sewer grates. Everything that was real existed here.

One could live an entire life in this memory and never know the difference.

To stay in the memory, we followed the paths that the other Charlotte had followed in life. We could only go where she had been. And as I walked with her, I noticed the world around us changed dramatically.

We crossed the street and the sky darkened suddenly. We kept walking and the trees turned to brilliant reds and oranges. Then the air grew cold and snow gathered on the ground. People around us changed. The fashion of their clothes changed. I realized that we were passing through levels of time. We would skip years, then fall back years. Pass through seasons as easily as turning pages in a book.

This was a scrapbook of memories all pieced together from the beginning of Charlotte's life. And as we walked, we followed Charlotte. I could see her change through time. Lines appeared on her face, then vanished. Her hair grew long, then short, then long again. For a time she was pregnant. And then she wasn't. Every so often she would appear holding hands with a man. In the moments he was there, her face was illuminated and when he was gone, there was sadness.

"Muninn Travel Agency," Charlotte said. "That's where we're headed?"

"Yes."

"Muninn and Huginn were two ravens that belonged to the Norse god Odin. Every day at dawn they would leave their god and fly all around the world, seeing everything, and then return at dinnertime bringing him all sorts of information about what was happening everywhere. Huginn was the Old Norse word for 'thought' and Muninn came from the word for 'memory.' So Muninn Travel Agency literally translates into Memory Travel Agency."

I smiled at this unexpected information. "How much do you remember about your previous life?"

"Just what you've seen," she said. "And there are certain things, feelings I guess, that I have. Deep feelings. Love."

"That's good."

"Hate. Fear."

"Oh."

"There are memories I've blocked. I've worked to forget. Sometimes I feel terrified. And I don't know why. It's like I've just woken up from some horrible nightmare. And I can't remember any of the details. But I'm sitting in bed in the dark still feeling terrified. And filled with this . . . I don't know . . . deep sadness. Like something happened to me, or was going to happen. And it made me afraid and sad at the same time."

"Could you find out what it was?" I indicated the city around us. "It looks like you lived in New York too. It must be out here somewhere."

She looked up at the buildings along Canal Street. "Maybe. But I don't know if I would want to find out. I think eventually the feelings will go away. I'll forget the sadness in this world. But if I knew what caused it, I would never be able to forget that. The feelings will melt away eventually, like spring snow, but the memory of the events that caused them . . . that will be up here." She tapped the side of her head. "For life. And maybe I don't want that."

"So I guess for now we're just a couple of New Yorkers, wandering around our old haunts together."

She smiled. "I'm sure between the two of us, there must be a few happy memories here. It can't be all the sad stuff. We've both loved very deeply. And you need a lot of happy memories to fall in love. That's the way it works. Might be we'll run into one of the happy times. Friends. Laughter. Something normal for a change."

"I'd like that."

We reached the intersection of Canal Street and started heading east. When we reached Broadway we encountered the wall, an old brick barrier about fifteen feet high and topped with barbed wire. It stretched from building to building, cutting off Canal Street completely. Set in the middle of the wall was an iron door.

"I guess we ran out of memory," I said.

"Yeah . . ." Charlotte said, running her hand over the hard surface. "I guess so. I never made it down here. Did you?"

"I don't remember," I said, then realizing how stupid that sounded. We both laughed. "I guess we'll find out." I reached out to her. "Here, take my hand."

Charlotte's hand in mine, I reached for the door. The knob turned in my hand and pushed forward. We passed through the doorway to the other side. We were now back in my memory, but it must have been old memories. In contrast to Charlotte's city, teeming with details and life, my city looked abandoned. Doors falling open. Windows broken. Sometimes entire facades of buildings were gone, leaving just bombed out ruined shells. The streets became more and more uneven until finally we reached a roadblock. An entire side of a building had collapsed. Brick rubble and twisted metal blocked the entire street.

"We could try and climb over it," Charlotte said.

I shook my head. "No. I think the memory ends here. We better find another way around. I've been down here before, it's just all faded."

"Erased or faded?"

"I don't think we can blame the system for this one. I think these are just old memories. I forgot about these neighborhoods."

We backtracked up Canal and found an opening onto Centre. Most of the buildings were still wrecks, but the street remained passable. We picked our way over rubble-strewn avenues until we reached Bowery. We passed a massive apartment building complex, all faded brick and overgrown with weeds, like photographs of the abandoned city around Chernobyl. The street beneath us was getting increasingly broken and rutted. I imagined that I must have passed through this way only a handful of times, maybe looked out the window of a speeding taxi, retaining only fragments of the surroundings in memory.

We reached the edge of Chinatown and witnessed a maze of narrow, winding streets and red awnings covered in Chinese lettering over hole-in-the-wall restaurants, massage parlors, and beauty salons. The buildings crowded over us, almost blocking the light above.

The entrance to Doyers Street was so narrow we almost walked past it in the warren of Chinatown. Doyers was a narrow road that wound its way out of view, surrounded by old curiosity shops and empty windows with placards. A small green sign on the corner advertised the street name. For an area I had rarely visited, the minutiae of the scene were quite sharp, and I had the sense that someone had spliced this street into the fabric of my existing memories.

The street itself was far more detailed than the rest of my Chinatown. The building looked shining and new compared to the collapsing, abandoned structures that lined the rest of the area. Even the lighting felt different. Brighter somehow.

"Something is different here," I said. "This isn't natural."

"I see what you mean," Charlotte said. "The street looks like someone just unwrapped it."

"I don't think this is my memory," I said. "I don't think I've ever been down this street in my life. The only way this would be in my brain is if someone put it there."

Cautiously, we walked between the buildings, the pavement beneath our feet smooth and unblemished. There was something welcoming about this section of the city. It felt very lived-in, different from the large, abandoned commercial blocks near Central Park. The structures here were more human in scale, with their multitude of oddly shaped doors and windows. Doyers curved sharply, and among a restaurant, marinated ducks hanging from a window, and a beauty salon lined with mirrors and barber's chairs, a dented metal door had the words Muninn Travel Agency stenciled in red lettering across the front.

The neglected door was set back from the street and seemed to connect to an office. I peered through the dusty glass, but a tattered green velvet curtain had been drawn over the window. I surveyed the street behind me. Empty, but without the overlay of memory that seemed to haunt the rest of the streets we had passed. There was nothing for me here. It felt liberating to be in a place with no attachments. I could float free from my past and perhaps, through one of these doors, find an alternate ending to my story. A rewritten history where my wife might be waiting for me with her usual smile. The warmth of her hug. The smell of her hair. And maybe I could forget what had happened to her.

"What do we do now?" Charlotte asked.

I took a last look around. Then with one hand holding Charlotte, I reached with my other and turned the knob on the Muninn Travel Agency door.

"Wait," Charlotte said. She leaned forward and kissed me on the lips. "For luck."

I stood surprised, unable to say anything. She smiled, and squeezed my hand. "Whatever happens, promise you won't forget me."

"What are you talking about?"

She let go of my hand. "I'm not going with you. I'm staying here. There's nothing left for me out there. Here, I have my son. My memories. Maybe someday I'll come find you. But for now, I'm staying."

"But this isn't real," I said. "None of this. You're in a machine."

"I don't care. Most of life out there isn't real. It exists in memory. Everything after the moment is just memory. Gone forever. We spend most of our lives in memory. Now that's all I have left."

"No, no . . ." I shook my head. "I can't accept that. Out there is real life. We can leave together. We can live."

"Without hope, there is no life. You have your wife. You can find her. You can live. Everything that gave me hope is in here now. Once I leave this place, it will slowly fade away until I'm left with nothing. My memories are stored here."

I felt a desperate energy inside me. Something I hadn't felt in a long time. "I need you."

"You know where to find me. I'm in your memory now."

Somewhere out there, I might find my wife. Or I might not. But in here, I would always have the memories of her. Perfectly captured. Just like Charlotte and her son. And maybe that might be enough for me. If I left this place, I might find nothing.

"You have to try," Charlotte said. "Your wife is in prison. As long as she's in that place, she can't know you. You need to find her and set her free. My son is dead. If he was alive and out there someplace, I would leave this city and find him." She reached forward and hugged me. Her lips close to my ear, she said, "Good luck. And don't forget me." I looked at her and she was crying. "That's a joke. Lighten the mood."

"If I can, I'll come back to see you."

She nodded, kissed my cheek, and stepped away.

I turned from her. The door opened into darkness. I had a brief vision of a wooden desk, travel posters of exotic destinations hanging from the wall . . . then the blackness reached out for me, like a living creature. It moved toward me, surrounded my vision, wiping out everything, filling my eyes and ears with a dark liquid.

The liquid seemed to spread across my body, down into my lungs. I felt an intense weight on my chest, an almost unbearable heaviness that made it difficult to breathe. Something hard and cold was pressed against my skin.

I felt like I was diving beneath the water. Descending into a Marianas Trench, pressed flatter and flatter until my head would crush inward, like an aluminum can beneath a boot.

And then the pressure lifted. I could breathe normally again. I was still in darkness, but realized the darkness came from closed lids. My eyes were shut, but through them I could sense light. I took a moment to regain my senses. I was standing, held in place it seemed, and I felt cold air on my body. Thankfully I could breathe normally, but my body, chest, and lungs felt weak, like I was breathing air at a new altitude for the first time.

8

Parker gasped for air, his body covered in sweat, his mouth dry. He sat motionless, disoriented, his mind still trapped in the nightmares of just moments before. Too afraid to move, he sat still, his eyes slowly making a survey of his surroundings. He was in a rundown corner office of an indeterminate time. A handful of mismatched filing cabinets were pushed against the wall, leaning on each other like drunken friends. A mesh wire trash can was nearby, overflowing with papers that spilled onto a faded Persian rug the color of soggy cardboard. A fan rotated on the sill of an open window, moving stale air and muting the traffic noise from somewhere outside.

He sat in a torn office chair, his feet kicked up on a desk. He scanned the desk: a green felt pad, a mug that read "Moonlight Diner" filled with pencils, a hospital-green telephone. He opened the desk drawers. Inside were more papers, a battered revolver, a holster, and a handful of loose silver bullet rounds. On the wall hung a calendar, a black and white photograph of a pinup girl with a month and year in bold across the bottom.

June 1953.

Parker had done it. He was inside the system.

"Selberg, come in," Parker said. "You there?"

There was nothing.

"Chan, Blake, anyone?"

Silence. Parker appeared to be truly alone. He had never been in a system on his own. He had always had help from the outside. Someone to guide him through the world. But now . . .

He wondered what had happened to the rest of the team. Charlotte had stayed behind. And if Selberg and Clayton had made it into the 1950s system, they could look like anyone.

He should have thought of that before they went through the back-door. He should have realized they might be separated. He should have thought of a meeting place. Now the others were out there somewhere. In a city of a million people. Just as lost as he was.

Parker stood up, braced himself against the desk, and moved each leg. He felt like he was in good shape. He had no idea what body he was in, but it felt solid. He opened the desk drawer again, pulled out the revolver and the loose rounds, and dumped them on top of the desk. Beneath the revolver was a shaving mirror. He studied his reflection as he loaded the gun.

He was handsome in a vintage tough-guy sort of way. Like a character from a dime-store crime novel. He had a heavy jaw that looked like it could take a punch, with a cleft in his chin and a thin line of stubble. His hands were big and thick, and he wore a loose-fitting gray suit.

There was a frosted glass door on the far side of the room, and when Parker opened it, he saw the words PRIVATE INVESTIGATOR sten-ciled in gold on the front. Parker had to laugh. Whoever set this scenario up, Chan or Selberg, had put it together perfectly. In his wallet he found seventy dollars in cash, a driver's license, and a private investigator card, complete with his name and photo. The PI card allowed him to carry a pistol and was valid through 1955. Two years. He hoped he wasn't going to be here two hours. But at least now he could move around, ask questions, and carry a piece without attracting too much attention.

Parker wondered why they would even need private investigators in this place. But he figured most of them must be guards. Sort of gave them a good cover story and allowed them to snoop around and look for breakouts.

But it also allowed him to snoop around. And nobody would raise an eyebrow.

Aside from his wallet, he had a key ring with a Chevrolet key and a couple other silver pieces that looked like they might open an apartment.

He went to the window and looked out on City Hall Plaza. A strip of grass meant as a park was surrounded by a wrought iron black fence, and beyond that was the cluster of old stone federal court buildings. A fountain in the center of the plaza lazily bubbled water from a centerpiece shaped like a Greek god. Traffic flowed up Centre Street. They were all big, boxy American-made cars, land cruisers like coupes and DeSotos. The women wore dresses and skirts, the men, suits, rushing to and from the diners along Broadway on their lunchbreak from the offices on Centre and Wall Street.

Just from a glimpse, Parker could tell this was a stable system. At least downtown, people seemed to thrive in their new identities. The other systems he'd visited always had an undercurrent of violence. Every dark alley was filled with menace. Characters just waiting to sandbag your skull. Arch villains disguised as regular people. But here, these prisoners seemed acclimated to their new locale. Almost made you feel like the Panopticon worked.

Parker sat down behind his desk to arrange his thoughts.

He remembered everything.

His mission was to find Andrew Scott, the wealthy son of Senator Ted Scott. Parker had no idea what Andrew had done to warrant his stay here. This time around, he was paid to not know. This fact weighed heavily on his conscience. And that burden made him angry . . . angry at the Senator Ted Scotts of the world who had money and thought they could buy their way out of everything. And the Andrew Scotts who felt above the law and got away with it because of Daddy.

Unfortunately, Parker didn't have the luxury of a conscience on this one. Because Andrew Scott knew where Parker's wife was being held. This fact made Andrew the most important person in Parker's life right now. And he was going to do everything he could to find him.

So, here's what Parker knew.

Fact 1: Andrew Scott. Male, white, rich, 22 years old.

Now in this system, Andrew Scott could look like anyone. But he would still always have the mentality of a spoiled 22-year-old. Which meant he would be impulsive, immature, self-centered, and generally most likely an asshole.

Fact 2: Andrew knew he was a prisoner.

This was the first time Parker had broken someone out who actually knew he was in prison. He wasn't sure how self-awareness would affect prison life. But he felt confident that whatever he was doing on the inside, Andrew was probably not keeping below the radar. He was going to attract attention somehow.

Fact 3: There was a guard on the inside who was helping Andrew.

This was what Parker had been told, and it was the only logical conclusion. Andrew could not have accessed the system with any awareness of the truth, ergo, he must have learned he was a prisoner from someone on the inside. The only ones with this immediate knowledge were guards. So, Parker felt it was a pretty reasonable guess that there was a crooked screw on the inside who had gotten paid off to help out Andrew.

Which led Parker to fact 4, which was less of a fact and more of an educated guess.

Fact (Educated Guess) 4: Andrew led a pretty cushy life in this system.

If Scott Senior had the money and clout to pay off guards to help his son, he probably also had the same ability to ensure his son was living the high life on the inside. Parker seriously doubted Andrew was doing his time as a clerk for Liberty Mutual or a stock boy at Gimbels. Andrew was going to be something important here. Probably had a lot of pretty girls around him. Nice cars. Nightclubs. Apartments. The best the 1950s had to offer.

Which meant Parker couldn't take for granted that Andrew would even want to come back out.

Parker started by opening the phone book and seeing if there were any Andrew Scotts listed. Maybe he would get lucky. He didn't. No such luck.

Fact 5: Andrew was a big boxing fan.

Now that fact was something Parker could use. The Panopticon had always looked at sports as a healthy diversion for the prisoners. So every system was always filled with athletics. Boxing. Baseball. Basketball. Every game they had on the outside, they played on the inside as well.

And that gave Parker something to work with.

He holstered the revolver and clipped it to his belt, hidden on the inside of his pants. He left his office unlocked and made his way down to the sidewalk below. Outside, he found a newspaper stand and bought a *Post*. He sat on a bench, opened up the paper, and scanned the Sports section. There was a heavyweight title fight tonight at the Garden. If Scott was going to be anywhere in town during the evening, it would be there.

Cars were parked along Broadway. Parker calmly walked down the line, trying his key in every Chevy he found. Eventually he found his car, a nice, cream-colored '51 Fleetline Deluxe. Inside the glove compartment he found the registration and a set of brass knuckles. He pocketed the knucks and left the registration where it was. A couple of cops in blue reefer coats and black patent leather shoes crossed Broadway. Parker kept an eye on them until they disappeared into a Ham n' Egg joint on the corner, then he started up the big Fleetline 105 horsepower engine and pulled off down Broadway.

The address on Parker's new license was just off Forty-Second Street. He headed uptown, the radio playing Rosemary Clooney, the windows rolled down, that artificial air feeling pretty fine on his face. That was the problem with these systems. Sometimes the fake world was better than the real one. Sometimes it was better to live in a dream. Being awake could be the hard part. *One of these days I might just retire here,* he thought. Maybe he could find his wife and just kind of stay on. Try and make a go of it in 1953. Pretty good time for America. Top of the world. Just won a world war. Jobs aplenty. No AIDS, no crack, crime down, wages up. What wasn't there to like?

Yeah, Parker thought, *maybe I'll just decide to stay on.*

Times Square was still a bit seedy around the edges. Almost like the real thing, just with the sound turned down. A couple of hookers worked the corners while their pimp kept watch behind the wheel of a big cherry-red Eldorado parked up the street. There were a few dancing girl spots, a couple sports bars, and some diners, all while big bright neon signs advertising Gordon's Gin and Admiral television sets and Canadian Club and Pepsi-Cola splattered yellow and red and green wattage over everything.

Parker found the address listed on his license, a sort of flophouse building sandwiched between a tiki bar and an all-night jazz joint, parked, and walked up two flights of stairs. The yellowing halls were spiderwebbed with so many cracks it looked like someone had taken a baseball bat to the plaster. He jiggled a few of the keys in the lock on his door and was rewarded with the clunk of a dead bolt turning back.

To describe what lay beyond as an apartment was a gross disservice to the word. It was a single room with a Murphy bed pushed up against the wall, a sink, a writing desk and chair, and a closet. And there was apparently a phone somewhere, as Parker could hear it ringing as he entered the room. For some reason the phone was tucked under the desk, almost beneath the radiator, which hung from the wall like the ribs of a starving dog.

Parker answered and Chan's voice came on the line. "You made it out?"

"Looks that way," Parker said. He felt a surge of relief that he wasn't alone in here.

"I'm connecting you with Clayton," Chan said. There was an electronic buzzing sound, then another voice came on the line.

"Hey, buddy," a voice said.

"Clayton?" Parker asked.

"Yeah, it's me. I know my voice is off. I look a little different."

"What happened? How did you get in here?" Parker asked.

The voice of an old woman came on the line. "He got in here because of me."

"Who is this?" Parker said.

"Ohh . . . yeah, it's Selberg. I came into this world as an old woman. It's the only body I could find."

"Kinky," Parker said.

"Selberg and I found another backdoor out of the underground Manhattan," Clayton said. "Where's Charlotte?"

"She's gone."

"What happened?" Clayton said.

"I don't want to talk about that now," Parker replied. Instead, he told Clayton about the fights tonight at the Garden.

"You think our guy will be there?" Clayton said.

"Don't know. But I think it's the best chance we have right now."

"All right, partner, come pick me up."

Clayton gave him an address off the West Side Highway just south of the Meatpacking District. Parker was there in ten minutes. The building was an old, down-on-its-luck brownstone. A grizzled-looking white man in a dingy T-shirt with jeans sat on the front stoop. His arms were heroin-junky thin, laced with veins, his skin pulled tight as parchment across his face. He stood up uncertainly as Parker pulled along the curb. "That you?"

Parker studied the man, trying to read some sign of his friend. "Sam?"

"Yeah, yeah," Clayton said as he headed to the passenger side door. Clayton joined Parker inside the Fleetline. "How come you get to look like you, only like a more handsome, more in-shape version of you. And I also gotta look like you, only a skinny, wasted-away version of you."

"Most times, it's just luck who you get," Parker said as he pulled away from the curb. "Next time maybe you get to be Billy Dee Williams."

They headed north on the West Side Highway. There were plenty of other cars on the road. Everyone seemed to be living their lives. The entrance for the Holland Tunnel was closed due to construction. Parker had a feeling that construction project was going to last an eternity. There was no New Jersey in this world. And that tunnel would never connect anywhere. Neither would the Lincoln or Washington Bridge.

They pulled off the highway and headed east on Thirtieth Street. The last time Parker had been here, the giant beast had chased him and Charlotte across the avenue before they escaped into Penn Plaza. He had lost Charlotte not too long after that. Ahead, he saw the familiar Hotel Pennsylvania. There were so many memories locked away in that building, Parker could imagine them now, playing on an endless loop that only a few could see. People long dead still walked those halls, ghosts of the mind forever trapped inside.

He and Clayton pulled up across from the hotel, and Parker turned his attention to the stadium. His brain whirled in surprise like a fighter on the ropes. The stadium was gone. He turned to check the street signs to make sure they were at the right place.

"Uh, buddy?" Clayton said. "What happened to the Garden?"

In place of the familiar circular domed stadium was a massive, rectangular, beaux arts-style building with plenty of columns and steps and statues that stretched two entire city blocks. People moved quickly in and out of the main entrance, a steady stream of pedestrians who hustled about their business, oblivious to the erasure of the most famous arena in the world.

"Damn . . ." Parker said. "Stupid."

"What is it?"

"Madison Square Garden wasn't here in 1953," Chan's voice sounded in his ear. The connection sounded strong.

"Where was it?" Parker asked.

"I have no idea where it was. That's why we have an Archivist. I'm working to get Selberg a direct connection to you guys now."

Parker studied the impressive structure. It was obviously something famous in its day. The people who moved in and out of the entrance appeared to be commuters or travelers.

"Hello, idiots." An old woman spoke suddenly, her voice sounding in their ear.

"Selberg?" Parker said, still thrown by the Archivist's new voice. This character shifting wasn't unusual when moving into new worlds. But it always took getting used to.

"That's right. Miss me?"

"Yeah. In a bit of a historical maze here."

"You're looking at the original Pennsylvania Station, built by the Pennsylvania Railroad in the early 1900s."

"Oh great, thanks for the history lesson. I played Monopoly too. We just need to find the Short Line and the B&O Railroad and that other one and we're going to win," Clayton said.

"The original Garden wasn't constructed for another fifteen years or so from when you are now. You're actually looking at a pretty amazing piece of history."

"School's out," Clayton said. "Where's the Garden in this time?"

"There have actually been four different Madison Square Gardens in the last hundred or so years. In 1953, Madison Square Garden was the third of its kind and was located at Eighth Avenue and Fiftieth Street. Maybe if you two idiots knew anything about history, you would know that."

"Clayton tells me you're an old woman. How's that feel? Because I'm like a really handsome, fit guy. I look like a cross between a Stetson model and a former high school quarterback," Parker said as he started up the car and headed north again. "Maybe later I can push you around in your wheelchair."

They took Eighth Avenue north. Traffic grew thicker around the Garden. A cop stood in the middle of the avenue, furiously blowing his whistle and waving a white gloved hand, trying to get the traffic to bend to his will. But the cars weren't moving, jammed up all the way east for blocks. Parker found an empty parking spot and dropped the Fleetline into it.

"You got a piece?" Parker said.

"Brother, I came alone in nothing but what God gave me," Clayton said.

"I got a revolver and some brass knuckles," Parker said. "I don't mind sharing. Which one you want?"

"I'll take the brass knuckles. Boxing is all muscle memory anyway. I still remember how to throw a punch."

Parker handed him the brass knuckles. Clayton concealed the weapon in his pocket, then left the car and headed toward the Garden. There was a large crowd outside the sports complex and they headed into it. Over the main entrance was a curving marquee that illuminated the iconic words MADISON SQ GARDEN in bright, white neon. The entrance was flanked by a men's hat store on one side and a Nedick's fast food on the other. The crowd was filled with fight fans, bookies, hawkers, hookers, and cops, all packed together on the sidewalk and spilling onto the avenue.

The main heavyweight event was advertised on the sides of the marquees. Both fighters were from Manhattan, of course, both probably prisoners, never knowing that their championship belt only existed in this collective dream world. Parker bought two tickets from the box office, then they entered through the main gates.

A couple of cops lounged around by the doors, but nobody bothered to check visitors for weapons, and Parker passed right through, the weight of the revolver heavy on his belt.

Inside, the Garden was sweltering hot and wreathed in cigarette smoke. The smoke haloed the lights and tickled Parker's lungs. This was a smoker's world, and everyone around him puffed away. He and Clayton pushed through the backed-up lines at the concession stands, then found their way onto the main floor. The eighteen-thousand-seat venue was almost at capacity; two middleweights limbered up in the middle of the ring, bouncing back and forth on their toes while the announcer proclaimed the undercard bout statistics.

The first line of seats near the ring looked to be all press types. Older men in fedoras bent over portable typewriters, the stubs of cigars crammed into crooked mouths. The next row was the money, women in fur shawls despite the tropical heat, and men in tails.

"You think he's in the second row?" Clayton asked.

"Not sure."

Parker scanned each of the faces. He wasn't sure what he was looking for, but nothing jumped out at him. He was confident their man would be bigger than this. He looked upward, scanned the VIP box seats along the outer edge of the Garden. There, the big money enjoyed air-conditioning and privacy, watching the fight from above. But even that didn't seem grand enough for a senator's son.

And then it occurred to him.

Parker flagged down one of the vendors and bought a program. The front cover featured a stencil drawing of two fighters landing hooks on each other. Inside were a few pages of ads for men's fashion and electric razors, and then a couple pages dedicated to each fighter. Parker turned to the main event page.

Thomas "Granite" Granville versus Andrew "The Empire" Adams.

There were small black and white photographs of each. Granville was a bruising man in his mid-thirties, a punchy face, half-swollen like mashed pizza dough. Adams was a good, clean-looking kid, movie-star handsome, in his early 20s. Parker touched the photograph of Adams and showed it to Clayton. "This is our guy."

"How do you know that?"

"Our kid was a big boxing fan. I thought he'd be here to watch the fights, but in this place, where you can be anything you want if you have the money, why just watch when you can actually be the fighter? You can be heavyweight champion."

"I don't know," Clayton said. "Maybe."

"And the nickname. Empire. His father is a New York senator. The Empire State," Parker said. "And look at this. He only turned pro a year ago. That's exactly when this kid came into the system. I really think this is our guy."

Up near the ring, the bell clanged and the two heavyweights charged each other, banging away, the thump of glove against flesh carried across the floor. The crowd cheered.

"Even if he is our guy," Clayton said, "what's our next move? It's a heavyweight title fight. What, you're going to shoot this guy when he steps into the ring?"

"No. We're going to go down to the locker room. That's where he'll be. That's where we'll get him alone." Parker tapped his ear. "Selberg, you there?"

"Oh, now you come crawling back," Selberg replied.

"I need you to find me a way into the locker room," Parker said.

"That's not my area," Selberg said. "Chan, can you help them?"

"I'll figure something out," Chan said.

The fighters entered the ring through a long lane that cut through the crowd and led down between the rows of stadium seating. Clayton and Parker worked their way around the seats, then moved up the aisles toward the fighters' entrance. In the ring, someone scored a knockdown. The crowd rose to its feet as the referee began the ten second cadence.

A security man stood at the entrance.

"Walk toward him now," Chan said. "I'll handle it."

As Parker and Clayton approached, a phone behind the guard let out a shrill ring. The guard turned his attention to the phone and walked a few steps backward to answer it. With his back to them, the duo slipped by and moved quickly down the long corridor. Around them, the roar of the crowd reverberated through the concrete of the building. The feeling was intense, like being inside a thunderstorm.

The hall turned sharply right and ended with a single door. Another security guard stood out front.

"You're on your own with this one," Selberg said. "I'm out of ideas. He's a prisoner, though. You can probably put him to sleep without raising too many alarms."

"Got it," Parker said.

Parker stepped ahead of Clayton and waved his hand to the guard. The guard moved slightly away from the door, his face surprised and confused. Hidden behind Parker, Clayton slipped the brass knuckles onto his fist. When they were just a few feet from the guard, Clayton stepped out from behind Parker and swung, the metal around his fist connecting flush with the guard's jaw. The man's eyes rolled back and he dropped to the ground.

Parker pushed open the door.

The locker room was small and stank of old sweat. Open-faced, wood panel lockers lined the wall, with a large mirror in the back of the room. A table stood in the middle of the parquet floor and a fighter sat on the edge of the table, in a robe, his gloves being laced up. Around him were clustered a half-dozen other men in his entourage, trainers and a couple of heavies who looked like bodyguards. The group was laughing about something when Parker and Clayton entered. The laughing ended. The men turned to face them.

The trainer stepped away from the table and Parker could see the fighter for the first time. Blocks of muscles were slapped onto his body like mounds of clay. His skin had a light sheen of sweat, his hair slicked back and tight on his scalp. His face had a sharp animal cunning and smile that made you feel more afraid than anything else. Parker could tell he was a mean, cruel kid who liked beating up on people, didn't matter who it was. Men, women, kids . . . probably all the same to him. The kind of guy that got his kicks from giving pain.

"I think you got the wrong room," one of the trainers said. "No press."

"We're not press," Parker said. "We're looking for someone."

"I don't care who you're looking for. He ain't here. Now beat it."

"Looking for Senator Scott's son. Any of you boys know him?"

"Now I said beat it," the trainer took a step forward.

Still seated on the table, the boxer cocked his head slightly. The atmosphere in the room shifted imperceptibly. He held out a gloved hand and restrained his trainer. The entire entourage turned to watch.

"What would you want with him?"

"We've come to take him home," Parker said.

"Says who?"

"Says Senator Scott. He paid us to do a job."

"Who the fuck is Senator Scott?" the trainer said. "Now, out you two bums go before I have security throw you."

The boxer patted his trainer's shoulder. "It's okay, Jimmy."

Though it looked more and more like this was their man, Parker felt something was wrong. "You know these guys?" the trainer said.

"Yeah. Friends of my father. They came here to kill me. Isn't that right, gentlemen?"

Parker shook his head. "Not exactly. We came to get you out."

"Oh right, right. Of course." The boxer smiled. "Why the fuck would I want to leave? I'm a king in here. Out there, I'm just some guy."

"Because your family misses you."

"Because Dad's sad, I have to give up all this?"

"Listen," Parker said, "I don't really give a fuck what you want. We're paid to come get you and bring you back. You want to stay, fine. But you have some information I need. You give me that, we'll be on our way."

Scott look surprised. "What information?"

"I'm looking for a prisoner. Her name is Susan Parker. I don't know what she'd look like in here, but on the outside she was about five foot seven, hundred thirty pounds, brown hair. She'd have been in this system for about two years," Parker said.

Scott's eyes narrowed and he stared as if Parker were a riddle he was trying to figure out. That look was not what Parker expected. He started feeling a deep, nameless anxiety spread through his system. Something definitely felt wrong here. "Did Scotty K put you up to this?"

Parker slowly shook his head. "I don't know a Scotty K."

"Come on fellas, what's the gag here? Susan Parker? Who is she to you?"

Parker clenched his hands into fists. He wanted to smash this pretty boy's face until it wasn't so pretty anymore. "She's my wife."

Scott's head went back and he laughed. He laughed so hard his sides shook and tears formed at the corners of his eyes. It was a bully's laugh, and his entourage joined in too, not really sure what was going on, but just taking their boss's lead.

"What's so funny?" Parker said through gritted teeth. "Maybe I missed the joke."

"My old man sent you here? Oh, that's rich. Real fucking rich. Susan Parker. Of all the people in the world."

"Hey, listen," Clayton said sharply. "Cut the shit and tell my partner where she is."

"She's not in the system," Scott said. "She's not a prisoner. She's dead, man. She died two years ago. The only way you're breaking her out is with a shovel and some smelling salts."

Parker suddenly felt lightheaded. The heat of the room, the smoke, the people . . . everything rushed through his brain at once like rocket fuel. That couldn't be true. His wife couldn't be dead. He could feel her out there somewhere. Like a part of him that was in the system. This had to be a mistake.

"She's not dead," Parker said. "She's in here. Somewhere. And you're going to tell me where she is."

Scott looked serious for a moment. "Why did they tell you about me?"

Parker took a moment and answered truthfully. "They didn't tell me anything."

"They didn't tell you why I'm in here?"

Parker suddenly knew what was coming. Like a skier caught in the path of an avalanche, there was nothing he could do to avoid impact. He wanted desperately to back up in time. To rewind himself out of this room. Back to the beginning when he still had hope.

"No . . ." Parker said quietly. "They didn't."

"I'm in here for murder. I killed Susan Parker. I killed your wife," Scott said evenly. His voice didn't waver for an instant. And Parker knew this man was telling the absolute truth. "Oh man," Scott held his hand to his forehead as if suddenly remembering something. "I know you. I know who you are. I didn't recognize you. You're the husband. I remember you from the trial. You were in the back looking all sad. Your wife was out with her friends at a bar when I first saw her. Sexy.

"I tried to buy her a drink and she told me she was married. But then later, when I ran into her in the parking lot, I followed her home. To your sad, little depressing apartment. I caught up to her at your front door. Little bit after nine at night. Papers said you were still at work. She had the keys in the lock and had the door open when I pushed her inside. She fought a little, you know, but yeah, I fucked your wife. I raped her right on your bed, then I beat her head in and choked her until she died. And that's why I'm in here. Living like a champion.

"And now you're here because my dad is paying you money to get me out. That's fucking perfect."

This man was evil. He wasn't just a rich man son's that bullied the weak. He was a psychopath. He was a murderous lunatic and deserved to die. Parker thought back to the apartment overlooking Columbus Circle. The bloodstains on the floor. The broken glass. The photographs of him and his wife on the refrigerator. That had been his apartment. That had been his memory. That was the crime scene. That was what he had found when he'd come home from work that night. Only his wife had been there. She was dead already.

My wife is dead.

The truth of it knocked the wind from him. He couldn't think. He . . .

"You okay, buddy?" Clayton said. His hand lightly touched Parker's shoulder, but his face was hard as stone as he stared at Scott. Clayton leaned in toward Parker. "Whatever way you want to go, I got your back."

Parker couldn't answer him. His hand slowly went to the gun in his waistband. His fingers wrapped around the grip. Parker had murder on his mind.

But there was no murder in this place. You couldn't kill what wasn't real.

But Parker just wanted to spray lead. To see this man die. To remember that at least.

Help me. Help me, please.

The words he had heard on the pay phone with Selberg. The same words that had lured him into the tunnels. The voice had been familiar. But now he knew. It had been his wife's voice. He had come home that night and found her. She was still alive. Those were her last words.

And the big band music that had been playing on the telephone in The Dakota. That same song had been in the apartment the night he found her. Oddly playing on the bedroom radio.

He understood everything. There had always been memories trying to seep through. And only now did he grasp them.

Parker pulled out the revolver.

"I told you, I'm not going back," Scott said. "I'm never going back."

Parker's finger tightened on the trigger. With incredible speed for a big man, Scott vaulted off the table and shoved his trainer forward right into Parker, who fired. The bullet struck the trainer center mass. The man grunted in pain as a flower of blood blossomed on the front of his white shirt. He collapsed to the ground.

Scott was out the back door of the locker room in an instant. Parker waved the revolver at the entourage, holding them back. Then he sprinted through the doorway after the boxer. Outside was another long hall that ran deep beneath the Garden. Scott, in great shape, had a thirty-yard lead on Clayton and Parker. He was pulling away. Parker fired once while running, but missed, the shot heading wide. These were silver bullets he was firing, and he only had a half dozen. He had to be careful with his shots, or nobody was leaving here.

Clayton and Parker chased Scott into an underground parking garage.

Scott slid behind the wheel of a light blue Chrysler Royal. The engine turned over and the big car accelerated with a roar down the length of the parking garage. Parker ran after it, chasing the car in a blind fury.

"Selberg, Chan, I need some help here."

"Got it," Chan said. "Third car up on your right, should be a black Dodge Coronet. There's a mailbox drop location nearby. I'll leave the keys there for you."

On the curb stood a U.S. Postal mailbox. The small access door was unlocked, and inside Parker found a set of keys. He hit the car running, pulled open the door, and threw himself behind the wheel. The keys jangled into the ignition and the engine turned over the first try. Clayton barely had the car door closed when Parker floored the accelerator, bottoming out on the ramp leading up to street level.

They launched out of the parking garage onto Forty-Ninth Street. A whistle-blowing cop jumped out of their way as the car screeched over the curb and sideswiped a box truck, sending the truck crashing up and into the plate glass of the Nedick's. Scott was a few car lengths ahead, the Chrysler weaving in and out between cars.

Scott hit the West Side Highway and headed north. Parker followed behind, the Dodge engine struggling to keep up with the larger Chrysler. Parker's hands were tight on the wheel as they sped by piers stretching out into the Hudson. The taillights of the Chrysler were the only thing that mattered now. He would have time to think later on, but now he had only the chase.

"Maybe he was wrong," Clayton said. "Maybe he's lying."

"No. He's telling the truth. She's dead. And he killed her. She was never in the system anywhere. They lied to me. They used her as bait. The first job was all a setup. The 1880s job. That's when they got access to my brain. When they removed the memories of my wife. Of the trial. Of her murder. Put in false memories. Described a story that made sense. That she was in prison. But that never happened. You remember when we were on the outside, and we found the dead junkie in the building in the East Village?"

"Yeah, I remember. Overdose."

"I know why that guy was familiar now. I remembered him."

"Who was he?"

"That was the target from the 1880s job. After I got him out of the system, they murdered him. The point wasn't to get him out, the point was to get me in. So they could work on my brain and take away my fucking memory. Made me think, just one more job and I can find my wife."

The Chrysler flew past the Soldiers' and Sailors' Monument set up on a ridge in Riverside Park. They had reached the block of the West Nineties and still headed north. Parker had never been this far up in the system before. Scott was running out of room. Only Parker still wasn't sure what would happen when they caught up with him. The mission had been to kill Scott. Kill him to wake him up. So killing him was exactly what the senator wanted. Parker couldn't give that to him. But just leaving him here in 1953 wasn't an option. Rich and powerful. He was living out his fantasy here. He was convicted of killing Parker's wife, and this was his punishment. This wasn't how it was supposed to be.

The Upper West Side rolled over into Harlem. Beautiful old apartment complexes flashed by on their right. They were in the 150th Street block and still headed north. Ahead they reached the Columbia-Presbyterian Medical Center. Scott's car swerved suddenly, taking the exit ramp off the highway and vanishing for a moment on the sharp turn.

"You're losing him," Clayton said.

"I got him."

Parker accelerated and hit the ramp, the lights of the Chrysler visible again in the distance. The ramp widened out, cutting along the edges of old brick buildings, the highway slowly rising in elevation until Parker felt like they were soaring out over the city. Above them flashed a sign. They were on the ramp to the George Washington Bridge, headed across the Hudson River into New Jersey.

They swept past a large sign flashing BRIDGE CLOSED. Scott crashed through the wooden gate of a toll booth, shards of wood flying through the air like confetti. The cars were gone now, the entire road empty except for the two speeding vehicles. The glorious span of the George Washington Bridge seemed to rise up before them like a castle in a dream. The Chrysler hit the bridge hard, Scott lost control, and the big car swiped the guard rail. One of the tires popped and the car began vibrating wildly, a brilliant cascade of sparks arcing out from the metal rim.

The Chrysler was losing speed. Parker accelerated, and his Dodge rammed its rear bumper, spinning Scott's car out of control. The Chrysler twisted sideways and then, like a skier catching an edge, flipped suddenly, the roof hitting pavement and sliding twenty yards along the length of the bridge.

Just ahead, the bridge was there. And then it wasn't. The roadway ended in a flat line in midair, a six-hundred-foot drop straight down to the Hudson. This was where the prison ended.

Parker hit the brake hard and the tires screeched on pavement. They kept skidding forward, too fast to stop in time before they reached the edge. Parker spun the wheel and the car turned. The cliff of the bridge came up fast, and the auto's back end went over. The two men hung suspended in space, the car teetering dangerously, the back half off the edge of the bridge.

Slowly Parker eased open the door.

"Let's move together slowly," Parker said. "On three, we'll jump from the car."

Clayton nodded. Parker calmly counted down. When he reached three, they both launched themselves from the car. Their combined weight gone, the Dodge slowly pinwheeled backward off the edge of the bridge. Parker watched the car fall toward the Hudson, but just before impact, the entire vehicle disappeared. The river below flowed quietly by, the water completely smooth.

"Jesus, you guys okay?" Chan said.

"Yeah," Parker replied. "What happened to the car? It just vanished."

"I saw that. I'm tracking it back to the 1970s system. Hopefully it landed on a few zombies out there. I told you, there are backdoors all over this place that connect the different systems. That must be one of them. Never made it up this far to check the bridges."

Parker heard a groan of pain. Scott slowly crawled from beneath the overturned Chrysler. He was still in his silk white and red boxing robe, fragments of glass caught in his hair. Blood streamed down the side of his face from an open gash above his temple.

"Looks like we both made it," Scott called out. "Good. You haven't had much luck with driving."

Parker advanced toward Scott, pistol out, ready to pull the trigger. But something in the man's words bothered him. "What do you mean?"

"I read about you," Scott said. "After the trial. You were so upset over your wife's death, you started drinking. What a fucking loser. You remember?"

"No . . ." Parker shook his head. He didn't remember. His memories were out there somewhere, he hoped. But this one he hadn't recovered.

"Oh man, they really fucked you up, didn't they? Who'd you let into that little brain of yours? You have no idea the things you did."

"What do you mean?"

"Sad little you wanders into a bar. Pounds like ten beers and shots, gets in your car, and does a head-on at fifty miles an hour with a minivan. You ever seen what that kind of wreck does to a minivan filled with a family of four? Little kid body parts were all over the road. God. It was disgusting. So in a way, I guess, you're more of a murderer than I am."

"That's not true. That's a fucking lie."

"No, I never lie. The truth is too good in this case. Oh the judge went as easy as he could on you, being that you were in mourning and all over your dead wife. But you can't kill a couple little kids and their parents and not go to prison. That's not happening."

Parker suddenly remembered the crumpled minivan on the street in the abandoned Manhattan. That had been part of his memory. A family car, with the inside streaked with blood.

"Before I went in, my father told me all about you," Scott said. "He said there was this crew that could break me out. Best in the world. And they don't even know why. But I do. You never wonder why you're so good getting into these prison systems? It's because you're already inside. You're already in prison. There is no real world for you. Whatever world you think you're living in, that shit's not real. Or should I say, it's as real to you as this world is to me."

No, no, no . . .

Parker was a cop.

Clayton was his partner.

The year was 1986.

That was real. That was his life. That wasn't a computer system.

He wasn't one of these people. He wasn't a prisoner.

He knew what reality was. He had experienced it.

He turned toward Clayton.

Clayton looked at him uncertainly. "I thought you knew."

"Knew what?"

"We're all prisoners. Every single one of us. Selberg. Charlotte. We never talk about it, but it's true. I thought we all knew," Clayton said. "I've been in and out of prison my whole life."

"Why didn't anyone talk about it?" Parker asked. He felt his body begin to shake.

"It's just not something we like thinking about, I guess. You talk about the prisoners that know. The glitches, you call them. We were all glitches. Except for you."

"But in the abandoned Manhattan, you were what, just pretending?"

"No. I had my memory wiped of everything. Same as you. I thought we were all 1930s explorers. But when I left that place, my memories came back. Now I remember. We all knew."

"No. No. Not all of us. I didn't know," Parker said. "So if I put this gun to my head and pull the trigger?"

"You wake up in your prison system. 1986. That's where you keep going back to every time. I mean, think about it, if 1986 was real, they wouldn't have this type of technology."

"So what's the date? The real date?"

Clayton shook his head. "I'm not sure. Sometime far in the future."

"But what about all those people I assassinated? All the prison breaks?"

"Sure, you got them out. But it only works if you've got someone on the outside. Someone to pull you out of the machine," Scott said. "They've been using you for years on these breakouts. You get all your assignments by phone, don't you? That's because it's easy to call into the system. It's a lot harder to actually get a person inside. This agency you work for, how many of their employees have you actually met?"

"Dunbar. I met him. He gave me this assignment."

"James Dunbar works for my father. They sent him into your prison system to evaluate you. Because it was the boss's son you were going after. To make sure you could get it done. But think about your life. What you think is real. Have you ever actually left Manhattan?"

Parker closed his eyes. He remembered his apartment near the bridge. The Chinese food menu of the place in Queens. Thinking he'd never visited there. The phone numbers that never seemed to pick up. An apartment filled with stuff that he didn't ever remember buying. The Malone kids always outside on the street, forever playing stickball like they were on some kind of loop.

"You don't have anything," Scott said, his voice sounding miles away. "When you get killed, you don't wake up in the real world, you just move to your old system. 1986. 1953. It's all the same. We're all living a fantasy. At least in this one, I get to live like a king. But you know what, fuck it. You want to shoot me. Go ahead. I can go back to the real world."

Parker took a few stumbling steps forward.

His wife had been real. Once she had existed. She loved movies and autumn. She snorted when she laughed. She made a scrapbook of precious moments and had a scar near her eye. They had built real memories together. And those memories were out there.

He turned and looked out over the bridge. Far below them, the Hudson flowed south, and in the distance, the million lights of Manhattan glittered against the black. That was the stuff of dreams. Bright lights and big dreams.

"So what's it going to be?" Scott said. "Light me up. Let's get it over with."

Parker lowered the gun. He turned back toward Scott, his mind set on a course of action. He flipped the pistol around and cracked the cruel boxer hard across the jaw with the butt end. Hard wood struck bone and Scott grunted. Parker grabbed him by the neck, and then, half-choking him, half-dragging, he pulled his wife's murderer toward the edge of the bridge. Through the blood and the haze, Scott saw what was happening and his eyes grew wide. He began to fight back. Scott was a big man and strong, but Parker was running on another level. No man on Earth could stop him now.

"No, no, wait, wait, wait!" Scott clawed at Parker's face. He felt skin tearing, but there was no pain. "I've got money. Whatever you want. We can get you out of here. Back to the real world. I promise you."

They reached the edge of the bridge. Far below them was the Hudson, the water swirling in deep eddies.

"My wife was my world. You took her from me. I don't have a world to go back to."

Parker hurled Scott over the edge. Scott screamed, his hands and legs reaching out wildly for holds that didn't exist. He plummeted, shrieking the entire way, Parker watching him, adding this moment to his memory palace. And then, just before he hit the water, his wife's killer vanished.

Gone like a memory lost in time.

ABOUT THE AUTHOR

Matthew B.J. Delaney published his first novel, *Jinn*, in 2003. Winner of the International Horror Guild Award, the novel was optioned for film by Touchstone Pictures, was featured as *People* magazine's "Page-Turner of the Week," and received a *Publishers Weekly* Starred Review.

Following the attacks of September 11, 2001, he left a career in finance and moved from Boston to New York City to join the New York City Police Department. He has been a member of the NYPD for thirteen years, and he continues to write in his spare time.